Venice 23. Mozzies (handwritten)

LONGEST WAY UP, SHORTEST WAY DOWN

Steve (signature, handwritten)

STEFAN WILD

www.tales-of-stefanwild.uk

CONTENTS

Preface
Acknowledgements

Chapter 1   The round up
Chapter 2   The interview
Chapter 3   Dead man's breeches and boots
Chapter 4   Eyes, nose and dock
Chapter 5   New breeches
Chapter 6   Settling in
Chapter 7   Heads I win, tails you moo's
Chapter 8   Then there were two
Chapter 9   Big Ben strikes twice
Chapter 10   Blankets, banks and superheroes
Chapter 11   Testing times
Chapter 12   The quiet Welshman and
                         the angry Cockney
Chapter 13   Spurs and stairs
Chapter 14   Walking tall to Duke Street
Chapter 15   On patrol
Chapter 16   The outstations
Chapter 17   Tears of laughter, tears of sorrow
Chapter 18   Name that tune
Chapter 19   Up the Albion
Chapter 20   The Lone Ranger
Chapter 21   They think it's all over

Epilogue
A Final word from the author

PREFACE

This is a story of stories. Stories of the West Midlands Police Mounted Branch of the 1970s. Stories that have been re-told many times about things that really happened. Re-told by the men that were there, re-told in pubs and canteens by the men that weren't there, and re-told again years later at re-unions, wakes, and other venues where old comrades meet, drink, and inevitably reminisce. They are stories that make people laugh; funny because they involve animals and really happened, but funnier because multiple renditions have added drama, humour and plenty of other frilly bits to the tale.

Stefan Wild, at the age of sixty-five, began to write them down, and what began as a collection of vignettes, unexpectedly morphed into one story and eventually into this book. The story is set in 1979, itself a time of change, so the male dominated environment, attitudes, and some of the dialogue may raise eyebrows among younger readers.

The author wanted a book that could be read by all members of his family so excessive foul and abusive language, indicative of the time, has been moderated; hopefully this has not diminished the authenticity of the narrative. It is the author's first book and his only writing qualification is a fifty-year-old O-level in English language.

The characters' names in this book are all fictitious. The characters themselves are a mixture; some are generic, others are hybrids, and some are the product of the author's fading recollection and vivid imagination. Similarities to real people, living or otherwise, are probably coincidental.

Some of the horses' names are real, but where the name of a horse could lead to the identification of a real person, that name has been changed.

The author is a real person and is the main character in the book; Stefan Wild is a pseudonym.

ACKNOWLEDGEMENTS

The ability to hold court and spin a good yarn in friendly company, with your hand warming a nice glass of red, is a very different undertaking to writing down stories with the intention of creating a book. This became blatantly apparent to me during the very early stages of this long-pondered project. The very fact that this book is now in print, and is being read by yourself, is tribute to a band of loyal friends and helpers who have educated, supported, cajoled, and encouraged me throughout my literary ramblings. I really could not have done this alone, and would like to use the next few lines to introduce these people and to express my heartfelt appreciation.

Firstly, my long-suffering wife, **Becks**, who has patiently endured my lengthy bad-tempered battles with 'Word', the laptop in general, and my caveman like keyboard skills. Her oils on my troubled waters have been constant and free flowing.

My thanks too to **Alex Lainsbury**, my young, enthusiastic, and patiently supportive editor who pruned my work by four thousand words, introduced me to the wonders of 'Track Changes', and injected another level of readability into my manuscript. I've never actually met you Alex, but in my vision, you have wings.

A special mention in despatches for leading the charge with such alacrity, against numerous dissident apostrophes, and armed with only a sharpened red ballpoint, goes to one of my oldest friends **Carolyn Jones**. It was good to have you on my side Carolyn; I'm just glad that I wasn't in your class at school, I would never have been out of detention.

Respect too, to **Simon Hill** who, despite such a frantic workload, took my manuscript to the anvil and hammered it into its final format for print. Cheers Simon the cheque is in the post.

My website www.tales-of-stefanwild.uk is the creation of **Steve Moore**; his perpetual patience with my IT incompetence is truly remarkable and greatly appreciated.

The book cover is the work of **Sarah Hilliar.** Thank-you Sarah for your hard work, artistic talent, and for presenting my old boots in a shinier condition than they ever were back in the day.

And finally my daughter **Claire** (Little Mel) who, whilst quietly rolling her eyes and occasionally raising an eyebrow, has cajoled many of her professional colleagues to freely assist in preparing my words for print. This may be a good time to warn her that I'm thinking of writing another!

Thank you all; thank you for cracking the whip, ensuring my dressings and keeping me 'trotting on'. I couldn't have done it without you.

Stefan
July 2021

CHAPTER 1

THE ROUND UP

"Two control calling Panda One-Two. Over."

"Go ahead. Over."

"Where are you Stef? Over."

"Just finishing that statement at the Co-op. Over."

"Smashin' thanks. While you're down there can you pop into Canal Street? The 'osses' are creating havoc again. Over."

"Nooo! Groan, groan, and double moan... Over," I replied in desperation.

"Leave it with you Tonto," I could hear laughter in the background, "try not to get trampled. Over."

"I'll do my best. Over."

It was sometime in the spring of 1978. I was a young uniformed copper, only twenty-two years of age, with just over two years of service behind me. I had only recently been posted to a regular position as a panda driver[1], working in a small working-class town located in that part of the industrial Midlands known as the Black Country.

---

[1] *Seen on UK streets during the 1960s, 70s, and 80s, small police general patrol cars were widely known as panda cars. The name is believed to have originated because they were originally painted black and white, but later more commonly blue and white.*

I had spent most of my two years' probation patrolling on foot around the local town centre, and was still eagerly learning my trade, but now also enjoying the independence, freedom, and variety of work that came with being mobile.

I was a local lad, a typical townie, so knew next to nothing useful about horses. My previous experience with them was limited, but had already convinced me they were large, smelly, awkward, and slightly scary creatures. Feral horses had lately become a regular problem on the patch, resulting in a growing number of calls and complaints from the locals. These horses tended to mysteriously appear overnight, tethered and chained on any available piece of waste land or grass verge. Neglected by their unknown owners, they usually happily munched away, minding their own business until they had eaten all of the reachable grass. When all of the grass was gone, boredom or hunger pains encouraged them to slip their chains and move on to richer pastures – invariably, someone's front garden.

The area was predominantly made up of pre-war social housing, and the community endured far more serious issues than the nuisance of feral horses. A high percentage of them lived in large families of the long-term unemployed, not because of recession or economic downturn, but simply because aspirations were low and employment of any sort was not on anyone's agenda.

The whole area was a mess; large gardens, originally provided by optimistic planners for people to grow their own vegetables, were now overgrown jungles concealing scrap cars, derelict pigeon pens, and other decaying debris. The streets were littered, sometimes with burned out car shells, and kids routinely roared around on noisy uninsured motorbikes. Petty crime was rife, especially assault, theft and criminal damage, with domestic violence, sadly, just widely accepted as a miserable fact of life.

Education was a low priority, heavy drinking was endemic, inverted snobbery too common and personal aspiration rare. As a consequence, a large proportion of the local lads had substantial criminal records before they finished their teens. We were kept busy, fighting a losing battle, and were largely disliked and mistrusted by our public.

On this occasion I didn't need to use my radio to confirm the house number of the caller because from the end of the road I could see a typically large and shaggy black and white horse, head down devouring the shrubbery of a rare impressively maintained front garden.

"Panda one two; I'm at Canal Street. Over," I reported.

"Cheers Stef. How's it looking? Over."

"Carnage to be honest sarge; lawn wrecked, covered in shite, and it seems to be pruning the roses now. Unfortunately, he's chosen the best garden in the street. Over."

"Not much you can do, Stef. Just some charm and charisma please. Smile sweetly, love 'em up, and smooth it over. Over."

Mulling over the last instruction as I walked up the garden path, I saw a man and woman, standing with arms folded by the front door. As I approached them, the horse - right on cue - dropped a huge pile of green, steaming poop onto their neatly cut lawn.

"Hello, I'm PC Stef Wild. What seems to be the problem?"

"If you can't see a problem mate, you'd best piss off and get yer eyes tested," replied the man of the house.

"You'll never be a bleedin' detective, will ya?" added the female support act.

"I don't know why we wasted our time calling. You'll just say you can't do anything, and then bugger off. Don't know why we pay our taxes!"

Reeling from the verbal assault with my pride dented, I was tempted to question the suggestion they had ever paid any form of tax in their lives - however, given the circumstances, it was difficult to argue with their frustration.

"Look I'm here to help. I know you're angry, but-" I was cut short.

"Too right we're bloody angry! We try to keep the place nice and it ain't easy in this shit-hole; I work hard on this garden. Now look at the bloody state of it."

There had been so many recent calls regarding this very problem, that the issue had been raised and discussed at every divisional management meeting for the last year. Much coffee and many doughnuts were consumed before it was agreed something definitely needed to be done. What was to be done hadn't yet been decided, but it was agreed that something, when it was agreed what, would have to be done.

This is where the management policy regarding feral horses stood, as I was being verbally lashed by two genuinely aggrieved and very frustrated people. A more experienced and thick-skinned officer would probably have just followed instructions and smoothed the situation over with false promises before rapidly leaving the scene. However, still wet behind the ears, sympathetic, and slightly stupid, I decided to be cavalier and stick my neck out.

"I agree with everything you say."

"You agree that you're a shit detective and you need your eyes testing?" asked the woman with some surprise.

"No. I agree that something needs to be done."

"Well that's a start."

"I agree. This *cannot* carry on," I empathised.

"Big words young man, but what are you going to do about it?"

It was a good question, because I was clearly under instruction to placate these people, record the incident, and leave the scene. After careful consideration, I made my decision.

"I'm going to seize this horse and take it to the police station," I heard myself say, "and we will prosecute the owner when he collects the horse."

Not having the slightest idea of what to do next, but to the obvious delight of the couple, I led the horse out of their garden using the rusty chain that was fastened around its neck. I knew if I reported my intentions back to the controller I would have been ordered to leave the animal where it was, so I said nothing. Then, with the tow rope from the boot of the Panda I made a lead rein, and leaving the car parked in Canal Street at the mercy of the locals, set off to walk to the police station. It was only five minutes away; what could possibly go wrong?

The most direct route to the police station was along a main road that led directly through the centre of a busy industrial estate. I walked steadily on with my tethered prisoner reluctantly lagging slightly behind, and found myself listening to that slightly unpleasant muffled crunching noise made by unshod horses walking on tarmacked roads. At first our journey was plain sailing and full steam ahead, until the horse stopped without warning and confirmed I had never actually been in control at all. I tugged at the rope in vain.

"Come on Dobbin. Giddy up. Giddy up," was the limit of my horse-talk.

The horse, head raised, showed no sign he understood my commands. His full attention now seemed to be drawn to the gates of the scrap yard located on the opposite side of the road. Suddenly, without word or warning, the horse simply made off, and walked straight across the main road, dragging me behind, ignoring all of my desperate efforts to stop him. I heard a car horn but didn't look, and was greatly relieved to find myself still alive when he stopped abruptly outside the scrapyard.

His motive soon became apparent when he lowered his head and began chomping on the tall bushy weeds growing either side of the scrapyard gates. Just inside the gates, an oily Alsatian guard dog stood on its hind legs, stretching at the end of a rusty chain. It was all teeth and bulging eyes, working itself into a killing frenzy, but the horse, unimpressed, completely ignored him and continued to devour the litter strewn foliage beside the gate.

I held onto the horse but kept a wary eye on the dog, which was now wildly lathering at the mouth. Thankfully, an equally oily but friendlier face in overalls and a flat cap came out to investigate. Ecka Rushton, as scrap men go, was a nice bloke, and was well known at the nick for keeping a stock of handy spares for use on our Austin 1100 panda cars. In those days accidental minor damage to a panda car was treated like a capital offence, so it was often easier to spend a pound note replacing a missing hub cap or broken wing mirror than it was to confess any mishaps.

"Oroight Stef? Day know yo'd got an oss?" laughed the jolly scrapman.

"Sort your dog out Ecka, I'm bricking it here!" I replied.

Laughing loudly, he dragged the snarling dog into the yard and wrestled it into the back of a wheel-less van before slamming the doors shut behind it. The van, which was the bottom vehicle in a tower of three, began to rock sideways as the frenzy continued

13

from inside, making the whole stack quiver precariously from top to bottom.

"Got to watch him Stef. He's a vicious bugger. He'd do you some bloody damage, he would."

"You need to be careful, Ecka. That new Guard Dogs Act has just come in. They'll throw the book at you if he bites a burglar." I kept a worried eye on the howling van, and the stack of cars that was now practically gyrating behind the oblivious scrap man.

"They're all bloody burglars around here Stef. Serves the buggers right if he ripped 'em up - and he would! Thievin' bleedin' toe rags. All of 'em," he ranted.

"Luckily, I can't hear a word you're saying Eck; the dog's making too much racket. Just be careful." I started slowly retreating away from the gate, eager to put some distance between me and the jelly like car tower.

"Where'd you find yer oss Stef?" he asked, skillfully changing the subject.

"Over in Canal Street. I'm trying to get the bugger back to the nick, but I don't think he's too keen."

"What's he done Stef? Are you going to charge him?" he laughed.

"I'd bloody shoot him if I was armed!" I pulled vainly on the rusty chain in an effort to distance myself from the now Leaning Tower of Ecka's Yard.

"He's enjoying them weeds Stef," he said, still laughing.

"That's for sure. I can't get him away from them."

"Shall I whack his arse Stef?"

Before I had time to fully consider his kind offer, my helpful friend had taken the initiative and belted the horse hard on the backside with his huge, oily, callused hand.

The horse leapt forward and crashed down on my foot.

"Aaaaargh! OW! Bloody hell!" I cried.

I'm sure it would have been worse if he had been shod, or if I had been standing on harder ground, but it still hurt like crazy. However, it also did the trick, and whilst I was still hopping in pain, my prisoner decided it was time to leave. We were once again en-route to the police station; this time with a little more speed and me limping along behind, still valiantly holding on.

"Whoa! Whoa! Slow down you great lump. Whooooa!" I howled in vain as I was pulled along, skipping, limping, and hopping my way down the road.

With only a furlong to go and the finish line almost in sight, our only remaining hurdle was the Rugeley to Birmingham railway line. The level crossing barrier, which in those days was still operated from the adjacent signal box, was open as we approached. As we were on a roll and making such good progress, I decided to go for the sprint finish. With plenty of tongue clicking, "Giddy Ups", and other verbal encouragement we trotted briskly onto the crossing.

The going was good; his head was now up and, floating like a Lipizzaner[2], we glided along - until without any warning he stopped dead right in the middle of the crossing.

The roadway was made of worn, wooden railway sleepers, and whilst yanking the rope I slipped and fell heavily onto my backside. I sat there cursing and swearing, still holding the rope, when without casting me a glance, his head went down, and he began chomping on the solitary weed bravely growing amongst the ballast between the lines.

It had flourished against all of the odds, in spartan conditions and unnoticed by the world, until my eagle-eyed companion decided to eat it.

[2] *A majestic breed of grey horse suited for advanced dressage and closely associated with the world famous Spanish Riding School of Vienna.*

I got up with a groan and yanked the rope again in an effort to get him moving, but only managed to hold him so that his lips were a tantalizingly two inches from the now seriously endangered plant.

I knew the signal man quite well. He was a friendly bloke, made a fair cup of tea, and enjoyed some company at quiet times. More importantly, he used to let me operate, whilst under his supervision, the row of levers that controlled the signals and points along the line. As well as being a grown man's train set, the signal box was also a great observation post, with a clear view of the crossing and passing traffic - so it didn't take long for our presence to attract his attention.

"Hoy up Stef! You can't stand there. It's very dangerous," came the familiar voice out of the window.

"Only two minutes - I'm doing my best. He'll move when he's eaten this bloody weed!" I shouted back.

I had to admire the horse's tenacity, because while I'd been keeping him out of reach of his snack, his actively puckered lips appeared to be sucking and drawing the leaves towards his mouth.

"Two minutes is stretching it, Stef. The coal train's due any time now."

Armed with this latest piece of information, I frantically resumed our tug of war.

"Come on Dob, you dozy sod," I yelled with some urgency, hauling on the rope. "We're going to get flattened in a minute!"

I know now, after years of experience, that if I had uprooted the weed, held it in my hand, and used it to entice the animal forward, we would have been out of danger in no time at all. Such knowledge was yet to be gained however, so the horse stubbornly continued his quest, and I seriously considered abandoning him to his impending fate.

The crossing lights started flashing red, warning bells rang, and in my panic I didn't see the signal man reappear at the top of the steps carrying a hand-held fog horn.

BAAAAARRRP!!! BAAAAARRRP!!!

I'm not even sure if I heard the loud double blast first or if I felt the blow-but the horse threw his head up straight into my face. I fell heavily on my behind again, dazed but still clutching determinedly to the rope, I was only partially aware of being dragged along at a canter by the spooked horse. Lost in a carefree haze of mild concussion, I remember being vaguely impressed at the unexpected turn of speed as I went with the flow, hanging on, barely noticing the blood pouring from my nose.

Somehow, we eventually found ourselves standing on the forecourt outside the familiar Victorian frontage of the police station. Both sweating and out of breath, we stood looking loathingly at each other from opposite ends of the tow rope. We were both hot, disheveled, sweaty, and covered in snot, but I suffered the additional indignity of a sore foot, black eye and a bloody nose. There also seemed to be more white hair stuck to my black tunic and trousers than there was left on the horse. I looked a mess.

The peace, or at least the lull in hostilities, was suddenly broken when a window opened and PC Ted Jenkins' face peered out. Ted was a typical front office man; he was long in service, scruffy, miserable, consistently unhelpful, and had a well-earned reputation for being the gaffer's earpiece.

"What the bloody hell have you got there?" he sneered.

"It's a horse, Ted. What does it look like?"

"I can see it's a bloody horse. What's it doing here?"

"I seized it from the job in Canal Street."

"I heard them tell you to square it and leave. Where's the panda?"

"I'm going back for it now. Will you book the horse in for me?"

Rolling his eyes despairingly, and shaking his head in his normal patronising way, he replied, "One. Where do I put the bloody horrible thing? Two. Where do you suggest that I book him in? We ain't got a bloody oss book! You, young Wild, are in the shit, so I suggest you take him back to where you found him before anyone else finds out."

The advice was sound, and he had a fair point about the lack of a horse book, stable, or any other means of keeping a horse, but I had no intention of releasing my prisoner. I certainly didn't relish the thought of repeating my experience again in reverse - nor did I want a further confrontation with the angry residents of Canal Street - so I made a desperate final plea to his better nature.

"Give us a break Ted. Something has to be done about these horses. They're making people's lives a misery. I can't take it back again. You're the man Ted, you know everything, you can sort it."

His ego, I believed, had been generously stroked, but there was still an uncomfortably long silent pause, whilst my desperate plea for help and mercy was fully considered. Eventually, and with raised eyebrows, he replied, "Go on then. Tie the damn thing up round the back. Then go and get your car before it gets wrecked. I'll sort it out, and make you a brew for when you get back."

Result! I'd never seen him smile before. Was I was privileged? Or was it wind? Perhaps he wasn't such a slimy git? Maybe he actually liked me a little?

Half an hour later, I returned to base with the car. Feeling better but still looking like I'd fallen out of a tree, I strode back into the front office ready for my cuppa, and ready to express my forever gratitude to our surprisingly helpful and misunderstood office man.

I was unpleasantly surprised to be greeted not by Ted, but by our unit inspector. The inspector was a big, barrel-chested, imposing man; well over six feet tall, always super smartly turned out, and because of his intimidating booming voice was commonly known as "Shout". He had a habit of getting in really close, nose to nose, and spraying you with spittle, when he was 'having a quiet word', and despite his immaculate appearance he had breath like a bear. Shout only normally visited our station once a day, so I had been extremely unlucky to be caught red handed in my disheveled state. Or was I?

"A quiet word in your 'shell like' Wild," he boomed.

"Sir?" I meekly replied.

"Look at the state of you; covered in blood, snot and white hair. You look a right bag of shit. And where's your cap?"

In all honesty my cap had been the least of my concerns, and I had no idea where it was. But I had no intentions of confessing to Shout that I'd lost it. I would worry about my cap later.

"It's outside in the car. Sir," I lied.

"Are you responsible for that monstrous hairy shit machine that is outside fouling the back yard?" he demanded.

"I did seize a horse Sir."

"Seize a horse? Seize a bloody great big stinky horse? And what part of your dim, immature, little pea brain told you it was a good idea to tie him by the back door? And then… and *then*, to flippantly enter him into the official found dog book as a black and white Saint Bernard?" he roared, liberally spraying my already mucky face.

The penny dropped with a loud clang. I had been 'stitched' good and proper, and was now fighting back the urge to punch our devious, smirking office man in the face.

"We haven't got a horse book Sir," I mitigated meekly.

"Exactly, you little turd. That is because this is the police station, not The High Chaparral[3], and we don't take horses. You stupid little prat."

"Sorry Sir," I cringed.

"Sorry! Bloody *sorry*! You, young man, are a constant and chronic pain in my arse. When are you going to grow up?

When are you going to earn your wages?" he roared.

"I-"

"Don't speak! Listen! If you hadn't got a wife and new little babby at home, I'd seriously consider dispensing with your services."

"I-"

"Don't speak! Listen! Do you want to continue as a police officer? Or would you rather be an Ostler[4]? Think young man. A copper or an Ostler?" he demanded.

Embarrassingly, I had absolutely no idea what an Ostler was, nor what the job description involved - but Shout became increasingly animated, and stomped gesticulating around the room. My uncomfortable predicament sent slimy Ted into sniggering laughter.

"Ostler. Good one Sir. Very good indeed," he smarmed.

"What?" boomed Shout.

"That's one of your very best, Sir. Bravo Sir. Love it Sir."

"What?"

"Ostler Wilde, Sir. One of your best. Ostler Wild. Very, very good Sir."

[3] *The High Chaparral was a popular TV western shown throughout the 1970s.*

[4] *A man employed to look after horses at an inn.*

"Ostler Wilde? Oscar Wilde? You have to be joking. Have you ever read this moron's paperwork? Have you? That bloody oss out in the back yard could do better!" he shouted, cruelly reminding me that my paperwork and reports were not only a mystery to me, but were a constant source of amusement to many of my older colleagues. I was now, without doubt, floundering, punch drunk and on the ropes.

I was momentarily relieved from the thunderous verbal onslaught when the bell at the enquiry window rang.

Shout stopped shouting while Ted opened the window, and there was a pause in hostilities as we all looked, smiling quietly, towards an old man who was peering at us nervously from the waiting room.

"Sorry to bother you officers. I know you're very busy, but I've just found this down at the level crossing." To my horror he was holding a battered, barely recognizable police cap in his hands. "I think it's been run over by a train. I do hope the officer is alright," he added.

I think it's fair to say that the following five minutes proved not to be the most enjoyable of my career. I endured a beasting of seismic proportions from Shout, who ranted without drawing breath for what seemed like forever.

To this day I'm not sure if it was the seizure of the horse, or lying about the destruction of my cap, that was the graver offence - but I certainly needed to wash and dry my face when he'd finished.

I honestly cannot remember how the 'horse in the yard, posing as a Saint Bernard' situation resolved itself, but it must have done, as things inevitably settled down and life returned to normal.

It was never quite forgotten, however, as from then onwards, because of my infamous battle with a feral horse, and a nuclear bollocking from Shout, like it or lump it, I became 'Ostler Wild'.

It's very easy, all of these years later, to look back through rose tinted spectacles, but those crazy 1970s years of policing were special, and thinking of them always brings a big smile to my face. Days of under-manning, long hours, few rest days, and of course - shockingly low pay. Days of black humour, constant ribbing and piss taking, when you took yourself too seriously at your peril, and unlike today, were allowed to earn yourself a nickname. A nickname that sometimes stung like a nettle, but one that you accepted and wore like a badge of pride, because deep down you knew that it was also your membership badge to a very selective club.

The wider club was the 'job' itself, but our exclusive member's only club was 'the shift'; our shift was very close; a second family where all our wives knew each other, everyone knew everyone else's kids, and we supported each other emotionally when it was needed.

My wife then, and miraculously still, forty odd years later, is my long-suffering Rebecca. At the time we had only been married for three years, and lived happily in a police house on the patch with our beloved nine-month-old daughter Melanie. Like most new moms of those times, Becks had happily given up work to become a full-time housewife and mother. She was the perfect police wife. She tolerated the shifts and my moods, never complained about us being permanently broke, supported me through thick and thin, and consequently had been warmly accepted into our tightly knit police family. We were very much the youngsters in the group, and I was constantly reminded by my elders that Becks was 'just the job', a 'proper police wife', and a 'little cracker' that I needed to look after.

We worked a full week of seven nights once a month, and would all routinely sit down at about 2am for a meal cooked by the station sergeant. Everyone would supply ingredients for the nightly feast, and Becks was renowned and very much appreciated for her bread pudding and apple pie. During afternoon shifts everyone generally brought sandwiches from home to eat for their meal; one memorable afternoon, whilst opening my sandwich box, I remember telling my colleagues that unusually Becks and I had had a major row that morning, but she obviously understood who was the boss because she had nevertheless quietly but dutifully prepared and packed my meal as normal. However, and much to the obvious amusement of everyone around the table, my aura of authority was shattered when I bit into my finger roll to discover the filling was a 'Bonio' dog biscuit.

When the laughter subsided to a manageable level, I was given some sound and profound advice by our wise old sergeant;

"Ostler my son, the next time that you put that girl in her place and show her who is boss, you need to step outside first so she can't hear you."

Laughter erupted again, and there was much speculation regarding what the dog would be enjoying for his tea that night. The truth was that I was still just a gangly youth, very much the baby of the shift, and any steps taken in an effort to prove my maturity and manhood to my elder peers, needed to be trod very carefully.

Several weeks after the horse debacle, I was sitting with Becks watching TV, when I showed her a document I had brought home from work. That afternoon I had been summoned to Shout's office, where I was handed a report and given the news that I had been selected for interview for a nine-week riding course with the Mounted Department. I was absolutely sure that I had never applied for the course, and Shout was sure that he had never approved or forwarded the application. We both knew it was a continuation of the 'Ostler' incident, and that some joker had forged and submitted the application on my behalf. Fortunately, we had both seen the funny side of the joke and I had taken the report home to show Becks, after which I was going to retract my application. It wasn't a problem, but was just another harmless piss-take to sort out. Her reaction, however, was unexpected. After reading the report intently several times, she spoke.

"I don't want you to retract it Stef."

"What? Are you joking?"

"No. I think you should go for it," she said with some feeling.

"But I don't know anything about horses."

"They'll teach you."

"But I can't ride."

"They'll teach you."

"The bloody things scare the life out of me."

"Impossible. You're Ostler Wild. Remember?"

"Ha! Bloody ha! And it's miles away in Brum. And I hate the Brums."

"And it's also nine weeks off shifts with weekends at home; *and* it would be a lovely break for the three of us," she argued.

"It was a joke, for God's sake."

"Stef. Please think about it? You'll be able to ride a horse when you've finished. How much do people pay to learn to ride?" she reasoned.

"But I don't want to learn to ride."

"How do you know until you've tried?"

"No. Sorry. I won't do it."

"I think you'd look really hot on a horse," she said, shamelessly changing tactics.

"What? I see what you're doing. Stop it! It won't work. No."

"Please Stef. Give it a go. For Mel, and for me. Pleeeease."

She threw her arms around me and hugged my neck, and despite all of my misgivings, I crumbled and gave in.

Was it her power of argument, or her big brown eyes that swayed my decision? I'm not sure, but I do know that I reluctantly surrendered without further debate, and promised not to withdraw the bogus application.

I now had an interview to attend. An interview in Birmingham, with the 'Brums', for a job I had never applied for, knew absolutely nothing about, and definitely didn't want. I would have to tell 'Shout' tomorrow too. What could go wrong?

CHAPTER 2

THE INTERVIEW

I was going to be late and there was nothing I could do about it. The interview date had arrived; I had set out in good time, but now my newly acquired red Mini Clubman Estate was helplessly sandwiched between two large lorries in stationary traffic on the southbound M6. It is very easy to think of unexplained hold-ups and traffic congestion on the Midlands M6 as a modern-day phenomenon, but it was still a very regular occurrence back in the 1970s.

The little red estate was our first grown-up car, the first we had bought together, and was also the first item that I had ever had to take out a bank loan to buy. Since passing my driving test at the age of seventeen, I had been happily driving, and become emotionally attached to, an old Minivan. The van had been registered in West Bromwich, so the first three letters of the registration number were TEA, and inevitably it became known to friends and family as 'Stef's tea van'. I misspent my youth in the tea van, carried out my courting in the tea van, and even after Becks and I were married, the tea van still provided sterling unwavering service as our family car. Unfortunately, its days were numbered from the moment we learned that Becks was expecting our first baby. These were the days before any legislation regarding the use of baby seats, child harnesses and booster seats, but even so I was unable to convince Becks that it was acceptable for our new baby to slide around, unrestrained, in a carry cot in the back of a van.

It had been the sad demise of a loving relationship when I finally waved goodbye to the tea van, as well as the beginning of a life of bank debt, as we took possession of our first grown-up car together. Little did I know that I was waving goodbye to far more than the tea van as it disappeared at the end of the street. I didn't understand the significance at the time, but the final threads of my carefree youth were still locked in the back, and they were disappearing too.

My interview with the Chief Inspector of the Mounted Department was scheduled for 2pm, at the central stables at Duke Street, Birmingham. I knew that parking in the yard at Duke Street was going to be a problem, so I had planned to arrive early enough to find a space, take a look around, and brush down before my interview. Despite my forward planning I was now sitting, helpless, in stationary traffic just three hundred yards short of my planned exit at junction seven. I could almost see Spaghetti Junction and my route along the Aston Expressway into the city centre. With nothing else to do, I inevitably began to question why I was here at all, given I didn't even want the job or the interview, and had only agreed to please Becks. Even so, I was stressing about being late. I couldn't help it - even now, years into retirement and with the days of interviews far behind me, I still hate to be late for anything.

I was just reaching the point of giving up any hope of making my appointment when, without warning, the traffic began to move. I was suddenly on my way to Duke Street, mentally debating whether I could still make it on time if I put my foot down.

It was exactly two o'clock when I drove through the gate, passing the security man in the shed without looking. I recklessly abandoned the Clubman alongside the petrol pump, and jumped out of the van with helmet in hand. I could hear the protests from the shed window as I strode across the yard towards the stables.

Duke Street stables were a rare remnant of Birmingham's past. Originally built in Victorian times as the City Ambulance Stables, they now sat, tucked away, at the back of a very busy car park used by both the central garage and the traffic department. Parking was a problem, always crowded and always chaotic, the fine old stable buildings had long been swallowed up, surrounded, and hidden away by ugly 1960s industrial units. The juxtaposition was stark.

I first saw the sergeant with the clip board as I looked up from tucking my too long hair up into my helmet. He was impatiently studying his wrist watch as I approached.

"Are you Wild?" he snapped.

"Bloody furious!" I joked.

"What?"

"Yes, I'm Stef Wild. I have an int-"

"You're late Wild," he snapped again.

"Yes. Two minutes. I was stuck on the-"

"I will open the door, you will march in, you will salute, you will give your name and then you will be interviewed by Chief Inspector Stuart Hancock and Inspector Benjamin Scott. Ready?"

"Sorry Sarge. Slow down a bit. What were their names again?"

"-left right left right left right. PC Wild Sir. Should have been here at 1400hrs Sir," he bawled as he opened a large blue door.

The door clunked shut behind me and I was in. I found myself standing with the door and window behind me, and two men in uniform sitting looking at me from behind a large oak desk. Behind them was a large glass cabinet displaying silver cups and other trophies. The room smelled of smoke, and on the desk were several used cigarette ends in an ash tray that had been made from a dead horse's hoof. The Chief Inspector was a smallish man with glasses, a pasty face, and greying sandy coloured hair. He had papers in front of him and spoke first, in surprisingly, a cockney accent.

"Don't you salute your senior officers in the Black Country?" he snapped.

The truth was that we didn't very often. The Black Country, then titled the 'Western Side' of the newly formed West Midlands Police, was without doubt less starchy than the central divisions, which consisted of the more traditional former Birmingham City Police. The force was now huge, second largest in the UK, but was still in its infancy after being formed in 1974 by the amalgamation of Birmingham City Police, West Midlands Constabulary, and the city of Coventry. There was an ongoing management struggle to smoothly blend three, long established, and very different organisations into one. Officers from all three regions were very parochial, still working to long established local practices, and this was one of the reasons that I would never knowingly have applied for a job with the 'Brums'.

But here I was in the very heart of Brum. 'When in Rome' I thought, as I stamped a foot and threw up a salute, or what I remembered from training school, a salute to be.

"PC Stefan Wild. Sir!" I said with raised voice.

"You're late Wild," he replied without looking up.

"It was the traffic on the M6…" I began to explain, perhaps a little too fully.

All of the time that I was twittering my apologies he never looked up from his papers. The inspector, sitting silently next to him, stared straight at me. He was a much bigger man, sitting ramrod straight, and I couldn't take my eyes off him. Ben Scott, who I would later get to know as 'Big Ben', had a face that you couldn't easily ignore. He had thinning greying hair, a neatly trimmed moustache, and a big red face which framed a slightly purple beer drinker's nose. His piercing eyes, below generous expressive eyebrows, completed the image of a slightly potty colonial colonel. The chief inspector spoke without looking at me, whilst his deputy looked at me but didn't speak to me.

"Do you know my name?" asked the Chief Inspector.

"I'm afraid I don't," I apologised.

"Do you know the inspector's name?"

"Sorry. No," I grovelled.

"How tall are you?" he asked, finally looking up.

"Six foot in thick socks," I replied, attempting to lighten the mood. The only response was the raising of the big inspector's right eyebrow.

"How heavy are you?"

"Just under twelve stone if I breathe in," he raised the eyebrow again.

"Your sick record is excellent. I trust it will remain so?"

"I'm pretty lucky with my health. So far," just seemed to redden the face as well as raise the eyebrow.

My attempts at humour were failing miserably, and not having been offered a seat, I was still standing uncomfortably to attention. I was beginning to think that the next question was going to involve a look at my teeth, when he asked:

"If accepted, would you be prepared to see out your service with this department, forgoing all opportunities of future promotion?"

"Crikey! That's a funny question. I've only done four years." The inspector's eyebrow now seemed permanently raised to full mast, and the reddened face deepened into a purple glow.

"It is a perfectly reasonable question, and is reality for most of the men on this department," snapped the chief inspector, finally looking up.

"I have no plans to take my promotion exam yet. I'm sorry, but I can't see into the future." I had been wrong. This provoked the eyebrow to rise to new levels.

"I see that you are married?"

"Yes."

"Do you have children?"

"We have a daughter, Melanie. She isn't a year old yet." I answered like a proud new father, and for a moment I was under the misapprehension that he wanted to talk about my lovely daughter. Fortunately, I resisted the urge to take her photograph out of my tunic pocket to show to him, as he cut me short again.

"I take it Wild that your wife doesn't work?"

"I'm sorry. Is that relevant?"

"I'll decide what is and what is not relevant, Wild. It is a very relevant question. Children get sick. It is your wife's job to look after your child, not yours. I won't stand for time lost for child care."

The attitudes of the 1970s were very different to those of today, but even by 1970s standards his comments were really very Dickensian. I straightened to my full height, and was considering some form of appropriate response when he asked:

"Do you have hobbies?"

"I play football on Sunday mornings."

"That would have to stop," he said dismissively.

The interview went on in the same vein, and after several more abrupt questions, all of a personal nature, I was asked if I had any questions of my own.

"I don't ride," I said.

"Good. We don't like bad habits."

"In fact, I know nothing about horses," I apologised.

"Good. We have our own ways here. Traditional ways; the right ways. Now if you have nothing further to say you may leave."

The abrupt end to the interview came as a surprise. I had made up my mind that they were going to play the 'nice cop/ nasty cop' double act, and that the big inspector with the over active eyebrow was, after all, going to follow his boss' blunt and overt rudeness with some friendly reassurance. It seemed not.

Feeling a little shell shocked, but relieved the interrogation was over, I stamped my foot, saluted and was about to turn for the door when the previously silent inspector suddenly leapt from his chair onto his feet. His eyes were glaring, face reddening, and the veins in his nose were pulsating into a deep purple. But more alarming was the fact that, although immaculate in his uniform tunic, below the waist he wore tan coloured flannel trousers and brown slippers. He had obviously not planned to get out from behind the desk during the interview, and had forgotten he was improperly dressed. I couldn't take my eyes off him, and was barely able to suppress a laugh. My self-control proved to be very fortunate however, as a fit of the giggles would certainly not have been the most appropriate course of action - 'nice cop/nasty cop' were about to become 'nasty cop/bloody indescribable cop'.

"IT WON'T DO!" fumed the inspector.

"Sorry?" I asked, smiling nervously.

"Don't bloody larf! It's not a bloody joke!"

"Sorry. I didn't mean to laugh, but I'm not sure what won't do?"

"You attend an interview needing a haircut! You were late! And you salute like a drunken sailor. Stand up straight. Put your shoulders back. Now salute again. PROPERLY!"

The Inspector was not as big as Shout, and lacked a little of his volume, but he looked meaner. When not angry, Shout could be funny, even jocular, and supportive. I could see no such qualities in this man's contorted face or eyes, so I obeyed, stamped my foot and saluted again

"No! No! No! I won't have it! I won't have it! Look and learn." He stood up to his full height, straight as a die, oblivious to the fact that he was only half properly dressed and wearing slippers. His face was aglow to the extent that I thought his head would explode. He launched into a saluting frenzy; up and down, up and down, went his right arm.

"Longest way up. Shortest way down. Longest way up. Shortest way down. Correct saluting. Begin!" he barked, looking more demented by the minute.

I was beginning to suspect a setup. Were they both in on the Ostler Wild joke? Was there a hidden camera? Was I on the telly? Nevertheless I stamped my foot, and threw up my arm again, but with more gusto than direction, and managed to poke my thumb in my eye and knock my helmet sideways.

"Whoops. Sorry." I blinked.

"NO! NO! NO! Say the words this time. Say the words. Longest way up, shortest way down. Longest way up, shortest way down. Do it! Say it! CORRECT SALUTING BEGIN!"

This man, half uniformed, half civvies, with a face like a boiling kettle was obviously a raving maniac, and to be honest immediate flight was my first instinct. I didn't want to be there anyway, and to this day I have no idea why I didn't just turn around and walk straight out of the door. I'm not sure if it was fear, intrigue, or the promise that I had made to Becks, but I stood my ground, with my helmet sloping, right eye watering, and returned his crazy salutes in a frenzied, uncoordinated panic.

Saluting is an activity best delivered with a mixture of control and some panache, and my efforts must have looked a sorry sight. I was, in effect, still a tall gangly youth, with long skinny legs and arms, and well known for my uninhibited and sometimes dangerous dancing. Now, with my helmet listing dangerously to port and my right arm flying in all directions, I think it is reasonable to assume that my salutes were falling well short of the madman's required standard.

"Carry on! Carry on! Don't stop! Longest way up, shortest way down. Longest way up, shortest way down - shout it out, shout it out."

The pasty chief inspector, papers still clutched in his hands, thankfully brought an end to the embarrassing performance.

"Thank you Mr. Scott, that will suffice. I think he has the message. Wild, you may leave. Please don't salute again, and shut the door behind you."

I stood for a moment with both arms firmly tucked into my sides. My temper was rising, and I tried to eyeball Inspector Crazy but thought better of it. By this time his face was blood red, his nose seemed to be throbbing, and he had the eyes of a man about to kill with an axe. I turned around and left with some haste, clumsily shoulder charging the sergeant outside of the door.

"Steady man, steady," he laughed, rearranging his clipboard.
"That seemed to go well. Would you like to look around?"

"No thank you. Nice of you to ask but I don't think I'll be visiting again," I answered as I strode rapidly back across the yard.

Behind him I could see through a large window into what was obviously a saddle room. Inside six or seven men wore white aprons over blue uniform shirts. They were all industriously polishing bridles and saddles; all quiet, all engrossed in their labour. All very Victorian. It looked like a scene from a TV period drama. What *was* I doing here? I turned around again and hot-footed it towards my car.

"HOY. Don't leave that car there again. You need a report for that," came a voice from the shed.

"No worries mate. I won't be back again! Trust me," I said, getting into the car.

"You been for an interview with the Donkey Wallopers?"

"Yes, I have," I replied to the talking shed.

"Good luck - they're all bleeding barmy. It's like a nut house in there."

I was still digesting this last bit of advice as I drove off, asking myself if the last fifteen minutes of my life had really happened, or if I had bumped my head earlier whilst getting out of the car.

Later that night, in the comfort of our living room, I was reliving my interview for Becks. I was just going through the actions for the third time when she held her hand up.

"Stop! Don't do it again, I'm going to pee myself laughing!"

"Please don't."

"You *must* be exaggerating Stef. God, I wished I'd been there."

"I wish I was exaggerating. It was unreal! Like Monty Python meets Basil Fawlty." I burst into my newly learned 'longest way up, shortest way down' one sided exercise routine again.

"Stop it. Your arm will fly off in a minute."

"That inspector should be in a straightjacket. That would put a stop to his bloody longest way up, shortest way down," I suggested.

"Poor Stef. Why you?" she giggled. "You do make me laugh."

"It may be funny now, but I thought he was going to sentence me to a flogging."

"Poor Stef. Poor Wild-thing; what did you think of the horses?"

For the first time it occurred to me that throughout the whole crazy visit to Duke Street, and my interview for a position on the Mounted Department, I had at no time actually seen a horse.

"I didn't see any horses." I meekly confessed.

"Stef! You went all the way to the stables at Birmingham, for an interview to be a Mountie, and you never saw a horse? What are you like?"

"I did try. Are you really disappointed?"

"A little; it would have been a nice break, but never mind. I know you; you would probably have ended up being executed by firing squad if you had got the job," she said, still laughing.

Giving the firing squad scenario some serious consideration, I clutched my chest and fell to my knees groaning.

"Come on you, don't die on me yet, let's go to bed," she said grabbing my hand and hauling me to my feet. So, we switched off the telly, and tip toed up the creaky uncarpeted stairs, giggling and 'shushing' each other with raised fingers, desperately trying not to wake our sleeping child.

And that, as far as I was concerned, was thankfully the end of Ostler Wild's adventure, and of any further involvement with the West Midlands Police Mounted Department. Or was it?

❖

CHAPTER 3

DEAD MAN'S BREECHES AND BOOTS

The summer was over, the leaves on the trees had gone, and life as a Panda driver at our little sub-station opposite the church was, to me, as interesting as ever. I was at that stage in service where I had become confident in myself, was able to deal with most of our jobs independently, but I hadn't yet become cynical and hard faced like some of my older peers. I was enjoying myself. Life was good, and the horrors of my interview at Duke Street had finally been filed into the deeper archives of my mind.

My posting was perfect. I could walk from our police house to work in five minutes along the High Street, so Becks had full use of the car, and I enjoyed the atmosphere at the small, crumbling, Victorian police station. The team was small, consisting of a sergeant, two panda drivers, sometimes a probationer to patrol the High Street on foot, and of course the ever-slimy Ted Jenkins in the enquiry office. We all got on together, backed each other when required, and were only occasionally visited by 'Shout' who was happy to spend the majority of his time at the sub–divisional headquarters, six miles away on the other side of town.

Working at such an outstation was a position of trust, which of course we collectively abused when it suited us. Being such a small team, we were all required, by the sergeant, to make up the numbers for a decent daily card school. So instead of dividing our meal breaks into two sittings of forty-five minutes each - thus providing constant operational cover - we generally all sat together, in front of the mess room coal fire, for about two hours every day.

It was during one of these extended social breakfasts (and a very serious game of 'niggle'[5]) that the phone rang in the front office. Ted, as usual, was glued to his chair with cards in his one hand and his third sausage sarnie in the other, so I, being the only one unable to ignore a ringing telephone, got up, walked into the front office and answered it. Forty-five years on, and I still can't ignore a ringing telephone.

"Front Office. PC Wild."

"Mornin' Ostler. Aren't you early, snap? Shouldn't you be out on patrol?" a familiar voice boomed out.

It was 'Shout', so I covered the mouthpiece and signaled for everyone to be quiet.

"Hello Sir. Just popped in to pick up some statement forms."

"Yer sure. Do you think I'm stupid? Who's winning?"

"Winning, Sir?"

"Never mind. When you've finished get yer skinny little arse over here. I need a quiet word in your shell-like little eary-ole."

"Anything serious Sir?"

"No. Don't worry. All of your dreams have come true. You been wishing on a star Ostler?" The tone of his laughter worried me.

Shortly afterwards, almost without a care in the world, I drove over to the big house, topped the car up with petrol, filled in the fuel book, and then made my way to the Inspector's office. I knocked on the door and walked in.

[5] A popular card game played in police canteens throughout the 1970s. The stakes were only pennies but the game provoked a level of competition that sometimes got out of hand.

"Hello Sir. You wanted to see me?"

"Sit down Ostler, and pin your ears back."

He seemed to be in very good humour, but I waited with bated breath whilst he pulled a white report form from a brown envelope. Was it a complaint? Worryingly, he began grinning from ear to ear.

"It seems, young man, that despite all of your self-doubt, you have triumphed and been successful in your application. You've been selected for a riding course at Tally Ho, and you start in the New Year - 2nd January. Congratulations."

I was absolutely gob smacked, and it took a moment or two for my thoughts to process into intelligible words.

"You're joking? The interview was a disaster. They hated me! I don't want to go on the Mounted Branch. I'll call them and withdraw my application," I spluttered.

"I don't joke about personnel matters, and you'll do no such thing. You'll go and you'll enjoy it. Take it as an opportunity to spend some normal person time with Becks and that little babby for a few weeks. And look on the bright side," he smirked "the bloody oss can do your paper work for you." driving home the paperwork jibe again.

I drove back with the report folded and tucked into my pocket book. I couldn't really believe it, and still hadn't completely ruled out the possibility this was another joke at my expense. If someone could apply for the job without my knowledge, then it was possible that my unexpected success could be a follow up plot. However, if this really was the case my team mates were well rehearsed and disciplined, because they genuinely seemed as shocked as me when I told them the news.

Predictably, initial shock was soon replaced with hilarity, and within a minute or two I was laughing uncontrollably as a handful of policemen, caps on backwards, pranced around the mess room snorting, whinnying, and scraping the floor with their feet. The gymkhana inevitably developed into a show jumping jump-off, with the aid of the kitchen mop and two wooden chairs.

This daftness was the side of policing that was unknown and unseen by the public, and I don't think people would have believed, if told, some of the antics we got up to. I often think that, because of our total lack of health and safety awareness, YouTube would have been much funnier if we had all had smart phones in the 1970s.

A short telephone call confirmed the authenticity of the report, and I found myself making an appointment to return to the dreaded Duke Street. There I would be issued with all of the kit required for a nine-week riding course.

A few days later, I was back in the Clubman retracing my steps south along the M6. There were no unexplained hold ups this time, and I had plenty of time to stop at the Duke Street entrance gate and formally seek permission, from the speaking shed, to park in the yard. So far things were going much more smoothly. However, I was careful to give the office, where my interview from hell had taken place, a wide berth, finding my way instead in through the main door to the actual stables.

My first impression was that I had walked through a time tunnel and gone back a hundred years. It was an airy old Victorian building, with a high vaulted roof and small dormer windows. There was a row of about ten stalls, all separated by cast iron partitions brightly painted red. Each partition had a large, obviously aged but highly polished brass ball on a post at the rear end, as well as a cast iron manger and hay rack at the front. Every surface was spotlessly clean and dust free, so that the assortment of highly polished brass fittings gleamed against the red painted background.

About half the stalls were occupied by large well-groomed horses, all wearing matching badged rugs. It was the first time I had actually seen a horse at Duke Street, and they were all facing the wall contentedly, steadily munching hay. They were bigger than I had imagined, but even with my complete lack of knowledge, it occurred to me that these impressive animals had very little in common with the shaggy, smelly, feral creature that had caused me so much anguish just a few months earlier. The walkway at the back of their straw covered stalls was cobbled with blue brick and worn smooth in parts by age, but had been scrubbed until it shone. The whole building smelled cozily of dry straw and hay, with a subtle background hint of disinfectant. The aura was one of ordered calm, efficiency, and well-being. It was a totally alien environment to me, but I felt strangely comfortable, almost at home. I liked it.

I found and introduced myself to a man dressed in overalls and wellies. He was carrying a broom, and seemed to be responsible for the agreeable scene. He in turn led me out of the stables, through the saddle room, and into a large room furnished with lockers all around the walls and a large wooden table and chairs in the middle. Sitting at the table, mug in hand, was the man I had come to see: Arnie Parfitt.

"Hello, I'm Stef Wild. I've come to collect the kit I need for a riding course in January," I explained.

"You're early. The gaffer said you'd probably be late," he looked me up and down.   "You'll have to wait, my coffee's hot."

He stood up, mug in hand, and I noticed collar numbers on his overall jacket denoting that he was a police officer and not civilian staff. Arnie Parfitt was, without doubt, the oldest looking PC I had ever seen. He was wiry, tanned, and fit looking despite his age, dressed in a dark blue two-piece stable suit with police shirt and tie, and well-polished shoes. He had weathered, aged features, short-cut pure white hair that must have been parted with a ruler, and a matching neatly clipped white moustache. He looked like he belonged in another age, and could easily have just stepped straight out of a black and white 1950s war film.

"Yes, I was late for my interview. I'm afraid I didn't make a very good impression. I can't believe I'm here to be honest; I thought it was a joke at first," I laughed, apologetically.

He looked me up and down again, and was obviously considering some comments that someone had made about me. "It's no joke. The gaffer didn't want you, but Big Ben persuaded him to give you a go."

That was not expected.

"If you mean the inspector, I don't believe it. He was raging at me all through the interview."

"That's Big Ben. He goes off every hour on the hour, and rages at everyone. Never stops. He's mad. He wouldn't do you a bad turn though, he's just mad. Liked the look of you, though. He reckons you'll look good on a horse." He looked me up and down yet again, as if undecided about the inspector's selection.

I was still digesting this unexpected information when he walked away. I followed him, passing the dreaded office window without looking in, across the yard, and up a set of stairs into a large store room. This room was packed with uniforms and all sorts of leather equipment that, at that time, meant absolutely nothing to me. There were buckets, mops and brooms, lances, swords, and even a large set of drums mounted on a leopard skin covered saddle. It could have been the quartermaster's store for Kitchener's Army, and smelled evocatively of leather and soap.

I was presented with a cardboard 'Vim' box to carry whilst following Arnie around the stores. Before too long it was getting heavy, pieces of kit dropped casually inside: polish, both black and brown. Brushes for black polish on, brown polish on, and brushes for black polish off and brown polish off. One hoof pick. Two yellow dusters, one small can of 'Brasso', one bar of saddle soap, one pair of size nine wellies. And finally, a white apron like the ones worn by the men I had seen cleaning saddlery on interview day. I stared at it in dismay. What on earth was I doing here?

"OK. Put that over there. We need to fix you up with some uniform now. What waist are you?"

"Thirty-two," I replied.

He rummaged through a rail of garments before passing me a pair of black breeches. They were a heavy serge material with buttoned waist, buttoned fly, and lace up legs. I put them on, fastened them up, and was surprised to catch sight of myself in the mirror. They ballooned out to the sides in the style of a World War Two Gestapo officer.

"How old are these things? Do they really still wear them like this?" I asked with some concern.

"I know who those were made for. They've never even been worn. He retired fifteen years ago. He's dead now. They don't make them like that anymore, and they fit you."

"They just seem a bit old fashioned to me. Have you got anything a little more fitted?"

"What's the matter with you young blokes? You're never satisfied! It's not a bloody fashion parade, and they're not going to allow you outside of the riding school anyway. They're fine, and they'll do for you," he said, raising his voice and reddening in the face.

Arnie was typical of a lot of older PCs of the time. He was coming to the end of his service, and was quite rightly being looked after with a cushier, less physical job. However, like many of his peers, once issued with a clip board his level of self-importance had risen to that of Admiral of the Bathwater. He was

43

the same rank as me, so it was tempting to bite back and put him in his place, but I had learned back in my cadet days that it paid not to upset the store man. The consequences were not a pretty sight, so I smiled sweetly and graciously accepted my dead man's breeches.

"What size foot are you?" he asked.

"Nine? Ten? It differs. I'm not sure." This earned me a filthy look.

I tried on a couple of pairs of boots that looked almost new, but even after tugging at them with metal boot hooks, I couldn't pull them over my calf muscles. The third pair went on more easily, but were cracked, patched, and very much on the roomy side.

"I think these are a bit on the big side. I look like a pirate. They look like they've seen lots of action, too."

"What do you expect? The real blokes have them made to measure. You can pack them out with thick socks. They're fine. They don't make them like that anymore."

"I guess you're right," I said with some doubt.

"Good, that's it then. Chuck them in your box and follow me."

"Do I wear my own tunic and cap?"

"No. In the riding school you will wear what I've given you, with uniformed shirt and tie. You will have to provide your own checked sports jacket, and checked cloth cap."

This came as a big surprise.

"A checked jacket and cap? I'm only twenty-two. Where the bloody hell do I get those from?"

"You can buy them from proper men's shops like Dunn's[6]. I wouldn't spend too much though; most blokes don't last the course," he reassured.

[6] Dunn & Co was a very traditional men's outfitter seen on most busy High Streets.

"Dunn's! I can't go into Dunn's, it's a museum."

"I don't care where you go, but you'll need a jacket and cap."

"How about a hard hat?"

"They're for pony club pansies. Not here. Try not to fall on your head."

I didn't seem to making much of an impression on PC Parfitt.

"Don't I need some spurs?"

"No. Recruits don't wear spurs. You win your spurs by successfully completing the riding course. If you do complete it, that is, and if we decide to keep you."

With that ringing endorsement, I left Duke Street Stables for the second time. Not quite as agitated as before, but perhaps more than a little disappointed with my 'Vim' box of cleaning products, and my meagre, ancient, and rather tatty riding attire. I wasn't feeling any happier about this unwanted development in my career, I certainly hadn't warmed to Duke Street, and I couldn't help worrying - what was I getting myself into?

Later that night, at home, we were enjoying that comfy period - just the two of us lying on the sofa in front of a nice warm coal fire, slowly roasting and watching TV.

We applied and adhered to a strict rule, that when Mel was fast asleep, we cleared the decks before settling down together. The washing up was done, the drying washing moved from the fireguard, and all of the toys packed away. It was our time together, and I think it's now known as quality time. The tranquility was interrupted by Becks, who I suddenly realized was looking at me intently whilst propped up on her elbow.

"Go and put them on then."

"What?"

"Go on. I want to see you in those sexy breeches and boots."

"Absolutely not."

"Come on Wild-thing. I want to see you in your kit."

"Trust me. No, you don't," I insisted.

"I doooo."

"Shut up and watch the telly."

"Stef, you are a grumpy git. Go and put them on."

She then, with surprisingly little effort, pushed me off the settee onto the floor. Dutifully, I got up, quickly got changed in the kitchen, and burst back into the lounge with my hands on my hips in typical Hollywood hero style.

"TA-DA!" I slapped my thigh for further effect, and it was only when I didn't feel the slap that I remembered the volume of material that had been used in constructing the sides of my breeches.

The result, though perhaps not the desired one, was instant. Becks sat on the edge of the sofa doubled up, and rocked with laughter. The tears ran down her face as she snorted uncontrollably.

"It's not supposed to be funny, Becks."

"Sorry Stef. I can't help it! You look such a *tit*."

"Not like a swashbuckler?" I asked in my most pathetic wounded teddy voice.

"No! Like Benny Hill."

"That's not very nice. You know I didn't want to bloody well do this. Anyway, it's not funny," I snapped.

"Now you look like a pompous tit with your hands on your hips. And it *is* funny. You aren't sitting here looking at what *I'm* looking at..."

I knew she was right, because I hadn't been happy when I tried the kit on earlier in the stores. I couldn't make my mind up if PC Parfitt had selected me for special attention, or if everyone was going to be kitted out so badly.

"I suppose all the others will look stupid too? Perhaps I won't be on my own," I asked, craving reassurance.

"Give us a twirl, tiger," she laughed.

I did a double twirl and paraded up and down the lounge, hand on hip, in true camp catwalk style.

The nasal giggling from the sofa resumed.

"Now what's so funny?"

"Well you used to have a fit bum, but it seems to have left home!" she laughed. "They could have made a tent with the material in those breeches."

"Not too sexy for you then?" I asked, adopting my most pathetic cuddly puppy pose.

The snorting abated as she got up, squeezed my bum and said, "Put the fireguard up 'Swashbuckler'. I'll turn off. You can take me to bed."

It seemed the old adage "make 'em laugh" had worked its wicked way again, so without too much of a struggle I obediently followed. We crept up the creaky wooden stairs again, both giggling at my hopeless attempt to do it quietly in such oversized, clumpy pirate boots.

One day, sometime in the future and overtime permitting, we hoped to buy a stair carpet.

CHAPTER 4

EYES, NOSE AND DOCK

It was 7.45am on the 2nd of January 1979, as I pulled into the car park at Tally Ho. Tally Ho was, and still is I believe, the main training centre of the West Midlands Police. It is situated in large leafy grounds opposite the Warwickshire County Cricket ground in Edgbaston, which is on the wrong side of the city of Birmingham for where I lived. A journey of over twenty miles each way, through busy city centre traffic, was a very different commute to my usual five minutes' walk along the High Street.

I had been to Tally Ho several times before, but was not familiar with the riding school. I found it in a large, flat roofed, brick-built building located next to the drill square. There was no one to be found in the yard, except for four horses looking over their stable doors, so I unloaded my 'Vim' box kitbag from the car and found my way to the first floor via a concrete stairway.

I walked into a large room laid out in the same fashion as that room at Duke Street, with lockers around the outside and a large table and chairs in the centre. I would learn, at some later date that this layout was to be found in all of the Mounted Department buildings within the force. Whatever the location, this room was commonly known as 'The Bunk'. The Bunk was always the 'centre of many things', where mounted men took their refreshments, and indulged in current affairs, politics, gossip, and general arsing around.

There were three men sitting at the table drinking tea from dubious looking mugs. They all looked in my direction, and the older one of the three stood up to greet me.

"Ahh. Now we have three. PC Wild I presume?"

"Yes, that's me. Good morning." I nodded to all.

"We are honoured. I was warned that you would probably be late, Wild. My name is Derek Joiner. I'm the sergeant and trainer for your course."

I looked at my watch and was relieved to see that it was only 7.55am, and that I hadn't yet confirmed my unfairly earned reputation. I stowed my "Vim" box alongside two similar looking cardboard boxes of kit, and was invited to sit down and have a cup of tea. I took my place at the table.

Derek Joiner was of average height, slim build, and spoke clearly in an authoritative voice. He had dark parted hair, and a neatly trimmed dark moustache. He wore a brown cow gown over uniform shirt and tie, and even in work gear he looked smart and efficient.

"Gentlemen, after today you will be expected to begin grooming at 8am sharp. Today I want to lay down a few ground rules, so we will begin at 8.30am when you have finished your tea. You will require your wellington boots and your aprons, and you will collect a grooming kit from a hook on the wall halfway down the stairs. The kit you choose will denote the horse that you will groom."

He carried on with our briefing and timetable for the day. Most was of a mundane nature, but my ears pricked up as he made his final point.

"Gentlemen, these horses are well trained. They are animals that thrive on, and enjoy, routine. If you handle them properly and professionally, they will cooperate with you and all will be well. If you are sloppy, they may stand on you. If you mess them about, they may bite you or even kick you. This, of course, may hurt you and injure you, so I suggest that you pay attention when I demonstrate the morning grooming routine," he looked us all up and down as if to emphasize the seriousness of his warning. "Does everyone understand?"

Everyone nodded solemnly. He then marched out of the door and down the stairs, grabbing a hessian bagged grooming kit from the wall, and carrying on down to the stable yard. The three of us followed, each taking our own bag from a hook on the wall. We gathered at the door of the first loose box, where a large bay horse stood looking at us. A groom dressed in a blue stable suit placed a bucket of steaming water and a cloth at the sergeant's feet.

"Gentlemen, this is Mr Durran. Mr Durran is our civilian groom; he looks after the horses and stables, and a very fine job he does too. He is not a servant, nor is he your skivvy. He has his own duties to perform. He will assist you, in these early stages, if you need help, but he is not here to do your work for you. Do you understand, gentlemen?"

We all quietly agreed, and during the next half hour watched intently whilst the sergeant groomed, demonstrating the method we were to use. We learned to always turn the horse around away from ourselves, and how to fasten him by his head collar to a stable chain with a quick release fastener. We were shown how to unfasten the heavy jute night rug, and draw it backwards along the horse's back following the lie of the hair before removing it. We watched quietly whilst he groomed the horse firmly from the ears to the tail with a stiff body brush. As he groomed he scraped the brush with a metal curry comb, occasionally knocking powdery grease from the curry comb onto the stable floor. He continued methodically, covering the whole of the horse including the belly and legs. All throughout the procedure the horse stood still, contented, and compliant. As I stood with my own grooming bag on my arm, quietly growing in confidence, I compared this well-mannered gentle animal to the shaggy, riotous creature I had battled a few months earlier. This, I thought to myself, is going to be much easier than I had imagined.

After the body brushing, we learned how to hold the tail while brushing it out thoroughly from top to bottom with a dandy brush, before binding the top of the tail with a navy blue tail bandage. After completing the tail, he unfastened the horse from the chain, and without any command it dutifully turned around for the sergeant to remove the leather head collar. He stood calmly with his head lowered for it to be gently groomed with the body brush, then without instruction raised it to a convenient height for his mane and forelock to be brushed and laid flat with the dandy brush.

The brushes were finally put back into the bag, before he took a heavy grey cloth out of the bucket of hot water. He wrung out the cloth and approached the horse's head again.

"I've almost finished, gentlemen. We now go on to 'Eyes, Nose, and Dock'. Pay special attention, because it is desirable for the horse that this procedure is carried out in the correct order."

We watched in silence as he first gently wiped the horse's eyes, then nostrils, before finally lifting its tail and wiping its arse with the cloth.

"Remember the order gentlemen. Eyes, Nose, and then Dock."

The head collar was wiped clean and replaced, then the horse was secured to the wall again, and a smartly badged day rug was put on and fastened.

"Finally, gentlemen, we pick out the horse's feet. You will need your hoof picks for this procedure. More information regarding the care of the horse's feet will be forthcoming, but in the meantime, you will pick out their feet after grooming, and always before leading them out into the yard. Mr Durran is not paid to follow you around picking up shit every time you leave the stable."

He nodded to the smiling groom standing close by. We were then shown how to stand to the near fore of the horse, and run our hand down the back of the horse's leg. He calmly lifted each front leg in turn while the sergeant picked the underside of the hooves clean with the hoof pick, showing us the frog, cleft of frog, and explaining which way to work the hoof pick so as not to injure the horse. He then moved and bent towards the back of the horse, following the same routine with the hind legs. Again, without fuss, the animal lifted each hind leg alternately whilst his hooves were picked clean. The whole grooming procedure had been quiet and efficient. The animal's behavior and level of compliance throughout had been impressive, and for this reluctant novice, very reassuring.

"Gentlemen, I am going upstairs to catch up on my normal duties. I'm leaving you in the capable hands of Mr Durran, who will advise and assist you if necessary. Don't hang around; you have just half an hour to complete grooming. You will then be shown how to saddle up before changing into your riding gear."

The riding gear instruction was unexpected. All of my previous training courses, of which there had already been many, had seemed to involve at least one day of classroom work and form filling. It suddenly dawned on me that I was going to be sitting on a horse in just over an hour's time. My thoughts were disturbed by Mr Durran.

"Okay guys. Forget the Mr Durran; my name's Steve. Look at the name on your grooming bag and find your horse's name over the door. Just get cracking, I'm only outside if you need me."

I dutifully read the name printed on the grooming bag: "Bijou." What sort of girlie name was Bijou for a police horse? Over each door a smartly painted name plate identified the occupant. "Coronet II" was the sergeant's horse that we had just seen groomed, next, both with their heads looking out over their doors, were the impressively named "Grenadier" and "Brigadier". I walked to the last door in the line, which didn't have a horse's head looking over it, and mentally prepared myself for my appointment with Bijou.

The doors were typical stable doors, with a separate top and bottom. Opening the bottom door, I could see there was a metal bar running across the middle which prevented the horses from escaping while the doors were open. I was greeted by Bijou's bottom. His head was facing into the darkest back corner of the stable, and he didn't acknowledge my presence as I ducked inside. I noticed immediately that Bijou was much darker than his neighbours, looking almost black in the darkness. He was also much smaller than his stablemates. Typical; while everyone else rode a manly war horse, I had drawn the short straw with a "my little pony" named Bijou.

Remembering what the sergeant had said about talking to the horses when you approached from behind, I formally introduced myself to my steed of the day.

"Bijou. My pretty little jewel. Morning, mate! I'm Stef and- AAAGGGHHH!!!"

There was a deafening clatter of hooves as Bijou spun to greet me. Ears flattened back, and eyes wide, white and wild - with his huge teeth bared, pretty little Bijou lunged for my throat! For a split second I was looking straight into the face of Satan.

I scrambled on hands and knees outside the stable door, and slowly became aware of a row of concerned faces looking at me from over the neighbouring doors. Steve Durran helped me to my feet.

"What happened there then?"

"The bastard attacked me! Went for my throat," I spluttered.

"Did he bite your forehead? You've got a right old lump on it."

"No. I hit it on the bloody bar in my panic to get out," I replied, poking at the fast-rising bump.

Bijou glared at us over the bar, his ears still pressed flat back. He had the look of a striking rattle snake about him.

"He can be a naughty little tinker with the new blokes sometimes."

"Naughty little tinker? He's an evil dangerous bastard! He'd have killed me if I hadn't got out."

Chuckling to himself, Steve walked into the stable, took hold of Bijou's head collar, turned him around, and fastened him to the back wall with the chain.

"There you go; he can't bite you now. Best hurry up. Time's getting on."

I gathered my scattered grooming kit and slunk warily back into the dragon's den. I unbuckled the surcingle on the rug, and then reached forward for the breast strap. He immediately swung his head, teeth gnashing, towards my hand.

"Hoy. Gerroff you bastard!" I said whilst jumping backwards.

Much to my relief, I was out of reach and managed to remove the rug without any further injury. I began the same body brush and curry comb procedure that the marvelous Coronet II had, a little earlier, stood so calm and still for. Bijou scraped and stamped his hooves on the cobbled floor, and continued with his best efforts to take a bite out of me.

"Bugger off you little shit!" I shouted with feigned bravery.

Brushing down the neck, along his back and towards the top of his rear end continued with me out of reach and only mildly terrified. However, every time I ventured to the top of his neck, I'm sure I could hear the links in the chain straining, as he constantly swung around with flashing eyes and grinding teeth.

"Steady. Steady. Bloody hell! That was close."

There was little relief to be found at the other end or down below. Every time I began to groom his rump or flanks, he stamped his hind feet so hard that they sparked on the cobbles. I wasn't aware at the time, but between his snapping and stamping, and my shouts, we must have been creating a right old din.

Steve's head reappeared over the door, and Bijou immediately stood angelically still and calm.

"What's happening in here? You're making a right racket."

"Sorry mate, but he's still trying to kill me. He's alright whilst you're here, but the minute you turn your back…"

"I'll hang around and watch you while you pick his feet out," he reassured me.

I took my hoof pick and moved forward towards the sharp end. As we had been shown, I bent down and ran my hands down the back of his lower near fore leg. Nothing! I did it again, more firmly. Nothing!

"BIJOU!" Steve said loudly.

One after another, both front legs were calmly raised and held while I cleaned his hooves with the hoof pick. Running my hands down his side, I moved towards the back, again bending before running my hand down the front of his near hind leg. Nothing! I tried again. Nothing!

"Try again, but this time lean your weight against him at the same time," suggested Steve.

The leg came up, and up, much higher than I had expected - it hovered menacingly above my lowered head. I froze with fear, convinced the swine was going to kick my head off.

"BIJOU! You little shit!" came the welcome voice from over the door.

He immediately lowered his leg to the appropriate height and I completed my picking of the rear hooves. I stood up with sweat beading on my brow.

"You need to show him who's boss. Who's in charge," he explained.

"That's easy to say. But how?"

"You need to command. Be authoritative."

"I think he's already worked out who is in command today," I conceded.

"He's just trying you out; I'll leave it with you," Steve replied, stepping back out of sight.

Following these words of wisdom I needed no further encouragement. With a newly found but bogus confidence, I happily gave Bijou an authoritative cuss and a swift dig in the ribs with the wooden body brush.

"Go on! Get over!" I commanded.

The result was instant. He swung towards me, lifting me off my feet, and pressed me with a thud against the back wall.

"Aaagghh!" I gasped, as all the air vacated my lungs.

I stood squashed and winded, unable to move, peering pathetically at Steve from over the back of the devil horse.

"That worked well," he laughed, coming in to rescue me. Bijou was again calm and compliant in Steve's presence. He restored order, released me from my embarrassing confinement, and left me alone with the enemy once more, with one final task before completion.

Now I'm not usually a sly person, but I was bricking it and my pride was severely dented - so I felt not an ounce of guilt as I checked to confirm I wasn't being watched, and wrung my cloth out of the bucket.

The coast was clear and I struck swiftly - with the element of surprise, I completed the personal wiping before Bijou had time to react, or Steve returned to check on me.

"That'll teach you to mess with the Ostler, you evil little bastard. Job done. 'Dock, Nose, and Eyes' complete." I smiled to myself as I hung my grooming kit on the hook, halfway up the stairs.

Bijou was now standing quietly; groomed, rugged, and tied in his stable; he was oblivious to the fact that I had, at the last moment, snatched a moral victory literally from the jaws of defeat. He didn't need to know. Only I knew, but it made me feel a lot better.

CHAPTER 5

NEW BREECHES

I walked into the saddle room. The others were standing studying a saddle on a saddle horse. Everyone went quiet and there was a collective swivel of heads as Sgt. Joiner turned and looked at me.

"Ah. Thanks for joining us Wild. Okay if we start now?"

"Sorry. That devil horse tried to kill me."

"Did he bite your head Wild? You seem to be wounded."

"No, I hit it on the door bar. I'll live."

"You must be quiet and more careful or you'll upset these horses. They're used to calm in their stables."

"Sorry," I protested, "but I was expecting to groom a horse, not fight a duel with a dragon."

Joiner shook his head, and my two fellow trainees looked at me in that sympathetic sort of way that is often used for patronizing inferiors. I was beginning to get the feeling that so far, I hadn't created the greatest first impression. I also didn't believe it was entirely all my fault.

I joined the gathering around the saddle horse, and class resumed. For the next ten minutes we were shown the saddle: pommel at the front, cantle at the back, seat, flaps, straps, girth, and how they fastened. Then we were shown a bridle, with the bit and reins. We were to take the saddles downstairs, saddle the horses, and return upstairs. After changing into our riding gear, we were to go back downstairs, bridle up the horses, and lead them into the riding school.

We watched while the sergeant 'saddled up' Coronet. First he removed the rug, pulling it backwards, and folded it neatly over the door. Then he lifted the saddle onto the horse's back just a little too far forward, sliding it backwards so that it laid the coat flat before finding the correct position. The girth was fastened but not tightened, and the horse, finally, fastened with the chain to the wall.

"Right gentlemen, it's your turn now. Mr Durran, will you supervise Wild please? I'll keep my eye on the other two."

Already having been identified as requiring special attention, I picked up my saddle and followed Steve into Bijou's stable. I think in the interests of speed and efficiency, he stood arms folded, watching whilst I warily saddled up. The cursed animal, fully aware he was under surveillance, never moved or even blinked an eye, but stood politely and patiently throughout the whole procedure.

"I don't get it Steve. Why does he hate the sight of me, and try to kill me, but behave when you're about?" I complained.

"He's a grumpy git with everyone, but you're new and he can smell the fear. You've got to be firm with him."

"You mean pretend I'm not shitting myself?"

"Something like that," he laughed.

Back upstairs, we were allocated lockers, emptying our 'Vim' boxes into them before changing into our kit for riding. Becks had bought me a smart new cap from Dunn & Co. for Christmas. A 'Rutland County Cap' no less, which had caused much mirth among family and friends during the Christmas festivities. Flat caps have enjoyed one or two returns to fashion in recent years, but in 1979 they were still regarded very much as a grandad or Prince Philip accessory. Family finances had decided I couldn't justify the cost of a new check sports jacket, and unlike more recent times, charity shops were still something of a rarity, so my parents had come to my rescue and found one that had belonged to my late grandfather. It was new, hardly worn, and because grandad had been a slightly built chap, fit my puny juvenile chest perfectly. Unfortunately, grandad had been only five feet six inches tall and I was six foot, so it was very obviously too short in the arms and body.

With the dressing up completed the three of us stood waiting, a little self-consciously, for the sergeant to come back.

"Bloody Hell Wild. What are you wearing?"

"Just my riding kit. Is there a problem Sarge?"

"Problems Wild, not problem. Are you storing winter fuel in those breeches and boots? Did you upset Arnie in the stores?" he asked.

"I'm only wearing what he gave me. Sorry."

"I haven't seen breeches like that since the old king died," he went on, "and that jacket? Who did that belong to, Norman Wisdom?"

"It was my grandad's. It's hardly been worn," I replied indignantly.

"I can see why too! You're aspiring to be a Mounted Man Wild, but you look a complete tosser. This is my course, and it is supposed to be a serious business, not the bloody circus. I've got both of my eyes firmly fixed on you, Wild. Be careful."

Once again I could feel my credibility plummeting ever faster ground wards. The others were looking at me in that condolent manner again; it seemed I was somehow already on borrowed time without having yet sat on a horse.

Back downstairs, we were shown how to bridle the horses. It was explained that the bit fit into the mouth and sat in the gap between the horse's incisors and molars. We were shown how to open the horse's mouth using our thumbs, how to fit the bridle behind the ears, and how to straighten everything, before finally fastening the throat lash. Again, the whole procedure was carried out quietly and without drama.

Thankfully, I entered Bijou's lair under the watchful eye of Steve, so I took advantage and quickly unfastened the head collar and turned him around while still under his close protection. I held the bridle to his head with the bit close to his lips and gently pressed my thumb into the corner of his mouth. Nothing! Those teeth that had previously been so active were now firmly clamped shut. With trepidation, I slid my thumb a little further into the corner of his mouth and squeezed more firmly. His ears immediately flattened onto his neck, and I felt his jaw tense and close even more tightly.

"Am I doing this right Steve?" I asked.

"BIJOU!" growled Steve.

I felt his jaw relax, his teeth opened, and the bit slid effortlessly into his mouth. The bridle was already adjusted appropriately, so the bit sat comfortably in the gap between the two sets of teeth. With relief, I pulled the bridle over the top of his head and began to fasten the throat lash.

"Check it out Stef. I don't think that that's going to stay on very long before it falls off," observed my minder.

I looked at the horse and bridle, and after a moment or two spotted my mistake. The top of the bridle, instead of sitting comfortably behind the horse's ears, was sitting on top of Bijou's, which were still flattened onto his neck. With the ears flat and his wide, wild eyes, he looked comically demonic.

"Does this bloody horse ever cooperate?" I asked irritably.

"He's taking the piss Stef. Just reach up and gently pull them forward so the bridle fits behind them."

I reached up in an effort to carry out the adjustment, but he immediately stepped back and raised his head high out of reach. I stared at him loathingly, and I could see in his eyes that the feelings were mutual.

"BIJOU!" growled Steve.

He lowered his head without further fuss, so I took the opportunity and pulled his ears into the correct position, before fully fastening the bridle. On refection, I probably wasn't as gentle as I could have been, but I was now determined to show him who was the boss. Finally, all saddled and bridled, I led him out of the stable, joining the others who were waiting patiently in the yard. In single file we led our horses through large double doors into the indoor riding school.

The riding school was an impressive purpose-built, high-roofed brick building, measuring the regulation forty by twenty metres. It was light, with high windows and hardwood paneled walls. The ground was covered in a soft mixture of sand and wood shavings. Waiting for us inside were Sgt. Joiner and two uniformed men on horses.

The three of us stood in line in the centre of the school. During the next ten minutes we were shown how to stand next to our horses, and how to 'stand to' our horses. 'Standing to' involved standing directly in front of the horse with the reins held high, close to the bit with both hands, looking at your horse face to face. Bijou's ears flattened back, and his teeth seemed to grow, every time we made eye contact. I was, however, more confident than I had been in the stable, because here there was safety in numbers. We were then shown how to fully tighten our girth straps, which inevitably provoked further castanet-like gnashing of teeth by my grumpy steed. Finally, we adjusted the length of our stirrups, measuring them by the inside length of our arms. The moment had arrived, and amazingly, I was about to sit on a horse for the very first time. We had all watched carefully while one of the uniformed lads demonstrated how to mount, and I was pleased to find that I could manage to lift my left leg high enough to place my foot in the near-side stirrup. We all stood on one leg, left hand on the pommel, right hand on the cantle, waiting to kick ourselves up into our saddles on the order to mount.

"Gentlemen, prepare to mount your horses," came the warning command.

"Whole ride - MOUNT!"

"AAAARGGGHHH! BLOODY *HELL*!"

"Wild. You don't appear to be on your horse?" observed the sergeant.

"BASTARD!"

"What the hell is the matter with you Wild?" he snapped irritably.

"He's bit my arse!"

"What?"

"The bastard bit my arse."

The initial shock had passed, but the pain lingered. I reached back to the seat of pain, finding a tear in the seat of my voluminous breeches. Further exploration revealed a trickle of blood from my left buttock. Impressively, and without anyone witnessing the attack, Bijou had managed to swing around and ravage my rear. My two fellow trainees were sitting on top of their horses looking down on me in amazement, and both of the uniformed riders were leaning forward in their saddles, making no effort to suppress their laughter.

"Wild. Are you going to disrupt my riding school all day?" enquired Joiner.

"He bit me on the arse," I protested. "He's drawn blood."

"*Wild*. What are you doing to that poor horse? You must treat him more kindly; you're frightening him."

"He bit me on the arse! I wasn't even looking at him," I replied indignantly.

"Don't be such a brute Wild. He's obviously afraid. Poor Bijou." His face began to crease with suppressed laughter.

The sergeant came over to view the evidence and soon joined the others in their hearty laughter. After the initial shock, it became pretty obvious to me that sympathy was not on the agenda, so I joined them all and had a good laugh at my own expense.

"Right gentlemen, drama over, time to press on. Wild, get a grip and mount up. Bijou, you are a bad little bastard, and one day I shall enjoy having you shot."

I mounted up without further incident, and within a few minutes we were lined up, one behind the other, at the side of the riding school. One of the uniformed guys took the front, 'leading file', while the other took the back.

"Whole ride, four feet nose to croup[7]. Walk march," commanded the sergeant from the centre of the school.

The leading file walked away, and the rest of us followed in a shambolic sort of manner. We circled the perimeter of the school while the sergeant attempted to encourage us into some sort of order.

"Keep up, keep up. Four feet nose to croup. Four feet! Four feet!"

We halted by feeling the reins, and walked on by squeezing with our legs. The principle seemed simple, but the process felt clumsy and unnatural, and I had little doubt that any sudden movement would probably have me on the ground. After a few minutes we numbered off from the front, enabling us to be identified without using our names.

---

[7] *Area between the top line of the horse's hind quarters and the dock of the tail.*

I shouted out number three.

"Heels down, toes up everyone. Look ahead everyone."

"Number three! Heels down and move your legs back."

"Try to relax at the waist everyone, shoulders back, look up and to the front."

"Number four, shorten those reins. Don't yank them like that, that horse has a mouth. Squeeze him with your legs now. Heels down, toes up."

I dread to think what we looked like, but we continued our amble around the perimeter of the school while our riding positions were scrutinized and amended.

"Leading file, at the diagonal change the rein."

Upon reaching a quarter marker, the leading file walked diagonally across the riding school from corner to corner, and we all followed, finding ourselves walking around the school in the opposite direction. I'd later learn that was what was meant by "changing the rein". The constant flow of instructions continued.

"Number two, lower your hands. Head up. Don't slouch. Head *up* man!"

We continued our circuits for several more laps, until I realised I was falling behind the horse in front. My squeezes developed into frantic kicks, but the effects were unfortunately minimal.

"Four feet, number three. Four feet nose to croup. Keep up man. Keep up!"

I was working hard, but to no avail. My ride seemed to be running low on fuel.

"Wild, keep up. Give that lazy slug a kick. Keep your hands still; don't flap them when you kick. Keep up. Keep up!"

After a few more laps we were called to a halt in the centre, dismounted, and watched as one of the uniformed guys rode around the school.

"Gentlemen, pay attention. Look at the leg position, look up through the seat, nice and straight in the back, shoulders back, chin up. Look at the hands. Nice and low and still. A nice bend at the wrists, and a nice bend at the elbows, look how relaxed his hands are," commented Joiner. "You are striving for a natural seat and true independence between hand and leg."

The rider went around the school effortlessly. He was a tall, skinny bloke, who looked like he had been born on the back of the horse as he sent the animal from a walk into a trot without any visible movement. Unlike our lumbering and swaying, he sat easily and proudly upright. It seemed unlikely to me, at that moment, that I would ever be capable of attaining such standards.

After a short break we prepared to remount, but before doing so the rider who had just delivered the demonstration rode over to me. I was immediately on the defensive because, watching him, I had mentally labeled him as snotty and aloof. He stopped alongside, leaned down, and with a face that was so creased in laughter that his eyes were invisible, offered me some useful advice.

"Sorry to laugh at you mate, but that was the funniest thing I have seen for ages. Next time, shorten the reins and hang on to them with your left hand while you're gripping the saddle to mount, and he won't be able to reach you."

I was more than grateful for the useful advice, but even more appreciative because these were the first friendly words anyone had spoken to me, since the first day at the interview from hell at Duke Street.

"Cheers mate. I'm not doing very well so far, am I?"

"You're new and he's taking the piss something rotten, but it'll be someone else's turn tomorrow." He gave me a nod and rode away.

Heartened by these words of encouragement, I remounted without incident and rejoined the ride. The remainder of the morning was more of the same, before, to my great relief, we were finally called to a halt. It wasn't a moment too early, as my backside was stinging and grumbling, telling me it was time to rest. However, instead of giving the order to dismount and return to the stables, Sgt. Joiner explained that we were, in fact, moving on to the trot. Following a short explanation of the transition, we were told to sit up and gather our reins.

"Whole ride. Walk march," he barked.

We resumed our unsightly amble around the school. It took a few minutes, but eventually our positions and dressings were deemed to be good enough for us to progress.

"Whole ride prepare to trot... Whole ride quietly away... Terrrrrot! Squeeze with the legs; ease the pressure on the reins. Come on! Squeeze with the legs."

We did, eventually, move into the trot, but not as one. Everyone in front of me did, but Bijou didn't - and consequently neither did anyone behind me. I began kicking my legs frenziedly, to little effect. Bijou plodded on sullenly; head down at a slow walk.

"Number three. Terrrrrot. Get him going Wild, get him going. BIJOU! TERRRROT!"

I'm sure it had more to do with the sergeant's verbal encouragement than any skill of mine, but eventually Bijou decided it was time to trot, and the ride commenced. The three of us bounced around, lap after lap, all completely out of time with the horses. Try as I might, it seemed impossible to avoid going down at the same time as the horse was going up. This was not as easy as it looked, and also not helped by the fact that the moment I stopped pedaling, Bijou stopped trotting. I was tiring, and constantly falling behind despite the aggressive and constant verbal encouragement from Joiner to keep up.

I bloody hated that horse.

Eventually the torture ceased, and after unsaddling, drying and rugging up the horses, we gathered back in the saddle room. We were shown how to strip and clean the kit, before reassembling and hanging it in the proper fashion. Following a debrief of our morning in the riding school, I was invited into Sgt. Joiners office. I thought that I was in for a bollocking after the morning's dramatic events, but instead was offered a replacement pair of breeches.

"Try these on. They're an old pair of mine, but they've got to be better than the panto ones you've been wearing. Try not to damage them," he said, throwing them at me. He raised an eyebrow, and I couldn't tell if he was serious about not damaging them or if he was winding me up, but I gratefully accepted his offered breeches. I took both pairs home that night, hoping the replacements would fit - if not, I was going to have to ask Becks repair the old ones.

Later that night, feeling like I had been trampled by a herd of rhinos, I updated Becks on my progress. She had already inspected and 'germolened' my forehead and buttock, and was keen to understand exactly why I was feeling so disheartened.

"It's really hard and physical, Becks. Every bone and muscle is killing me."

"I get your aches and pains Stef, but I don't understand why you are so knocked about. Shouldn't you just ride these horses? Why do you always have to fight them?" she asked.

"I don't. They just don't seem to like me," I whimpered.

"They're supposed to be such gentle creatures. You've only met two, and they've both beaten you up!" She tilted her head to one side in a pitying manner.

"I guess I've been unlucky. It'll be better tomorrow, I hope. If I survive!"

I went into the kitchen and tried on the replacement breeches; happily, they fit perfectly and were made of a much lighter fabric. I pulled on the boots and returned to the lounge, hand on hip adopting my finest catwalk strut for inspection.

"Wow! They look much better. They really suit you, actually. Give us a twirl. Hmm, nice bum Wild-thing!"

I walked up and down enjoying the attention and a feeling of freedom that hadn't been evident with the heavier baggy pants. Unfortunately, the thinner, lighter material emphasised just how much leg room I had in my saggy boots, which were floppier than ever. I tried on a second pair of football socks in an effort to pad out my legs, but found I couldn't get my feet into the boots while wearing two pairs of thick socks.

"That's weird Stef. I know you've got skinny legs, but that bloke must have had legs like a snooker table and feet like a fairy."

"You know what they say about blokes with little feet?" I joked.

"Yes, they wear little shoes, you smutty sod," she scolded.

We laughed over the peculiar shape of the unknown previous owner of my boots, and both concluded that what I desperately needed was something that thickened my legs without enlarging my feet. I didn't think anything of it when she left the room, but just flopped out flat on the sofa to rest my weary legs.

I must have nodded off for a few minutes, and woke up startled when she burst back into the room. She stood, giggling, with her hands behind her back - obviously hiding something.

"What have you got?"

"Nothing."

"Show me what you've got."

"Nothing for you here," she teased.

"Don't make me get up and get you. I hurt too much."

Giggling, she produced something pink and fluffy from behind her back.

"What the bloody hell have you got there?"

"They're my old keep fit leg warmers."

"You have to be joking. I'm not going to work in those," I said firmly.

"Give them a chance! No one will see them under your boots. Stop fussing and try them on."

I'm not sure why I ever actually considered the possibility, or why I bothered to examine the pair of bright pink, wool knit ladies leg warmers. They may have been a very fashionable accessory to accompany leotards, worn by trendy ladies in keep fit classes, but I doubted they would be understood by the earthy blokes at Tally Ho. Nevertheless, I gave in, trying them on and pulling the boots back over the top. I couldn't deny it. The boots fit closer, the leg warmers couldn't be seen, and that there was no flopping noise as I paraded around the lounge.

"See, I told you! That's much better."

"I'm not sure, Becks... I'd never be able to show my face if anyone saw them."

"No one will see them. They're completely hidden. You wore long johns on cold nights last winter," she reminded me.

"Yes, but no one knew."

"Exactly, and no one will know about these unless you tell them."

I gave in. I had pains in every muscle as we tiptoed up to bed, but my biggest discomfort by far was the promise I'd just made. It would appear that tomorrow, at my new testosterone-loaded workplace, I would be wearing pink ladies leg warmers under my riding boots. No one would know, of course. What could go wrong?

CHAPTER 6

SETTLING IN

I woke at 6am to the sound of the alarm clock, and leaned across to silence it before it woke little Mel in the next room.

"Ow! Ow! Ow! Ouch!" I groaned as I leaned out of bed.

"Are you OK?" replied the sleepy voice from under the pillow next to mine.

"No, I feel like I've been run over. I think I'm dying."

"Don't die before you've made me a cup of tea…" she yawned.

"Bloody hell Becks. This is murder. I'm in agony! I can hardly move."

"Hmmm. See if you can find a biscuit while you're down there."

I got out of bed, tottered to the bathroom, and then struggled downstairs. It was January and we didn't have central heating, so the house was always freezing cold when I got up. Not being a pyjama man, I usually sped around the kitchen putting the kettle on the gas and lighting the coke boiler, so the house was a little warmer for when my girls got up. Today, however, speed was not an option. I finally crept back upstairs, shivering, with two mugs of tea, wincing with pain and trying to avoid the danger of exposed carpet gripper with my cold-numbed toes.

"Hmmm. A cuppa tea, *lurv*ley. You're doing a lot of moaning this morning, Wild child?"

"I'm in pain. Like I've been battered," I complained pathetically.

"Like every week after you've played football?" she asked, sipping her tea.

"No. Much, much worse, so I need a bit of 'there, there, there' from you."

"Couldn't you find a biscuit? They were by the cornflakes."

It was obviously far too early for empathy or sincere sympathy, so I soldiered on alone, got ready, and left quietly for my commute to Tally Ho.

It was 7.30am when I pulled up outside of the riding school, at the same time as one of the other lads from the course. His name was Paul Garrett from Coventry, and much to my relief he was also hobbling about and complaining of all of the same ailments as me. We walked up the stairs together, comparing notes on the pain stakes and reflecting on our experiences of the previous day.

Paul, when compared with the average 1970s policeman, was a small lad - slightly built with small sticky out ears - but in my opinion, he had performed best out of the three of us on our first day in the riding school. I couldn't decide if this was due to the fact that he looked more like a jockey than me, or because I had been riding with a bigger handicap, having had to cope with Bijou the devil horse.

Our colleague and fellow trainee was sitting at the table as we walked into the bunk. There were no mugs of tea waiting, and the kettle was still sitting cold in the corner of the room.

"What's this? No tea?" asked Paul.

"No, sorry. I really couldn't find the motivation to move. I'm in terrible pain."

"Well, that's all three of us then. Couldn't you even lift the kettle?" enquired Paul.

"I really can't see how I can ride today. I hurt from head to toe," he whimpered.

I listened while I filled the kettle, switched it on, and prepared the mugs. It was obvious that this lad, whose name I really cannot remember, was already in a different place to Paul and myself. The two of us were aching all over, but had been laughing, groaning, and making light of the situation. Our colleague - we'll call him Smith - already seemed to be struggling mentally.

As I poured the tea the door opened, and Sgt. Joiner and Steve Durran walked in.

"Ah, tea, the nectar of life. Good man Wild, you're not so bad after all, you'll go far in this job. We'll make a mounted man of you yet. How is everyone today? All raring to get aboard and tame those hairy beasts, I hope?"

"Could I have a private word please, sarge?" apologised Smith.

The rest of us drank our tea as the sergeant and Smith disappeared into the office. Paul, Steve and I recapped the previous day, laughing at my injuries, torn breeches, and speculating about who would draw the short straw for the devil horse today. It was almost 8am, and we were already changing into our aprons and wellies when the door opened and the sergeant and Smith came back into the room.

"Gentlemen," he harrumphed, "I think we need to re-establish the rules of the game. This riding course runs five days a week, Monday to Friday. You will, therefore, ride these horses for five days a week, Monday to Friday. (Harrumph). Five days a week *without* exception. If you have a doctor's note for a genuine illness or injury, you may, I repeat only *may*, be excused. But if you are merely wracked from head to toe with aches and pains, or your delicate little bottoms are merely saddle sore and bleeding, you will not be excused from riding. You will, gentlemen, *not* be excused from riding," he cleared his throat again whilst eyeballing the three of us. "Do I make myself clear?"

Paul and I nodded in silence alongside a very sheepish Smith, as the sergeant looked at us. It was the first time I had noticed Joiner's propensity for clearing his throat and repeating himself when laying down the law. He spoke clearly, authoritatively, and pompously. It certainly wasn't the last time we would hear the sharpness of his tongue over the coming weeks.

"You are being paid for the privilege of completing this course. If you are unable or unwilling to complete the course, the door is over there, and you are most welcome to walk through it, return to your respective divisions and resume the wearing of your tall hats." He cleared his throat again. "Return to your divisions. Are we all very clear gentlemen?"

We all nodded solemnly in silence.

"Good. Very good. It is now time to groom these horses. Wild, you will ride Grenadier, Garrett you will ride Brigadier, and you, my delicate little friend," he said, smiling at Smith, "will ride Bijou."

Back downstairs, I opened the stable door and walked in to meet my ride of the day. Grenadier loomed like a giant compared to Bijou. He stood over seventeen hands high, was liver chestnut in colour, with a huge head, a massive arched neck and a hogged mane, which made him look tough like a muscle-bound skinhead. A hogged mane is a term used when the horse's mane is clipped completely off. It is normally done when the mane is weak or perhaps unruly, and tends to suit heavier type horses. Because of my previous day's experience, and the sheer size of this animal, I was feeling far from confident. Steve Durran looked over the door to check on me, obviously sensing my trepidation.

"Just crack on, Stef. He's a gentle giant, a true gent. Call him Garth for short."

So I cracked on, following the previous day's routine. A true gent was the perfect description, because Big Garth was as gentle and compliant as Bijou was aggressive and truculent. He stood perfectly still as I body brushed him, lowered his head when I touched his ears, moved over at the lightest touch, and lifted his massive feet when asked. The whole experience was a total contrast to the horrors of the previous day - I never felt for one moment that he was going to bite, kick, or kill me, and consequently my confidence rose to new levels. I liked this horse.

There were, however, familiar and disturbing noises coming from next door. There was the same clattering and stamping of hooves on the cobbled floor, but this time, punctuated with howls and shrieks that suggested Smith was having an even worse time than I'd had the previous day. I heard Steve Durran:

"You can't leave him like that, the sergeant will go nuts. His mane's still full of hay, and his back legs are covered in shit."

"Would you do it please? I'm so afraid of him," pleaded Smith.

"I know you are, and worse, he knows you are. Come on man, get on with it. If I do it for you, you've lost."

I listened with interest and not a little smug satisfaction, knowing now, I hadn't been singled out for special treatment the day before.

"Oh, *please* Bijou. Be a good fellow," came a whimper from next door.

"Just hold his head collar with your left hand and brush that mane out."

"Down! Bijou down! Oh, you are a brute."

"Down? He's not a bloody sheepdog. Get a grip man. Have you picked his feet out yet?"

"Do I have to? Will anyone know?"

"I'll know, because I'll have to sweep up after you. It's also to make sure there's nothing in them to make him lame. Come on. I'll watch."

"Good boy Bijou. Please pick your foot up. Please don't kick me," he begged.

"For God's sake, I've already told you…"

I took my leave, closing my stable door quietly and making my way up the stairs. It may not be very nice, but I couldn't help shamefully enjoying the fact that someone else was attracting all the drama and unwanted attention today.

Paul and I were finishing preparing our saddles when Smith walked in. He was stooped, head down, completely ashen, and looked like he had been ravaged by wild animals. He remained silent, trying to catch up.

After saddling up, which was again punctuated with the noise of howls and squeals for mercy, we changed into our riding gear. Feeling happier and far less conspicuous in my new breeches, I almost forgot, and began to empty my boots onto the floor. At the very last moment I remembered the fluffy pink leg warmers tucked inside with my football socks. I picked up my boots and shut myself in the toilet to finish getting dressed.

Two hours after our arrival, we finally lined up in the centre of the riding school. Two new uniformed riders joined us to assist with our training.

At this time there were several small stables dotted around police station yards in the city of Birmingham. Most of them were small three horse stables, mainly located at the older stations, and our daily ride leaders rode to Tally Ho from these outstations. We had no idea at the time, but some of these riders, who to our untrained eyes looked so professional, were trainees themselves who had only completed their own riding courses a few weeks earlier.

Mounting up proved to be less eventful than the previous day. With pain and stiffness in every joint, it was a struggle to lift my foot high into the stirrup of the much larger Garth - but on the order to mount I surprised myself at the ease with which I sprang up into the saddle. Gathering my reins, adjusting my seat, and looking down at Smith next to me on the much smaller Bijou, I felt tall and far more positive than I had the previous day. Shamefully, I was more than a little disappointed that Smith had managed to get onto his horse without suffering the indignity of being ravaged around the buttocks.

"Gentlemen," announced the sergeant, with a characteristic harrumph, "today is your second day. Yesterday was nothing more than a gentle introduction. Today we will increase the tempo. There is only one way to learn to ride these horses, and that is to ride, ride, and ride some more. Keep your dressing, four feet nose to croup, do not drop behind. You are aspiring to become Mounted Men and the pain is only in your mind. By the time I have finished with you all, you'll make Genghis Khan look like a mommy's boy."

I could have argued that my pain was in fact in my legs, pelvis, arse, back, and just about every other part of my body, but I thought better of it and remained silent like the others.

We fell in along the side of the riding school, with me at number two, directly behind the uniformed leading file. My fellow trainees were behind me, and the other uniformed officer took up the rear. On the order to 'walk march' we began to circle the riding school, while the sergeant corrected our riding positions, hands, posture, and general shambolic appearance.

"Sit up number three. Put your shoulders back. Lower your hands. Are you listening, number three? Catch up - you're already dropping back. Four feet, four feet! Get some leg on him, number three. Catch up!"

With all of the instructions being barked at number three, I didn't have to look to know that Smith and Bijou were the partnership riding directly behind me. Big Garth, in contrast, was a positive delight. He walked forward immediately when the order was given, and seemed to know exactly how far to stay behind the horse in front, keeping a constant distance without me having to apply leg. The difference between the two horses was like comparing a new motorcycle to a rusty old bike with no gears. This was so much more enjoyable, and after a while our dressings were deemed good enough to progress.

"Whole ride, prepare to trot. Whole Ride! Quietly away - TERRRROT!"

The horse in front broke into a trot, and without any encouragement from me big Garth followed suit. My ability had certainly not improved overnight, and there was absolutely no empathy of movement between horse and rider, but not having to pedal every inch of the way was a luxury in itself. I concentrated hard on keeping my hands down and still, and also strived to decrease the height to which I was bouncing every time my bum and the saddle made contact. Nevertheless, for the first time since my arrival at Tally Ho I was enjoying myself. The tone of the orders streaming from the centre of the riding school told me that not everyone was in such a happy place.

"Catch up number three! Four feet! Four feet!"

"I'm trying! I'm trying," came a feeble reply.

"Get up there Smith. Catch up! Leg! *Leg*! LEG!"

"He won't go. I'm trying."

"Don't you dare screw up my riding school Smith! CATCH UP. FOUR FEET, *FOUR FEET*!"

"I'm so sorry. I'm trying, I'm really trying. He's so naughty."

"Whole ride prepare to walk. Whole ride, WAAAAALK."

We came to a halt, and without further word a furious looking Joiner stormed out of the riding school, leaving us alone. We tried to offer a little encouragement to Smith, who looked absolutely broken. He was hunched forward over the saddle and completely drained of colour. The two uniformed officers gave him various words of advice, but he seemed washed out, unable to absorb any information.

A few moments later the sergeant returned carrying a large long handled whip. To my untrained eye it looked like the sort of thing used by a circus ring master, but I now know that it was a lunging whip, and something I have since used many times when exercising horses on a lunge rein.

"Right, gather your reins and prepare to walk. Whole ride! Walk march!" Snapped an angry sounding Joiner.

We resumed our circuit, moving up into the trot when ordered, with all of the riders and horses maintaining their dressings to the obvious satisfaction of the sergeant. It seemed remarkable to me, at the time, that he hadn't used or threatened to use the whip in any way, yet all the horses had mysteriously gained new energy. In no way, shape, or form did I feel comfortable or secure in the saddle at this stage, but I was enjoying myself. This was fun.

We moved on to turns across the school. On the given order "left turn" or "right turn", the whole ride turned inwards, crossing the school in a line knee to knee, before turning back into single file on the other side. It was early days, only twenty-four hours since we had sat on a horse for the first time, but I was surprised by the unrelenting intensity and pace of the riding. For the first time in my life I knew what it was to be saddle sore, and realised the sooner I learned to stop bouncing around out of control, the sooner the pain levels would subside.

Relief finally came in the form of Steve Durran, pushing through the door with a tray full of tea mugs. Morning tea was a break enjoyed by both men and horses alike. For the men, apart from the tea, it was relief for the backside and an opportunity to take a pee in the corner. For the horses, their girths were slackened and reins loosened, letting them put their heads down and give their necks a stretch. The break was over all too soon, and after barely ten minutes we were back in the saddle, in line, ready for more torture.

We were soon trotting again, and numbered off in the same order as before. I was struggling to achieve some sort of rhythm between bum and saddle, in a vain attempt to alleviate the pain, when the sergeant broke the silence.

"We are now going to see who is riding their horse, and who is merely a passenger," announced Joiner after clearing his throat for the umpteenth time, "when I give the order, the rear file will overtake the others and become leading file. Trot on everyone. Don't slow the pace when you take up leading file."

We continued precariously at a fairly brisk pace awaiting the order.

"Number five. Trot on and take leading file. TERRRROT."

I kept looking ahead, and was satisfied that Big Garth was four feet from the croup of the leading file. After a few moments, the uniformed officer from the back of the line appeared to my left, trotting briskly past everyone. He took up leading file, maintaining a steady pace.

"Number four. Trot on and take leading file. TERRRROT."

It took a while longer, but a few moments later a gallant Paul Garrett and Brigadier comically appeared alongside of me. Paul's legs flapped wildly as he bounced high out of the saddle, first to the left and then to the right. His hands were all over the place, but you could see the determination set in his reddening face. It wasn't pretty but he did eventually reach the front of the line, and took up leading file without reducing the pace.

"Well done Garrett. Well done. Good man. Number three. Trot on and take up leading file. TERRROT," commanded Joiner from the centre.

We trotted on around the school, but no one appeared.

"Number three. Get a grip, and kick that horse on. TERRRROT."

No one appeared, and the orders from the centre gradually increased in volume, escalating into abuse.

"Wake that bloody horse up Smith! He's taking the piss. TERRRROT!"

We completed another lap, but still no one appeared to my left.

"Catch up! Catch up you lazy bastard! Push him on! Leg! Leg! Leg! TERRRROT!"

Without further warning there was a loud crack of a whip from behind me, closely followed by an explosive fart that shook the school - and the sound of a man screaming in terror.

"EEEEEEEEAGGHHHH!" howled Smith, as Bijou hurtled past, head up and wild-eyed on my nearside as if he had been fired from a cannon. Poor Smith was thrown completely forward out of the saddle, feet free of the stirrups, with both arms gripping tightly around Bijou's neck. Bijou bucked with his hind legs as he galloped around the riding school. Every buck was accompanied by another extended blood curdling wail as Smith was pushed forward ever closer to his horse's ears.

I was amazed at the speed that the previously bone-idle Bijou reached whilst still following the track, banking dramatically around the bends of the riding school.

"EEEEEEEEEEEAAAGGHHHHH!"

"Whole ride, prepare to halt. Whole ride… HALT!" shouted Joiner from the centre. "That includes you Mr Smith. Stop showing off, Mr Smith."

Smith howled again as Bijou shot past us, starting yet another lap. We sat in silence, watching in horror as Smith's screams of terror increased in volume, and he hung around Bijou's neck for dear life.

"Mr Smith this is not the wall of death. You may stop now. You are frightening the horses!" Joiner called from the centre.

It became, literally, a vicious circle around the perimeter of the riding school. The further forward along Bijou's neck Smith found himself, the tighter he gripped with his heels, and the more the wildly flapping stirrups banged into the horse's sides, the faster Bijou galloped. The faster Bijou galloped, the tighter Smith gripped, and the louder he screamed. It must have been terrifying, but he was beginning to sound like a gang of little girls on a fairground waltzer. Mr Smith was, without doubt, a bit of a chicken.

Eventually, but suddenly and without warning, Bijou screeched to a halt by the exit. Smith, unable to hang on any longer, flew over the horse's head almost in slow motion, landing heavily to the sound of a muffled thud. For what seemed an age there was no sign of life, and I began to fear the worst; thankfully, Smith eventually shifted with a low-pitched groan, confirming life was not yet extinct. He made no effort to get to his feet.

"Thank you for that daring display of horsemanship, Mr Smith. Now, please get up and remount. You are delaying my lesson," said Joiner as he approached the curled-up figure on the ground.

"I can't. I can't," groaned Smith.

"Get up man. Dust yourself off, and get back on your horse. Now!"

"I can't do it. I can't," he repeated, shocked and trembling.

"You are conveniently lying next to the door Mr Smith. You can get up and get back on your horse, or you can walk out now," Joiner said, voice low and dangerous. He cleared his throat. "If you walk out, you won't be allowed back. The choice is yours. Now whatever you decide to do, get on with it."

"I'm not sure," he whimpered pathetically from a disheveled heap.

"The door is there. Make your mind up."

Smith, covered from head to toe with sand, shit, and shavings, slowly got to his feet. To his credit, though accompanied by a great deal of whimpering and moaning, he slowly got back onto Bijou and collected up his reins.

The lesson finally resumed, but poor Smith fell off again on several occasions. Every time we turned to the left or right he fell sideways, out of the saddle, before thudding heavily to the ground. He remounted every time, but his head gradually dropped, and he sagged further and further forward as the lesson progressed. It was pitiful to witness, but evident to all that his spirit had gone as he reluctantly and feebly went through the motions, just hanging on until the end of the session.

We began to settle into a routine, and at the end of the lesson we picked out our horse's feet, before leading them back to their stables. The horses were always looked after first, so after un-saddling we dried the sweat patches on their backs before putting on their rugs. Each horse was given two full buckets of fresh water, which they eagerly drank while we all carried our saddlery back up to the saddle room. The cold, grey concrete steps always seemed steeper, gloomier, and more numerous when carrying heavy saddlery after a hard morning in the school. Smith moaned, groaned and whimpered with every step, and at one point I thought we were going to have to carry his saddlery for him, but he did eventually make it to the summit under his own steam.

After putting the saddles on the saddle horse, and hanging our bridles on the large iron hooks that hung down from the ceiling, we were issued our meal tickets by the sergeant. I'm not sure why, and I don't think it happens these days, but we were always provided with a meal when attending training courses away from division. Meal tickets in hand, we went back to the horses, removed their water buckets, and tied them up by their mangers before feeding them. When they were all happily feeding, we walked across the large drill square towards the canteen.

Tally Ho was a large busy training centre, and the canteen at lunch time was always full of officers of all ranks enjoying their free lunchtime meal. It occurred to me, as we stood in the lengthy queue of chattering people, that we must have looked a strange sight. There were uniformed senior officers attending management courses, suited CID officers from the detective school, young fresh-faced cadets in their track suits and trainers, and then us in our checked jackets, flat caps, and ill-fitting breeches and boots. I don't think 'nose blind' was a known phrase in 1979, but as the weeks went on, it perfectly described the reason why no one was ever keen to share a table with us.

After lunch we made our way back to the riding school, and cleaned and polished our saddlery ready for the following day. After kit cleaning, we gathered around the 'bunk' table with the sergeant for a theory session, in preparation for a written exam we had to take towards the end of the course.

Poor old Smith looked like a beaten man. He had hardly spoken a word during kit cleaning or lunch, and played no active part in the afternoon theory session. He seemed to have descended into a sulky trance, and I had a growing feeling that we wouldn't see him again after the end of the day.

I, however, drove home that night in high spirits. It had been physically hard; my limbs ached, my buttocks were really very sore, and it was a concern that despite the pain, I had to get on and do it all again day after day for nine weeks. But on a positive note, I was at least now enjoying it. For me it had been a much better day, in fact a very good day, and for the first time in this unwanted adventure, I was looking forward to tomorrow.

CHAPTER 7

HEADS I WIN, TAILS YOU MOO'S

It was mine and Becks' quality time again, and for the first time since the crazy interview at Duke Street, I had returned home in a very positive frame of mind. During our evening meal, and throughout Mel's bath and bedtime routine, I had updated Becks on the highlights of my day. I had enthused about the gentle and wonderful Grenadier, described in detail how I had improved and performed in the riding school, and rejoiced that apart from aching limbs and a very sore rear end, I had managed to escape any further humiliation or injury.

I had conducted a fingertip search of the cupboard under the kitchen sink, and found a half-used bottle of surgical spirit. Its former purpose had been to rub on my feet when breaking in new football boots, and new walking boots during my police cadet expedition days. I now found myself lying face down on the lounge floor, half naked in front of a roaring fire, with Becks kneeling beside me.

"Are you sure it's okay to rub this stuff on your bum?" she asked.

"The sergeant and a couple of the blokes told me it's what they used when they started riding. It's supposed to harden the skin."

"Well it smells really strong," she said dubiously, removing the cap, "and I'm not sure I want you with hard skin on your bum."

"It'll be fine. Just be careful, and don't spill any on my nuts," I warned.

"I know a song about that."

"What song?"

"Goodness gracious! Great Balls of Fire," she laughed.

We giggled like a couple of kids whilst she dutifully began to rub my buttocks with surgical spirit. The first application made me wince - it stung like nettles, but soon settled down to a rather pleasant, warming tingle which had me purring like a lap cat.

"How did you get on with my leg warmers?" she asked, breaking the spell.

"They worked a treat. I got changed in the loo and no one seemed to notice."

"I told you it would be fine," she said. "Is that enough, or shall I carry on?"

"Noooo! Don't stop. Carry on. It's absolute murder, but if you stop I'll have to kill you."

I lay there by the fire, oblivious to the potential fire hazard, milking the moment for all it was worth. With my eyes shut, the fire gently toasting my side and my bum tingling pleasantly, I began to reflect on how my life had changed so dramatically during the last few years.

It seemed like no time at all since I was a teenaged police cadet living happily at home with my parents, and now, in the blink of an eye, I was married to, and still learning to live with a young woman and our baby, in our very own home. It made me smile to think that the girl happily rubbing my bum with surgical spirit had in fact been unknown to me for the biggest portion of my life. Life was certainly pleasant at that moment. With the warmth of the fire and the pleasure of the massage, I began to feel dozy, warm, and more than a little nostalgic.

It was a Monday night in the early summer of 1974, when the chain of events leading to my blissful tingly massage had begun. Monday night was disco night at The Three Crowns, a regular weekly hunting ground for me and a group of fellow police cadets. It was a difficult time for a young lad to live with the smart, short police-issue haircut, because the youth at that time were generally either skinheads or grew their hair long down to their shoulders. Neither style was acceptable to the West Midlands Police Cadet Training Department, so even when dressed to impress in our high-waisted flares, platform-soled boots and penny-round collared shirts, cold-shouldered rejection by the local girls was sadly the norm.

It had been my turn to drive, so six of us wedged ourselves into my dad's old Humber for the journey to the pub. On our arrival four of the lads propped themselves against the bar for the night, whilst myself and a lad that we all called Doris preened ourselves, prepared for a night of cruel rejection, and boldly went on the prowl hunting for girls.

Very few lads were dancers in the 1970s; I was no exception, and generally danced like a baby giraffe on ice. I was already a gangly six feet tall, but was rendered even more top heavy due to my liking of fashionable but ridiculous platform-soled boots. The girls usually danced together, forming circles around their handbags. It was an almost impossible task to break into these impenetrable circles, so we tended to focus our attentions on pairs instead, sometimes asking if they would like to dance, and sometimes just smiling cheekily, before clumsily shuffling and shaking a leg next to them.

This night, sadly, soon began to follow a familiar pattern. Rejection is a bitter pill, and you could almost hear the sound of air leaking from our deflating egos. The nice girls generally smiled weakly before saying, "No thank you", the not so nice usually retorted with, "Piss off freak", while others who just felt harassed, raised their eyebrows and turned their backs.

There is a limit to the level of rejection that even a randy teenage lad can absorb before giving up and joining the boozers at the bar, so we both agreed to try once more before throwing in the towel and admitting defeat. There were two girls dancing together at the edge of the dance floor. One was petite, with short dark brown hair. She was wearing a short skirt, and looked cute. The other girl, wearing trousers, was taller, skinnier, with lighter hair, and looked neither cute nor like she was enjoying herself.

"Let's have one last go. Let's try those two over there," suggested Doris.

"I want the little dark haired one in the skirt," I replied firmly.

"No way. It was my idea. I get first pick!"

"We'll toss then. The winner gets the pretty one."

"I suppose I'll lose and get the miserable looking one again?" grumbled my partner in crime.

"No. We'll stick to the rules. Winner gets first pick. Loser hangs on in with the other one. It's a team sport Doris, and you don't always lose," I insisted.

"Well I'm not snogging her," he grumbled.

"We haven't even tossed yet. You might win! Cheer up you grumpy git."

So he tossed the coin. I called heads, and smiled smugly when the coin fell and landed with the Queen face up. Doris' face fell, but he dutifully followed me, slouching across the dance floor towards our chosen prey.

"Can we dance with the two best looking girls in the room?" I smarmed.

"No," snapped the miserable looking one.

"Yes. Why not?" smiled the pretty one.

Having successfully breached their first line of defence, we danced for a while making small talk, and when she didn't cold shoulder me or openly laugh at my enthusiastic but spasmodic dancing; my confidence levels began to rise. Things were looking up, and I was feeling lucky.

The chance of any growing intimacy ended when the room suddenly began to throb to the sound of Noddy Holder 'Feelin the Noize'. Everyone started to go 'Wild Wild Wild', and our conversation inevitably developed into a shouting match. The situation was thankfully saved however, unintentionally, by the grumpy friend.

"I want to sit down," she moaned.

"Good idea. Let's sit in that quiet corner over there. I'll buy you both a drink?" I suggested.

"No," said the grumpy one.

"Yes please," replied the pretty girl, her big, warm brown eyes looking lovelier by the minute. "I'll have a port and lemon."

I bought the drinks, the four of us sat down, and two of us talked non-stop for the rest of the night, while Doris and glum girl sat in stony-faced silence. We laughed, flirted, and cheekily made fun of each other until the end of the night, when the DJ began to play the kind of smoochy bum feeler music which traditionally signaled the end of a 1970s disco. We got up, embraced, and shuffled around the dance floor hidden amongst a swirling crowd of other groping couples.

"If you insist on keeping your hands on my bum, you're going to have to tell me your name," she laughed.

"It's Stefan when I'm in trouble with my mum, but you can call me Stef."

"I take it that you're Stef the soldier?" she asked looking straight at my hair.

"No," I laughed. "Nothing that exciting, I'm just a police cadet. Your turn now, what's your name?"

"Taking down my particulars, are you?" She smiled before answering my question. "I'm Rebecca, you can call me Becks, and I'll kick your shin if you call me Becky."

Freshly introduced, Becks and I walked back to the table hand in hand, where our two grumpy friends were waiting with their coats on. Doris to be fair, remained stoic in keeping his side of the bargain and sullenly continued to hang on bravely, showing loyalty beyond the call of duty.

"Well, you two girls have won the jackpot tonight, and the first prize is a lift home with two handsome chaps in my car," I said hopefully.

"No," replied grumpy girl.

"Don't speak for me; I'm going with them," snapped Becks.

"We don't know them Rebecca. I'm not getting into a car with two strangers!"

"Don't you 'Rebecca' me; they're alright. I can tell, and I'm having a lift home. You can walk home if you like."

The decision made, we left together and walked out to the car park where I suddenly remembered the other four lads, who were now all noisily drunk and leaning against the car. The grumpy girl chilled by several more degrees, and stood next to Becks taking in the scene. Both of them looked at the gaggle of lads and the big old Humber.

"You told me you were a police cadet?" she said, probing my face with her big brown eyes.

"I am. We all are. Straight up," I explained in my most reassuring voice.

"Look at you all. Look at the car!" she laughed. "You look more like gangsters than coppers."

I couldn't argue with her description, because we did look a motley crew. The two girls stood back and entered into a private debate as to whether they should still accept the lift given the change in circumstances. Getting into a car with six strange lads, four of them drunk, was obviously a different prospect to accepting a lift from two. I opened the car, the drunks crammed themselves onto the back seat, and Doris got into the front. I waited patiently outside for the verdict, convinced that the sudden appearance of extra bodies had blown my chance of ever seeing Becks again.

Eventually, following considerable deliberation, the foreman approached the car with the verdict.

"I trust you Stef the police cadet," she said, looking straight into my eyes. "So *you* mate, had better look after us. Now let's get into the car."

The seating plan, for eight, proved a little difficult, because the grumpy girl understandably refused to travel in the back with the drunks. After some further discussion, Doris and I picked Becks up off her feet and posted her horizontally through the back window onto the laps of the four delighted boisterous youths, while grumpy girl, arms folded, sat in the middle of the large front bench seat. I got in, started up, and we all chugged away in the old Humber. It was a lively ride back into town, but apart from some cheeky banter there was no real harm in the lads on the back seat. I watched with admiration through the driver's mirror, and listened as she endured their banter, giving back as good as she got and never appearing intimidated. I liked this girl.

Becks was my first drop off of many that night, and we drew up outside of a large Victorian house at about half past midnight. I pulled her from the back of the car to the sound of cheers and heckling from the occupants of the back seat. We stood together by her front door, both 'shushing' at the rabble in the car, who were noisily offering suggestions as to what we should do next. It was only a matter of time before they woke the whole street.

"Well, Stef the police cadet, thank you for the lift. It's been interesting. It's been a laugh," she smiled.

"I want to see you again," I blurted out.

"Good, because I want to see you again too. Will they all be with you next time?" she asked, nodding towards the baying mob in the car.

"No. Not tomorrow," I assured her. "It's their day off."

Tomorrow, it's fair to say, was genuinely the beginning of the rest of my life. I truanted from college and picked her up from home just after lunch time. I whizzed her away in the tea van to Sutton Park, a large leafy park on the edge of The Royal Borough of Sutton Coldfield, to the north of Birmingham.

It was a beautiful warm sunny day, so we walked hand in hand, talking, flirting, laughing, and eagerly getting to know each other. After a while I bought a couple of ice creams, and we sat on the grass to eat them in the warm sun, overlooking a large pool. Eventually we lay down, side by side, and just talked. I closed my eyes because of the sun, and lay there not able to believe my luck. I hadn't yet known this girl for twenty-four hours, and here we were lying together on this lovely warm sunny day, listening to the birds, and getting along wonderfully. Inevitably I began to ponder my next step. What would be her reaction if I leaned over and kissed her? What if she rejected me? Perhaps if I waited a little longer, she might lean over and kiss me instead. That would be fantastic, so I lay a little longer, warm, comfortable and happy, waiting patiently. Eventually I felt warm breath on my face, and pursed my lips in anticipation.

"MOOOOO!"

I felt a spray of warm spittle, and sat bolt upright to the sound of a loud scream. It took a few seconds, but when my eyes focused I was gazing into the large brown eyes of a large brown cow. There were, in fact, seven of them, and they had inquisitively formed a tight circle around us, moving in for a closer look before loudly announcing their arrival.

"Oh my God Stef, do something!" cried Becks, throwing her arms around me.

"Just sit still. They won't hurt us. They're only cows," I said, trying to disguise my terror.

"What are they doing? What do they want? I'm scared Stef," she said, strengthening her grip around my neck.

"I don't know. I've never met a cow up close before. Let's get up before they stand on us."

As we stood up the cows took a step back, and feeling more confident I decided to take positive action, so I held my arms out to look bigger, and shooed them away.

"Off you go. Shoo! Nothing here for you. Bugger off now. Shoo!" I ordered in my bogus scariest voice.

Thankfully they complied, and calmly walked away in their carefree way, starting to munch the grass a few yards away. With the crisis over, we dusted the grass off our clothes. With her arms still tightly wrapped around me, and my street cred soaring sky high, we laughed as we made our escape.

The final ice had been broken, and from that day onwards we spent every possible moment together, without a single day off. We went out, we stayed in, we laughed, we played, we wrestled, we argued, and soon found that we were completely unable to keep our hands off each other.

My granddad ran a garage very close to the Walsall Football Club. I worked the petrol pumps two nights a week to supplement my meagre wages, and Becks had taken to joining me and working as my unpaid assistant. My granddad was sadly very ill, and unknown to anyone at the time was suffering from that shocking illness that is now known as motor neurone disease. Driving was his passion, and he had become quite depressed at being unable to drive his beloved car, so my parents had begun to take him and my Nan out for a weekly drive in it. I hadn't yet told any of my family about my fledgling relationship, so I was horrified to see the big white Jag roar onto the forecourt on one of our garage evenings. After their refueling, I cringed as my four closest family members walked into the shop to see me, and show their surprise that I wasn't alone.

"Hello you lot," I said nervously. "Have you been out for a spin? Oh, and this is my friend Becks."

The two men were quite content with this explanation, but of course the two women were far from satisfied with the lack of detail and general brevity of my report.

"Becks? What sort of name is Becks?" began my Nan.

"It's short for Rebecca, really," replied the cornered suspect.

"Oh, I see, and what do you do Rebecca?" persisted the old matriarch.

"I don't work at the moment. I'm only here helping Stef tonight."

"You don't work? You aren't a gyppo are you?"

"No, I'm not a gyppo, and I live in a normal house with my parents," laughed Becks.

"I told you! I told you - I knew he'd got a girl because he's started to have a bath every day," chipped in my Mom for good measure.

"Well that's a sure sign," agreed Nan. "So where do you live Rebecca?"

The probing interrogation continued, with Becks batting skillfully and answering a flurry of personal questions without actually revealing any secrets. Fortunately, and as usual on cue, my Dad intervened and saved the day, skillfully herding everyone back out of the shop and into the car, before returning alone.

"Goodnight you two. You know they won't shut up about this now, so you'd better bring Becks around for tea and another grilling soon!" He laughed on his way out.

"I think I've just been well and truly interrogated. Who are those crazy people, and why do they know your bath night routine? Are they regular customers?"

"Don't you know?" I grinned. "I thought I'd told you. That's my family, and you've just been well and truly Wilded!"

A few days later, we were happily chattering away in the tea van on the way to my parents' house, for Becks' first formal introduction. I explained to her that we used to live in an old Victorian terrace, but had recently moved to a new build on a new development on the edge of town. Thinking about the new house and its open plan design, a thought suddenly sprung to my mind. I looked at the lovely, smart, but very short dress she had put on especially for the occasion.

"I never gave it a thought, but maybe you should have worn trousers for tonight," I casually remarked.

"Why? Don't you like my dress?"

"I think it's absolutely stunning, and it doesn't matter. I'm sure it'll be fine."

"Won't they like it? Is it too tarty?"

"No, I love it. It's class. Forget I said anything," I said, back-pedaling like crazy.

We pulled onto the drive, and being conscious of her nervousness, I squeezed her hand as I unlocked the front door. It opened directly into the lounge, and to the bottom of an open plan staircase. I showed her in, and we were immediately met by my parents. My worst fears were realised, when immediately after the introductions, with no delay or advance warning, my Dad came out with the question that I had been dreading:

"Do you think you can go backwards on your hands and knees to the top of the stairs?"

She laughed and looked at me quizzically.

"Don't look at me. I'm afraid he's serious. Just say no, and then we can all sit down."

"I don't know. You'll have to show me how to do it first." It wasn't what I was expecting to hear, and wasn't the wisest of answers because he really didn't need the extra encouragement.

After a brief but impressive demonstration from my Dad, we all watched for the next ten minutes whilst Becks, with her bum in the air and her face glowing increasingly red, mastered the art of climbing our new stairs backwards on her hands and knees. To her credit, she finally reached the peak without supplementary oxygen or injury and established her reputation as a 'good girl' on her very first visit. When I relate this tale to people they look at me in disbelief, but in the new 1970s home of the Wilds, this initiation ceremony for visitors was a fairly common occurrence.

The evening went wonderfully well. Conversation came easily, everyone gelled, and my parents took to Becks right away - but I was aware of a little tension in the car when driving her back home.

"I may be wrong, but I feel in trouble?" I tentatively enquired.

"Why didn't you warn me?" she asked. "How could you let me wear this short dress?"

"Becks, you look drop dead gorgeous. It looks lovely, and I really like it."

"I know you really like it, I really like it, and I'm pretty sure your Dad really liked it too, but I didn't think I'd have to display my knickers to your parents on my first visit," she scolded.

"If it's any consolation your knickers looked lovely and clean, and they're sure to have noticed, so my Mom will be impressed and will now file a favourable report to my Nan." This earned me a quick punch.

"Your parents are lovely," she said approvingly. "I really like them, but they're completely nuts, and you're just like them!" she laughed.

"Welcome to Wildlife," I warned with a smile.

My introduction to her family was a little less eventful, but equally successful; they accepted me like another son from our very first meeting. My parents idolized her, so our new and exciting relationship developed rapidly, bolstered by the enthusiasm and obvious approval of both sets of parents. We had a truly wonderful summer, which we enjoyed to the full, and I was blissfully happy in my new situation. There was, however, a massive and depressing black cloud looming on the horizon which threatened to spoil everything.

Becks had left home at the tender age of sixteen, and had spent the previous two years in Canada, where she worked as a live-in home help and child minder. She had, in fact, only arrived back home for a holiday a couple of weeks before we met at The Three Crowns. She was due to return to Canada in September, but before doing so was going on a European camping holiday with her family for the whole month of August. My wonderful summer was rapidly approaching an early and miserable autumn, and I had no idea how to stop it.

I had only known her for six weeks. I waved them all off as they left for the South of France, and was absolutely miserable as

I watched their old Transit mini bus disappear towards the M6. A full month away seemed like a lifetime - but knowing that only a week after that she would disappear again, possibly forever, was unbearable. Years later, my mother used to delight in telling people about this time. Apparently I was lost, 'moping about like a dog that had lost his tail'.

It's very easy to forget, in this amazing modern age of cheap and easy communications, that in the 1970s there were no such things as mobile phones, texts, Facebook or WhatsApp. International telephone calls were still difficult to arrange, and crazily expensive. So I wrote. Mostly mush and nonsense, but I wrote and posted a fresh letter every single day, addressed to the camp site they had booked. I had no idea how long they would stay there, and no real belief the letters would reach her, but I wrote anyway. It made me feel better.

After the longest and most miserable month of my life, I decided I had waited long enough. On a lovely sunny afternoon, and with a bag of clothes but no plan, I drove south. Inevitably, and after a long drive, I found myself waiting on the quay side at Portsmouth as their ferry docked. Half an hour later they were taken completely by surprise as I waved down their minibus. Even I had no more idea how this was going to go than I had had on the night when Doris flipped the coin at the Three Crowns, but I found myself at the side of the road, face to face with Becks and her astonished parents.

"Hello everyone; welcome back. It's great to see you all," I clumsily blurted out. "I want to take Becks away for a few days."

"I don't think so Stef. Her Nan would go mad," replied her mother.

"This is a bit of a shock, Stef. Let's think about this for a minute or two," reasoned her dad.

Without any nastiness and with surprising calm, negotiations began regarding my sudden and unexpected appearance, and the morality of my shocking request. Parental attitudes were very different in the 1970s. Appearances were everything, and had to be fully considered, but her parents' consent became irrelevant when Becks took her suitcase from the back of the minibus and calmly transferred it into the waiting tea van.

"Love you Mom, love you Dad. Love you kids. See you soon," she said, before calmly climbing into the tea van's passenger seat. "Now you, you crazy nutter, let's get out of here before they realise what's happening. Where are you taking me?" she laughed.

"To be honest I have no idea. I just want you to myself," I confessed.

So, without further delay we took advantage of the confusion, and headed east in the direction of Brighton. We laughed and talked non- stop nonsense, until at the first opportunity I pulled up at the side of the road, where we hugged until it hurt.

"Becks. I really don't want you to go back to Canada," I poured out.

"Good, because I'm not going back, you Muppet!" She hugged me tightly by the neck.

"Really? Really? Why not?"

"Because I've been thinking in France, and decided if you asked me not to, I wouldn't go back."

Unbelievably, after having known each other for only six weeks, she had changed all of her plans for the future. We spent a couple of fun filled brazen days in Brighton, before sheepishly returning home and nervously announcing to our families that we were now engaged to be married. Happily, and surprisingly, given we were both so young and had only known each other for such a short time, both sets of parents seemed delighted.

Shortly afterwards, on the day she should have returned to Canada, we hosted a party at Becks' parents' house to celebrate our sudden betrothal. Showered with the love and generosity of our closest family and friends, we began our preparations for future life together as the proud joint owners of three toasters, two kettles, four sandwich makers, an assortment of nonmatching crockery, and an eclectic collection of domestic bric-a-brac. It was very early days, with exciting times ahead - but forward planning was a concept we definitely needed to work on.

Becks, having given up cosmopolitan Toronto for the drudgery of the West Midlands and wearing a ring bought with money loaned from my dad, settled back down to live at home with her parents. She found work, initially in a shoe shop and then a petrol station, before securing a full-time clerical position with the local health authority. She learned to drive, passed her test, and in a symbolic gesture of trust and true love, was presented with her own set of keys to my beloved tea van.

It was in March 1975 that I turned nineteen, and automatically metamorphosed overnight from police cadet to constable. It was what I had aspired to since I left school at sixteen, and it meant that, as well as wearing a much taller hat, my wages rose from £10 to almost £50 per week. Police pay at this time was a national disgrace, but for a carefree young couple enjoying life with few financial responsibilities, this was a significant increase in our fun fund. We knew that my work – now with nightshifts, weekends, and bank holidays on the rota – was going to have a much bigger impact on our lives, but had discussed it and were prepared to adjust accordingly.

In April I went away to the district police training centre at Ryton-on-Dunsmore, near Coventry. It was a twelve-week residential course where we learned police law and procedures, how to march, unarmed combat, and a multitude of other skills necessary for modern policing. Ryton was a dump. It had been built poorly and rapidly during the war, and was used as a displaced persons' camp until its transformation into a police training centre in the 1950s. We marched and paraded every morning before room inspection, but no amount of discipline, paint, and camaraderie could disguise the despondent lines of the cold grey Nissen Huts that made up the camp. To compound the misery, the food was notoriously appalling. After homework, we spent our evenings at the bar in the mess, drinking too much beer, complaining about everything, and buying meat pies and cheese cobs to supplement our meagre diet. I was very homesick.

Just outside of the bar were the only two public telephone booths on the site, and every night there were lengthy queues of dutiful students waiting patiently to call home. It was one such night that I finally managed to shut myself into a booth with a fistful of ten pence coins, and call Becks for our nightly chat. Like every other night we swapped news, flirted, and compared our levels of misery caused by separation.

"It won't be much longer now Stef," she consoled, "you're nearly halfway through."

"Some of the older blokes have sorted their police houses out today."

"How do they get a police house?" she asked casually.

"You have to be a policeman, and you have to be married, and then you can apply to your division for a house."

"Well, we're halfway there, because you're already a policeman!"

"So… if we were married, we could live together in our own house," I explained.

"Yes."

"I know it's a crazy idea because we're so young, and we've got nothing…"

"Yes."

"…but I don't think it would be impossible if we put our minds to it…"

"Will you belt up and ask me properly?" she laughed. "I've already accepted twice!"

"Sorry, I'm twittering away here. What did you say?"

"This isn't the violins and champagne proposal I've always dreamed of, but I've just accepted twice. If you'll shut up and listen," she explained patiently.

"Bloody hell Becks. Have I proposed?!"

"You proposed in Brighton, but I think you've just suggested we get married straight away. Well, I thought you had. Have you changed your mind already?"

"No! No, I haven't, I just didn't know that I had, but if you think I did, then I did. So let's do it. Why not?" I twittered again.

"Wow Stef! You're such a romantic. Not!"

"Sorry; I can't get down on one knee because the pips are about to go, and I've run out of change, and there's a big ugly bloke banging on the window. I need to go. Love you. Speak to you tomo-"

We were cut off mid-sentence to the sound of 'peep-peep-peep', so in a daze, I went back into the bar. I told the blokes my unexpected news, and as the cheering subsided, they put their hands in their pockets and set about making sure I had a splitting hangover for the following morning's muster parade.

We arranged our entire wedding that weekend. It wasn't easy booking a church wedding at short notice, but Becks' family were known to the vicar, so he kindly agreed to marry us at the unusual time of 6pm on the 6th of September 1975. Unlike the meticulously planned, super lavish, and eye wateringly expensive weddings that we all know today, we married on a shoe string budget. Following the ceremony, we and the guests just walked across the road to the room above the local pub. My parents' neighbour had prepared a substantial buffet, and we danced the night away to music provided by a friend's disco. It was a night to remember, we were officially Mr and Mrs Wild, and I was penniless and still only nineteen.

We spent our first night of married life together in our very own three bedroomed, semi-detached police house. The divisional admin had been very good, and had given us our keys early after seeing proof from the vicar of our forthcoming wedding. Our parents had helped us to redecorate, so all was ready for the big day. Our bed and bedding was a wedding present from my parents, and Becks' Dad - a carpet fitter by trade - had provided and fitted new carpets in the lounge and bedroom. We'd bought, on hire purchase, a trendy stripy three-piece suite for the lounge. Together, that numbered all of our new possessions. Everything else was given to us by friends and family, so we began our new life surrounded by second hand, mismatched furniture and curtains, and uncarpeted floors and stairs. By today's expectations our house must have looked awful, but we were oblivious and didn't care to boot, because it was our crazy adventure. We were together in our own home, and full of the excitement of suddenly finding ourselves grown up.

I became vaguely aware of being dragged away from my cosy memories and pleasure induced stupor. Reluctantly, I was slowly returning to reality, but it took a few moments to wake myself fully, and a few more to work out where I was. The warm ambiance was giving way to some sort of panic.

"Stef. Stef, wake up. I can't rub any more. Your bum's all red like a monkey's! I think I've overdone it…"

"Well it feels okay. A little warm, but okay."

"Oh no! You should see it. It's glowing. Oh! I hope the skin doesn't peel off?" she nervously giggled.

"How can I see my own bum? You fool," I laughed.

"It's not funny. What if I've scarred you for life?"

"Don't worry, it feels fine." I yawned. "Let's go up to bed. I'm sleepy."

We switched off, put the fire guard up, and tiptoed up the wooden hill to our bed. Before reaching the top I heard familiar snorts of mirth from behind.

"Shush! You'll wake Mel. Now what's the matter with you?" I asked.

"You didn't need to put the light on," she whispered.

"What are you twittering about now?"

"Keep going. Don't stop. The glow from your bum is leading the way!" she blurted out, descending into fits of laughter. I pulled her into the bedroom and we both fell onto the bed.

CHAPTER 8

THEN THERE WERE TWO

I arrived at Tally Ho nice and early for my third day. When I got out of the car and walked across the yard, and then up the two flights of concrete stairs, I began to understand what it felt like to be old and arthritic. I was only twenty-three years old, but groaned with every step, and genuinely ached in every muscle and joint from head to toe.

Inside, Paul Garrett was sitting at the large table, already clad in his apron, drinking a mug of tea.

"You're walking like I feel," he laughed. "There's a cup of tea over there."

"Good man," I said, supping my tea. "I feel like I've been run over by a bus."

"Me too, but it must have run me over in bed, because I felt worse when I woke up than I did when I went to sleep."

"Is Smithy here yet?" I asked, looking around. "He must be in a right state."

"I haven't seen him yet."

We sat drinking tea while comparing our pain levels, waiting for our colleague to arrive and speculating about what horses we would be riding that morning. We both looked up as the office door opened, and Joiner walked into the room. He picked up a mug of tea and sat down beside us.

"Good morning gentlemen. I have some news for you," he said, pausing for effect. "That big girl's blouse Smith has thrown in the towel, so now there are only two of you."

"Is he injured? He did fall off a lot," I asked.

"He's not injured. He's just hurting. What did he expect? Bloody wimp! He's just frit. Never make a Mounted Man so long as he has a hole in his arse," he said with undisguised contempt.

We discussed our aches and pains, and listened while he reassured us that they were perfectly normal, and would improve as our bodies became used to the extensive and unfamiliar exercises. We just needed to bite the bullet and trot on. While pain was the topic of conversation I told them about my massage of the previous evening and of Becks' unintentional over-application of the surgical spirit. For the first time since the start of the week, I saw Joiner laugh. He obviously thought it was hilarious, because he spluttered into his tea and had tears in his eyes.

"So let's get this right, Wild. You got Mrs Wild to rub your arse with spirit? Then you went to sleep? And she dutifully carried on rubbing until your arse glowed like a baboon's?" he asked.

"Yes. That's about it; and afterwards, I led her upstairs to bed glowing like an emergency beacon," I confirmed.

"Well fair play to you man. I'm damn sure my missus wouldn't rub my arse with anything. How is the zone in question this morning? Is it raw?"

"No, it's fine now. I had to keep it outside of the duvet all night in case it ignited the bed clothes, but it was fine when I woke up this morning."

He roared with laughter again, and seemed to forget all about poor Smith.

"Bloody hell Wild, it's only eight o'clock and you've made my day. That is so bloody funny," he paused for breath. "Right gentlemen, (Harrumph) we digress. Let's get those horses groomed," he laughed all the way out of the room and down the stairs.

Downstairs it was all change again, and my steed for the day was Brigadier. The most obvious thing about Brigadier was that he was white, with a large pink nose. He was larger than Bijou, smaller than Garth, but was obviously well fed and quite rotund. He didn't attack me when I entered the stable, which was a bonus, and was indifferently compliant as I removed and folded his rug. However, the moment I removed his head collar, he carefully turned around and began to search my apron pocket with his large pink nose. I laughed and scratched his ears, before noticing Steve Durran watching over the door.

"Well this one seems friendly enough Steve," I said with obvious relief.

"He's fine. Like an old worn shoe. But he's a greedy sod. He'll eat non-stop if you let him. Make sure he's tied up when you've finished, or he'll scoff all of his bedding, shit and all."

"Do I have to do anything different because he's a white horse?" I naively asked.

"Shush. Don't say that. There's no such thing as a white horse, Stef. He's a grey." He went on to explain that white horses are usually born almost black and grow lighter with age, but whatever shade they are, they are always known as greys -never called white.

Carefully considering my newly acquired knowledge, I came to the conclusion that Brigadier, given his unmentionable but obvious whiteness, was not a particularly young horse. I carried on grooming, following the routine learned from the previous two days, and soon found that horses that cannot be called white can still shed an awful lot of white hair. It was everywhere, and was soon clogging the body brush. The more I groomed, the more came off, and when I groomed again, even more came off. I soon had piles of white hair that I had knocked out of the curry comb, dotted all around the stable floor. Steve reappeared at the door.

"I think he's going bald Steve. I'll be able to stuff a cushion in a minute!"

"It's the curse of the grey, Stef. Their hair gets everywhere. They get shit stained too - look at the big patch on his belly, and his hocks. You'll have to give them a scrub before you've finished."

My education continued, and I soon discovered that greys were much harder to keep looking clean than bays. I learned how to scrub soiled patches with a stiff brush and soapy water until the stains were gone. Also, importantly, I learned they must be dried thoroughly after scrubbing to prevent cracked heels, especially in winter.

With grooming complete we prepared our saddlery before saddling up our horses. Between the saddle and the horse's back we used a saddle shaped cushioned pad called a numnah. Each horse had its own personal numnah, the purpose of which was to absorb sweat, cushion the saddle and prevent rubbing. It was obvious, even without reading the number, which was Brigadier's, because it was ingrained with the dreaded white hair. Even a vigorous scrub with a stiff brush failed to remove all of the evidence.

After saddling the horses, I quietly snuck into the toilet to change into my breeches and boots. It occurred to me that it was only a matter of time before someone noticed my unusual morning routine and apparent shyness. I looked hard at my sexy leg warmers before pulling them over my socks and breeches, and for the first time noticed that the fluffy pink knitted wool was actually patterned with delicate silvery stars and glittery moons.

They were even more 'girlie' than I'd realised. The thought of someone seeing them was beginning to worry me.

We made steady progress in the riding school, without the presence and hindrance of Smith. Brigadier certainly wasn't as eager as Grenadier, but he was a dream when compared to Bijou. He was an 'old sweat', had obviously been in the job for a long time, and knew exactly how much or how little effort he could get away with. Unlike Bijou, he walked when he should and trotted when he should, but still required considerable pedalling to maintain the pace and dressing.

The orders from the centre were beginning to make more sense, and our dressings when riding and turning across the school were definitely improving. Unfortunately, I couldn't say the same for the actual riding of the horse. There was still little evidence of the required independence between hand and leg, and my inability to sit still and comfortably into the saddle without bouncing up and down, meant that my hands and reins were also jiggling up and down clumsily.

It was certainly no fun for the horses either. Having someone without rhythm, bouncing clumsily and heavily, up and down on your back, is irritating. But when the effect is transferred down from the hands, through the reins and into a metal bit that is sitting in your mouth, it can become demoralising, and, I imagine, painful. To compound the problem, we were taught to ride from scratch whilst using a full military style bridle. Novices normally learn to ride using a single rein with a very mild bit known as a 'snaffle', and often never progress to anything more sophisticated unless they later move on to competitive riding. We learned to ride from day one with two reins and a heavy, severe military bit known as a 'universal reversible port mouth bit', however. It was little wonder that some of the horses were grumpy in the riding school, and although I didn't know it at the time, we would not be allowed to ride the 'better' ones until our skills had developed to a higher level.

We ended the session without any undue drama, with neither Paul nor I having yet fallen off. We were upstairs, having already seen to the horses, and were hanging up our saddlery before going over to the canteen for lunch. The sergeant walked into the bunk.

"Do you think you need to brush down before your meal, Wild?" he asked.

I turned to look in the large wall mirror, and was amazed to see I was covered from head to toe in white hair. I couldn't have looked any worse if I'd laid down on the floor and deliberately rolled in a pile of it.

"You're right. Look at the state of me! I look like a moulting polar bear," I groaned.

It took me a full five minutes, and a very stiff brush down, to get rid of sufficient hair to allow me to go and stand in the canteen queue for lunch. Looking at my scruffy appearance in the mirror, took my thoughts right back to the very start of this story, and my battle with the feral piebald horse back on division. Remembering the problems, pain, and embarrassment of that day cheered me a little - because on reflection, my confidence when handling the animals was without doubt improving, and my outlook for the future of the course was far more optimistic than it had been at the start of the week.

However, I still couldn't see myself continuing my career as a mounted man. All of the polishing, cleaning, drill, shouted orders, and daily routine weren't my cup of tea, but I was now enjoying the riding, and could hopefully see myself successfully completing the nine-week course. I would then quietly return to division, and put the previous nine weeks down to experience. In the meantime, I would play the game, trot on, and hope that no one realised I was 'only here for the ride'.

Every afternoon we sat around the table with the sergeant for our theory session. There was no blackboard, flip charts, or power point projectors, and because of the small size of our group, it was pleasantly informal. We drank too much tea, and used it as a welcome wind down after the usual vigours of the morning. The syllabus, however, was comprehensive and interesting. We were all townies, born and raised in the urban sprawl of the West Midlands, so none of us were familiar with the care of horses or any other form of animal husbandry.

We learned the points of the horse[8], colours of the horse, and markings of the horse, how to recognise lameness, the workings of the digestive system, an endless list of diseases and illnesses, and their treatments and cures.

We studied shoeing, clipping, cold hosing, poulticing, bandaging, and the forward movement of the horse, including the footfall patterns at the walk, trot, canter and gallop. We learned how to age a horse, or sex a horse by examining the teeth, care of the teeth, wear of the teeth, rasping the teeth, and, of course, in my case - how to avoid the teeth. All the information was new, interesting, relevant, and had to be learned because we had to sit and pass a theory exam before the end of the course. I had never previously been naturally attentive in classroom environments, but I enthusiastically applied myself to this subject, soaking up everything I could. It was much more interesting than law.

One afternoon during the second week, the sergeant dropped a pile of expenses forms on the bunk room table.

---

[8] *Equine term for the anatomy of the horse. Usually learned from a point's of the horse poster.*

"Gentlemen, don't forget to complete your travelling expense forms on a weekly basis for me to sign. You will have to claim the money from your respective divisions, but I will need to sign them for you. They will not appreciate it if you try and collect the lot, and empty their petty cash tins, at the end of the course."

Being notoriously dozy with money matters, I hadn't even been aware we were able to claim travelling expenses for training courses. The amount was 10.7 pence per mile for the total travelling distance, less the distance normally travelled to your usual place of work. As I normally walked the few hundred yards to my local police station, I was able to claim the complete return journey to Tally Ho, which was forty four miles per day.

"Have I worked this out right? I've got this to over two hundred pounds for the whole course. That's about three week's wages!" I asked, with some surprise.

"That sounds about right to me Wild, you do travel a fair distance, and if you've got any sense you won't tell the missus about it either. (Harrumph) After all every man needs a secret fun fund," the sergeant winked knowingly.

Two hundred pounds was quite a sum in 1979, and Joiner's advice had given me food for thought.

It was early days, but the domestic effects of working regular hours had already been noticed at home. It certainly had its benefits, and the evening bum rub and accompanying debrief of the day, was, in my opinion, a very welcome addition to our domestic routine.

"You're getting to like this, aren't you?" she asked.

"Hmm, what's not to like? Don't stop."

"Not just the bum rub. I meant everything else too."

"What else is there at this moment?" I purred.

"Well the three of us have eaten together, for a start."

"Yes. That's been nice," I conceded.

"And you've joined in with Mel's bath time, and you've read her bedtime story. She loves it when you read the story, because you do the silly voices," she gave me a teasing pinch.

"OW! You're dicing with death, lady," I laughed.

"Don't change the subject Wildy. I'm being serious. We've been like a normal family. And you'll be here with us at the weekend again."

"Make the most of it. It's only for a few weeks. It will be back to normal soon," I said, trying to restore a little reality.

"Unless you get to like it, and unless you change your mind, and try to stay," she retorted.

"It's not going to happen, sorry. Now be quiet woman, rub on, you're spoiling the moment with all of this tattle!" I laughed and braced myself for another pinch.

There was less giggling and flirting than usual that night, as we climbed the wooden stairs carefully avoiding the carpet gripper. I knew she was serious about the benefits of me working normal hours, and I knew that she was quietly and secretly debating the whole situation in her head. I needed to handle this carefully, because even though the working hours were attractive, I knew my future didn't involve being a mounted man. I would have to be firm about this from the start. It would be wrong to build false hopes.

CHAPTER 9

BIG BEN STRIKES TWICE

It was Monday morning, the first day of the second week of the riding course, and having enjoyed a rare family weekend at home to recuperate, I had a spring in my step. I made my way up the gloomy stairs to the bunk two at a time.

As usual, Paul Garrett was already sitting at the table, the tea was made, and much to my surprise he was sitting opposite to someone I had known well for several years. Jim Hardwick had joined the cadets with me in 1972, straight from school, when we were both sixteen year old boys. He was about the same height as me, but much heavier. He had always been a big hefty lad, built like a rugby union prop with a red complexion, and was one of the nicest people that you would care to meet. I couldn't imagine what he was doing here at Tally Ho riding school, so early on a Monday morning.

"Hello Jim, what are you doing here?" I asked. "You're a long way from home on a cold winter's morning."

He stood up, smiling like he usually did, and shook my hand in a warm, genuine, and enthusiastic manner.

"Morning Wildy! What you really meant to say is: 'I can't believe that a fat bastard like Hardwick is able to get on a horse.' Don't hold back mate. It's not like you to be so polite," he laughed.

I was completely taken aback. He was right, though - because of his size, and given how I had been questioned about my weight at my interview, it would never have occurred to me that big jolly Jim was Smith's replacement. He went on to explain that he had started his riding course in October, but had fallen and injured his leg after five weeks, and had to take sick leave while he recovered. He had just about given up any hope of returning, but jumped at the chance to join our course as a last minute replacement for the unfortunate Smith. I was still trying to imagine Jim on horseback when the door opened, and Joiner came into the room.

"Good morning gentlemen. I see you have all met," he said, sitting at the table with a mug of tea in his hand. "Young Hardwick here is taking over from that useless wimp Smith. I'm aware that he's a little in front of you two, but he's been away for a few weeks, so hopefully there won't be too much difference and you'll soon catch up."

We talked for a few more minutes while finishing our tea, then eventually, following the sergeant's lead, got ready to begin grooming.

"Ah. Gentlemen, (harrumph) I almost forgot. Unfortunately I have an appointment this morning which I cannot cancel, so Inspector Scott is kindly coming over from Duke Street to take the first half of today's riding school. It is a little earlier in the proceedings than is normal for him to partake, but I'm sure you will all be fine. Just do your best gentlemen. Don't let me down, (Harrumph). Please don't let me down," he repeated as we all followed him down to the stables.

This, as far as I was concerned, was not good news. On a positive note I was grooming big Garth as my ride for the day, so I at least would be able to keep up in the school, but I hadn't seen Big Ben since the day of my interview. If a weak salute could send him into a frenzied rage, what heights of fury could he reach in the riding school? I wasn't looking forward to finding out.

Grooming, unusually, was a quiet and uneventful affair. Jim Hardwick had Bijou, and for the first time since I had started, there were no shouts, screams, swearing, or clattering of hooves coming from his stable. I couldn't help myself, and had to go and see how he was doing. I watched quietly over the top of the stable door, surprised by the level of calm, tranquillity, and general lack of drama coming from within Bijou's lair. There was still the grumpy flattening of ears and flashing of eyes, but Jim just ignored him and got on with the job, occasionally replying quietly, "alright. Cut it out," or "give over man and behave." I couldn't believe my eyes.

"What's the secret Jim?" I asked. "He tries to kill me as soon as I walk in!"

"He was the same with me when I first started; used to chase me out of the box. I think he enjoys the reaction, so now I don't react. It seems to work, but I still keep my eye on him." He calmly carried on with the grooming. I told him about my first day, when I had smacked my head on the door bar whilst running away, and how Bijou had then bitten the seat out of my breeches before I'd even sat on a horse.

"Only you Wildy, only you," he laughed. "Does everyone here know the Ostler Wilde story?"

"No. They bloody well don't, and if they get to hear it I'll have to kill you painfully with a big stick," I warned whilst laughing.

The Bijou behaviour theory was food for thought. I returned to finish grooming my own horse feeling a little more optimistic, because if Jim Hardwick could tame the savage beast, then so could I.

Back upstairs, it was time to change into riding gear, so I snuck into the toilet where I secretly covered my sexy pink gym wear with my oversized boots. I decided this was going to be the last time. It was only a matter of time before someone noticed my unusual morning routine, and I was living in dread of anyone seeing my pretty leg warmers. I would have to think of another solution.

Suited, booted, and back in the bunk, I looked at the others. Collectively, it occurred to me, we looked rather comical. One fat one, one thin one, and one little short one, all dressed in granddad hats and coats, and ill-fitting second hand riding clothes.

"There must have been at least one other fat bloke on the mounted branch, because his boots fit me perfectly," observed Jim.

"Yes, and he had two pairs, but the second pair certainly don't fit me," I complained.

We entered the riding school a little early, because no one wanted to upset Ben Scott by being late. Only Jim Hardwick had any previous experience of a Big Ben riding school, and that was on the day he had fallen off and injured his leg. The only advice he would give us was to 'hold tight, shut up, and keep up'. Our two uniformed leading files were already inside waiting for us, and after walking the horses around to warm them up, quickly got us into line, ready, waiting for our instructor. There was definitely an air of tension about the school that wasn't usually apparent, and we waited apprehensively side by side, in line, with a uniformed rider at either end.

Quietly talking amongst ourselves, we learned a little more about Inspector Ben Scott from the two regular mounted men. Before joining Birmingham City Police about twenty five years ago, he had been an NCO in the Household Cavalry. There was some disagreement as to whether he had been a Lifeguard or a Blues and Royal, but whichever, it explained his obsession with saluting and his love of drill of all kinds. Later, he had enjoyed success as a sergeant in police horse competitions around the country on a horse named 'Grey Storm'. He had even one year, won the best police horse trophy at The Horse of the Year Show. Now he only rode infrequently, because he had a chronic back condition.   The varying levels of back pain that he suffered tended to determine the mood of the day.

It was just after 10am when the large door opened and Big Ben walked in. My thoughts immediately went back to the day of my interview, and of that strange juxtaposition of civilian and uniform clothing, because today he was following a familiar theme. If I'd had the courage I would have probably let out a laugh, but I didn't dare. The inspector was wearing a uniform overcoat with his two pips on the shoulders, but had added a paisley patterned scarf. Below were grey flannel trousers tucked into his socks and brown brogue shoes, whereas above he wore a trilby hat, complete with feather, perched on his head.

He walked along the line, obviously inspecting us. He acknowledged and greeted the two uniformed lads by name, whilst nodding and smiling at myself and the other trainees. He was carrying the lunging whip that had terrorised Smith a few days earlier, and I watched him closely, trying to judge the mood.

"WHOLE RIDE SHUN!" he bawled without warning.

Without thinking, I threw both of my arms down by my sides, and in doing so dropped my reins. Rein-less and brainless, I looked along the line and could see that Paul had done nothing, but Jim and the uniformed men had their right arms down by their sides, whilst still holding their reins in their left hands. The inspector stopped in front of me. He looked at me with a raised eyebrow, obviously unable to believe my stupidity, before speaking.

"Whole ride at ease. We'll try that again."

"WHOLE RIDE SHUN!"

This time I was ready, and managed to follow, in a fashion, the example of the rest of the line.

"WHOLE RIDE! RIGHT DRESS!" came the next order, like rapid fire.

"Not good. Not good," he muttered, walking along the line shaking his head.

One of the uniformed lads spoke up and told him that we hadn't yet covered right dress in our previous lessons. He seemed surprised and unimpressed, but didn't persist any further with the drill, and within a few minutes we were trotting around the school in a familiar fashion. We numbered off from the front and I found myself at number four, immediately behind Jim Hardwick and Bijou.

We were soon back into the routine, and performed our turns and circles in a reasonable fashion. He did, however, appear increasingly concerned about our actual individual riding ability, and continually barked instructions in an effort to improve us.

"Sit down number two. Get your arse into that saddle!"

"Sit still number four. Keep your hands still. Give that horse a break. SIT STILL MAN!"

"Keep up Hardman. DRESSINGS! DRESSINGS!"

We thundered on, lap after lap, with the inspector still continually shouting out orders in an effort to improve our skills. I could hear what he was saying, but try as I did, I just couldn't sit into the saddle without bouncing up and down in a clumsy manner. I wasn't alone, because I could see that Paul Garrett was having the same problem. In trying to keep up with the furious pace, he too was bouncing high into the air with every step of the horse. He appeared to be spending more time mid-flight than sitting on leather.

Jim Hardwick, despite having a much better seat because of his extra weeks of experience, was having problems of his own. He was suffering from the Bijou factor, struggling to keep his horse up to the required 'four feet nose to croup', and Big Ben was already on his case.

"Hardman! HARDMAN! FOUR FEET! FOUR FEET!"

The barrage of instructions was relentless, the pace frenetic, and I could see that Jim was working his hardest but also getting increasingly frustrated.

"DRESSINGS! HARDMAN! DRESSINGS!" barked Big Ben.

"WICK. WICK," replied the harassed Jim.

"PRICK? PRICK? WHAT ARE YOU BLABBERING HARDMAN? CATCH UP HARDMAN. CATCH UP!"

"WICK! It's HARD*WICK*!" shouted Jim.

"Shut up Hardman. CATCH UP YOU BLOODY FOOL! Pick? Hoof pick? SHUT UP AND TROT ON MAN!" roared Ben.

Getting redder in the face by the minute, he raised his whip, and with admirable precision, let out a loud crack just behind the flagging Bijou. The effect was instant. Big Garth shuddered in shock at the cracking whip just before his eyes, but Bijou immediately went up a gear and caught up with the horse in front. We continued, with now perfect dressings, at our non-stop rattling pace, for lap after lap after lap. I was fighting a personal bouncing battle against gravity, trying desperately not to fall off, but also to keep my eye on our instructor, who seemed to have descended into a wild eyed trance. Every time anyone looked like dropping behind, the whip cracked again, the pace increased, my stress levels rose, and the horses began to steam.

Around and around we went, and just when I thought things couldn't get worse, they did.

"Trot on! Trot on! Everyone knot your reins. On the order to drop your reins, drop your reins."

Having not the slightest idea what to do, I watched the leading file as he gathered his reins short and tied a knot in them. I followed suit, and with great difficulty, eventually succeeded in knotting my reins without falling off, despite the fast trot. Just in time for the next order.

"Whole ride. Drop your reins and put your hands on your heads."

I was astonished. After only five days of experience in the saddle, I was hurtling around on horseback, hands on my head, with no control, brakes, or steering. The whip cracked loudly again in front of me.

"Catch up Hardman! CATCH UP!" barked Ben.

"WICK! WICK! HARDWICK!" shouted Jim.

"Shut up Hardman. Forget your bloody hoof pick. Don't whinge man. CATCH UP. CATCH UP!" was the wild-eyed response from the centre.

The whip cracked again, and within a few minutes, whilst still thundering around out of control, we further progressed to holding our arms out horizontally, and then clapping hands over our heads. Eventually, still at a blistering pace, we were told to remove our jackets and put them back on again. We dressed and undressed three times before he again changed the rules.

"Buttons, buttons. DON'T FORGET THE BUTTONS!"

So we fastened and unfastened our buttons several more times, before finally removing our jackets, and holding them in our outstretched arms towards the centre of the school. Then he had us swirl them around above our heads and fling them into the centre of the school. How I kept on the horse I'll never know.

"TROT ON! TROT ON! CATCH UP! SIT DOWN! TROT ON!"

With grandad's jacket lying steaming in a sweaty heap on the wood shavings and sand, I trotted on, hands on head, arse on fire, and my energy levels sapping rapidly. I could see in front, Jim and

Bijou had started to lose ground again, and the gap between him and Paul Garrett at number two had started to grow. Big Ben raised the lunging whip.

"HARDMAN! FOUR FEET! FOUR FEET! LEG, LEG, LEG!"

I saw him lunge the whip at the same time as I saw him trip forward over one of the jackets. The sharp end of the whip missed Bijou's hind quarters and soared forwards, almost in slow motion to my horrified eyes, to land heavily with a loud 'THWACK', across Jim's back.

"AAAAAAAAGGHHHH!" screamed Jim.

"Whole ride WOOOALK… Whole ride HALT!" ordered the inspector.

"Oh! Oh. Oh. You've bloody whipped me," howled Jim as he turned Bijou into the centre of the school. He instinctively dismounted and stood in the middle, groaning and tentatively feeling his back with both hands.

"Are you okay, Hardman?" asked the inspector, examining the dirty welt mark running from right shoulder to left hip on Jim's shirt.

"It's bloody Hard*wick*! And no, I'm not alright. You whipped me, and it hurts like shit," complained Jim.

"Now, now. Arley-Barley, Hardwick, Arley-Barley. It was an accident. Man up, Hardwick, man up. Accidents happen to mounted men all the time. They do you know." This was perhaps the closest to an apology that Jim was going to get from the now reticent, scarlet-faced inspector.

It took several more minutes for calm to be restored. Everyone still mounted, including the two uniformed guys, looked horrified at the obvious stripe rising beneath Jim's shirt. I'm ashamed to admit, that although shocked and concerned for my friend, those precious minutes were a much welcomed reprieve. I'm not sure I could have carried on much longer without falling off to join

Granddad's jacket in the dirt. Further respite came from Steve Durran, who appeared at the door with a tray of mugs.

"Tea time, Sir?" he cautiously enquired.

"WHAT? WHAT? Ah the tea. Yes, yes, carry on Mr Durran," Ben replied. "Take a five minute break everyone. Slacken the girths and let them stretch their necks," he left the school hurriedly through the large doors.

The five minutes stretched to ten, but unfortunately seemed like only two. The horses stood motionless, heads down and slicked with sweat, steam rising like they'd run the Derby. The conversation was more animated, a raucous exchange of opinions regarding the inspector's mental stability, and the two uniformed lads agreed that although he often 'went off on one', this 'one' had been a particularly spectacular 'one'. One of them referred to it as a 'full on purple noser'. The three of us retrieved our jackets from the dirt, dusted them off, and put them back on. I took stock while we drank our tea, and concluded that we all looked a right mess. Everyone was physically exhausted and a little dazed, but even so, we were still managing to laugh at the situation.

Any further sense of levity disappeared when the doors opened, and the purple nose walked back into the school, nodding and smiling to no one in particular. I had hoped that after the break he would return in a more subdued mood, and the second half of the lesson would be easier. My optimism was shattered, and my heart sank even further, when he spoke.

"Prepare to change horses and mount up. Four to three, three to two, and two to four. Mount up!"

I couldn't believe it. I was devastated. I had wondered how Jim Hardwick had lasted the previous hour's nightmare whilst riding Bijou, and I was now about to find out.

We were soon trotting around the school again, but this time I was at number three, and pedalling like crazy to keep Bijou up to the pace. The going was hard, but having no wish to be subjected to a stroke of the cat, I was determined not to drop behind. My miserable situation worsened considerably following the next order.

"Whole ride prepare to quit and cross… WHOLE RIDE QUIT AND CROSS!"

Again, I had no idea what he was talking about. I watched dumbly as the leading file took his feet out of the stirrups, and crossed the stirrup leathers across the horse's neck close to the saddle pommel. I clumsily followed suit, and immediately realised that even the worst nightmares can get worse.

This was an entirely new experience. Bouncing around, high out of the saddle, because of my lack of 'seat' had been tough going - but now without the stirrups for support, the whole impact caused by my lack of coordination shot straight up my spine. I feared the fillings in my teeth were about to shake loose.

There was no let up, nor respite, as we continued to thunder around the school at a fast trot, turning, circling, and keeping our dressings as before. The orders from the centre were as prolific as in the first session, but to me were becoming increasingly secondary, as my mind was now concentrating on a new, more pressing problem. With no stirrups to support my feet, my big, baggy boots were beginning to slide gradually down my legs. I slowed down their descent by wrapping my legs around Bijou's belly and gripping tightly, but he was still bone idle, and in order to avoid the whip, I had to give him a regular kick with my heels. Every time I did, the boots slid down my legs a little further.

The question was simple. Whip or pink leg warmers? What would be the worst option? I carried on gripping, with my toes raised as high as possible, in a desperate attempt to hold on to my boots.

"Good leg position, Wild. Keep those toes raised. Well done man," encouraged Ben.

My toes were raised so much, and my legs gripping so tightly, that I was now suffering cramp in my calf muscles. It was a nightmare, but hope of any imminent relief was shattered by the next order.

"On the order to 'trot on', rear file trot on past the ride and take up the lead. NUMBER FIVE. TROT ON AND TAKE LEADING FILE!"

I hung on grimly, toes pointing up, legs cramped but still gripping, while the uniformed rear file glided effortlessly past and took up the leading file. When he had taken up his new position, he was closely followed by a red-faced Jim Hardwick, boinging clumsily past on the willing Big Garth. It was my turn next, and my moment of truth had arrived.

"Rear file, take up leading file. TERRRROT!"

I kept up my grip, but squeezed harder with my heels. Nothing! So, with every muscle in my lower body protesting and hurting, I squeezed even harder, using every ounce of strength I had left. Still nothing! Bijou, the shit, simply refused to increase the pace, and so, we remained as rear file.

"TERRROT! TERRROT! COME ON WILD. GET ON WITH IT! TERRROT!"

Thinking of Jim's back, I was left with no alternative. I kicked frantically with both legs and he slowly began to move forward and pass the others. I was barely holding on to my boots when he began to slow again. I could no longer keep my toes curled up because of cramp pain, and despite all of my efforts, when I moved my legs to kick him on again I felt my right boot leave my leg and plop to the floor. Thankfully no one seemed to notice, because my right leg was school side, and my left leg, which was visible to the centre, was still booted.

I may, with a little luck, have got away with it - but Bijou had other ideas, and predictably began to slow before we quite made it to the front. I tried to raise my toes and kick at the same time, but the body was now far weaker than the mind. As I moved my legs to kick my toes dipped, and inevitably my remaining boot fell gracelessly from my leg and hit the dirt of the riding school. My cover was blown, my murky secret was out, and I was exposed.

"Whole ride, waaalk. Whole ride, HALT!"

I was invited to ride into the centre of the school, and did so whilst squeezing my miserable horse with calves clad in pretty pink, fluffy, leg warmers. My shame was complete, and my peers looked on in jaw-dropped amazement. Ben's face turned from red to crimson, a contorted picture of confusion. Disbelief, anger, concern – all flickered across his face as his eyebrows rose to new heights, eventually disappearing beneath the brim of his trilby hat.

I braced myself for a massive verbal tirade, and wasn't completely ruling out the possibility of a flogging with that bloody whip. There was an air of tension while everyone waited for the speechless Ben's reaction, which thankfully was suddenly broken when the door opened and Derek Joiner walked into the school.

"All correct, Sir," said the sergeant. "Are you okay to carry on, or shall I take over?"

"No. No. I'm leaving now. You can take over Derek," replied Ben, still eyeballing me.

I saw the sergeant clock the steaming horses, and our exhausted, dishevelled and chaotic condition. He also, obviously, sensed the uncomfortable atmosphere within the group.

"Is everything okay Sir?" asked the sergeant.

"Yes Derek. Everything is fine. No problems here. No problems here at all. I've thrashed Hardman, and Wild is a closet fairy, but there's nothing else to report. Just sort it out Derek, sort it out, and I'll call you when I get back to Duke Street," he said shaking his head, and twitching as he rapidly left the riding school.

The sergeant looked at me sitting on Bijou, looking resplendent in my sexy pink fluffy leg warmers, and shaking his head with disbelief, chose not to comment. I got off the horse, collected my fallen boots, and put them back on in an effort to hide my embarrassment. No one said a word. It was awful.

"Gentlemen, (Harrumph) it looks like everyone has had enough for today, so let's put these horses away. Wash their backs, and Mr Durran will show you how to layer straw under their upturned day rugs. Do not water them yet, they're far too hot. Wild, my office - before lunch, please," he added rather sharply, walking out of the school.

Ten minutes later in the sergeant's office, I explained my unusual choice of clothing. I showed him the big baggy boots, how they flopped about when I walked, and how the leg warmers packed them out without increasing the size of my foot. He laughed out loud with obvious relief, until tears appeared in his eyes.

"You, Wild, are a trial," he said, still laughing. "You are going to send the inspector's blood pressure through the roof. Bugger off now and have your meal, I'll call him and calm him down."

The three of us were hot, moist and over-ripe when we sat down in the canteen, so no one chose to share our table. It gave me the opportunity to clear the air by explaining my leg wear, and for us to discuss the morning's session. Jim's back was still very sore, and we were all feeling battered, bruised, and slightly traumatised. The walk back after lunch was slow and deliberate, because we were all in pain and completely dishevelled. In fact, we looked a total mess - a mass of creases, shirts hanging out of the tops of breeches, and our sweaty damp jackets were covered in a dusty film of riding school surface.

As we limped in the direction of the drill square, we paused and groaned because there was a drill session in progress, which meant we had to extend our painful walk by deviating around the edge of the square. There was a squad of young cadets, all shiny, pressed, and smartly marching in step to the orders of the drill sergeant. He was wearing a red sash, carrying his pace stick tucked under his left arm, and bellowing out orders as we approached.

"LEFT ROIGHT, LEFT ROIGHT, LEFT ROIGHT LEFFFTTTT. SQUAD!   ROIGHT TAARN. LEFT ROIGHT, LEFT ROIGHT, LEFT ROIGHT LEFFFTTTT."

We paid no attention, continuing to support each other as we chatted and shuffled our way around the edge of the drill square.

"SQUAD! ROIGHT TAARN. LEFT ROIGHT, LEFT ROIGHT, LEFFTT."

I only became aware of the approaching cadets when I heard the increase in volume from the crunch of their boots on the tarmac. They appeared on our right, shiny buttons glinting and arms swinging

"SQUAD! SCARECROWS TO THE LEFT. SQUAD EYERS LEFT!"

The squad of cadets all turned their heads smartly to their left and smirked at us as they marched past. Their drill sergeant also turned his head to smartly face us, saluting as he grinned and they all marched past.

"SQUAD! EYERS FRONT!"

I had been tempted to return his salute, but at the last moment had a flashback to my longest way up and shortest way down fiasco, and thought better of it. I'd never felt so wretched and really hadn't got the energy to enter another saluting competition. So, looking like we had all been run over by a combine harvester, we increased our pace and conspicuously hobbled our way back to the riding school.

Safely back upstairs the sergeant had made a pot of tea, and sat us down to debrief the morning's events after his conversation with the inspector.

"Gentlemen, I have spoken to the inspector, anointed his troubled brow, and calmed his concerns, of which there were many. (Harrumph) Hardwick, he wanted me to assure you that your thrashing was unintentional. He tripped over a jacket, and is sorry, but it's unlikely that he will ever say so. Also, he was bitterly disappointed with all of your abilities in the riding school after five weeks of training, and was striving to improve your seats. I reminded the old fool that you have been here for only five days, not five weeks, and I think he now believes that he was too hard on you all - but again, it's unlikely he will ever say so. Wild, your sexy stockings, or whatever they are, disturbed him deeply. Apparently, he was still twittering and gibbering about them when he arrived back at Duke Street. I have now fully explained the situation, he is both relieved and sees the funny side, and I think there may be a development with your boot situation very soon. Now, you rabble, let's get those kits cleaned. They'll need a good dig out after today's debacle."

Back at home that evening, I was again laid out in front of the fire, with my bare bum pointing skywards. I was completely knackered, and hurting from head to toe. I could have slept for a year, and was only half paying attention to what Becks was saying.

"That horrible man is a maniac. He should be in an asylum! Look at the state of you Wildy," she said angrily.

"You should see the others. At least I wasn't whipped."

"Poor Jim and he's such a nice bloke too."

"At least he's got a new name. He's 'Officer Hoofpick' now!" I laughed until it hurt too much.

"Your poor little bum is in a right state, so you can forget the white spirit. I'll use some of Mel's cream. Now lie still," she fussed.

I didn't need telling twice, and lay half asleep while she rubbed my buttocks with zinc and castor oil cream. Not very manly, I thought, but at least I wouldn't get nappy rash.

"This is all my fault Stef."

"How's that then?" I asked.

"You never wanted to do it in the first place. I nagged you, and now look at you," she said with genuine concern.

"Shut up. I'm fine," I reassured her. "And as strange as it seems, I'm enjoying it. So stop being daft, and keep rubbing."

"I see that you've got some shiny new boots. Are they any better?"

"They're great, really smart, and they fit too. I haven't got the energy to put them on for you though. Sorry," I murmured sleepily.

"I've never seen you like this, Wild Child. I hope you don't stick like it."

"Hmm. Don't worry, I'll be fine tomorrow.   At least you can have your pink fluffy thingies back now," I yawned.

"No, you can keep them. I like you in them," she giggled. "They look much better on you. You've got the legs for them."

"Brave talk little one, brave talk. You know I'm helpless, but I'm going to punch your lights out tomorrow, when I can stand up."

"Be careful matey; I have the cream. I'm in charge, and you are at my mercy.   I may just give it a slap," she threatened, continuing to carefully rub my weary numb bum.

I smiled helplessly. We enjoyed a good play fight, but I just didn't have the energy. I was drifting into that comfortable dozy state, where the pain and the tiredness seem to blend perfectly, creating a sort of weary apathetic stupor that was strangely pleasant. I was at that point where I just didn't give a monkey's.

I don't remember going upstairs that night, nor getting into bed. I must have slept like a log, too tired to even dream, and thankfully too tired to worry about the potential horrors that may be in store the following day.

CHAPTER 10

BLANKETS, BANKS AND SUPERHEROES

I slept deeply without waking until the alarm rang loudly the following morning, and it wasn't until I leaned over to switch it off that I realised I was alone in bed. This was not normal, so I lay there for a few moments, collecting my thoughts, groaning and slowly moving my limbs to make sure they were still in working order. I had just about satisfied myself that I was wholly intact when the door opened, and my wife appeared carrying two mugs of tea.

"Wakey-wakey Wildy, tea's up; how are you feeling?" she whispered.

"Bloody hell Becks, is the house on fire?"

"No. No it isn't, but I thought you'd need to take your time this morning, so I made the tea. Are you sure you're okay to go to work?" she asked, intently studying my face.

"I've got to go, or they'll chuck me off the course. I'll be fine once I get up. This is a lovely surprise though. We should do this more often," I suggested between slurps.

"The house is really cold this morning," she shivered, "and there's no hot water."

"That's because it's six o'clock, and the boiler man hasn't lit the stove or switched on the immersion heater yet. That's all part of my morning duties. Come here and get back in bed, let's give you a warm up while Mel's still asleep."

I got up, creaking, hurting, but smiling and feeling loved. I completed my morning chores, and as I left Jim Hardwick, as arranged, pulled up in the road outside of the house. This was going to be a bonus. Jim only lived a mile away, so we had arranged to share lifts. It meant our travelling costs would be halved while our expenses stayed the same, and our girls would have more use of the cars during the day.

"How's Officer Hoofpick this morning?" I greeted him as I gingerly lowered myself into the car.

"I was wondering if that was going to stick," laughed my driver. "Officer Hoofpick is as stiff as a poker, and you look like you need oiling this morning."

It was good to have company on the way to Tally Ho, and the conversation inevitably focused on the dramatic events of the previous day's riding school. Big Jim's back was still really sore, and he ached in all of the same places that I did - but I still couldn't get my head around the fact that he had actually been whipped, albeit accidentally, by the inspector.

"He gave you a right old whack, Jim. I was right behind you. I nearly fell off in shock."

"*You* nearly fell off! It brought tears to my eyes, I can tell you. He's raving mad you know, but I don't think he can help it," he said - a little too benevolently, in my opinion.

"Well I heard that he got chucked out of the army for the same thing. Did you know?"

"No. What happened?" he asked, looking at me with new interest.

"Apparently he was court martialled when he got caught furiously thrashing his privates!" I laughed.

"You're a daft bugger Wildy. I like that though. I like that," he sniggered, "but you definitely stole the show, mate."

"Me?"

"Those bloody leg warmers! I thought his head was going to explode when he saw them. I think it was only the trilby that kept it all together. He didn't know what to say or do. I nearly pissed myself." He laughed loudly.

"Don't," I groaned. "I thought I was going to die. It was Becks' idea. I can't believe I agreed, I must have been nuts. They were rather pretty though, don't you think?" I asked, puckering my lips and fluttering my eyes at him.

"Oh yes. They were well hip. You looked like Nureyev on the coalmon's oss," he continued, laughing loudly.

"Well he doesn't frighten me, so the next time I see the barmy bugger I'm going to lay into him and give him a right old bollocking," I interrupted.

"Really?" asked Jim, looking across at me.

"Absolutely, but I'll go into the wash room first so he won't be able to hear me," I laughed.

The conversation continued in the same vein, and the normally mundane, miserable, dark winter's morning journey along the slightly manic M6 seemed to fly by. Jim's chosen route was exactly the same as mine, but it seemed much shorter than normal with some pleasant like-minded company sharing the ride.

We were sitting in the bunk drinking tea with Paul, comparing our pain levels and laughing about the horrors of the previous day - Jim had just removed his shirt to show off his wound - when the sergeant walked into the room.

"One, two, three - a full crew, well done gentlemen. I'm impressed. I didn't know who or what to expect this morning after yesterday's enduring adventure. All credit to the three of you, we'll make mounted men out of you yet (harrumph). Yes, we'll make mounted men out of you yet."

The three of us gradually gelled into a close team. We were comfortable in each other's company, happy to give and take the banter, but ready to support when the going got tough. As the weeks progressed we improved, the course became more technical, and there was something new to learn all of the time. We didn't know it at the time, but the horses that we were riding in the school were the old timers of the branch. They were known as schoolmasters, and had seen it all before. Their mouths were hard and spoiled after years of work with a multitude of different riders, and it was easy to see how they had become miserable and difficult with the trainees.

We learned to walk, trot, and canter, and how to deliver signals to the horses by using our hands, legs, voice, and seat. These signals were known as natural aids. A simple analogy is to compare the signals given to the horse to that of the controls in a car. When learning to drive, you must practice and develop a feeling for the bite of the clutch. When riding a horse you need to develop a balance between your hands and legs in order to stop, start, and move the horse forward smoothly at the required speed and pace. Unlike learning to drive, a horse is a living, breathing animal with a personality and a mind of its own, so the required level of application of the aids varies greatly between individual animals. With experience came the ability to assess each horse and apply the required level of aids accordingly. Or alternatively, in Bijou's case, just keep kicking him until your boots fall off.

With the use of these aids we also learned to move the horses sideways to the left and to the right. Moving sideways and forwards at the same time at an angle of about forty five degrees was called a half-pass, and moving the horse fully sideways to the left or right was known as a full pass. Moving the horse backwards in a straight line - a rein back - was achieved by applying forward aids with the leg, but at the same time resisting with the reins, a little like finding the bite on the car's clutch.

When applied correctly, it caused the horse to move quietly and smoothly backwards without moving left or right. All of these movements were learned by trial and error, plenty of repetition, and were, of course, just a few of the absolutely essential skills required to safely work a police horse in crowds of people. There was definitely more to this mounted man business than had initially met the eye.

We worked from 8am until 5pm from Monday to Thursday, but finished early on Fridays, and because they were shorter these days were designated as blanket days. When the concept of blanket day was first explained to us I was convinced it was a joke, but it wasn't - after the first couple of weeks we routinely rode on Friday mornings with just a blanket between us and the horses' backs.

Friday was the designated blanket day because the school horses were used on Saturdays at any one of the six football clubs within the West Midlands area. It was less strenuous, meaning the horses weren't tired on Saturday, and it also meant we had less kit to clean before our early finish. Our reduced kit consisted of the normal bridle but with the bottom rein removed, which meant that unusually we rode with a single rein and no kerb chain.

On our first blanket day, while congregating in the school and waiting for the sergeant, I was feeling pretty smug. I was holding onto big Garth - always everyone's first choice ride. It wasn't until the order to mount was given that I realised I was actually at a considerable disadvantage. Whilst holding onto the reins with my left hand, I found there was absolutely nothing else to hold onto with which I could pull myself up onto the horse. The other two had thrown their arms over their horse's back, and Paul had managed to wriggle himself up the side of and eventually onto the back of the much shorter Bijou. Jim was in limbo on Brigadier, with his arms clinging and his legs kicking frantically, but both still on the nearside of the horse.

"Come on Hardwick. You're nearly there. Pull yourself up man, you're nearly there," encouraged the sergeant.

Jim was a big guy with a fair amount of body weight, but after a lot of grunting, swearing, and verbal encouragement, he finally hauled himself up and threw his right leg over to the other side. His face was blood red, his forehead wet with sweat - but he was on his horse, and I wasn't.

I was a lot lighter than Jim Hardwick, but had never been blessed with excessive upper body strength, and at well over seventeen hands, Garth was much taller than the other two horses. The knack was to grip the horse's mane at the withers with the left hand, reach the right arm as far as possible over the horse's back, spring as high as possible from the legs, and pull yourself up with your arms whilst scrambling your knees up the side of the horse.

My first problem was that Garth had no mane. The second was that any spring left in my legs had already sprung from previous day's riding. The biggest issue by far, however, was that the horse was just too big. Despite a lot of verbal encouragement, I was embarrassingly the only one still with my feet planted firmly on the ground.

"Come on Wild, we haven't got all day. Make an effort man; it's a horse not a bloody elephant. Spring up!" goaded Joiner.

Despite all of the instructions, banter, and encouragement, it became obvious that I wasn't going to be able to get onto my horse without assistance. The sergeant strode over to me.

"Right. Get a grip, man. Hold on and bend your left leg."

I dutifully obeyed, and bent my left leg as he gripped my left boot. Then, as I sprang from my right leg, he flung me upwards with both hands.

"WOOOOHAAH BLOODY HELL!"

CRASH!

I'm not sure how high I actually reached, but I would probably have been able to mount the aforementioned elephant without touching its side on the way up. I clattered into the wooden boards on the wall of the riding school and then crunched heavily onto the ground, but I don't recall making contact with a horse en route.

I sat momentarily winded, listening to the sound of laughing, but couldn't understand why everything had gone dark, muffled, and more scarily - why I was unable to see.

"I can't see. I can't see! I've gone blind," I heard myself groan.

"It's no good you hiding Wild! We can all see you under there. Please come out so we can carry on." laughed an unsympathetic voice from the darkness.

Eventually normal daylight was restored as I pulled the blanket from over my head, and found myself sitting on the ground to the offside of the motionless and ever-patient Garth.

"Ahh, he's now playing peek-a-boo with us gentlemen. Come out from under that blanket and re-join the rest of the school, please. All in your own time Wild, of course."

I slowly got to my feet, with nothing damaged apart from my pride, and joined in with the general hilarity. It was, of course, the only thing to do, and I guessed that this incident was probably a regular feature of every course, and I knew that it would, hopefully, be someone else's turn next time.

Nonchalantly trying to maintain an aura of cool composure, I picked up my blanket and purposefully put it back onto my horse. Without any further fuss I quietly bent my left leg as Joiner grabbed my boot and lifted me skywards again. This time, fully prepared for take-off, there was no further drama, so I gathered up my reins whilst sitting on my blanket. I had never sat on a saddleless horse before, so wasn't sure what to expect, but something didn't feel right. This wasn't going to be a comfortable experience.

"Are you ready now Mr Wild?"

"I'm not sure. Something's not right."

"You can say that again. *You*, Wild, are definitely not right. Where is your cap man? Get a grip now and hurry up."

His question, thankfully, was the remedy to my problem. The penny finally dropped with a clang. I didn't say anything; it was better not to, but just quietly leaned forward, lifted my backside, and managed to retrieve my missing cap from beneath the blanket. As soon as I returned it to my head I could feel that it was full of shavings, but I didn't dare take it off again. I would have to suffer.

Riding a horse without a saddle was very different, and I certainly wasn't the only one to hit the dirt that day. We began by going through a fairly normal routine of turning and circling at the walk, trot and canter, but it was definitely a completely different experience. Initially it felt very unstable when changing pace or speed, and slowing from the trot to the walk was particularly unnerving, but we all adapted more easily than anticipated.

After a while, the whole tone of the lesson changed and we actually began to play games. We played tag, ran relay races, and raced around obstacle courses put together with cones and wooden jumping poles. We cantered around with our hands on our heads; turning around backwards on the move and at all of the paces, falling off at regular intervals, and climbing back on without any thought or assistance. To the casual observer it must have looked like grown men playing pony club gymkhana games, but though the psychology wasn't immediately apparent, the results were impressive.

Our inhibitions disappeared along with the formality of the drill, and with the introduction of games came competition and a natural determination to win. The fear of falling off seemed to have been left upstairs with our saddles, and by the end of the morning all three of us were completely covered in muck and shavings, all having hit the dirt on countless occasions. Everyone had a smile on their face, and we chattered eagerly as we climbed the stairs to the bunk to begin cleaning the kit. It had been a very enjoyable morning.

The informality of blanket day was a great way to end each week. It improved our seats, raised our morale, and developed a good team spirit as we all threw caution to the wind - and the horses enjoyed it too.

As the weeks passed by, our riding skill levels improved. Our 'seats' became more natural, and the pain and soreness lessened, so the necessity for my nightly bum rub had diminished. It was a shame; it was a pleasant domestic routine that had been too readily suspended, and was something I quietly considered one evening whilst lying on the sofa during quality time. I was just about to raise the issue when I began to sense a little tension in my unusually quiet wife. I looked at her, delaying a little in order to assess the mood, before a little probing eye contact confirmed my suspicions.

"Go on. What's the matter?" I nervously enquired.

"Are you in a good mood? Or are you going to shout?"

"Why should I shout? Have you been a naughty girl?" I asked with a raised eyebrow.

"Don't you raise your eyebrow to me Wildy," she laughed, trying to push me onto the floor. "It's you too, we've both been naughty."

"Naughty?"

"You've had a nasty letter off Hooperman," she answered with a pained expression.

"Oh shit shit shit! Not again. I'll bet he's not wishing us a Happy New Year?"

"We're sixty pounds overdrawn, so he's charged us fifteen pounds, and he wants to see you."

"What! Fifteen quid?! The bastard! He's got no chance of seeing me now I'm on this course though, unless he wants to work the weekend. What does he want, blood? Doesn't he know we've just had Christmas and Mel's first birthday party to pay for?"

"I knew you'd shout, don't wake her," she said, raising a finger to her lips.

"I know, I know. I'm sorry, but what the bloody hell does he want? Half of our overdraft is because of his bloody charges," I answered in a loud whisper.

My anger wasn't aimed at Becks, and was purely down to my frustration. We just couldn't seem to live on my income. We were constantly overdrawn towards the end of every month, and it was only the amount that varied. It was a subject we had discussed at length many times before, and it was the only real issue that created stress in our otherwise happy lives. As usual, my mind went into overdrive when our financial plight was raised, but though the causes were obvious, any solution seemed unreachable.

Police pay at the time was pitifully poor, and since Becks had given up work to look after Mel, it had been a constant struggle to make ends meet. We certainly didn't waste our money, had few material possessions, and the only time we ever went out was for an occasional get together at the police club, where the drinks were very cheap. Everyone at work was feeling the pinch. Some of the older guys' kids qualified for free school dinners, and several experienced officers had recently abandoned their careers to take up better paid, often low-skilled work in factories and on building sites. There was a worrying and constant haemorrhage of manpower and resources from the job, which wouldn't begin to end until after the conclusion of the Lord Edmund Davies inquiry which, unknown to anyone at the time (and to the horror of the Government), would increase our pay by 45% the following year in 1979.

We had opened a joint account at The National Westminster Bank just after we married, and our local branch was only a couple of minutes' walk away on the High Street. It was a small branch, with only a manager and two or three staff in total, and I'd had a very comfortable relationship with the manager, Mr Longstaff. He was a nice old chap who I had got to know through the job, and had first met him whilst attending an alarm call at the bank in the middle of the night. We had further cemented our friendship, sometime later, when I arrested the man attempting to steal his Vauxhall Viva from the staff car park.

Ron Longstaff was old school, a relic of quieter times, and carefully counting the weeks to retirement. He smoked a pipe, wore leather patches on the elbows of his jacket, and if he saw me at the counter would often ask me into his office for a chat and a coffee. He used to ask about what I had been up to at work, chuckled at my heavily embellished stories, and told me he envied my exciting work, because he had been bored for forty years at the bank.

In our conversations he always referred to me as 'Young Stef' and never forgot to ask about Becks and Mel. He had learned about Mel when we opened a bank account for her shortly after her birth; he had personally dealt with the application, and had added a discretionary £10 to the account because she was born on New Year's Day. Recently, and much to our amusement, he had adopted the habit of adding a personal written message to the bottom of our monthly printed statements. Sometimes it would be a simple 'Don't forget to pop in for a coffee', or 'Hope you, Rebecca and Melanie are well', or, if we were overdrawn more than normal, he would add a friendly warning like 'Tut-tut Stef' or 'Careful Stef, you're not a superintendent yet'. In short, we were charmed and 'got away with murder' with Uncle Ron. We were completely unprepared for what unforeseen horrors may be lurking in the future.

Our nightmare began on a lovely warm sunny afternoon when I was still a probationer patrolling the High Street beat on foot. Nothing was going on, so I took the opportunity to pop into the bank to withdraw ten pounds in cash. In the 1970s ATMs were uncommon, few people had a credit card, debit cards, chip and pin, and contactless were things of the future, and goods were generally purchased with either cash or a cheque, so it was a regular occurrence to sign a cheque for cash at the bank and be given your money over the counter.

I wrote out my cheque, handed it to the familiar lady behind the screen, and smiled at her when she looked up.

"Hello PC Wild. I'm glad you're here, because the manager would like a chat with you. If you have the time of course?" she asked returning my smile.

I looked at my watch, confirmed that I had plenty of time, and happily agreed to share a coffee, chat, and the fumes from the puffs of Uncle Ron's pipe smoke. She disappeared for a few minutes before letting me in through the staff door. She then knocked on the manager's door before opening it and showing me into the familiar office.

I spotted the trap at the moment that I fell into it. There was a man sitting behind Uncle Ron's desk, but it wasn't Uncle Ron. It was a much younger man, smartly suited with Brylcreemed hair, a stern face, and a brown folder in his hands. I assessed the unexpected situation and quickly formed the impression that this man wasn't going to be interested in listening to any of my amusing yarns of the local constabulary. In order to take control and gain the upper hand in whatever discussion was about to take place, I spoke first.

"Hello I'm PC Wild, Stef Wild," I began.

"Mr Wild. Thank you for popping in to see me," was the unsmiling reply. I began to develop the cold alone feeling, that I remembered so well, before receiving a belting in the headmaster's office.

"I was expecting to see Ron Longstaff. He's a very good friend, we get on like-"

"Sadly Mr Longstaff is no longer here, Mr Longstaff has gone Mr Wild. My name is Hooper and I am the new manager. The party is over Mr Wild. Please sit down so that we can discuss your account."

I made no reply.

"Mr Wild, your constant overdrawing is causing me deep concern, and it is something that cannot go on any longer without a penalty."

"I don't see a problem with it myself. You have a bit of mine at the start of the month, and I have a bit of yours at the end of the month," I sheepishly grinned.

"Yes. Unfortunately, Mr Wild, the bit of yours that we have is diminishing, and the bit of ours that you have is rapidly increasing. As I said, the party is over, and we are going to work together to get you back on track."

He wasn't joking. The party certainly was over, but the end of my coffees and chats with my friendly bank manager was the least of my problems. The much-debated long spell of government austerity inflicted upon the nation during recent years, is nothing new to us, because we had been subjected to similar measures in the 1970s by the dour, miserable, and humourless Mr Hooper. Unlike his kindly old predecessor he chose not to share his first name with me, was totally immune to my youthful cheeky chappy charm, and from the very start began to rule our finances with a rod of iron.

There was precious little left of my salary after the monthly bills were paid, but he still imposed a harsh budget and repayment plan which accounted for almost every penny of it. If we wanted to buy anything deemed frivolous, like a pair of shoes for the rapidly growing Mel, I had to call and convince him that we weren't squandering our money on anything that may have brought joy into our lives. If we dared to exceed our meagre agreed overdraft by a single penny he came down on us like a ton of bricks, writing letters and heavily charging us for the privilege. We often joked about the situation in an attempt to lighten our worries, and for some reason which I now cannot remember, christened our detested bank manager 'Hooperman'. Hooperman may, in our nightmares, have worn his pants on the outside of his trousers - but he was the nemesis of Superman, not our superhero, and most definitely not on our Christmas card list.

Any shortage of money in an economy inevitably filters down to all levels, eventually affecting everyone, and our situation was not unique. I have an uncomfortable memory of a very embarrassing incident one Saturday morning when the Co-op milkman called at the house for his money. Howard was an excellent milkman, reliable, a really nice chap, and was the brother of a sergeant at our nick. He was always considerate, understood my shift pattern, and would always take steps not to wake me if I was in bed after nights.

On this particular morning I was unable to write a cheque because we were completely skint. It would have been bounced by 'Hooperman', who would have then charged us for the privilege. We were too embarrassed to answer the door, so decided to be quiet and lay low until he went away. We both stood in the kitchen whilst I held Mel, playing a shushing game in an effort to keep her quiet. After two knocks on the door and a short pause, we both looked in horror as the letter flap opened and a pair of eyes stared straight at us along the hallway.

"Ah! There you are. 'Oroight'? I knew you were in because the car's outside. Don't worry about the money; I'll come back on Wednesday after pay day. Tara-a-bit," he cheerfully announced, before whistling back to his milk float with just the empties.

It was an embarrassing moment which still raises my colour over forty years later, but it perfectly reflected our financial hardship at the time. We had no credit cards, couldn't dream of a new car, and had no expensive designer clothes, iPads, smartphones, or any of the other technology that is taken for granted with today's modern life. I had never been abroad, stayed in a hotel, or even been on an aeroplane, but we were still skint and with very little to show for it.

Forty-five years later, with hindsight, it is plain to see that Hooperman's efforts prevented us from getting into serious and permanent debt. He wouldn't let us spend money that we didn't have, and wouldn't allow us to borrow money that we couldn't afford to pay back. I don't know where he is now, or if he still wears red pants over his trousers, but I feel pretty sure that a lot of modern life's financial anxieties could be sorted by short periods of 'rehab', whilst being restrained and force fed with regular double doses of 'Hooperman'.

However, back on the sofa in 1978, and without the wisdom of hindsight, Hooperman's virtues were as yet unrecognised and I had been summoned to endure yet another humiliating and emotional beating. The same office where I used to lounge in a comfortable leather chair, supping filter coffee with a warm friendly man, had now taken on a new persona. The smell of St. Bruno had gone, as had the coffee, and had been replaced by the ambience of an interrogation room. It was also cold, because the miserable sod had turned the heating off too.

"So shall I phone and book you an appointment to see him?" Becks asked, interrupting my thoughts.

"No. I'm not going."

"You can't keep putting him off Stef. You know what he's like."

"It's pay day next week. Leave it until then. I'd rather talk to him when there's a bit of money in the account. Just forget it for now. I'll sort it out, so please just forget it."

We went up to bed that night, climbing the same wooden stairs, and avoiding the teeth of the redundant carpet gripper, without the usual giggles, shushing, and play fighting. Our money problems always made me grumpy, because they worried me.

How did I work so many bloody hours and have so little to show for it? When was it going to get any better? Would it ever get any better? Would we ever be able to afford some carpet on these stairs? Would we ever be able to take Aunty Sue's old curtains down from the lounge and buy some that matched the room? It isn't good getting into bed with a head full of questions and money worries. It creates a head worm that keeps you awake at night. I'd much rather just be aching and saddle sore. At least then, I'd get to have my bum rubbed.

CHAPTER 11

TESTING TIMES

The three of us had all arrived at Tally Ho unusually early, and we were sitting around the bunk table drinking our second mug of tea, when Derek Joiner made an unexpected announcement:

"Gentlemen, you are mid-course now and consequently I will be leaving you at the end of this week. Sergeant Owen from West Bromwich will take up the reins from Monday, and will see you through until the end of your course."

This was a bombshell. It came as a complete surprise, and caused me some concern. I had become comfortable around Joiner and had grown to quite like him. In the early days of the course, I had identified him as a pompous arse and was convinced that he 'had it in for me'. However, as we all had progressed and got to know him, his sense of humour became far more obvious. He explained things simply and plainly, and although there was never any doubt that he was the boss, and that the job had to be done properly, he was approachable, personable, and enjoyed the banter of the bunk. To coin a phrase of the times, he was a bloke's bloke.

We all expressed some concern, and came to the conclusion that something had happened that we were unaware of, and that someone was being moved as a consequence.

"No, no not at all, nothing is amiss," explained the sergeant, in an effort to allay our fears. "It's quite common for us to change instructors at this stage in your training. I've started you all off from scratch; you are now familiar with the drill, and your riding abilities have developed very nicely. Now in the later stages you will move on to more active riding, and will be doing more pole work and jumping. Dai Owen is far more experienced than I am in that field. I'm sure you will enjoy the change, and benefit from his wealth of experience."

So that was that. Derek Joiner was to move over the weekend, with his horse, and take over the section at the West Bromwich stable, while the mystery West Bromwich sergeant with the very Welsh sounding name came to us. It is important to keep an open mind in life, but I've never been a natural embracer of change. I have often been guilty of 'getting my feet under the table' and staying too long in a job when it was obviously time to move on. Only time would tell whether this change was for the best - I would have to wait until Monday to form an opinion of our new trainer.

During morning grooming, the three of us cornered Steve Durran, who was grooming the sergeant's horse. We wiped the grease from our horses' head collars with cloths and hot water, and took the opportunity to have a bit of a chat.

"What's Dai Owen like then, Steve?" I asked.

"He's very quiet. He's not like Sergeant Joiner at all."

"In what way?" asked Paul.

"He's a bit shy really. He's all for the horses. The horses come first, last, and in between with him. He is sort of tuned into them, like he understands them," he tried to explain.

"I bet he doesn't understand that black hearted bugger over there?" I replied, nodding towards Bijou's loose box. "I don't think he's too bad now, to be honest." Everyone looked at Paul in surprise. "In fairness, I think he's better now that I've got to know him. He's been as good as gold today."

"Well I've got to know him too, and I still wouldn't trust him an inch," I said emphatically to nodded agreement from Jim.

"You just need to cool it, Stef. Stop going in with your guard up, just treat him quietly and firmly, but show him a bit of respect and you'll get a positive response. He's only flesh and blood after all."

I looked closely at Paul, trying to decide if he was really being serious, or if he was cleverly playing 'devil's advocate', and winding us all up. I couldn't tell.

"He's a miserable bugger whichever way you look at it, Paul. I don't trust him either," replied Jim, taking my side.

"I don't agree, we should be beyond this now. We're not first week recruits anymore! I personally feel confident in my ability, and the horse detects that and responds accordingly. You two just don't help yourselves."

I was still mulling over this pompous little lecture, trying to work out if he was being serious and whether we had been told off or not, when the sergeant suddenly appeared at the bottom of the stairs. We all, as one, dried off our head collars and walked quietly back into our respective stables to finish the grooming of our horses.

"AAAAAAAAAGGGHHHH!!!!" came a blood curdling scream from Bijou's stable only a moment later.

I ran out just in time to see Paul Garrett teetering out of Bijou's doorway. He was ashen faced and clutching his throat with both hands. The suspected offender was brazenly standing head over the door, ears flattened back and teeth bared, with a half fastened head collar dangling precariously from his nose. We looked on, amazed and speechless.

"He's had my throat! He's had my throat! The bastard's had my throat out!" The panicky words came out in a sort of demonic gurgle, as blood began to trickle from between his fingers.

After a moment's hesitation we composed ourselves and piled in to help. We sat him down on an upturned bucket, and whilst trying to calm him down, managed to force his tightly clenched fingers away from his neck. There was no spouting gush of blood, but there was a considerable flow, which in hindsight looked much worse because it was spread all over the front of his neck, his hands, and his shirt collar.

"I'm going to die! I'm bleeding to death!" gurgled Paul as we tried to decide just how serious an injury Bijou had inflicted. The blood continued to run, and the colour drained from his face as he twittered on senselessly, convinced his life was rapidly ebbing from the wound in his throat.

"I don't like the look of that at all. Best get it checked out; Wildy, Hoofpick, get the keys to the Marina and take him up to 'The Accy'," ordered the sergeant, now taking charge.

I ran upstairs and came back down with the car keys, before joining a debate about what first aid, if any, should be applied before the emergency run to 'The Accy'. The general consensus was that some sort of pressure bandage should be applied to the wound to stem the flow of blood before we began our dash to the hospital.

"There's nothing like that left in the first aid kit," admitted Joiner. "I sent an order to Arnie to restock it yesterday. There's only an eye patch and some milk of magnesia in there at the moment."

"Do you want to play pirates, Paul? Or have you got indigestion?" asked Jim in his best swashbuckling voice, in a clumsy attempt to lighten the mood.

Everyone burst out laughing.

"Bollocks to you Hardwick. I'm dying and you don't give a shit. Bollocks to all of you. Piss takers," gurgled Paul, whilst sinking deeper into a pit of despair.

As worried as I was, I found it difficult to suppress a laugh as our crises rose to another level, and began to resemble a Laurel and Hardy sketch. In the simple days before political correctness was invented, black humour was a common coping factor used to deal with the everyday stresses of police work. It wasn't uncommon for an officer to be lying on the ground injured, having to listen to his mates discussing who was to have his locker, torch, and what would happen to his share of the Christmas party fund. It was the way things were - no offence was ever intended, and none was ever taken.

The confusion was further compounded by Bijou loudly kicking his stable door in a noisy protest over the delay in morning feed time, so Steve Durran quietly walked over to his stable, re-fitted his head collar and turned the horse around before tying him to the back wall. He came back with Bijou's tail bandage in his hand.

"Here, you could use this," he suggested.

Sometimes, in the heat of the moment, and at times of genuine crisis, you do things that in the cold light of day seem less than wise. I honestly can't recall if I thought it was a good idea at the time, but I do know that I stood quietly by, without saying a word, while, in an attempt to stem the flow of blood, someone tightly bound Paul Garrett's neck with Bijou's rather smelly, dark blue cotton tail bandage.

Eventually, and with the dubious emergency first aid applied, we picked Paul up and lay him on his back on the back seat of the car. I jumped into the passenger seat and Jim drove us to Birmingham Accident Hospital.

It was morning rush hour, so the traffic was frustratingly slow as we drove towards the city centre along Bristol Road, and it probably took a full ten minutes to reach the famous old hospital in Bath Row. I kept a close eye on our back seat casualty, who apart from the occasional moan, had quietened considerably. For my own peace of mind, I gave him a sharp poke in the ribs to satisfy myself that he was, in fact, still alive and breathing. The sudden ungrateful outburst of foul and abusive language reassuringly confirmed that life was not yet extinct.

On our arrival Jim parked the car outside of the modern ugly canopy that covered most of the forecourt of Birmingham's Accident Hospital. The hospital itself was located in an old building that stood behind an attractive and impressive Victorian frontage. Affectionately known by Brummies as 'The Accy,' it was widely respected and internationally recognised as being one of the world's first specialist trauma units. Confident that he would now be in good hands, we took an arm each, helped Paul off the back seat, and dragged him through the main doors into the reception. The woman at the desk looked at us suspiciously as we held Paul on his feet at the window. On reflection, we must have looked rather strange dressed in our white aprons and mucky wellies whilst standing in a busy hospital in central Birmingham.

"Name?" she asked rather sharply.

"Paul Garrett," I replied.

"Date of birth?"

"I have no idea."

"Address?"

"Sorry I don't know that either," I apologised.

"Can't he speak for himself?"

"What's your address Paul?" asked Jim.

"Gluc... glorc... gluc..." replied Paul without opening his eyes.

"Is his face always that colour?" asked the woman, now showing a little more concern.

I looked at Paul and noticed for the first time that his face was indeed beginning to turn a worrying shade of blue. Before I could answer her question, the woman picked up her phone and spoke rapidly.

"I have a man at reception that is blue in the face, and he seems to be having difficulty with his breathing," she said with increasing urgency.

Almost immediately a nurse appeared from a set of double doors to the side of the reception desk. She looked at Paul in apparent disbelief. "What has happened here?" she demanded.

"He's been bitten by a savage horse, and we think he's bleeding to death," explained Jim.

"He's not bleeding to death. He's choking to death. Bring him through immediately," she snapped as she briskly walked back through the double doors.

Jim and I followed, dragging our colleague between us. We delivered him to a cubicle in the emergency room, where within a minute Paul was lying on a bed while the nurse removed Bijou's tail bandage from his neck with a pair of scissors. I waited, expecting the worst, to see spurts of blood when the bandage came off, but there were none. The only blood evident was already dry and congealed on Paul's neck.

A young male Asian doctor entered the cubicle, looked at Paul, and then spoke to the nurse. "Is this the choking that's just come in?"

"Well it was, but he's okay now. He's breathing normally, and his colour is returning," she replied, whilst scowling at Jim and myself.

"Have you removed a blockage? Are the airways clear?" he asked, looking into Paul's eyes with a light.

"There was no blockage doctor, just this tourniquet tightly bound around his neck." She shook her head and handed the doctor the now ribboned tail bandage.

"A tourniquet around his neck?" asked the young doctor incredulously. "What is this dreadful thing?" He held Bijou's tail bandage safely between finger and thumb at arm's length.

"It's a tail bandage," explained Jim. "You wrap it around a horse's tail to make it all neat and tidy."

"What are these stains on it?" asked the doctor, turning up his nose and obviously dreading the answer.

"Some of it will be Paul's blood," I said, after taking it from him and inspecting it more closely, "but I think this is a bit of shit."

"A bit of shit!" gasped the doctor.

"So, whose idea was it to put this excrement-infested tourniquet around an open neck wound? Don't they teach you any first aid in the police?" demanded the increasingly stroppy nurse.

"It was just a tail bandage when we started; I don't think it became a tourniquet until we were well down the Bristol Road," explained Jim in desperate mitigation.

"Brilliant! I have a simple bite on the neck, but nearly croak out because you pair of clots garrotte me on the way to hospital?" complained Paul, still lying on the bed and without opening his eyes.

"Shut your face, you ungrateful little git. It's all your fault anyway," snarled Jim in his best bedside manner.

"That's enough, please, that's enough," pleaded the doctor. "Nurse, just clean up his neck please, the wound will only require a butterfly stitch. The unfortunately administered first aid treatment, however, will require a tetanus shot and a course of antibiotics. If you arrange the shot I'll write out a prescription. Thank you. Goodbye," he added whilst beating a hasty retreat.

After watching Paul drop his trousers to be jabbed in the buttocks with an enormous needle by the icy nurse, and following a considerable wait in the hospital pharmacy, we shuffled back into the bunk at Tally Ho towards the end of the morning. Paul was unusually subdued and embarrassingly sporting only the tiniest of butterfly stitches to show for all of the morning's drama.

"Ah, the wanderers return. You're not dead then Garrett?" observed the sergeant, looking up from his paperwork.

We sat down for a cup of tea and related the tale of our adventure at 'The Accy' to Joiner, who roared with laughter when we told him about the stroppy nurse and the horrified young doctor.

"There's nothing wrong with an improvised field dressing, nothing at all. It's a good job they weren't at the Crimea. Load of pansies, that's what I say, (Harrumph), load of pansies," opined Joiner in between slurps of tea. "Look at the state of this bloody tail bandage Garrett. Arnie's going to have a fit when he sees this. They're a couple of quid each you know," he complained, provoking further laughter from Jim and myself.

"I'm very bloody sorry about the tail bandage, but look on the bright side - I'm still alive despite everyone's best efforts to kill me." moaned a sulky Paul Garrett.

"Yes you are Garrett, yes you bloody well are, and you are also aspiring to be a mounted man, so you can get your skinny arse down the stairs, all of you, and get your legs over those horses. They can still have half an hour's leg stretch before your lunch time." On that note, he picked up his saddle and strode down the stairs. We quickly followed him.

I retold the day's story to Becks during our evening meal that night. I included all of the groans, gurgles, and the snotty tones of the frosty hospital nurse in my exaggerated narration. As usual she shook her head in disbelief, laughing heartily at the latest of the comical sagas that seemed to occur all too often in my daily work life. After a succession of questions to clarify the finer details of the story, she eventually skilfully changed the subject.

"Are we going to watch the telly again tonight, or do you want me to test you out on the settee?" she casually asked as we settled down for another evening in.

"Ooh err missus, there's no contest there," I laughed. "There's nothing on the telly tonight anyway."

"What?"

"How will you score me on the settee; will you use cards like they do in the ice skating?" I asked whilst raising my eyebrow.

"What are you talking about Stef?"

"My test on the settee of course; will it take long, and how will you grade me? It won't hurt will it?"

It took a while, but the penny finally dropped with a clang, and I was rewarded with a sharp play punch to the arm.

"Wildy, you have a one-track mind, and you are a smutty old git," she scolded playfully.

"I plead guilty to the charge of smutty Ma'am, but not guilty to the slur of old git."

"Fair comment and plea accepted, but you've got this theory test soon, and I need to test you out 'young man'."

She was right of course, as she invariably was, so we settled down on the settee with my head on her lap whilst she read through my lesson notes. I closed my eyes and prepared myself for a rigorous, but sadly only theoretical, testing.

"What is seedy toe?"

"Seedy toe is a separation of the hoof wall from the underlying sensitive laminae."

"How do you recognise it?"

"Usually found when investigating a crumbling hoof wall."

"How do you treat it?"

"It's a job for the vet and the farrier, and involves paring back all of the damaged area to remove the decay, followed up by antibiotics, and regular cleansing."

"Hmmm. What about thrush?"

"Thrush is a foul stinking discharge from the cleft of the frog," I recited from memory, recalling Derek Joiner's exact words.

"A frog? Where do frogs come into it?"

"It's a soft cushiony bit on the sole of the hoof, and has nothing to do with toady frogs," I explained.

"Oh okay. How do you treat it?"

"Prevention is better than cure, so stable floors should always be kept clean and dry. You need to regularly pick out the feet, and keep them clean and dry too. Thrush is treated by scrubbing the foot clean, and daily scrubbing with a good antiseptic disinfectant or a copper solution. You may need the farrier to cut away any necrotic tissue."

"Hmmm. I'm impressed. What do you know about splints?"

"A splint is a bony swelling at the side of the cannon bone. It can cause extreme lameness, and is usually found in younger horses when excessively worked on harder ground."

"Like police horses?"

"Yes. Like police horses," I agreed.

"What's the treatment?"

"Rest or lighter work, plenty of cold hose, support with leg bandages, and maybe a course of anti-inflammatory pain killers from the vet. Once the splint is fully formed and calcified it is permanent, but there should be no further lameness."

She flicked through my notes, asking random questions on a full range of subjects, which thankfully, and somewhat to my surprise, I rattled through almost without error.

"How are you on these paces of the horse thingys?"

"Okay I think, ask me one."

"What are the paces of the horse at the canter?" she replied.

"Off fore or near fore leading?"

"What? Oh, hang on a bit," she said, reading a little more. "Off fore leading?"

"Canter is a pace of three-time. With the off fore leading it goes; near hind, off hind and near fore diagonal, off fore."

"What does all that mean Stef?"

"It's classified, and I'll have to kill you if I explain it," I laughed.

"You really know this stuff, don't you?" she said, putting the notes down on the floor.

"Why do you sound so surprised?" I answered. We both got up from the sofa, ready to make the trek upstairs to bed.

"Because you keep telling me you're too stupid to study for your promotion exam. I know you're not stupid, and this proves it. You, mate, are just plain lazy!"

It was difficult to argue or defend myself, because since we had been married, I had invested in too many books and several home study packages, in an effort to prepare myself to sit my promotion qualification exams. Sadly they had all had the same effect, and I had lost count of the times she had walked into the spare room with a cup of tea, only to find me snoring with my head resting on an open book.

"I just find this really interesting; it's all hands-on stuff and it makes perfect sense to me. Law is so bloody dull and boring. I read a page, and can't remember a single thing that I've just read. It just doesn't float my boat." I yawned.

She looked at me sternly in an all too familiar manner. I knew that look; it was a mixture of love, pity, and exasperation. It made me feel naughty, like a much loved cute puppy, just caught in the act of pooping on the kitchen floor or chewing the toe out of a favourite slipper.

"Well there's the answer. You should have been a vet and not a copper. We would certainly be a lot better off if you were," she scolded. "We may even have had some carpet on the stairs and a bit of money in the bank."

"You're right, but unfortunately I slept through school too. That's why I've only got one O level; and that's for woodwork. I don't think that would have got me into vet school." I engaged my most pathetic, quivery bottom lip look.

She was looking at me, with her head to one side, in that despairing, chastising manner that women are so good at. I knew I was walking on thin ice, but thankfully my continuing survival was confirmed when she gave in and burst out laughing.

"Remind me why I'm here with you, Stefan Wild? Remind me why I'm not living the life back in Toronto?" She accompanied her words with a flurry of sharp pokes and tickles to the ribs.

"Because I'm annoyingly irresistible, and super-super sexy too?" I tentatively suggested, rapidly retreating.

A playful beating with my rolled up lesson notes was a small price to pay to escape from the thorny subject of my refusal to apply myself to my studies. I tentatively pointed out that if I did change my mind, and stay on the mounted-branch, promotion opportunities would be so rare that any further studying for the exam would be a complete waste of time.

We didn't know it then, but in thirty years of service I never would pass my promotion qualifications. I just never found the time to sit down at home and dedicate myself to study; I could always find something more pressing or interesting to look at through the window. It wasn't something that I consciously thought about, or deliberately practised, but I always did have the ability to leave work at work whilst I was at home. It was often a great advantage, and I know of many friends and former colleagues who could never maintain that distinction, living for the job, and subsequently rising through the ranks whilst enjoying all of the challenges and financial benefits of a heady career - but not too many of them are still married, joking and play fighting with the same woman after forty-five years.

CHAPTER 12

THE QUIET WELSHMAN
AND THE ANGRY COCKNEY

It came as a shock when I looked out of the bedroom window at 6.30am on Monday morning and saw snow on the ground. It had come down in the night without warning, looked about three to four inches deep, and consequently all the cars in the street had a generous covering. I would have to 'get my skates on', because it was a long way to Tally Ho, and I had to pick up Jim first.

Fortunately, we always set out in plenty of time and were generally at Tally Ho with time to spare, but today was going to be a test. I was the first vehicle out of our side street that morning, and for the first five minutes the tyres of the Mini were cutting through undisturbed snow, but before I reached Jim's house I was in amongst the spray and slush with the morning traffic on the main road. I was, however, only five minutes later than normal when he got into the passenger seat after kicking most of the snow off his boots.

"Well done Stef. When I looked out of the window I thought you'd be well late."

"It's a bit of a bugger isn't it?" I replied. "I've dashed around and cut some corners this morning to gain a little time, and Becks has had to give up her cup of tea in bed."

"She won't like that mate."

"She won't know yet because I didn't wake her up," I laughed.

"Oh-hoh! There may be trouble ahead…" he broke out into song as I drove away.

Luckily the journey was much better than it could have been. It was over twenty miles to Tally Ho, but once on the motorway the traffic moved steadily along, albeit much more slowly than normal. Our conversation, however, was regularly interrupted as we took turns to wipe the condensation from the windscreen in an effort to maintain the view ahead. My Mini was typical of its time, and was annoyingly under equipped, with an inadequate, asthmatic ventilation system, and sloth-like windscreen wipers.

This weather was another consideration that would have to be taken into account before any final decision could be made regarding my future attachment to the mounted branch. A forty-mile daily commute, instead of a short walk to work, was a nuisance - but could prove to be a real pain in any extended period of this type of weather.

We arrived safely at Tally Ho with ten minutes to spare, and were quietly sitting around the bunk table, 'chewing the fat' and drinking tea with Paul and Steve, when I heard the steady rumble of a motorbike engine and crunching snow from outside.

A few moments later we all looked around as the door from the corridor opened and a dripping wet figure stepped into the room. Dressed in all black waterproofs, and faceless thanks to a motorcycle helmet with a badly steamed up visor, the figure walked across the room, past the table and into the wash room, leaving a substantial trail of water in its wake. There was no look to the left or right, and no acknowledgment of anyone else in the room.

We sat listening to the rustling of someone removing clothing coming from the washroom, but it was barely discernible above the sound of a steady and rhythmic cough.

"Someone doesn't sound very well at all," I whispered. "Do you think he's okay?"

"It's the sergeant," replied Steve very quietly. "He always does it. That's why the West Brom lot call him 'The Barker'."

"I don't think I'd have come on my motorbike on a day like this," remarked Jim.

"He comes miles; from somewhere in Staffordshire," replied Steve.

"He must be nuts. It's bloody horrible out there and well dodgy," I couldn't imagine how cold it must have been on a motorbike on such an awful day.

"He's not nuts," answered Steve. "Just as hard as nails."

We leaned in to whisper conspiratorially, and then suspiciously suddenly back again when the figure reappeared at the washroom door. The sopping waterproofs had been removed, and he was now wearing a cloth cap which was tightly pulled down onto his head. I suppressed a laugh as I inwardly debated whether he had taken the cap from his pocket, or if he had actually been wearing it all of the time beneath his helmet.

Without looking at anyone in particular, our new sergeant quietly uttered his first words to the room.

"Tea?" cough, cough, cough.

"There's one in the pot sarge," replied Steve.

He walked over to the tea table, quietly poured himself a cup, and headed back towards the sergeant's office. He looked absolutely frozen as he walked past us, tea in hand, again without looking.

"Five minutes," he almost inaudibly coughed. As he reached the office he took a swig of his tea and spluttered, "This tea's bloody cold," before shutting the door heavily behind himself.

"Well, he seemed pleased to see us," observed Paul.

"He's not a morning person," laughed Steve. "He's actually as good as gold, but don't expect him to be like Sergeant Joiner. It takes ages to get to know him."

Dai Owen looked like he had been sculpted with a hammer and a chisel from the grey slate found in such abundance in the place of his origin, North Wales. He wasn't a tall man, in fact he was quite short for a police officer of the period. He looked as old as the hills, but was only in his forties, and had heavy dark features, dark eyes and eyebrows, and a nose so misshapen that he could easily have been mistaken for a retired prize fighter. He was lean, but with broad shoulders, big hands, and a steely expression that made him look hard. In Dai's case looks didn't deceive, because he was hard; not nasty, quick tempered or violent, but quiet, shy, slow to anger, and just hard. I didn't know this at the time, but I would grow to respect him enormously and we would eventually become good friends - but it would take time and I was going to make a few mistakes along the way.

There was no announcement or verbal order like we were used to from Derek Joiner, and the only way that we knew the sergeant was heading down to the horses was the bang of his office door and the sound of coughing growing quieter as it made its way down the stairs. We had not been allocated our horses for the day, so just randomly grabbed grooming bags from the hooks. Being a little slow off the mark, I found myself once more paired up with everyone's favourite little jewel, Bijou.

Bijou's new next door neighbour was Dai Owen's horse 'Dunkirk', and I paused for a few moments and watched while the sergeant removed his rug to begin grooming. Even to my untrained eye Dunkirk was conspicuously different to any of the other police horses at Tally Ho. I was no expert, but this horse was obviously of a much finer build; a more athletic animal than anything else I had seen so far. He looked more like a race horse than a police horse. Dunkirk wasn't the sweetest natured of horses, and I watched with interest as he fidgeted, ears back and foot scraping, as the sergeant went calmly about his business. There was no obvious threat of impending bites or kicks from Dunkirk, but he was undisputedly miserable, spoiled, stroppy, and Dai Owen adored him. He just quietly got on with it, tutting under his breath, whispering to the horse between coughs, and generally ignoring the animal's bad manners.

At this time I knew very little about any of the characters of the department, nothing about the recent history, and even less about the politics. However, if I had known, I would probably have more fully understood Dai Owen's obvious lack of enthusiasm for being at Tally Ho.

Before the amalgamation of the midland forces in 1974, Birmingham City Police already had a sizable mounted department of over twenty horses. It was an old, well established department run on very traditional lines by a Chief Inspector, Inspector, and a full complement of sergeants. In contrast, prior to 1974, Sergeant Dai Owen had been in sole charge of the much smaller and definitely less traditional West Midlands Constabulary Mounted Department. In stables at the back of West Bromwich police station were four horses and a handful of officers that made up the small constabulary mounted department. Dai Owen had been in charge of buying the horses, training the horses, choosing and training the men, and the day to day running of the department. Dunkirk was very much Dai's horse. He had chosen him, bought him as a youngster, backed him, trained him, almost solely rode him, and without doubt regarded him as his own horse.

However, since the 1974 amalgamation he had found himself one of four sergeants - very much not in sole charge, and under the command of senior officers that he disliked and held in contempt. This much larger department was very different to his former little empire at West Bromwich, and although he disliked it there was nothing he could do about it, because he lived in constant fear of his beloved Dunkirk being taken away and reallocated to another officer. He had no alternative but to quietly comply, lump it, and get on with the job.

I moved on to the next stable and removed Bijou's rug. I hung it over the door ready to commence grooming, and looked him up and down whilst contemplating how different he was to his new next door neighbour. He really was a dumpy, stocky little brute, and actually looked quite comical with his teeth bared and his ears flattened to the back of his head. Grooming Bijou didn't induce the level of terror that it did during the first few days of the course, but remembering the throat biting incident I was fully aware I still needed to be careful. He still threatened to bite when being body brushed, and to kick when grooming out the tail or the hind legs, but I had learned most of his actions were bravado. If possible, he was better ignored, because reaction always escalated the drama. Sometimes, however, he still pushed it a little too far.

"Cut it out!" I growled when he began to scrape his near fore hoof on the floor.

"Enough!" I added, digging him in the ribs with the body brush when he began to lean against me.

Bijou, never quick to relent, clattered his hooves noisily in protest.

"Shaddap you prat! Behave yourself," I said in my firmest voice.

I was happily contemplating how much my confidence had increased since that first day when I had fled from the stable, when I became aware of someone watching over the door.

"What are you doing to that horse?" asked a quiet voice from beneath the tight cap.

"Just showing him who's in charge sarge, he's pratting about again."

"I see someone pratting about and it's not the horse. And I see someone in charge but it's not you," the sergeant replied, his voice barely audible. He bent down under the bar and joined us in the stable. "Why do you blokes have to fight these horses? What's the matter with you all?"

I was just about to reply when he turned his back on me and began a whispered conversation with Bijou.

"Poor Bij. Poor Bij. What are these fools doing to you, little man?"

Without further ado, Bijou lowered his head and sighed ecstatically whilst Dai Owen stroked him and whispered mysterious sweet nothings into his ears.

"Shush, shush lad. You're safe now. There, there Bij, take no notice, it's okay now."

I couldn't believe my eyes. The normally volatile animal was completely motionless except for a contented quiver in his bottom lip. All was peace. All was calm. He was almost in a trance.

"Now treat him with respect. Be kind. He's your friend." He coughed as he bent under the bar and returned muttering quietly to his own stable.

Even before he had completely disappeared Bijou's head was up, his ears were flat back and his eyes were flashing angrily, as he immediately and aggressively resumed normal service. I was under no illusion that he would return to his trance if I whispered sweetly into his ear, and I rather feared he would remove my face if I tried, so I pressed on with our morning sparring session - still determined, but a little more quietly.

Our riding school sessions were now very different. Dai Owen conducted his school from the centre, but on horseback. Gone was the clarity of short sharp orders; they had been replaced with barely audible mumblings which had us all leaning towards the centre of the school in order to hear them. Gone were the shouts and the crack of the whip, because Dai never carried one; now errors in our riding position were addressed in a more personal manner with the sergeant riding alongside, at whatever pace, quietly mumbling pearls of wisdom that were easily lost in the voluminous space of the riding school. Sometimes he would ride alongside for several laps, during which time the spoiled and stroppy Dunkirk would offputtingly snap and threaten my horse while I tried to absorb the information. I never doubted a word he said, or that he held a wealth of knowledge, but I often wished he would speak more clearly and leave his brat of a horse in the stable.

We were introduced to a lot more jumping. At first we concentrated on trotting poles, before progressing on to cavaletti, which were used singularly or stacked together to make higher jumps. We moved on to small courses of multiple jumps, some built with coloured poles, some rustic, and some with planks. We learned how to count a stride when approaching a jump, or between jumps, and how to lean forward in the saddle on take-off and when landing to assist the horse and save its mouth.

We ran relay races around small courses, sometimes with hands on head, sometimes sitting backwards in the saddle, and sometimes leading our horses in hand around obstacles and over low jumps.

The whole emphasis slowly moved away from repetitious drill and barked orders, and quietly toward more active riding. There was a lot to learn and the three of us were thirsty for knowledge, but had to concentrate to hear the quiet, moody mumblings of Dai Owen as he rode his race horse around the school. It would have been easy to label the new sergeant as a miserable man, but it became apparent that was a long way from the truth on the Friday at the end of his first week.

It was blanket day, and we had spent half an hour riding bareback while performing the usual turns and circles at the trot and canter to warm up the horses, when we were called to the halt and instructed to ride into the centre of the school. We formed a small circle and sat with relaxed reins while we waited for further instructions. Without saying a word, and very much to our amazement, Dai Owen turned his cap around so that his peak faced backwards and began to grin mischievously from ear to ear. Without further warning, and whilst we were still sitting open-mouthed, he darted forward, grabbed hold of Big Jim's leg and flung him out of the saddle, before riding away to the other end of the school. Paul and I sat dumbly looking down at Jim, who was dusting himself down and getting to his feet.

"Come on! Come on! Get away from him. He's it. He's it!" yelled the sergeant.

It took a while, but the penny dropped - we were now playing a game of equine tag! Paul and I rode away from Jim before he could climb back onto his horse. In no time at all we were all cantering in different directions in an attempt to evade Big Jim, who was determined, red faced, and looking for blood. I was his first victim, and unable to escape the trap as Jim cornered me, dragging me from the back of my horse. I hit the ground with a thud but managed to hold onto the reins, so remounted immediately and set off to seek my victim.

I chose Paul because he was the smallest. I cantered alongside him and leaned down to try and grab hold of his leg. He increased his pace, but I legged on and managed to keep up. Any sense of fear had disappeared and been replaced with a blind determination to unseat my friend.

"Don't run away, you bloody chicken! Fight back. Fight back!" goaded the sergeant.

The game had changed. My previously vulnerable prey had now become an opponent, and we cantered along wrestling and grappling, each determined to unseat the other. Eventually we hit the ground together, and sat stunned as our horses trotted freely, rider-less, around the school. Big Jim roared with laughter, and didn't notice the sergeant ride alongside him from behind. Inevitably, before he knew what was happening, Jim crashed heavily to the ground, and his horse joined the other two.

"Come on! Come on! Don't bloody sit there all day, get back on. Any horse will do."

We all remounted many times that morning, onto the nearest passing horse, without difficulty or any thought given to the lack of saddle or stirrups. Fear was forgotten because personal pride was at stake, and as we all repeatedly hit the ground we became increasingly caked in a mixture of sweat, sand and shavings. Looking back now, over forty years later, it seems ridiculous that we were being paid for having so much fun. At the time we never gave any thought to the obvious danger of injury; we wore no hard hats or any other form of protective equipment, and I dread to think how many modern health and safety rules would be broken by the use of these methods today.

The morning's activities eventually drew to a natural close as the three of us united and ganged up on the sergeant. He fought like a cornered tiger, and any inflated allusions as to our actual abilities were soon popped, because following a tremendous struggle involving much grunting, groaning and cursing, the sergeant, although cap less, jacketless and completely dishevelled, was still sitting astride Dunkirk while we were all, once more, rolling in the shavings. Any initial worries that we may have overstepped the mark were soon dispelled, however. His usual fixed frown disappeared to reveal a wide, almost ear to ear grin.

"Pussies. You're all hopeless. My granny played cricket better than you pussies fight," he laughed. "Now go put these horses away. Make sure you dry them properly and check their legs for knocks. Praise them too, they've done well." He coughed and rode towards the door.

Dai Owen was a true paradox. He was moody, introverted, often unfriendly, and a man of few words, but he was also someone that people, often unsuccessfully, wanted to be friendly with. He definitely preferred animals to people, and the horses seemed to sense it. Their welfare was always his first and last priority, and he always seemed happiest when he was in their company or in the saddle. He wasn't a man that mixed well in crowds, but would often sit, whilst rolling a cigarette, and happily converse one to one. He was a mine of information, but never offered unsolicited advice or opinion, and mumbled so quietly that listening to him was sometimes a real effort. He wasn't liked by everyone, but was widely respected as a natural horseman, and also admired as a fearless rider of untrained and difficult animals that much younger men went out of their way to avoid.

As a trainer of men, he couldn't have been more different to Derek Joiner. I got on with both of them, but I grew to like and admire Dai Owen and kept in touch with him for many years after his retirement. I drove past his house one day as he was lifting a bale of hay into his pick-up truck, so pulled up for a chat. He seemed to have shrunk, and I noticed he was showing pain whilst we were talking, so I asked him if he was fit and healthy.

"I'm fine. I'll live. It's just a cracked rib. I'm backing a two-year-old for a mate. He's a stroppy little bugger and he chucked me off last week," he said, grinning from under his cap.

"Backing a youngster? How old are you Dai?" I replied, shaking my head.

"I'm only seventy-four, I ain't dead yet," he mumbled.

"Seventy-four! Haven't you considered packing it in Dai?"

"What would I want to do that for? Bloody daft idea." He clutched his ribs and burst into a fit of coughing.

One afternoon, during the seventh week of our course, Chief Inspector Stuart Hancock arrived at Tally Ho with a folder containing the questions for our theory test. The test was going to take one hour, and Hancock was going to invigilate the test himself. We hadn't seen very much of him during our course, but he had visited twice before to take our afternoon theory sessions.

He was a humourless man, not well liked, and was without doubt a bit of a snob. He certainly considered himself of a different class to everyone else in the department, and saw our perceived lack of equine etiquette as a personal embarrassment. The truth was that the men of the mounted department were generally dedicated, competent riders and good horsemen, but were also undeniably city dwellers, so not always well versed in the fashionable horsey folk terminology found in the countryside. He lived in fear that, whilst attending some prestigious country show, one of his department's visiting display teams would say something daft.

Consequently, his input during our afternoon theory sessions tended to lean more towards a form of equine elocution than it did to any useful, practical information. He was, without doubt mind-numbingly boring.

One afternoon, following a particularly arduous morning session in the riding school, he sat at the head of the bunk table and began a lecture on the bloodline history of the British Thoroughbred. It was a nightmare. He waffled on in his tedious, monotone cockney accent, and with the heat of the radiator and a belly full of canteen dinner, it was a mammoth task just to keep my eyes open. I sleepily jotted down a few notes, and I could see that the other two were also desperately fighting slumber. It is fair to say that at the conclusion of his lecture, none of us were any wiser than we had been at the start.

The following week he came again, and we sat sulkily around the table mentally preparing ourselves for yet another never ending hour of purgatory; however, he suddenly woke us up with a sneaky opening low baller.

"Let us see what you have remembered from last week. Can anyone tell me the names of the three Arab horses, imported into Britain in the early eighteenth century that all modern thoroughbreds are descended from?"

I was clueless, sat right next to him, and looked down helplessly at the useless doodles and scribbles in my notebook. The silence was deafening. I looked anywhere but in Hancock's direction and in a vain effort to remain anonymous, fixed my eyes on Dai Owen, who was sitting in the corner of the room casually licking the side of a roll up. I couldn't have answered if my life had depended on it.

"Wild?" he asked, forcing me to look at him.

After several seconds of embarrassing silence I realised that honesty was my only escape.

"I'm sorry sir. I can't remember."

"I'm obviously wasting my breath on you Wild. Garrett?" he asked, moving his eyes across to Paul.

After a never ending painful silence Paul responded with a show stopping howler. "Was one of them Queen Anne, sir?"

"Queen Anne! Queen bleedin' Anne?! What the hell has Queen Anne got to do with it Garrett?" Hancock erupted, whilst blue in the face.

"I'm not sure, but I've written Queen Anne in my rough notes," whimpered Paul.

"In the *reign* of Queen Anne, Garrett. It happened in the reign of Queen Anne. A queen is by definition a woman, so how can Queen bleedin' Anne be a pedigree stallion?"

"I don't know. I don't really understand this sort of thing sir," mitigated Paul, sending Hancock into a new level of fury.

"You don't understand it, Garrett? You don't *understand* it? I feel very sorry for your poor wife Garrett! What the hell is the matter with you young blokes?"

The chief inspector was now in a full, incandescent rage. He stood, banging the table with his fist, with his red face now rapidly moving through the spectrum towards puce. I looked at Big Jim, who was obviously the next target and our only real hope of salvation. His face was unreadable and I couldn't tell if he had any idea or not.

"Tell them Hardwick. For God's sake let one of you know the answer," pleaded Hancock. He slowly came off the boil and gently lowered himself into his chair.

All eyes were on Big Jim, who sat silently and expressionless, scratching the side of his nose, obviously wracking his brains. You could almost hear the cogs whirring, as the clock ticked ominously.

"Well, Hardwick? Please tell us. We're all waiting," demanded Hancock, breaking the silence.

There was another uncomfortable lengthy silence before Jim finally gave his answer. "I'm just trying to remember the last one, sir. Bear with me - it's on the tip of my tongue."

"Hooray! Hoo-bloody-ray! At least someone was listening! At least one of you was awake! Enlighten your dozy stupid colleagues, Hardwick. Please tell us, what are the names of the first two?" Hancock sighed with an obvious sense of relief.

"Oh, I don't know the first two. I was just trying to remember the last one because it was the easiest," replied Jim, with a nonchalance that didn't fit the occasion.

Hancock sprang back to his feet, rampaging around the room and hurling a stream of abuse in our direction. The expletives flew in rapid fire, and we were all left in absolutely no doubt as to what he thought of us. Dai Owen was now vigorously tapping his newly rolled cigarette on the side of his baccy box. His head was down and all that was visible was the top of his cap, but from the gentle shaking of the brown county check you could tell that he was quietly in stitches of laughter.

"Have you any idea how busy I am? Have you? Any of you? Why do I waste my time trying to educate you thick Black Country oikes?" continued the chief inspector.

"I'm from Coventry," corrected Paul unhelpfully.

"What?" demanded Hancock, temporarily losing his stride.

"You said 'Black Country oikes'; but I'm from Coventry," insisted Paul.

"I don't bloody care if you are from Coventry, or even Calcutta or bloody *Cairo*; you're still as thick as the other two. Now shut up. How bloody dare you, how bloody *dare* you correct me when I'm bollocking the class? Who do you think you are, you little Coventry shit?"

Hancock was obviously not the healthiest of men, and he began to wheeze as his anger levels rose. He stormed out, slamming the door angrily behind him, and confirming to all in the room that whatever he may have known about thoroughbred bloodlines, he certainly wasn't as posh as he pretended to be.

The stormy atmosphere calmed when we heard Hancock's car finally leave the yard. Dai Owen finally lit his roll up and sat in the chair the chief inspector had so dramatically left a just few moments earlier. He took a couple of drags, and we all leaned forward intently, so as not to miss the words that he was obviously about to mumble.

"Thoroughbreds; what does he know about thoroughbreds? He wouldn't know a bloody thoroughbred if one sat next to him on the bus. Now let's talk about colic."

The Byerley Turk, the Darley Arabian, and the Godolphin Barb are the names of the three pedigree horses to which the bloodlines of all English Thoroughbreds can be traced. They were all indeed imported into Britain from the Middle East in the early 1700s, during the reign of Queen Anne. These three names are permanently etched onto my brain, somewhere deep in the rarely used archives, ready to be retrieved at a moment's notice and enabling me to impress any horsey toff I may happen to meet. I think the chance of that scenario is highly unlikely; however, I do live for the day that the question is asked in a quiz, and I am the only person in the room that smugly knows the answer. Sadly, I think that is an unlikely scenario too.

Predictably, after all of the drama, my newly acquired knowledge wasn't required for the theory test. The questions were limited to the syllabus that we had covered daily since the start of our course. I knew the stuff, as did the other two, so we all passed with flying colours. Not too bad for two Black Country Oikes and a little Coventry Shit.

The finish line was almost in sight. The final hurdle was the riding test, and it was only two weeks away.

CHAPTER 13

SPURS AND STAIRS

It was the Thursday of our ninth week, the final day of our course, and the day of our riding test. The nine weeks had flown by in the blink of an eye, and despite all the knocks, tumbles, pains, and sores, the three of us were all still present, correct, and ready to tackle the final hurdle. There was nothing in the riding test that we hadn't done many times before, and providing something awful or unexpected didn't happen, we had all been offered a further twelve weeks' attachment to the department.

A three month attachment meant working as a mounted officer, in uniform, out on the streets. It would involve some further training in the school at Tally Ho, but would mainly involve working alongside other mounted officers from across the variety of stables around the force area. It was not my original plan, and no one was more surprised than me when I had enthusiastically accepted the offer to stay for three more months. I had enjoyed my riding course far more than I'd imagined I would, and after a shaky start, and sometimes painful progress I was now keen to improve and develop my newly learned skills. I still, however, had no ambition to transfer permanently. As much as I enjoyed the riding, and even though the sociable working hours suited my family life, I really couldn't envisage spending the remainder of my police career in such a regimented, spit and polished, routine-orientated environment. A three month attachment would take me very nicely into summer, but after that I absolutely intended to return to the diversity of divisional duties.

We were in the riding school a few minutes earlier than normal, walking around warming our horses, when we were joined by three uniformed riders. The six of us lined up side by side in the centre of the school shortly before ten o'clock. Right on time, the doors opened and Big Ben Scott walked in. It was the first time I had seen Ben Scott in full uniform. Gone was the trilby hat and the grey flannel trousers tucked into socks; he was now dressed in a uniformed overcoat, cap, boots, spurs, and breeches, but - thankfully - he was not carrying a whip.

He immediately barked his first order.

"WHOLE RIDE. RIDE, SHUN!"

We all, as one, took the reins into our left hands, before slapping our left hands with our right hands, and smartly 'throwing' our right arms vertically down to our sides. It sounded good, it sounded crisp, and I thought that I detected a slight smile momentarily cross the inspector's face. I couldn't help but think of that infamous day when Ben Scott had previously ordered us to attention, and of the obvious progress we had made since. This time I didn't have fluffy pink leg warmers to worry about, and as he wasn't carrying the lunging whip, I surmised Jim Hardwick was feeling a little happier too.

"WHOLE RIDE! RIDE, RIGHT DRESS!"

We smartly turned our heads to the right, looking intently at the right hand man, and quickly manoeuvred our horses so we formed a perfect line, with a distance of six inches between the knees of the riders.

"WHOLE RIDE! EYES, FRONT!"

As one, we looked sharply to the front.

"Whole ride, sit at ease!" he said more quietly, nodding in apparent approval.

We rested our hands, right on top of left, on the saddle pommels.

"Good morning everyone. For you three recruits it is your final day and your final test. I know that you have all been offered further attachments, but those offers can be withdrawn if you do not perform adequately and are not seen to be competent today. I need to see, and to satisfy myself, that you not only have the required skills, but that you also have sufficient balls to become mounted men. So do your best. Yes, do your best," he nodded to no one in particular. "WHOLE RIDE, RIDE, SHUN!"

We smartly sat to attention again before numbering off from the right, and on the order followed the leading file around the perimeter of the riding school. I was riding Bijou, which at the beginning of the course would have been a definite handicap, but we now routinely changed horses regularly during sessions, which meant (hopefully only metaphorically) we all would receive a fair crack of the whip.

The session followed a familiar pattern, with us working as a whole ride whilst performing circles and turns, with stirrups and without. Initially, and as expected, I had trouble keeping up and had to pedal the sullen Bijou every inch of the way, but this wasn't such an issue as it had been in our early days. We were all fitter and had much more strength in our legs after nine weeks of intensive riding.

We progressed into a double ride, riding in half sections and then sections, before finally riding six abreast down the centre of the school, and halting in a straight line in front of Big Ben.

"Good. Good. Sit at ease everyone," smiled the obviously satisfied inspector.

We now had to, in turn, ride individually around the school, following orders from the centre. The object of this exercise was to show that we could control and direct our horses independently, without a leading file to follow. Horses are instinctively herd animals and will invariably follow the others if left to their own devices, so it is often quite easy to hide and follow the crowd whilst in a collective riding school.

The riding school was marked around the perimeter with reference markers; these assisted when schooling horses or performing riding tests. There was a marker at both ends of the school, and further markers along each side at the halfway points and in between at the quarters. The marker at the entrance to a riding school is always A, and if turning to the left and riding with your right side to the inside of the school, the letters around the school are: A,K,E,H,C,M,B,F. These marks are traditionally learned and remembered by using the mnemonic; ALL - KING - EDWARD'S - HORSES - CAN - MAKE - BIG - FENCES.

Paul Garrett went first, and we watched intently as he set the standard by performing well on the ever-steady Brigadier. I was to go second, and by the time it came to my turn, we *had* already changed, so I would be fortunate to be riding the ever-willing Big Garth, and would be able to concentrate on my riding without having to kick and pedal my way around the test.

In the meantime, whilst quietly watching Paul go through his paces, I reflected on our progress. I was certainly under no illusion that any of us were yet equine experts or brilliant horsemen, but watching my new friend and colleague riding around on the big white (sorry, grey) horse brought home to me how much we had improved since that terrible day when Big Ben had 'beasted' us during our second week. We were unrecognisable, and to confirm my theory, so was the inspector. He now seemed quietly satisfied as he called out his instructions from the centre. I was abruptly brought to attention when the voice changed in our direction.

"Right Wild; trot down the centre at A and at the end of the school turn onto the left rein at C."

I collected the reins, applied both legs, and we were away.

"Turn left at E and then onto the right rein at B," he continued.

I followed the directions, performing turns, circles and figures of eight to the left and to the right. All were repeated on both reins at the walk, trot, and canter, and after several minutes Garth was, as ever, obliging whilst we trotted up the middle of the school to halt at X in the centre.

"Rein back four paces, then forward four paces, and then halt again. In your own time – begin," instructed Big Ben.

I sat deep into the saddle and squeezed with both legs, until I felt Garth ready himself to move, then I resisted with both hands to prevent him from stepping forward, and as I applied further resistance with the reins he began to step steadily backwards in a straight line. One, two, three, and four, I counted the steps in my head before relaxing the reins causing him to stop. I didn't look down or back but he felt square, so I squeezed again with both legs and counted the four forward paces in my head before feeling the reins to halt again at X in the centre.

A few minutes later, having completed a nice full pass to the left and then an acceptable half pass to the right, I found myself sitting next to Paul Garrett on Brigadier at the far end of the school. We whispered a few words of mutual encouragement, and both agreed that we were glad it was Jim Hardwick who now had to perform his independent ride on Bijou and not us.

We watched and listened, our fingers crossed, as Big Jim followed the inspector's directions and frantically pedalled Bijou around the riding school. Bijou, as reluctant as ever, dawdled around the school with his nose poking forward and his ears flattened back onto his neck in a continuing gesture of surly defiance. He suddenly reminded me of 'Mutley,' a truculent cartoon dog that regularly appeared on children's TV, and I had to suppress a laugh as I imagined Bijou adopting the famous 'Mutley' snigger on his way around the riding school. Big Jim, to his credit, though red faced, legs flapping, and puffing like a steam train, never gave him an inch and kept his miserable steed moving throughout the whole test. With his ordeal eventually over, you could hear him deflating with relief as he pulled up alongside us at the end of his test.

"Well done you three recruits. Stand easy everyone. It's time for tea whilst the entertainments are prepared," nodded Big Ben, as he looked us up and down. I saw the nod and thought for a moment that I noticed a smile of approval, but it may only have been wishful thinking.

We watched patiently, drinking our tea, whilst a small basic jumping course was built. There was a sequence of trotting poles along the one side of the school, a row of three cavaletti jumps along the opposite side, and a three-foot-high brush jump in the middle.

"I'm going to watch from the gallery, so will now hand over to Sergeant Owen for the fun and games. Thank you Dai, carry on please," said the inspector as he left the riding school to make his way upstairs to the viewing gallery.

The course was basic and very simple, but when I looked back to the day we started only a few weeks earlier, it seemed miraculous that we would be able to do this kind of active riding without falling into the shavings and sand.

Paul started first, and Jim and I watched with interest as he broke into a trot and successfully negotiated the trotting poles, before breaking into the canter to jump the three perfectly-spaced cavaletti at the other side of the school. As he reached the end of the school, he turned down the middle and effortlessly popped Brigadier over the brush jump. Turning right at the end of the school, and now trotting, he approached the poles from the opposite direction but this time with his hands firmly clasped on top of his head. Successfully clearing the poles, he continued around the school with his hands on his head to jump the three cavaletti, before taking up the reins and turning down the centre to finish the course over the brush jump. He had a big grin on his face as he drew alongside of us.

It was my turn, and all I had to do was follow exactly the same route Paul had just completed. It was as simple as that, because if I could remember the way, Garth would just go through the motions without the need for extra leg or any other encouragement. He was by far the biggest and heaviest horse in the school, and had huge feet, but was surprisingly an excellent jumper. We had all jumped far bigger jumps during the previous few weeks, and I felt a bit of a fraud as I effortlessly sat aboard on auto-pilot, while Big Garth thundered successfully around the course before returning us safely to the other two.

I sat quietly alongside Paul as Big Jim struggled and eventually managed to break Bijou away from us to begin his final round. You could see the effort and activity in Jim's legs, and the redness in his face, as he negotiated the poles and then the cavaletti, before turning down the centre for his first pop at the brush jump. So far so good - he was nearly there. The second run over the poles and cavaletti with hands on head was completed without incident, and all looked good as he cantered down the centre towards us for the final hurdle over the brush jump. It certainly looked to be a formality as he approached the jump, and we all relaxed accordingly; until suddenly, without warning, at the take-off point, Bijou broke down from the canter to the walk. With nonchalant arrogance he strolled around the jump and casually began to make his way towards us and the exit door.

"HARDMAN! Get a grip man!" came a verbal explosion from the gallery. "Ride that bloody horse. Who's in charge down there, you or that damned horse?"

Everyone watched as Jim turned him around, and with unexpected speed cantered Bijou back around the school to make a second approach at the brush jump. This time, the normally placid Jim had a face like thunder, and let out a tirade of verbal abuse and encouragement before kicking his legs into Bijou's side with some force at the take-off point. The result was impressive and the horse responded by rattling the school with an explosive fart before taking off and clearing the jump by about three feet. When he finally slowed and came to a halt beside us his ears were planted flat and his eye flashed angrily at anyone who wanted to look.

"Well done man! Well done, that's the spirit! That's balls; balls are what we need," exclaimed Big Ben happily from the gallery. Jim leaned forward and patted Bijou's neck in the recognised congratulatory manner, and the horse responded in his normal way by further flattening his ears and gnashing his teeth. I smiled to myself, and couldn't help thinking again of 'Mutley'.

A few minutes later the three of us sat on our horses waiting for Ben Scott to come down from the gallery and address us. It wasn't much of a speech, but I felt a strong sense of personal achievement as he reached up and handed me my hard-won set of spurs. He did the same to the other two, congratulated us all for our hard work, and told us that we all had a long way to go before we could be regarded as real 'Mounted Men'. I didn't doubt what he was saying for one moment, because although I was amazed by the progress we had made, I was under no illusion that I, as yet, had any real idea of what I was doing.

After picking out their feet, we led our horses out of the riding school in single file for the last time, under the eagle eye of Big Ben. I caught his eye as I walked past, and was surprised when he nodded, smiled, and spoke:

"Trot on Wildy."

"Sir?"

"Trot on wildly Wildy," he said, laughing at his own joke.

"Sir?"

"Longest way up Wildy; shortest way down," he said, still chuckling to himself. I watched, astonished, as he turned and made his way to his car.

It was a nice early finish for everyone. After the kit was cleaned and the horses were put to bed, I felt strangely melancholy whilst emptying my kit from my locker and loading it into the back of the Mini. Jim Hardwick followed the same routine, and when fully loaded, we set off ahead of the normal rush hour traffic, back home towards the Black Country.

"Well, that's that then," observed Jim as we crossed the traffic lights by the cricket ground.

"I know. It feels weird, doesn't it?" I agreed.

"I've got the whole weekend off, and I start at West Bromwich on Monday. That'll be interesting."

"Bully for you Jim. I may have the whole week off, but then I've got to go to bloody Duke Street. That's going to be fun, with all the gaffers there, watching my every step."

"A whole week off? Be careful mate, your arse will be all soft and squidgy to start over again," he laughed. "You'll have to buy Becks some more surgical spirit."

"That's not a bad idea," I dreamily agreed. "I can't believe I got through it to be honest. I really struggled for the first few days. I'm glad I stuck to it though. It's been good."

"I can't believe I got picked in the first place, because of my size. Hancock's glasses must have been steamed up when I was interviewed!" He laughed whilst shaking his head.

Well, to be honest, I think you've been the pick of the bunch mate. How heavy are you exactly Jim?"

"You don't need to know mate, but Joiner's already told me to shed a few pounds, so they must be keeping an eye on me," he replied thoughtfully.

"Hmm. Slim Jim, that'll be novel. Or they could just buy you a Shire Oss," I joked.

For the rest of the way home, we relived the funny stories, the ups and downs, and the rises and falls of the previous few weeks. The shouts, abuse, falls, bites, Jim's whipping, and my pretty leg warmers all provided good material for some excellent mutual yarn spinning, which seemed to shorten the journey considerably. Eventually I dropped Jim outside of his house, and looking at my watch while he unloaded his kit, decided I just had enough time to visit my divisional headquarters before going home.

It was almost 4pm when I walked into 'Shout's' office with a bundle of papers in my hand.

"Ostler, how are you son? I've missed you. I've lost my twitch and haven't had a single headache since you left us," he boomed, shaking my hand and showering me with spittle.

"It's been interesting Sir, very different, but interesting." Somehow, this man didn't seem anywhere near as scary as he used to be.

"When do you start with them?"

The week after next, but it's only a three monther. I'll be back after that."

"I don't think so Ostler. I'd gladly have you back; joking apart you're a good lad, but I don't think you'll come back if they offer you a full-time post. The choice will be yours, I wouldn't stand in your way, but we'll see. What have you got for me?"

I was a little dumbfounded at the warmth of his words. After three years of living in sheer terror of this man's mere presence, it dawned on me that he actually liked and rated me. For the first time ever, he was talking to me like a grown up, albeit in a paternal manner. He was, in fact, the second scary inspector of the day to speak kindly to me. It was all a little unsettling.

"I've got some expense forms for my travelling. Would you sign them before I take them upstairs, please?" I appealed whilst handing over my bundle.

"Shit Ostler! There's nearly two hundred quid's worth here. Admin Frank will have a baby when he sees this lot, and he may not have enough cash in the safe. Give them here though; I'll sign them. Best of luck lad."

Shout was right, I did have to endure the wrath of Admin Frank. It was indeed a considerable amount of money - for me almost a month's wages following deductions, and it virtually drained Frank's cash box dry. Frank was a typical ageing long served PC, whose uniform hadn't seen the street for many years, and like many others he did a good job - but instead of quietly enjoying the twilight of his service in a privileged cosy position, he never tired of telling everyone how busy and stressed he was. As I packed my wallet with five and one pound notes, I was fully briefed that the petty cash safe was now empty, the banks were now closed, there would be no money for tomorrow morning, and he was going to have to queue at the bank as soon as they opened. I sympathised and apologised for my sins as I left the admin, inwardly smiling as I felt the thickness of my wallet.

Back at home, everything was all systems go when I arrived, because Becks was going out for the evening. Not to a night club, a hen night, or anything so exciting, but to a 'Pippa Dee' clothes party with her mother. It was something that ladies did at that time, and involved visiting someone else's house with a group of women, and perusing new clothes which were presented by the 'Pippa Dee' lady. Refreshments were provided, and they all had a good natter and a laugh; it was very similar to a Tupperware party, but for clothing instead of plastic dishes. It sounded like hell to me, but the girls seemed to enjoy themselves.

"Look what I've got, and they're all shiny, shiny, shiny," I interrupted, dangling my newly won spurs in front of her face.

"Wow! Look at those," she said whilst awarding me a peck on the cheek. "Well done Stef, I knew you'd do it."

"Well that was a little bit underwhelming," I said whilst jokingly activating a sulky bottom lip quiver.

"Sorry Stef, but I'm a bit behind. Don't put them away - if you're still awake, we can have a good look at those when I get back." She smiled and raised her eyebrow.

Becks' preparation for an evening out was always finely tuned, and all had to be set fair after our evening meal before she would agree to leave the house. I was deemed perfectly capable of getting Mel ready and into bed, but everything else had to be shipshape before I was ever handed temporary command.

"Are you sure that you don't mind me going?" This was the usual routine before she left the house.

"No I don't mind you going. Why would I mind?"

"Because we've got no money, so I can't afford to buy anything, and you've been at work all day. Are you sure?"

"I'm going to put Mel to bed, and then I'm going to have the settee to myself, have a beer and watch Starsky and Hutch. You are going out with the girls, and here is a tenner to spend, so buy something nice, and sod off." I laughed as I handed her a ten pound note.

"What? Where have you had ten pounds from?"

"I drew it out today so off you go," I insisted as I pushed her out of the door.

"Stef, what about Hooperman?" she protested, and dug her heels in.

"Hooperman won't be there, so spend it, and buy yourself something nice, now go, go, go."

She carried on protesting as I herded her all of the way down the path, before she finally surrendered and got into the car. It was a close call, because just a few minutes after she turned out of the end of the road, her Dad's old mini bus pulled up outside of the house.

I didn't get the chance to watch Starsky and Hutch, because for the next two hours the house was turned into a noisy hive of activity; Mel enjoyed going to bed later, and sat quietly on my lap, intrigued as she watched her granddad busily fit our hall and stairs with smart new carpet. When the noise of the hammering and sawing was finally finished I took her up to bed, where after a short story and carefully administering the prescribed number of kisses, I left her and went back downstairs to help with the tidying up.

"Charlie, I have to say it looks really fabulous." I scratched my head whilst looking at the deep pile, luxurious carpet. "I won't worry about Mel falling down the stairs now, it's like a cushion. She's going to be so happy with it and good choice of colour too. It's perfect mate."

"I didn't choose the colour Stef, it chose itself. It was a roll end sitting in the corner of the warehouse so I got it really cheap. It's a top quality carpet and much better than you could really afford," explained my father in law.

I sat there patting it, watching the pile spring back every time I moved my hand.

"I didn't expect the carpet tiles in the hall either. How much extra are those?" I asked, secretly worrying if I had enough money in my wallet.

"They're my very best price Stef. Free! I stripped them out of a chemist's shop this morning," he laughed.

"But they look brand new?"

"It's an old trick of the trade Stef. The worn ones go in the skip, but the hardly worn ones from around the edges go in the back of the van. They're commercial quality so even you two messy buggers won't wear these out."

The transformation was complete, and after counting the cash out of my wallet I waved him goodbye. I sat at the top of the stairs looking down. It looked absolutely great, and that bloody savage carpet gripper was now safely hidden below the deep pile - so even if Becks didn't like it, we were still going to save a fortune in socks, tights, and Elastoplast.

It was just after eleven o'clock when I lay on the settee, feigning sleep, whilst listening to the key turn in the front door. The hall light clicked on, but I kept my eyes closed during a considerable delay, before the door opened and she burst into the lounge.

"What? Wow! How? What have you done?" she spluttered, shaking me in a way that would have woken the dead. Before I had chance to reply I was being dragged by the hand into the hallway.

Crikey! Who did that? When did that happen?" I teased in mock surprise.

"Stef it's lovely, really lovely. I love it. I really, really love it," she said, sitting down on the stairs. "But where did it come from? I know we can't afford it. How much was it? Where did the money come from?" The questions came in rapid fire, with barely a chance to answer.

"Don't worry, your Dad's put it down, and I've paid him," I smugly reassured. "No one is going to come and take it back up again."

"But I know we're broke, and what about Hooperman? He's going to go crazy; or have you won some money, what's happened Stef, tell me?"

"Don't worry; I've saved a shedload of travelling expenses from my course. I've paid your Dad for the carpet and he fit it for free, Hooperman is sorted, happy, and off our backs; hopefully you've bought yourself something nice tonight, and there's enough left for us to get a babysitter next week and go to 'The Berni' for a steak and a bottle of 'Blue Nun'."

I knew, though she never complained, that the lack of hall and stair carpet for three years had been quietly getting her down. It had looked an embarrassing mess when opening the front door, but whereas I was out of the house a lot at work, she was at home with Mel, so had to live with it far more than me. I don't think she could have been any happier if I'd have presented her with a million pound cheque, and I knew I had earned myself a mountainous pile of brownie points. Hopefully, I was going to be able to milk this for some time yet.

"I just love the colour Stef. Did you pick it?"

"I did, because I knew you'd like it," I replied with crossed fingers behind my back.

"It's perfect, perfect, and it goes with everything. I love it Stef."

"I knew you would when I chose it."

"And the carpet tiles go with it perfectly. They're lovely too."

"I thought that when I picked them, and they're really hard wearing too, so they'll be perfect for Mel to play on," I knowingly explained, with fingers still crossed.

"I can't believe this; you and my Dad keeping secrets from me. I love it. I love it. It feels like a real home now."

She was very, very happy, and our ascent of the stairs to bed that night was interesting, protracted and took much, much longer than usual, so when we finally fell into our bed I was pleasantly contented and ready for sleep. It had been a long, arduous, eventful day, and an anaesthetic-like weariness took over my mind and limbs. I began to doze as soon as I hit the sheets.

"Stef. Stef," whispered a voice from outside of my comfy cloud.

"Hmm?"

"Are you asleep yet?"

"Hmmm?"

"Where are those spurs?"

"No! Go to sleep."

"*You* are such a lightweight Wildy."

"Hmmm."

I may have won myself a whole bag of new brownie points, but I was also blissfully knackered, and had absolutely no intention of spending them all at once.

"Goodnight Becks," I yawned.

"Not funny Wildy. Not funny at all! Humph!"

CHAPTER 14

WALKING TALL TO DUKE STREET

The week's annual leave at the end of my riding course was a welcome break, and a great opportunity to spend valuable time with Becks and Mel. We had planned a trip to Dudley Zoo and other days out, which unfortunately had to be cancelled when the West Midlands was unexpectedly hit by a late freezing spell and a blanket of sticking snow.

In the middle of the week, despite the state of the roads, I managed to keep an appointment at Duke Street. I spent an interesting hour with Arnie Parfitt in the stores, whilst he topped me up with the required kit needed for my three month attachment. This time he obviously meant business, because I was immediately issued with two old cardboard boxes instead of the single Vim box I had taken away from my first visit. I was issued with a second pair of breeches, with no suggestion this time that I should accept a comedy pair of baggy pantaloons from the days of The Raj. I tried on a riding tunic, which fit very nicely, and was surprised to discover that it was beltless, fitted, flared and longer in the tail than my normal beat tunic. In contrast to beat uniform, most of the mounted garments were made to measure and of a very high quality - this, however, meant new officers had to make do with second hand clothes until after they had been measured at the annual visit of the tailor. There was certainly a lot more equipment required for uniformed duty than had been needed in the confines of the riding school. I had a reinforced helmet for use at football matches, fluorescent hi-vis items for both me and the horse, a battery operated red lamp for fitting to a stirrup at night, and most amusingly, a huge Gabardine belted raincoat that covered me from neck to ankles.

I put it on and stood looking at myself in the long mirror on the back of the door. I knew exactly what it was for, but couldn't keep a smile off my face because it looked so comical.

"Who was this one made for; The Jolly Green Giant?" I asked with tongue in cheek.

"There's nothing wrong with that mac. It's a good fit. It ain't for walking the beat in; it covers the horse as well," he replied sharply.

Arnie, I later discovered, was a genuinely helpful and thoroughly decent guy, but at this early stage of our acquaintance our senses of humour were definitely tuned into different stations.

I arrived home, and after lunch showed Becks the exciting contents of my two new goodie boxes. All was calm until I tried on the reinforced helmet that I was to wear at football matches. It certainly wasn't a purpose made public order riding helmet, but was in fact an obsolete 'Corker' motorcycle helmet that had gone out of use in the Traffic Department many years previously. They had only recently been resurrected as an alternative to the flat cap for mounted officers, who were beginning to experience the start of the disgraceful, and often bloody, football violence that was to besmirch the game throughout the 1980s. Soon to become obsolete for the second time, the likes of this helmet wouldn't become a common sight in public again until the period drama Heartbeat hit the TV screens sometime in the distant future.

"What is that Stef? You look like someone out of Dixon of Dock Green," asked Becks, trying to suppress the giggles.

"Oh you've seen nothing yet. Prepare yourself for a real treat."
I hurriedly fastened up my riding raincoat and started parading
up and down the lounge.

"Stop it, I'm going to wet myself in a minute!" she responded,
in fits of laughter. "Stop it! Pete's outside clearing the snow. He's
going to think we're raving mad."

I could see our next door neighbour, Pete, clearing the snow
from our pathway. Pete, middle-aged and a long serving scenes of
crime officer, lived with his wife in the adjoining police house,
and they were both the most wonderful of neighbours. They had
kids older than us, but instead of moaning about the noise and
disruption that inevitably arrived with their new young
neighbours and small child, they enthusiastically adopted us as a
surrogate family. They both adored little Mel, who was now
joining in with the fun whilst happily emptying the remaining
contents of my kit box onto the lounge floor.

"Come on; we're going to give Pete a treat and prove to him
that we really are raving mad. Put this helmet and mac on," I
said.

"Wildy, you're *not* going to make me look stupid in front of the
neighbours. No way matey."

"Don't be a mardy bum. Come on," I insisted. "Put this helmet
on - it'll make you look cool and really sexy."

"You have a strange mind Stefan Wild! I don't know where
these ideas come from sometimes…"

She eventually capitulated without too much further protest,
and began less than enthusiastically to get dressed. The helmet,
which was far too big, sat down low on her head covering her
eyes and ears, and when she climbed into the huge mac she
disappeared from sight completely. We both, to the wide-eyed
amazement of our small daughter, laughed like kids who had just
been caught playing in the grown-ups' clothes box.

After a fair bit of huffing and puffing in the hallway, I lifted her up so that she sat astride my shoulders, and with me completely hidden beneath the now knee length mac, we stooped and squeezed out of the door onto the front doorstep. Mel, always keen to get in on the act, followed us out and immediately ran to Pete who was now finishing off by the front gate.

"Mommy Big! Mommy Big!" she shrieked with enthusiasm as she ran towards our bemused neighbour.

I stood up straight, still completely hidden beneath the mac, and began to make my way blindly along the front garden path. Becks, on top, swung her arms briskly; marching at a completely different pace to that at which my legs were walking.

"'Ello 'ello 'ello; what's goin' on 'ere then? Do you need any help?" I heard her ask.

There was no immediate verbal response from our neighbour, who when confronted by a nine foot tall pantomime policeman in a huge helmet and ridiculous uniform, stood open mouthed, shovel in hand and completely speechless.

"Do you think these heels make me look too tall, Pete?" she innocently asked, tipping her helmet back as I peeped through the buttoned-up mac.

"Your Mommy and Daddy are absolutely raving mad," he spluttered to Mel between fits of laughter. "What the hell are you two wearing?"

I began to walk again, Becks smartly marching with her arms, whilst Pete, followed closely by Mel, ran to fetch his wife to share our performance. The three of them stood on the doorstep in fits of laughter, and a man walking along the street almost slipped in the snow and fell whilst looking at us in amazement.

"You can put me down now Stef. You don't need a cricked neck for next week," I heard the voice of the sensible one, say from above my head.

"I don't think so, not just yet. You, girl, are going for a little walk along the High Street – so hold tight and get marching."

"You *must* be joking. If you take me down the High Street like *this* you're a dead man. Put me down!" she demanded, in something of a panic.

"About turn! Quick march!" I laughed as I turned towards the direction of the road and continued along the path.

"You're going to die Wildy, you're going to die! Put me down! Do not take me down the High Street! Do not take me down the High Street! Are you listening to me Wildy?"

I recklessly ignored her commands and opened the gate, stepping out of our garden and setting off towards the High Street. I was immediately subjected to a cruel and determined barrage of hefty kicks to my ribs.

"Put me down! Wildy put me down! Joke over! You're dead mate! You are *dead*!"

I'm not sure if it was the obviously increasing annoyance in her voice, or the jabbing pain in my ribs from the frantic kicking, but something convinced me that a long tall patrol along the busy High Street was not such a clever idea. Whatever the reason, I turned around and headed back towards our garden, before bending forward and gently letting her down onto the path that our considerate neighbour had just carefully cleared of snow.

It is fair to say that I was on the wrong end of a fairly severe telling off, which I think was partially fuelled by the sheer relief of narrowly escaping an embarrassing involuntary walk along the High Street dressed as a nine foot tall pantomime policeman. Unfortunately, when standing just a little over five feet tall with only your nose and lips visible beneath a massive hat, and dressed in tent-sized clothing, it is difficult to maintain any real air of authority. Especially when your husband and neighbours are in fits of laughter at your expense.

"If you want me to feel properly told off, you'd better go and put your own clothes on and try again," I laughed, with all the courage of a man standing securely next to his neighbours, who were both still in fits of laughter.

"Please you two, don't ever move away from here. You do brighten our lives up. You're such a couple of clowns," laughed Pete. "Your Mommy and Daddy are a couple of real dafties. They are," added Pete to Mel, who he was now holding in his arms.

At the time we thought our act was unique, but over the years I've since seen the massive policeman trick involving two fools and a riding mac performed many times in a variety of locations, and always causing hilarity. But for me, none have been funnier than that first time with my angry wife, on a snowy day in our own front garden with just our lovely neighbours as an audience.

It was about 6.50am, my first day at Duke Street, and the first day of my three month attachment to the Mounted Branch. I had been looking forward to it, and now after a week's annual leave I was raring to go. I parked the Mini in a dark side street and began the short but perilously slippery walk to Duke Street Stables across the frozen compacted snow.

It was an unlikely location; sitting just on the edge of the city centre but now almost engulfed by the ever growing campus of Aston University, Duke Street certainly wouldn't have been everyone's first choice of a place to stable horses. Some of the older guys could remember when the whole area had been a labyrinth of Victorian terraced houses sitting in cobbled streets, and Duke Street Police Station had been an operational station. Now, in the 1970s, the whole police complex was condemned for demolition, surrounded to one side by modern high rise student accommodation, and by empty patches of rough derelict land on the other. On a positive note, it was far easier to park the Mini on the street than it had been on my previous visits inside the yard.

An early day shift at the Mounted Branch usually began at 7am and ended at 3pm. A late shift began at 10am and ended at 6pm, and the only time that later hours were worked was for evening football matches and other specific commitments. The working hours, when compared to my regular operational duties, were ridiculously cushy. I was considering this as I slipped and slid across the yard, weaving between a multitude of parked cars and laden down with two large bags full of kit, uniform, and a pair of boots and wellies. This was to be the 'curse of the attached man'; with no permanent place of work, no locker to call my own, and postings that might include three different stables in one week, I was going to have to carry my kit around in the back of the car for the foreseeable future.

It was shortly before seven when I eventually reached the door under the veranda, and after stamping the snow off my feet and a brief struggle, I managed to depress the handle with my elbow. Still holding onto my bags, I pushed the door open with my rear end and squeezed into the room backwards. Inside, I turned around to see about half a dozen men sitting around the bunk table. Some were smoking, some not, but all were drinking tea and after briefly looking up and down, none of them acknowledged me. This display of overt rudeness may have been a little more worrying if I hadn't been forewarned that the Duke Street lot were notoriously prickly with newcomers.

"Morning all, I'm Stef Wild. It's my first day. Where shall I stow this lot?" I greeted in my most friendly but humble manner.

There was no response, and I had to check and see my reflection in the window over the sink to confirm to myself that I was actually really there. With my presence confirmed, I now had to decide whether to meekly accept this moody and ignorant reception, or to throw an early morning hand grenade into the room. I chose the latter and without further conversation deliberately dumped both of my bags, my boots, wellies and my coat onto the middle of the table, creating mayhem with the mugs, tea pot, and newspapers. The proverbial hand grenade certainly had the desired effect as everyone immediately jumped to their feet, cursing and swearing in an effort to avoid spilled tea.

Any negative consequences of my action were delayed by the sergeant walking, in a timely manner, into the room. It was the big burly sergeant with the clipboard who I had last seen months ago on the day of my awful interview. This time, however, he had no clipboard, was dressed in scruffy stable gear, and was carrying a large and possibly the only full mug of tea in the room.

"Ah young Wild, thanks for joining us, chuck all your stuff over there in the corner, get yourself a cuppa, and I'll see if we can find you an empty locker later," he said, sitting down at the table.

I removed my offending baggage, poured myself a mug of tea, and sat down amongst the burning glares of the miserable bunch in total silence. After what seemed an eternity of no conversation, and at exactly 7.15am, the sergeant got to his feet. Everyone else followed suit, walking through the saddle room and into the stables. It suddenly occurred to me, that in all of my nine weeks at Tally Ho, I had never once mucked out a stable - and consequently I had no idea what to do. It hadn't been an oversight in the training, but the riding course had been pretty intensive and priority had been given to the riding and theory of the job. The morning mucking out had always already been completed before we arrived.

The morning routine at Duke Street turned out to be a well ordered and long practiced drill. Everything was done to the clock, in a laid down, almost cast in stone, order. Initially the unwavering rigidity seemed petty and annoying, but it was in fact a long established, tried and tested routine that got the job done in the quickest, cleanest and most efficient manner. Everyone but me knew exactly what to do, when to do it, and when to stop doing it. Unfortunately, no one's morning routine included showing the new bloke what to do.

The main double door into the yard opened, letting a cold blast of frosty air into the previously warm and cosy stable. Two men disappeared outside, whilst everyone else took a pitchfork from a rack on the wall and began to muck out the individual stalls alongside the standing horses. I had never used a pitchfork before, and it was easy to tell. The stalls were bedded with straw, which was obviously soiled because the horses had been unattended all night, and the object was to separate the dirty from the clean. The clean and dry was moved and piled neatly at the front of the stall beneath the manger, whilst the wet straw and muck was piled in the walkway at the back of the stall. The stall was then swept clean into the walkway by a man with a broom, who continued along the line in the wake of the 'muckers out'.

The two men who had not started mucking out the stalls, reappeared with a large, two wheeled barrow, which they filled with the dirty piles from the backs of the stalls. They systematically moved along the line, loading the barrow without delay, until they got to me. I was still intently, and slowly, striving to separate the clean straw from the soiled, but was unfortunately dropping most of it onto the floor. While the others were now working on their second stall, and moving rapidly down the line, I was in a mess - unready, under pressure, and under the glare of the two impatient barrowmen.

"Come on pal, come on, get a bloody move on. We haven't got all day."

"I've never done this before and it's harder than it looks. I think there's a hole in my fork," I laughed perhaps a little too apologetically.

"It's shit pal. It's not bloody rocket science. It's just shit. What's the matter with you?"

One of them grumpily barged in, joining me and the horse in the stall, and with his pitchfork rapidly began to make light of what I was finding to be so tricky.

The whole operation literally swept along the length of the stable. As the muck piles at the rear of the stalls disappeared into the barrow and out into the yard, the stalls were dry swept into the walkway, which was itself then swept dry clean by two men with stiff brooms.

In not much more than ten minutes the whole stable, of around ten horses, had been mucked out, swept clean, and completely cleared of soiled bedding. I stood with my pitchfork, still unsure of what to do next, taking in the pungent smell of the morning muck out. It was a unique concoction of warm horse, warm man, horse droppings, and the distinctive nose clearing whiff of ammonia that came from the urine soaked straw. On that first day it made a distinct and memorable impression, but over time it would become normal and barely noticed. The whole smell of the horses and the stable eventually impregnated your pores and clothing, but went unnoticed amongst the men, who whilst working, existing, and eating together, all smelled the same.

There were no toilets or showering facilities at Duke Street Stables; these luxuries would not be available until the move to more modern premises in 1983, so at the end of our working day we all took the lingering odour and evidence of our occupation back home. To us it didn't matter - we were conditioned and oblivious - but I would occasionally be reminded of my evocative occupational pong by the amount of personal space I enjoyed if I had to pop into the grocery shop on the way home.

"Shit pit or water?" I was abruptly jarred back to my senses.

"What?" I answered.

"Don't stand around gaping pal. Shit pit or water? Your choice but just do something."

Half of the men had begun to turn the horses around in their stalls whilst placing two buckets of water in front of each of them. The horses all drank deeply, most quenching their thirst with the two buckets, and some emptying both and being given a third. Finding myself surplus to requirements, I took my pitchfork outside into the yard.

The rest of the group were busily stacking the tippings from the barrow into what I now know to be, the 'shit pit'. The shit pit was a small, low walled enclosure with an entrance on one side. It measured about three metres square. The soiled bedding was tipped from the barrow into the entrance and then busily thrown by pitchfork into the enclosure, where it was skilfully stacked, patted, and carefully trimmed, so that at the end of the procedure it looked neat, tidy and upright, almost standing to attention. Having played little part in the creation of this organic masterpiece I stood back and admired the finished work.

"A tidy shit pit is a happy shit pit," remarked one of the younger men as I stood looking.

"Is that so?" I laughed.

"You'd better believe it," he replied. "It's in direct view of Big Ben's window, so if the shit pit's happy Ben's happy, and if Ben's happy everyone's happy."

I walked back into the stable and hung my pitchfork back on the wall, contemplating this latest piece of important and valuable information. Inside, the buckets had already been put away but the air of busy activity continued as men collected their day rugs and grooming bags. Each horse had two stable rugs; the night rug was a heavy, coarse jute rug which was worn, as the name suggests at night, which was replaced by the lighter and much smarter liveried day rug after grooming. It was easy to tell which horses had been groomed because they were wearing day rugs, whilst the un-groomed horses were still in their night rugs.

Apart from two loose boxes, one at either end of the block, all of the horses were kept in stalls, so were chained to and facing the wall. They were chained either 'short rack' or 'long rack' depending on their tour of duty and the time of day. When the bedding wasn't down in the stall, or they were groomed ready to ride, the horses were chained to a ring on the wall which allowed them to reach their manger and look around, but not lie down - this was known as 'short rack'. After riding, when the bedding was down and when wearing their night rugs, the horses were chained to a lower ring below the manger. The chain was now weighted with two wooden weights known as 'logs', which allowed the horse to pull the chain longer to lie down, but prevented any slack that could cause injury if caught around the front legs. This method was known as 'long rack'.

There were plenty of opinions regarding the stabling of the horses in stalls. I quickly formed, and still hold, the opinion that both short and long racking was an ancient, out-dated method designed to stable large numbers of working horses after long, arduous working days; horses who were content to quietly lie down and rest their weary limbs on return to their stable. Our horses, however, routinely worked for only three hours a day, which meant twenty one hours looking at the wall in the stable. The benefit to limbs, joints, circulation, and general health gained by being untethered and able to move freely around a loose box seemed obvious to me, but was equally disputed by a lot of the department's traditionalists; and in fairness, the horses never seemed bothered by their restricted existence. They obviously couldn't voice their opinions on the subject, but without doubt, most of them were always very keen to get home to their compact and restricted beds towards the end of their patrols.

"Look on the board to see what horse you're riding. Their names are painted below their saddles in the saddle room, and over their stall," said the friendly guy who had explained the rules of the shit pit to me.

"Cheers mate. I'm a bit of a little lost sheep to be honest," I gratefully replied.

"No worries. I was you a few months ago. You'll be on it in no time."

"I can't get my head around how bloody miserable everyone is. This one bloke is on my case already and keeps calling me 'Pal'. It's my first day and he's pushing his luck a bit," I complained.

"That's Bertie Rock. He's the same with all the new blokes, but he winds all the others up too. I had it in the neck just the same. Truth is he's not much of a problem when you get to know him."

"How do you think he'd respond to a punch in the throat?" I asked.

"You wouldn't be the first, and I don't think you'll be the last either," he laughed whilst walking away.

I stored this extra snippet of useful information as I found my way to the chalk board at the end of the stable and discovered I was riding a horse called Hertford. In the saddle room I located his kit, collected the grooming bag that was hanging on a hook beneath the bridle, and the day rug that was neatly folded and hanging over the saddle. Back in the stable I found Hertford quietly standing beneath his nameplate in the middle stall. He was a large horse, the only black horse in the stable, and I was extremely relieved to discover that he seemed docile. He didn't appear to harbour any ambition to bite, kick, or attack me in any other way.

I began to follow the same grooming routine I had been taught at Tally Ho, but became almost immediately aware that I wasn't going to be able to hang around if I was to finish at the same time as the others. Everyone was busy, grooming, cleaning head collars, chains, and mangers, which leant an industrious atmosphere to the place. I removed Hertford's night rug and hung it on the end of the stall partition in a neat fashion the same as the others, before detaching his head collar from the chain with the quick release fastener. As I walked back out of the stall the horse followed me, turning around to face me, so I removed his head collar and cleaned it before grooming his head. I was surprised how easily he had turned around within the width of the narrow stall, and also noticed that, unlike Tally Ho, I was able to keep my eye on all of the others, so hopefully I would be able to pace myself to finish at the same time as everyone else.

Despite working at a much faster pace than I was accustomed to, I was just giving Hertford's shiny black coat a final wipe with a slightly damp cloth, when the sergeant's voice called out:

"Two minutes!"

Everyone else was in their final stages, so I followed suit by turning Hertford around, putting on his day rug, fastening his head collar to the chain and packing the brushes and curry comb away into the grooming bag.

"Right; that's it. Brushes away. Swill down!" ordered the sergeant.

The atmosphere changed again as everyone left their individual grooming and moved in to the same finely tuned collective mode that had been so obvious during mucking out. The outside door was flung open again, as three men went out and began to fill buckets with freezing cold water from the two troughs in the yard. Everyone else picked up a broom and the swilling out began with gusto. The stalls were swilled first with the bucket men carefully emptying their buckets, so as not to wet the bedding, whilst the sweepers swept the stalls clean into the walkway. With all of the stalls swilled, the walkway was swilled and swept from either end towards the central entrance door. The worn old blue cobbled brick floor had been laid more than a hundred years earlier by the Victorians, who obviously knew their stuff, because it was perfectly sloped in every required direction. The stalls sloped gently back down towards the walkway, and the walkway sloped into a shallow central gully, which itself directed water downwards before channelling it through small holes in the brick wall and out into drains in the yard. When the stable was completely swilled, we moved out into the yard to repeat the process outside, with some of the men flinging buckets of water filled from the troughs, and others vigorously sweeping towards the drains. The yard was soon as sparkling clean as the stable. Finally, the wet, dirty sweepings were cleared from the drains and thrown into the shit pit, before everyone moved back into the stable with the large central double door closed behind them.

Back in the warm, some of the previously quiet horses began to scrape their feet on the cobbled floor, and the occasional kick of the wooden stall partitions could be heard as a sense of excitement took hold of the animals. It was feed time, and the obvious rising tension didn't abate until after the civilian stableman had completed his long walk with bucket and scoop and fed the last horse in the line. Eventually, with peace and calm restored, all that could be heard was the muffled sound of processed feed pellets being steadily crunched, in a mill like fashion, between large equine molars.

I stood and watched for a few moments as the rest of the men began to file out of the stable and into the saddle room. I was quietly impressed with the scene, and was contemplating how in just a short period of regimented activity, such a transformation had occurred. It was almost 8.30am, so in little more than an hour the horses had been groomed and the whole place had been transformed; it was now quiet, clean, fresh and airy.

"Don't stand around pal. You look untidy and you'll miss your breakfast," said a sharp voice, rudely interrupting my chain of thought.

"My name is Stef Wild. Either will do, but I'm not your pal. Do you understand?" I grumpily replied.

"Don't get shirty pal. Just short rack your horse, because if you leave him long like that he'll lie down on the cobbles after breakfast. Also you're just showing the sergeant that you haven't washed your chain. Alright pal?" countered Bertie bloody Rock as he smugly turned and left the stable.

I was mad with myself because I'd forgotten to short rack my horse and had left myself open to criticism by an annoying know it all. I quietly seethed back into the stall, unknotted the chain and removed the logs, before sliding it out of the lower ring and retying it onto the higher ring. Hertford, completely disinterested and unaware of my misdemeanour, continued to contently chomp his breakfast throughout the readjustment.

As I walked back into the saddle room everyone was changing out of their wellies and into shoes, before either making their way back into the bunk, or out of the door into the yard. The friendly lad who had advised me during mucking out explained that some were going to the canteen for a cooked breakfast, whilst others chose to stay in the bunk and eat their own food. Becks had prepared and packed me some sandwiches, but following the morning's activity I was absolutely starving, so I decided to treat myself and join him as he walked to the canteen.

The canteen was located upstairs in the main building, which also contained the garage workshops and the Traffic Department. It was a typical police canteen of its time, buzzing with conversation and laughs and whoops of frivolity as large men in uniform played cards whilst scoffing their cholesterol laden food.

As soon as our small group entered we were greeted by a tirade of loud but good natured abuse.

"Bloody hell, what's that smell?"

"Has someone shit themselves?"

"For God's sake somebody open the windows!"

The prevailing pong of the stable had followed us in, and the resulting protests and noisy barracking were coming from a large group sat at the back of the room. The row of crash helmets along the windowsill, the dripping wet heavy 'Belstaff' jackets hanging from hooks on the wall, and their heavy breeches and boots left their identity in no doubt. They were traffic motorcyclists, a notoriously rowdy group, and known widely as 'The Central Bikers'. To a passing stranger their behaviour would have been offensive and possibly intimidating, but there was no malice intended, no harm done, and the mounted men held their own by responding in a similar manner. There was closeness and an element of mutual respect between the two very different groups, which prevailed throughout my service on the Mounted Department. Despite some later, misguided attempts by modern management to eradicate the banter in the name of political correctness, the noisy rapport between the two groups of dedicated professionals continued unabated in its own friendly but abusive way.

To them, we were and always would be the 'Donkey Wallopers'. To us, they were the 'Dirty Scruffies' - and our bacon butties just wouldn't have tasted the same without each other.

Back downstairs in the bunk there was just time for yet another cup of tea before everyone got up to resume their morning routine. The activity commenced in the saddle room as everyone took their saddles down from the racks and sat them on the saddle horses in the middle of the room. There were a few unfamiliar items hanging with Hertford's kit that we hadn't used at Tally Ho on our riding course, and when no one offered any help or advice, I quietly watched the others and copied what they did.

I took the long baton, known as a sword stick, and fastened it to two loops on the left side of the saddle seat, before taking down the unfamiliar breast plate and badge and laying it across the saddle. I added a long slender chrome chain to my heavy pile, and carrying my load, followed someone else out into the stable. I was familiar with fitting the saddle, and watched through the bars of the stall partition as my neighbour added his breast plate and chain before copying him and following suit. I replaced the day rug loosely over Hertford's back covering the saddlery, and waited my turn before taking a can and brush and dressing his hooves with hoof oil.

Back in the bunk everyone was in varying stages of undress as they began to replace their scruffy stable wear with smart uniform. I noticed, with quiet amusement, that though there were several pairs of long johns being secretly worn beneath breeches, there was no evidence of any pink fluffy leg warmers in the room. Using a pair of metal boot hooks I pulled my now nicely fitting boots on over my breeches, before, for the first time, adding my recently won spurs. I completed the look with tunic, cap, and finally my huge riding mac. Everyone else was dressed the same, and looked the same, but I couldn't help but stand in front of the long full length mirror to take a look at myself. It was my first day in full mounted uniform, and in a few moments' time I was going to be out on the streets of Birmingham riding a police horse. A milestone indeed; but the silly smile on my face had actually appeared because I was thinking of the last time I had worn the ludicrous mac, with Becks on my shoulders, performing a double act at a private matinee for the neighbours.

Not for the first time that morning, my daydreams were rudely interrupted when I saw the frowning, punchable, face of Bertie Rock appear over my shoulder.

"Don't stand admiring yourself pal. You're not that pretty."

"I wasn't admiring myself, I was just-"

"Just hurry up pal. You're with me today, and if you keep fannying about we're going to be late out," he turned away, carrying his bridle, and walked towards the stable.

I followed him out carrying my bridle, with my quiet excitement having just taken a sudden dip. This rude, objectionable, supercilious bloke, who condescendingly insisted on calling me 'pal', was getting to be past a joke. I was going to have to sort him out, and soon, but alas not today. Today, I needed him. I had never ridden a horse in traffic; I had no idea where to go, what to do, or how to look after myself. He was my minder for the day - my life was in his hands - and I didn't like it one little bit.

CHAPTER 15

ON PATROL

We lined up outside in the yard just before 10am. There were seven of us, and I was on the far left of the line sitting astride Hertford, next to my escort for the day, Bertie Rock. He had nagged me whilst saddling up, and continued in the same fashion now that we were waiting outside for whatever was going to happen next. I had no idea; it was my first day.

"Sit up straight pal. You look like a bag of shit," he continued. "Come on, dress up, get in line before Ben comes out. Come on pal, get a grip!"

I didn't bite; just stared at him, eyebrow raised adopting my most sinister 'drop dead' look, while I quietly seethed inside. I was sitting much higher than my objectionable escort because Hertford was a sizeable horse, while his was much smaller, and I was actually looking down onto the top of Bertie Rock's cap. I was quietly checking the range, fantasising about trying out my sword stick, and bending it over my partner's head, when Big Ben suddenly appeared in front of us.

"RIDE SHUN!" growled the familiar voice. "RIDE RIGHT DRESS!"

Six of us looked across to the right-hand man and repositioned until our line was straight.

"RIDE EYES FRONT."

We looked to the front as the inspector walked along, nodding acknowledgement to everyone until he reached me at the end of the line. He stood directly in front, looking me up and down, before moving around to my nearside where he looked me up and down again. I continued looking ahead until he stepped forward and lifted my mac to look at my boots. Surprised, I glanced down at him just in time to see a nod of approval.

"Don't be alarmed Wild, just checking for pink frillies and petticoats," he laughed.

Everyone else joined in while I replied with a weak smile.

"Good man Wild, good man," he said, smiling smugly at my expense. "From the right walk march."

The man on the far right moved away, and we all followed in single file out of the yard and into the street. At the end of Duke Street, we split into different directions and I was suddenly alone with my mentor for the day.

"You ride on the nearside. I ride on the outside. You'd better keep up because these horses need some work today," he said as he legged his horse forward into a brisk walk.

I followed suit and we continued in silence side by side, until we reached a main road, where without word or warning he broke into a trot.

"Come on pal. Keep up. You're supposed be alongside. Come on pal! Come on catch up."

I eventually caught up and took up my position kerbside. I bit my lip tightly as we trotted along at a good pace, and quietly came to the conclusion that this was going to be a long and trying three hours. My knowledge of Birmingham in those days was not very good, and I had no idea where I was or where we were going until we reached a large traffic roundabout with an ancient monumental steam pump in the centre. I now know this roundabout, which was locally known as 'PUMP ISLAND', to be

Dartmouth Circus. It was, and still is, a very busy roundabout with lanes of traffic approaching and leaving in multiple directions; beneath it runs the A38M Aston Expressway, which is a busy motorway heading into the city centre. The traffic was fast and furious as we approached, and I really hadn't anticipated having to negotiate such challenging conditions within my first ten minutes on the street.

We entered the roundabout, without slowing, at a fast trot and moved towards the centre in a position to turn right. Vehicles were passing us closely on both sides. I said nothing, but I felt vulnerable, and was left in no doubt that I was being tested and tried out.

Much to my relief we left the roundabout, still at a brisk trot but also still alive, and headed out of city along Lichfield Road in the direction of Erdington. My regained composure, however, was short-lived, and within a minute my tension levels began to rise again as the road ahead ascended to the right, and we were soon crossing the A38M on a flyover. This was not at all like riding in the school at Tally Ho. The clatter of the horses' hooves on the hard metalled road surface was obviously louder, but I could also feel the concussion of every beat rising up through the animal, through my seat and finally up my spine. The noise from the traffic was also deafening, and even further exaggerated because although most of the recent snow had now been removed from the highway, the roads were still wet and dirty from the rock salt that had been spread on the icy surface earlier that morning.

Fortunately I had soon mastered Hertford's gait and found a steady comfortable rhythm as I rose and fell in time with the saddle. Any relief gained, however, was short-lived and immediately lost with the panic-inducing view developing on my nearside. I could clearly see my left stirrup, boot, and spur peeping from below the hem of my riding mac. I could also clearly see that my foot was less than one foot away from, and at the same height as, the steel railings at the side of the road. Even *more* alarming was the sheer drop of about forty feet on the other side of the railings, down towards the busy seven lanes of the Aston Expressway. I quietly but firmly fixed my eyes directly ahead, and concentrated on my rise and fall, which was beginning to play havoc with the watery lump in my throat as we clattered along the main road.

We eventually slowed and came to a halt at some red traffic lights at Aston Cross. Aston Cross was a busy junction - I had never been there before, and whilst waiting for the lights to change I was intrigued by the familiar but not immediately recognisable smell that dominated the local atmosphere. Looking ahead I could see the large shape of Ansell's Brewery a little further down the road, but the smell of fermenting beer was only a partial ingredient of the mysterious aroma that was entering my nostrils and teasing my brain. It occurred to me that this may be a good opportunity to build bridges and begin a more civilised rapport with my so far objectionable escort.

"What's the smell?" I asked.

"What?" he snapped in reply.

"The smell? I can't put my finger on it," I added, still trying to be friendly.

Without reply, or any further acknowledgment, he legged his horse forward and almost immediately broke out into the trot again. Caught off guard and slightly left behind, I could see the lights had changed to green, and as I legged to catch up I looked both ways at the junction and saw the large brick factory tower displaying the HP sign. The secrets of the peculiar pungent smell were unlocked, and I made a firm mental note never to try a cocktail which included both Ansell's Bitter and HP brown sauce; it just didn't smell right.

"You need to shape up and keep up, pal," he sneered, as I finally caught up and positioned myself alongside him.

I chose not to reply, but made up my mind that one way or another, I was going to confront this unpleasantness – and sooner rather than later. I, like many others, had gone through this cold shoulder initiation before, but back then I had been only nineteen and straight out of training school. I was still only twenty three, but had served my time as 'the sprog' and had largely earned the respect of my elder peers back on division. A lot had happened to me in four years; I had matured, I was a husband and a father, and I had learned a lot. I'd had to deal with some seriously nasty people along the way, so I wasn't going to suffer this bullying creep for another day longer. But this was still not the moment.

I settled into a steady rhythm of rise and fall as we trotted on, moodily, along the main road. The horses were beginning to steam a little in the cold air, but Hertford was still happily going forward without the need of excessive leg, and easily kept up with the smaller, lighter horse. He really was a strange looking little beast. He was barely sixteen hands high and very light-boned, with a scrawny neck, small head, and great big floppy ears which gyrated wildly in perfect time with his gait. His animated ears had earned him the nickname of 'Radar' with the men; he was a timid animal, not really suited for the job, and disliked by most within the department. I had no idea at the time, but before long he would be my horse - and if I had known then what an impact he would have on my future, I would have probably paid him a little more attention.

We continued in silence at an impressive pace, mixing again with heavy traffic at another large and busy roundabout at Gravelly Hill, where, as we trotted on, I was for the first time able to view the famous Spaghetti Junction and the M6 motorway from beneath the concrete structure. The route (which hadn't been shared with me, and therefore remained a mystery) continued on the main road for several more miles, passing through Erdington, Walmley, and finally into Sutton Coldfield, where we eventually entered Sutton Park through Town Gate.

The horses were beginning to blow now, and once inside the park we slowed down to the walk before finally halting for a rest. Without saying a single word he dismounted, crossed his stirrups over the saddle, and removed his mac to cover the horse's back. I quietly followed suit, and both of the horses began to relax and stretch their necks whilst they cooled down. The park was a different world from the busy main road and was white over for as far as the eye could see. The roadways were shiny and compacted, but on either side the snow was undisturbed, endless, and almost a foot deep. It looked absolutely lovely and, as the sun was now out and shining, was difficult to look at without squinting. It was also worlds apart from how Sutton Park looked on that day when Becks and I had been surrounded by cows on our first date.

Smiling to myself, I estimated we had travelled around eight miles in little over an hour since leaving the yard at Duke Street. I had absolutely no previous experience, so nothing to compare, but I doubted this was typical of a morning's patrol. I knew I was being tested out, but although the ride had been hard going, I had kept up, complained about nothing, and most importantly, had kept in the saddle. I was quietly pleased with myself.

"What have you got to be so happy about pal?" The voice of my companion suddenly disturbed my drifting thoughts.

"Why shouldn't I be happy? It's a beautiful day. What's not to be happy about?"

"Sorry pal, but if you don't know, I'm not going to tell you."

"If you can't say anything constructive you'd better bloody well keep quiet, and if you call me pal once more I'm going to punch you right in the gob!" I snapped, feeling the smile leave my face.

"Touchy touchy; so what would you prefer to be called, Aynuk or Ayli?" he answered, without acknowledging my threat.

Aynuk and Ayli are two flat-capped, beer-drinking, mythical Black Country characters that are the subject matter of a lot of local jokes. For many years the two characters appeared professionally on stage at local venues, where much of their humour stemmed from the Black Country culture and dialect. Their names are a local phonetical translation of the names Enoch and Eli. I had nothing against Aynuk and Ayli, they were funny and I had seen them several times at local functions, but I was in no doubt at all that this objectionable 'Brummie' was using their names to personally insult me.

"You know my name!" I snapped. "Use it or shut it." I turned my back, removed my mac and remounted my horse.

He sneered and remounted too, before turning away and carefully walking his horse across the slippery roadway and into the deep, undisturbed snow. Without any further warning he legged his horse forward and began to gallop away from me. It was the first day I had ever ridden out of doors, the first time I had ever galloped on a horse, and certainly the first day I had galloped a horse in the snow -but without further thought I turned the eager Hertford and followed in his tracks. I had no choice, because I didn't know my way home.

He had a start on me, and the little horse with the ridiculously independent ears came into his own with a turn of speed that the heavier Hertford could never hope to match. We followed in their tracks a few lengths behind, never gaining any ground and being showered with the clods of snow thrown up by the faster horse. I'm sure the intention was to terrify me, but if that was the plan it was a miserable failure. I was afraid in the way that a fairground ride creates fear, and any mild terror was completely outweighed by the exhilaration of fast flowing adrenaline. Hertford was enjoying it too. He was blowing hard but stretching out without any leg from me; my cap was hanging on by the chin strap at the back of my head, and I could hardly keep my eyes open because of the spray of snow flying into my face. It was fantastic, it was exciting, it was "Yee hah!", and I was being paid for it.

We eventually slowed and stopped at another park gate, where he dismounted and inspected his horse's feet. I silently followed suit and, whilst slipping and sliding on the roadway, found that the sole of the hoof was clogged with compacted snow. Fortunately I had had the foresight to put a hoof pick in my mac pocket, so I was able to get on with the job without having to borrow from my supercilious colleague. The snow in the hoof was surprisingly hard, packed so tightly that it stood proud of the shoe, and I could see the potential danger of slipping on the road if it wasn't removed. I hacked at it with the hoof pick, and following a little brutality it began to break up and come away from the hoof in frozen chunks.

"Hey! Be careful with that horse. You'll damage the frog, you clumsy Black Country oik; didn't you think to oil the bottom of his feet? You knew it was icy, what's the matter with you?" asked my helpful friend.

He was being rude and unreasonable; I wasn't about to damage the frog and I'd had no help or guidance from this arse of a man since the moment I arrived at work that morning. I chose not to respond. It was not the time or the place, so I bit my lip whilst I continued, silently asking myself if he was like this with everyone, or if I was being treated as a special case because I had spilled his tea earlier that morning.

We returned to Duke Street by a different route, and I was totally lost for most of the way. For the last ten minutes we slowed right down to allow the now tired horses to slowly cool down, and as we walked along Duke Street we lengthened our reins so that they could further relax and stretch their necks. We were late back and it was after 1.15pm when we rode into the yard. I knew I was a mess. I could see the dirty spray marks on the front of the horse and my mac, so my face and head would probably be the same. We had ridden hard in excess of fifteen miles on busy roads, and I was not used to it so was completely knackered. We were met at the trough by the anxious looking civilian stableman who had obviously been waiting for us.

"Where have you been?" he asked. "I've been waiting to feed up. Bloody hell you're both in a right state. Is everything okay?"

"Just open the door," replied Bertie Rock dismissively, whilst I just nodded and smiled.

When the horses were watered we led them to their stalls, dried them down with stable towels and then layered straw on their backs before putting their day rugs on upside down. This allowed ventilation whilst they dried and prevented them from getting cold. When we were finished, all of the horses were fed and the two of us made our way, with our saddlery, into the saddle room. We hadn't spoken a word to each other since we had left Sutton Park, so I had calmed down considerably and was ready for a drink and a bite to eat. I hung my bridle on its large hook and was making my way into the bunk when the silence was broken.

"Don't leave that like that, pal! I don't know why they send us you yam yams. You're all slow in the head."

'Yam yam' is a slang name used to describe a man from the Black Country, and is mostly used by Brummies. It was a regular greeting at the time and usually used in a light hearted manner

224

during harmless two way banter. On this occasion, however, I was in no doubt that it was intended as a personal insult, and was yet another snide attempt to provoke me. It finally worked. I turned around quickly and grabbed him by the throat with my left hand. He retreated rapidly against the wall and my right fist instinctively rose to give him a punch in the face. He didn't fight back, but just looked at me with widening eyes and began to gurgle some incomprehensible response. I didn't hit him, but just held on to him with my hand raised. I was contemplating my next move when I sensed that we weren't alone in the room.

Standing behind me and quietly watching with interest was a man that I later learned was named Len Hunter. Len, a tall lean man in his fifties with grey hair was by far the oldest PC at Duke Street; he was also notoriously grumpy, and I hadn't heard him speak a word to anyone since I'd arrived that morning. I hadn't seen him and realised immediately that I was probably in deep trouble. It was my first day, I was the new bloke, and I had been caught attacking one of the regular crew; I felt that I had been severely provoked, but really it was no excuse. I was still holding on to the throat of my victim, contemplating the possible consequences of my actions, when the old guy spoke.

"Are you going to throttle him to death son, or just punch his lights out?"

"I'm sorry, I'm out of order and I was just about to loose him," I feebly replied.

"No don't, hold on to him," instructed Len as he pushed past me and landed Bertie Rock a heavy blow to the belly. I immediately loosened my grip as he slid down the wall groaning and holding his middle with both hands.

"I could have done that myself; I didn't need your help," I complained.

"It's only your first day son. You'll have to wait your turn and get in the queue," he replied as he casually made his way into the stables. "The snidey little shit," he muttered as he went out of the door.

I related the episode to Becks later that night, after we had put Mel to bed. It had been a physically hard day; I'd had a week's break from riding, and it was probably the most challenging day since Big Ben exposed my pink fluffy leg warmers to the world during that crazy morning in the riding school. I was a little saddle sore, so was in one of my very favourite places; face down on the hearth whilst Becks rubbed my tender bum with surgical spirit.

"Stef, what are you like? I'm afraid to let you out of my sight sometimes."

"I know, it sounds bad doesn't it?"

"Which bit sounds bad, Stef?" she scolded. "The bit where you introduced yourself by attacking the whole crew with your kit bag, chucking their tea all over the place, or the bit where you assaulted your partner on your first day?"

"You don't understand what a miserable lot of sods they are," I sulkily mitigated. "It was awful. I hated it. I'm sorry but I can't see me fitting in."

"So you thought it would help things along to chuck your weight around and thump everyone? How did that help?" She dug her fingers in a little too hard.

"Ouch. Steady on girl. That's my tender bum you're taking it out of," I laughed, trying to lighten the mood.

"It's not funny Stef; you promised you were going to give it a try. They won't ask you to stay if you punch everyone all of the time," she continued.

"I didn't punch anyone. It was the old guy, and I now believe there's a rota so everyone can have a go at him. You can't imagine how annoying he is Becks."

"But it's not your job to punch the class bully Stef! You're not a nasty lad or I wouldn't be here with you. Stop pretending to be nasty; it doesn't suit you, and I don't like it."

I knew I had been told off, and that she really wasn't pleased with me. There was no fun and games on the stairs that night, and our goodnight conversation in bed was short, cool, and mainly back to back. I lay there thinking about what she had said; I knew Bertie Rock was a bully, and that he had deserved a little slap, but it had been my first day and I had overstepped the mark. Others had had first days too, and they had survived, so I would have to hold my tongue and try harder to get along with the morose and miserable Duke Street crew. I had mixed feelings about tomorrow, but before I went to sleep I made a personal resolution that I would keep my head down, my hands to myself, and try a little harder to fit in.

The next day began much the same as the one before, but this time I wasn't laden down with kit on arrival and I knew where my locker was, so had no need to ask directions as I entered the bunk. I just sat quietly at the bunk table, supping my tea, and pretending to be as miserable as everyone else. As I looked around, I began to wonder if I would end up just like them if I transferred and worked here for any length of time. I was and still am a morning person, and had often been accused of being too loud on early parade when back on division. This crew, however, took the art of morning misery to another level. I made my second personal resolution in the space of twelve hours, and began to consider ways that I could cheer the place up in the morning.

At 7.15am on the dot my drifting thoughts were interrupted when everyone stood up and silently filed into the stables to begin the morning mucking out routine. It was a much better experience second time around. I certainly wasn't completely familiar with the drill, but I didn't seem to get in the way so much either, and was able to play a more useful role in the proceedings. Strangely, neither did I endure any further helpful instructions from Bertie Rock.

After mucking out I checked the board and found that my ride for the day was to be Grey Storm. Grey Storm was a living legend within the department and I had already heard several stories about him. He was Big Ben's former horse and was the horse that he had been successful with at The Horse of the Year Show, back when he was a sergeant. Storm was twenty six years old, which is old for any horse, but is a truly great age for a working police horse. He had completed twenty two years' service, all of them at Duke Street, and his length of service on the department was only exceeded by PC Len Hunter. There was a feeling amongst the men that Storm should have been retired years ago, but it was also recognised that he was completely institutionalised, and Ben Scott was loath to retire him because he was worried he would deteriorate rapidly if sent out to pasture.

I collected my grooming kit and spoke to Storm as I entered his stall.

"Morning Storm. How are you old chap?" I asked. He immediately stepped to his right allowing me to walk in along his nearside.

I quietly untied his chain and walked back out of the stall to wash it in my bucket. Storm, without encouragement, followed me and turned around in the stall to face outwards. I compared his action to that of Hertford on the previous day, and it was plain to see from the obvious stiffness and effort involved that this was a much older horse. Even so, he was still a fine looking animal. He had perfect conformation, stood tall and square, and having been recently clipped showed a subtle greyness to his skin that disguised the pure whiteness of his coat, and belied his real age.

I began grooming him and found that his manners were faultless and impeccable. He moved left or right, raised and lowered his head just as required without any verbal encouragement from me. He just knew what was wanted, when it was wanted, and did it quietly - but in a rather snooty manner. It sounds ridiculous for a horse, but Storm was definitely aloof, and even though his behaviour was exemplary, he seemed to do everything whilst looking down his nose at me, which I found a little unnerving. I noticed that his skin lacked the elasticity of the younger horses, but completed grooming him without incident and was satisfied with the result. The final indication to his real age was an involuntary twitch which caused his lower lip to constantly flap. Grey Storm was indeed a very old chap.

I rode out that morning at 10am escorted by PC Len Hunter, who hadn't acknowledged or spoken to me since he had floored Bertie Rock whilst I shook him by the throat, the previous day. I didn't feel particularly offended, because I hadn't seen or heard him talk to anyone else during the morning either. I had been forewarned that he probably wouldn't acknowledge my presence while we were out on patrol together, but that I was to stay close because he was presently street training a new young horse. My understanding of the situation was that he would look after me because I was new and only partially trained, and I would reciprocate because his horse was only partially trained too. I never knew Len's view of the situation, because not only did he not speak to me, I don't think he had noticed I was there.

Len's young horse, which was known within the department as a 'remount'[9], was a large impressive-looking dapple grey named Jackson. Unlike the previous day with Bertie Rock, I knew exactly where we were going, what we were doing, and when we were going to do it, because although he completely ignored me, Len constantly told Jackson, and I sneakily listened in.

The whole morning was much quieter and calmer than the day before, and I watched with interest, and a growing respect, whilst this apparently miserable old man, who had hardly acknowledged any of his colleagues for two whole days, encouraged a young and inexperienced horse around the busy streets of central Birmingham. He told him when we were going to trot and when we were going to walk, when we were going to turn left and when we were going to turn right. He cooed, clicked, and encouraged him past street nuisances, and patted and praised him when he had successfully negotiated them. He allowed him to pause and inspect unusual sights, but legged him forward when appropriate - and all in a calm, fuss free and encouraging manner. It was an education, and though I was fully aware that it was not for my benefit, I was left under no illusion as to the yawning gap that still remained between what I had so far learned and what lay ahead of me, should I be given the opportunity to stick around any longer.

Storm, in the meantime, performed like a robot. He never moved from the young horse's side, stopping when he did and moving forward in harmony too. He was unflinching, and had, of course, seen it all before, time and time again. Looking at Storm it occurred to me he was actually older than I was, and had been a serving police horse since I was only a year old.

[9] A remount was a newly purchased horse. Usually previously ridden, but requiring further training before being suitable for police duties.

The proud old horse had certainly seen some changes in his time, and significantly, a fair few riders too. It was, however, becoming increasingly obvious to me that I was having very little influence on his actions - I was pretty much just a passenger sitting aboard an automated horse.

Towards the end of the patrol Storm began to jig jog with his hind legs. It wasn't a gait we had covered during our theory lessons at Tally Ho, and he wasn't moving any faster than Jackson, but he was definitely still walking with his front legs whilst slowly trotting with the hind legs. It became uncomfortable and irritating to sit into the saddle, but any feeling on the reins, in an effort to check him back into a proper walk, had no effect at all. Storm had 'no mouth'; he had been ridden by so many riders over so many years, that he had long ago lost any feeling and sensitivity in his ageing, long-toothed mouth. His head remained in a perfect position, his speed and dressing with Jackson remained exactly the same, but for the first time since mounting him that morning, it occurred to me that any signals I gave with the reins had absolutely no effect whatsoever. Storm was in charge; Storm was on autopilot.

My silent efforts had not escaped the attention of Len, who for the first time since we left Duke Street, began to pay me some attention.

"Get a hold of that old screw. Don't let him piss off with you. Remember you're escorting a remount," he said in a low voice.

I had no idea what he was worrying about. The rickety old horse was twenty six years old – geriatric! - hadn't put a foot wrong all day, and certainly wasn't about to take off with me.

We passed the woeful barks and howls emanating from Birmingham Dog's Home in New Canal Street, and as we reached the derelict frontage of the old Curzon Street railway station the jig jogging began to intensify. I had no idea where we were in relation to Duke Street, but looking at my watch, felt sure we were nearly back at the stables. The road ahead began to rise in the direction of a busy dual carriageway which ran left to right across our path, and as soon as we reached the foot of the incline, and without any sign or fair warning, Storm took off! In no time at all we were galloping up the hill towards the dual carriageway. He certainly couldn't match the speed I had reached the day before riding a much younger horse in snowy Sutton Park, but the main road was still approaching far too fast. My considerable hauling on the reins had no effect what so ever.

"Whoa Storm! Whoa Storm! WOO-OOO-OOOOOAH STORM! WOO-OOO-OOOOAH YOU BASTARD STORM!" I heard myself howl.

By this time I was leaning fully back into the saddle and pulling, in vain, with all of my weight on the reins. Storm thundered up the hill, - showing no signs of any intention to stop at the end of the road. The brakes had well and truly failed, so my only remaining hope was the steering. Still leaning back, I pulled with all of my might on the right rein in a final attempt to steer him away from the looming danger ahead. The steering failed too.

"WHOOA! WHOOA! BLOODY HELL WHOOA...! JEEEEE-WOOH-ZUZZZZ!" I frantically screamed as Storm reached the end of the road, clattered across the pavement and grass verge, and finally hurtled across the full width of the dual carriageway and central reservation at his fastest gallop. How close we were to the approaching traffic I didn't know, because my eyes were firmly closed as I braced for the inevitable crash.

I slowly opened my eyes. I was relieved to see we had safely cleared the dual carriageway, and were now in a quiet side road out of immediate danger. Storm, with no further signal from me, slowed down to the walk before calmly halting at the side of the road. My anxiety levels began to gradually subside, and my heart rate began to lower as Storm continued to stand square and perfectly still, as cool as a cucumber, and as if nothing out of the ordinary had happened. As I looked around I could see Len Hunter and Jackson behind, calmly walking across the dual carriageway in our direction. As they got closer I could see him patting and hear him talking quietly to reassure his horse.

"Good laaad Jacko, good laaaad. Well done Jacko, well done."

As they drew level with us, Storm quietly walked forward and carried on alongside of them, and it finally dawned on me that we were actually in Duke Street. He had been waiting for them to catch up before we continued into the stable yard.

Len Hunter never spoke to me, looked at me, acknowledged me, nor mentioned the incident as we watered our horses at the trough, and as far as I'm aware neither was it ever reported to anyone else.

Inside the stables I moodily removed Storm's saddlery, fitted his day rug, and walked to the front of the stall to short rack him before feeding. I took a long hard look at him as he stood motionless, tall and square.

"What did you do that for, you crazy old bastard? You could have killed us both," I whispered angrily.

Aloof as ever; I thought for a moment he winked at me, but it may have been just a raised eyebrow; whatever it was, it had an air of superiority about it and I had no doubt it was meant to put me in my place.

"You can wink all you like mate, but you're still just a horse, an old horse, and if you were human you'd be in old folks' home."

As I walked out of the stall he relaxed, lowered his head, and to confirm my opinion, began to noisily flap his bottom lip.

Back in the bunk I was pleasantly surprised to see Paul Garrett, who was busily changing into uniform and preparing to go out on afternoon patrol. He was working the later 10am until 6pm shift, and I hadn't seen him since the final day of our riding course at Tally Ho. He told me he had spent the previous week at Duke Street and that he too had initially found everyone to be as miserable as I had. He explained that it got much better though, and that I had been unlucky to be paired with the two most difficult personalities for my first two days.

"How did you get on with old Storm today Stef?" he asked.

"Don't tell anyone, but he's just pissed off with me," I whispered after checking there was no one in earshot, "straight across a main road. I've never been so bloody terrified in my life."

"You got away lightly mate," he whispered whilst getting closer, "because he took off with me last week down Washwood Heath Road, and it took me a quarter of a mile to stop him. We did two sets of red traffic lights. I thought I was a dead man, twice."

"Why does he do it? And where does the old crock get his energy from?" I asked. "It's a wonder that he doesn't have a bloody heart attack."

"The blokes reckon he's well and truly senile, and that Big Ben suffers from sympathy symptoms."

We had a quiet laugh together, both feeling better knowing we were in the same boat and that our early experiences weren't unique. I went home at the end of my second day in a lighter mood than the day before, and had nothing negative to report back to Becks apart from that I had almost been killed whilst galloping out of control across a busy road on a rickety geriatric horse. I was still in a conundrum regarding my future and had a lot of plusses and minuses to weigh up before I could hope to make a final decision; if, indeed, the final decision was to be made by me. I still had three months of my attachment ahead of me, and if the first two days were anything to go by, they were going to be interesting.

CHAPTER 16

THE OUTSTATIONS

In 1979, mounted branch life extended beyond Duke Street and Tally Ho; it would be some years until the opening of large new central stables at Aston Cross, so in the meantime there were horses and men dispersed around the force area and working from a collection of small out stations. The stables at Bordesley Green Police Station and Thornhill Road Handsworth were Victorian buildings, which predated the formation of the mounted branch, originally housing horses that drew police vehicles in the days before the motorcar.

An outstation usually housed three horses and was manned by a complement of four officers. The fourth man of the team was often a newly trained officer, yet to be allocated his own horse, who rode all of the horses on the rest days of their regular riders. It was this spare man role that made up a large proportion of the working life of the 'attached man', and was the reason that for the duration of my attachment all of my kit and uniform was kept in the back of my car, and not in a permanent locker.

Outstation life was very different to that at Duke Street. There were no sergeants or senior officers to supervise the daily routine, so the majority of officers working at the outstations did so because they were happy to escape the politics of the hub, and were also regarded by the bosses as steady, trustworthy and capable of working without close supervision. Hancock and Scott would randomly visit the outstations once or twice a week and sign the desk diary that recorded the daily routine. If the horses were out on patrol at the appropriate time, and the stables and bunk were kept clean, tidy, and dust free, life at an outstation could be cosy and stress free. If, however, Big Ben arrived unexpectedly and caught you going out late, found dust on a surface, or even more seriously, dull unpolished brasses, there would be trouble.

Trouble could take on several forms, but usually involved daily angry visits and the close inspection of horses, kit, and every inch of the building. He would forensically scrutinise every surface for dust by running his finger along the stalls, mangers and even door tops in an effort to pick fault. Big Ben could be a 'right pain' with his punitive inspections, and they came to be known as 'being in Ben's barrel', which was inescapable until a more recent miscreant was chosen to replace you. So to ensure a quiet life, it paid to keep the place routinely clean and tidy.

Back in the day, their pre-occupation with dust in the stables seemed to be just another petty rule made by two overzealous and out-dated officers to make everyone's day a little more difficult. It has since been scientifically proven, however, that airborne respirable stable dust contains pollen, mould spores, bacteria and plant fragments. A stable is not a natural environment for a horse and it is now commonly accepted that dust in stables can cause serious and long term respiratory disease, meaning modern professional stable management practice is now similar to what we were doing forty years ago. Perhaps, in hindsight, they weren't the old fools we all thought them to be?

I was often posted to Ladywood stable, which was tucked away in the back yard of Ladywood Police Station. It was the smallest of all of the outstations, consisting of only three stalls and a small bunk with two chairs and a desk for the men. Ladywood is a poor, heavily populated suburb of Birmingham located on the very edge of the city centre. Just across the Hagley Road however, a few minutes to the south of Ladywood, is leafy Edgbaston, which meant that the riding school at Tally Ho was only half an hour's ride away. In stark contrast to Ladywood, the route to the riding school passed pleasantly through some of the leafiest and most opulent streets in the city, and because of its close proximity to the riding school, when posted to early shift the Ladywood officers would regularly be used to assist with leading file in the school for the Tally Ho riding courses. These regular visits to the riding school gave me plenty of opportunity to further develop my riding skills during the course of my attachment. Taking part in the riding school was a good measure of the progress I had made in a relatively short time; riding in uniform and taking leading file seemed to be much easier than our struggles of a few weeks earlier. It was a good feeling to be in uniform, leading from the front and lording it over the new lads as they hit the dust, as I had often done myself only a few weeks earlier.

The largest of the outstations, and the only stable located within the Black Country and outside of the Birmingham area, was West Bromwich. It was still very much Dai Owens' domain, and even five years after the amalgamation of the forces, West Bromwich still stubbornly operated slightly differently to the other stables. It was more modern having only been built in the early 1970s, and comprised of four large loose boxes where the horses could freely move around and be left with water in buckets throughout the night. The priorities were different too, and it was immediately apparent that the levels of spit and polish found at the other stables were not so evident at West Bromwich. In some ways, however, it was by design more efficient. For example, the forage loft was located directly above the loose boxes so that all hay and straw could be dropped through trap doors, straight into individual boxes thus avoiding the need to sweep the yard several times a day. The whole working environment was without doubt far more laid-back than that at Duke Street.

On the morning of my first posting to West Bromwich I found myself sitting with Jim Hardwick and an older guy drinking our first cup of tea of the day. Whilst I had spent a lot of my time at Duke Street, Jim had spent most of his at West Bromwich, and having now settled in had already shown me where to unload my considerable pile of kit. In contrast to my first day at Duke Street, my arrival had been friendly and welcoming. Shortly before 7.15am, however, a loud banging noise began in the yard, and continued non-stop, increasing in volume, reminding me of the noise made by a team of police flattening a front door during an early morning raid.

"What the hell is that?" I asked, nearly jumping out of my skin.

"That's just Cuthbert sounding the breakfast gong," laughed the older man. "He's a minute early today. His watch must be fast."

We all got up together and walked into the yard, where looking over, and kicking the bulging door of the nearest loose box was a large, hog-maned, chestnut horse. It had probably the biggest head I had seen on a horse since the start of my riding course, and was certainly the ugliest. Most of the face of was covered with a large white blaze which framed a bright pink nose and muzzle. The horse was still furiously kicking the door as we walked into the forage room to collect our forks for mucking out. I was surprised when the other two passed the tools and began to fill buckets from the feed bins.

"Aren't we going to muck out first?"

"No, feed up first here. We muck out while they're feeding," answered Jim.

I was surprised, but quietly complied as we fed the four horses together before collecting our tools to begin the mucking out. I went into the second loose box and began to separate the clean and dry from the wet and soiled, whilst piling the clean at the back of the box and the dirty by the door. I had never mucked out around a feeding horse before, but the animal was too engrossed with his breakfast to pay me any attention. The loose box was big, and held a lot more bedding than was to be found in a Duke Street stall, but I soon found myself happily swinging my fork to the rhythm of a deep, smooth, crooning voice emanating from the first loose box.

"Send me the pillow that you dream on... git up son... Don't you know that I still care for you.. ooooh... gerover son... good lad. Send me the pillow that you dream on... oy up, that's it, good lad. So darling I can dream on it too, oooooh!"

"How are you getting on Stef?"

I looked up and saw Jim standing in the doorway, waiting to load my dirty bedding into the large wheel barrow.

"I was enjoying being serenaded," I laughed, "I'm finding it very soothing to be honest."

"Don't worry it's not for you, he does it for Cuthbert. He likes a song in the morning. It puts him in a good mood."

"Each night while I'm sleeping oh, sooooo lonely... good lad - I'll share your love in dreams that once were true... oooooh."

"Well, I don't think I've heard that anywhere else! Does it really work?" I asked.

"That's Cyril Riley. Cyril and Cuthbert have been together for fifteen years. The bugger bites everyone else, but never Cyril, and he reckons that it's because of the singing."

"Send me the pillow that you dream on… So darling I can dream on it tooooooooooo!"

Then the singing stopped, as Cyril left Cuthbert to his breakfast and joined us in the yard.

"You two got nothing to do apart from gossip? Have I got to do all the work?" he asked, whilst still smiling.

"Jim's just been telling me about how you sing to Cuthbert every morning. Does it really work?"

"Music calms the savage beast. Everyone knows that. Cuthbert never bites me so figure it out for yourself," he replied with obvious sincerity.

"I'm not sure Cyril," said Jim. "It may have more to do with the fact that you've always finished mucking out before he's finished eating."

"Have it your own way; you young blokes know everything. What do I know? What do I know?" answered Cyril before moving on to the last box.

We continued with the mucking out but unfortunately without any further serenading.

Cyril Riley was a proper Black Country bloke. He had completed his national service with the Household Cavalry, before joining Wolverhampton Borough Police in the late 1950s. He was now approaching the end of his police career, and had few remaining ambitions other than to see his time out quietly and retire, hopefully, at the same time as Cuthbert. He had a dry, droll sense of humour, and despite appearing cynical and disinterested, was actually a really nice guy who would quietly offer help and advice if asked, but never would do so unsolicited.

Cyril's other main responsibility, other than looking after Cuthbert, was to daily 'rinkatink' the stable cat. The stable cat, Sam, was a tabby that lived at night between the loft and forage room, where his reputation as a mouser was legendary. He moved stealthily between the floors by way of a ten foot high iron ladder fastened to the wall, and I never ceased to be impressed watching him slink sure-footedly up and down, between the narrow metal rungs. Sam spent many of his daylight hours sleeping in his basket in the bunk, where, with the occasional blink, he quietly watched his two legged colleagues go about their daily routine. It was during my first morning, while the three of us sat in easy chairs finishing our breakfast after grooming that the unusual ritual, which could have only been improved with a David Attenborough commentary, began.

Cyril's low baritone voice said, "Prup Sam!"

The cat lifted its head and opened one eye.

"Have waaaaarn?"

Sam's eyes opened a little wider but he didn't move from his basket.

"Have waaaaaaaarn?"

The cat slowly got up, paused, and stretched before slowly walking across the room to Cyril, where he circled and rubbed himself against Cyril's legs with his tail held high and vertical. The 'Have waaaaaarn' chant was repeated several more times during the circling ritual before Cyril finally reached down and picked Sam up, holding him upside down with his back against his lower legs. When the correct position was attained and the cat appeared to be ready, Cyril began to furiously rub the animal's belly in perfect time with another verse of the chant.

"Oh - rinka-tinka-tinka, rinka-tinka-tinka, rinka-tinka-tinka-tooooooo!"

Sam, still motionless and upside down, seemed to have fallen into an ecstatic trance.

"Oh - rinka-tinka-tinka, rinka-tinka-tinka, rinka-tinka-tinka-toooooooo!"

Unlike the beginning, the finale of the performance came suddenly, when Cyril put him down on the floor, patted his sides and sat back down in his easy chair. Sam walked slowly and giddily across the room, his tail still raised, before sitting down on the carpet to calmly groom himself. The 'rinkatinking' ritual was performed twice a day, once after breakfast and again after riding, but only ever by Cyril. I saw others try, but offers to 'Have waaaaaaarn' from anyone else were generally declined; Sam would steadfastly refuse to leave his basket, happy to wait for the next time Cyril was on duty.

West Bromwich, with its alternative routines, easy chairs and laidback practices, truly was a different world to that of Duke Street. The cat in the basket under the table added to the ambience, helping to create a warm and homely atmosphere. I have referred to Sam throughout as he or him because he was without doubt part of the team and one of the lads. However, a few years later, Sam was unusually out of sorts and McDougal the vet was called to examine him. Fortunately he recovered well after a feline hysterectomy. The revelation that Sam -, stable cat, good bloke, and one of the men - was in fact Samantha, created shock waves throughout the bunk. No one had suspected and after a while no one really cared, because whether boy or girl,

Sam was still Sam and still 'rinkatinked' twice daily - but only ever by Cyril.

Sometime later I was again posted to early shift at West Bromwich, and because Cyril wasn't on duty until 10am, found myself mucking out Cuthbert for the first time. I knew of the animal's reputation and didn't want to be bitten, so I decided to follow Cyril's lead and serenade Cuthbert whilst he enjoyed his breakfast. I rapidly set about separating the bedding, and at the same time sang my tuneless heart out. Cuthbert stood with his head buried in the manger, whilst I hurried in the hope that I could complete my work and be out of the box before he finished his breakfast, just like Cyril always was. I would have liked to have tied him up while mucking out, but he wasn't wearing a head collar because Dai Owen insisted that the horses only wore head collars during the day, after they had been groomed. If I had collected his head collar and fastened him up just to muck out, it would have been noticed and I would have been regarded as a chicken, so I conformed with the confidence of a man pretending to know what he was doing. Besides, this big, lumbering, ugly old chap was a pussy cat when compared to the evil Bijou.

I had mucked out half of the box without incident, and was left with just the area beneath and around Cuthbert, so I bent below his head and moved to his other side, squeezing between horse and wall, before pushing against his side to move him over.

"Come on son, over you go," I said, momentarily breaking from my song.

He never lifted his head out of his manger, but kicked out, sending his near hind hoof crashing against and shaking the back wall. I almost jumped out of my skin! I was never in any real danger, because I was still standing by his shoulder, and was confident the kick was more of a protest than an attack. The black and white painted bricks of the wall behind him were badly marked and chipped about four feet from the floor, confirming that this warning shot was something of a regular occurrence. I had mastered Cuthbert - he was a bit of a fraud, and his threats were all bluff and bluster.

"Enough! Enough! Get over now!" I responded positively, giving him another firm shove.

This time the big old horse moved away, pivoting on his front legs whilst still eating from the manger, allowing me to complete the mucking out. I was victorious, almost finished, had forgotten all of my fears, and still lost in song at the far end of the box, when I sensed hot smelly breath on the back of my neck. I carefully turned around and found myself face to face with a huge pink nose and the smell of masticated horse feed. His ears were flattened back, his teeth were bared, and he was now between me and the door. I had no idea how he had been able to turn around from his manger and creep up on me without me hearing him, but being far more confident than I had been in my early days with Bijou at Tally Ho, I just quietly pushed his head aside and walked towards the door. I calmly reached for the bolt to let myself out and was smugly complimenting myself on a job well done when I was stunned by a vice like grip and excruciating pain in my ribs just below my left armpit.

"JEEEEEEEEEEEE... AAAGHHH... ZUUUUZ!" I cried.

I staggered out into the yard to find Dai Owen exiting his office to see what the noise was about.

"Shush. What's the matter with you?"

"That bloody big ugly bastard has bitten me," I snapped back.

"Quieten down. You'll scare the horses. What do you blokes do to them? Always a drama; always a fuss."

I couldn't see the damage but the sergeant confirmed the skin was broken, so after mucking out was finished I drove myself to Sandwell General Hospital. I was painfully injected in my rear end for tetanus, and sent back to work.

Just before 10am, while getting dressed for riding and feeling very sore, I was looking in the mirror and inspecting a huge bruise that was growing by the minute below my left armpit; over the next few days it would balloon to the size of a large dinner plate, but it was still in the early stages of development when Cyril walked in the door.

"Bloody hell son. That's gonna be a good 'un! How did it happen?" he asked.

"Your shit of a horse bit me while I was mucking out!"

"Why would he do that?"

"You bloody tell me; he's your horse," I snapped.

"Did you sing to him?"

"Yes, I did sing to him, and a fat lot of good it did too!"

"What did you sing?" he calmly asked.

"What?"

"What did you sing?"

"I think it was Ob-La-Di, Ob-La-Da, or something like," I replied.

"Ah. That's why he bit you then," he nodded knowingly.

"Why did he bite me Cyril? Please tell me."

"Because he can't stand the Beatles at any time, and he expects a bit of Jim Reeves on Wednesdays."

I have no idea if Cuthbert really did enjoy Cyril's crooning, or even if he was genuinely offended at my poor attempt at a popular Beatles number. I have my doubts, but have to confess that I did take the trouble of learning a few country and western numbers, and that I often used them when mucking out in the future. I'm not sure if it is significant, but Cuthbert never did bite me again.

Except when a special commitment demanded the horses were generally rested on Sundays. Apart from mucking out, bedding down and feeding, Sunday was a day spent catching up on cleaning and the servicing of tools and personal equipment. It was traditionally a quiet day, and was also a rest day for half of the department. On Sunday afternoons only two men worked at Duke Street, with the remainder of the department finishing at lunchtime. At the outstations one officer would return to work at around 5pm to feed the horses. This return to duty was known as 'Water and feed', and as well as the obvious, involved checking on the horses' health, straightening rugs, and de-littering the stables. When the task was complete a call was made to Duke Street to confirm all was well, before they went off duty and left the horses alone again for the night.

My first Sunday 'Water and feed' duty was carried out at Ladywood stables, and inevitably, because of the novelty of the occasion, became an exciting family afternoon outing. With Becks and Mel in tow my five minute task developed into a half hour entertainment session. I turned the horses around one at a time, to be patted and fussed by my girls whilst I de-littered the backs of the stalls. Police horses, because of their sheer size, can be very intimidating to the inexperienced, and it was interesting to see that Mel was the bolder of the two despite standing only a little above their knee height. She was completely unfazed, and happy to feed them polo mints from the flat of her hand. She thought it was hilarious when one took her bobble hat from her head and held it swinging out of reach, and then happily sat astride them when I lifted her up, displaying far less fear and uncertainty than I had when I'd mounted on my first day.

I did countless more 'Water and Feeds' after that day and invariably had my daughter at my side to help. She had been captivated by the horses on that first occasion and her interest never wavered. Learning to ride at a very early age she progressed rapidly, through a succession of ponies, winning rosettes for gymkhana and show jumping at a variety of local shows. She was a natural and became a talented rider, only giving up her horses when she left home to go to university. Mel's riding became a big part of our lives, and we made lifelong friendships with many like-minded people, but if I could have foreseen the future financial sacrifices it was to cause, I may have been tempted to leave her at home when I did that first 'Water and Feed' at Ladywood.

Rotating around the outstations was a large part of the life of an attached mounted man. It was a nomadic existence but was also a good grounding, ensuring that skill levels were developed by the opportunity to ride a wide variety of horses. The easy atmosphere away from the rigid routine of Duke Street appealed to many, and some of the men were happy to hide away out of the spotlight. To others, who had ambitions to compete at shows and become part of the display teams, it was essential to be seen, and to be seen you had to be at Duke Street. It was down to ambition and personal choice, but as a mere attached man with no guarantee of a permanent position, it was, at the time, no concern of mine.

CHAPTER 17

TEARS OF LAUGHTER, TEARS OF SORROW

My faithful Mini had returned me and my bulky load of kit to Duke Street for a few days, where the current riding course at Tally Ho was the hot topic of afternoon tack room debates. Rumour travelled around the department at remarkable speed, even though man power was spread thinly around so many stables. Today, two of the men from Duke Street had ridden to Tally Ho to lead the recruits around the riding school, and had returned with more tales to add to the ones already circulating around the department.

All of the talk focussed on one of the new trainees, who was ex-forces, older than the others, and obviously struggling to cope with the riding. I hadn't personally seen any of the present recruits, and still clearly remembered my own recent struggles in the school, so chose to listen intently without adding any comment.

"He's all over the place. You've got to see it to believe it," reported one of the morning's eye witnesses.

"He can't be as bad as everyone says, surely?"

"Worse, much worse mate. Words can't describe it. He rides like a circus acrobat."

"Circus acrobats are bloody good riders, aren't they?" someone pointed out.

"Not the clowns, who keep falling off!" This provoked a roar of laughter in the room.

"He was on the floor more than on his horse," added another, "and he's as old as God's dog."

"That's nearly as old as Len Hunter isn't it?"

"Shut your face you cheeky little shit," growled the previously silent Len from the back of the room.

"You've seen him haven't you Len? What did you think?"

"Sod all to do with me," muttered Len. "Who cares what I think?"

"Come on you grumpy old sod; you must have an opinion."

"Well, if he is ex-army… thank God we've got a navy." This typical pearl of Len Hunter's wisdom reduced the room to further laughter.

Lively discussion and laughter continued in the same vein until all of the kits were finally cleaned and hung on the pegs. I hadn't added anything because I didn't want to leave myself open to any comment or comparison regarding my own limited abilities, but I was quietly looking forward to a morning at Tally Ho so I could witness the spectacle myself.

A few days later I was back at Ladywood; there were two of us on earlies, and we hurried through the mucking out and grooming so we could ride to Tally Ho to assist in the riding school. I was pleasantly surprised to find myself riding my old favourite Grenadier, who had only recently been rested from riding school duties. Following an early breakfast for both us and the horses, a brisk ride through Edgbaston's pleasant leafy streets brought us to Tally Ho shortly after 10am.

We discarded our swordsticks, chains, and macs before standing quietly side by side in the entrance passage, from where, sitting on our horses, we could see over the tall door and into the riding school. Inside the three trainees were walking around the perimeter while the familiar tones of Derek Joiner corrected and adjusted their riding positions.

"Catch up Rogers. Four feet, four feet."

"Hands down Lyons. Head up. Don't slouch man."

"Merryweather you're listing to port again man. Don't you dare fall off again Merryweather, we haven't even started yet!" he said, with what sounded like an element of despair. He finally noticed us waiting at the door.

"Good morning gentlemen, please, do come in. Let's see if we can breathe some life into this dozy lot."

Without dismounting we pushed open the heavy door and rode into the school, where my colleague took up leading file and I took up the rear. I could tell immediately that the hot topic of Duke Street bunk was riding directly in front of me. He was obviously much older than the other trainees, was stick thin and hunched forward precariously over the front of the saddle. Every movement he made was in complete contrast to the motion of the horse, and I immediately sympathised. I don't think I had ever seen anyone look quite so unnatural on horseback.

"Whole ride prepare to trot. Whole ride quietly away, terrrott!"

The horses moved away together into the trot and the entertainment truly began. The height of his bounce was enormous, and every time he came heavily back down, the horse came up, colliding with his meagre buttocks and launching him back into the air to ever increasing altitude. As the ride reached the end of the school and followed the track around to the left, he gradually slid sideways and began to lean to the left. I was mesmerised - he moved ever lower, and I began to wonder what angle he would be able to reach before he actually fell out of the saddle. As the ride reached the long straight along the side of the school he gradually raised himself to a more vertical position before sliding sideways again on reaching the next bend.

"Sit up Merryweather. Sit up man. You're not riding a motorbike, there's no need to bank around the corners!" shouted Joiner with more than a hint of desperation.

After a couple of laps we changed the rein by riding across the diagonal, and my curiosity was answered when I saw that he leaned out the other way, equally precariously, on the right-hand bends. The bounce never improved; there was constant daylight between his backside and the saddle, and there was little sign at all that he may eventually settle into a more comfortable rhythm.

"Whole ride right turn!"

I turned my horse to cross the school, looked across to my left to check I was in line with the rest of the ride, and immediately noticed the horse alongside was rider less.

"Whole ride halt! Merryweather, what are you doing down there again?"

I stopped alongside everyone else, looked behind, and saw the crumpled shape of someone lying on the ground against the wooden sidewall of the school.

"Merryweather, get up man. We'll never progress if you keep throwing yourself into the shit every time we make a turn. Get up man!"

The man got to his feet, dusted himself down, straightened his cap and quietly walked back to his horse. He was a mixed picture, because there was evidence of a well-polished pair of boots, but they were well disguised beneath a heavy layer of riding school dust, suggesting this was not the first time he had fallen today. He quietly remounted, took up the reins, and looked enquiringly along the line as if there had been some other reason for the delay.

"Whole ride walk march! Turn left at the end leading file. Let's try again."

We turned left back on to the track and following the next order, resumed trotting around the school.

"Sit up Merryweather! Don't slouch man! You look like you've been attacked by Apaches and have arrows sticking out of your back."

Riding behind, I was still mesmerised by his riding position. He was obviously awful, but I doubted if I would be able to attain the angle of his almost permanent lean without falling off. His bounce out of the saddle seemed to get higher, and I winced at the thought of the discomfort he must have been suffering at every stride of the horse. I admired his tenacity and shared his pain as I recalled my own nights on the hearth with Becks and the sting of the surgical spirit.

"Whole ride right turn!"

We turned in unison to the right and I heard a now familiar thud as Merryweather hit the deck again.

"Whole ride halt," groaned the now despondent Joiner. "Merryweather get up. No one told you to dismount. Get back on your horse."

Once again, he slowly got back onto his feet whilst dusting the ever thickening layer of muck and shavings from his jacket, before eventually remounting. He took up his reins, straightened himself in the saddle and looked straight ahead awaiting the order to carry on. I tried to judge his mood; he didn't appear dispirited or broken, in fact he didn't appear to appreciate that he was the cause of the delay or in any way different to the other trainees. I had taken my share of falls on my course just a few weeks earlier, but nothing like on this scale. Some had been minor, others had knocked the wind out of my lungs and rattled every bone in my body, but they were all infrequent enough to be memorable. For PC Merryweather, hardly a lap was completed without hitting the deck.

The ride resumed, and having changed the rein we were riding around in the opposite direction, with me now at leading file. Sometimes it is hard work maintaining a steady regular pace at leading file, because horses are naturally herd animals and many prefer to follow instead of lead, but big Garth was always happy to lead so it wasn't difficult. I kept up a brisk and steady pace and after a couple of laps Joiner gave the order for the rear file to trot past the others and take the lead. I was well versed with this exercise having practised it many times on my own riding course. It could be easy, it could also be very hard work - it really depended on the horse you were riding. Sailing past the line of other horses on a willing, forward going horse could be enjoyable, whereas furiously peddling a reluctant nag until your legs were fit to burst was no fun at all.

The original leading file, who was now at the rear, eventually appeared alongside of me. He was sitting into the saddle, looking ahead, and effortlessly overtook me to take the lead position.

"Well done, keep up the pace. Next one; trot on and take the lead!" ordered the voice from the centre.

One after another and evenly timed, the next three riders successfully rode their horses from the back of the line, past me and the other trotting horses to take up the lead. The whole ride had kept dressing, pace, and order throughout the exercise. Maintaining my position and looking forward I had watched everyone ride past me and take up leading file, so I knew there was only one left to go, and I also knew who it was.

"Okay Merryweather; hold tight, in your own time take up leading file!"

He was right behind me, but there was no sign of any movement coming up the side of me.

"Come on Merryweather take up leading file!"

Again there was no sign of activity to my right, but Garth began to feel a little agitated and move too close to the horse in front. The dressing distance in single file order is four feet nose to croup[10], and riding any closer to the horse in front runs the risk of injury from the hooves. I increased my feel on the reins to resume our proper position, but had become aware of unusual activity from behind.

"Don't you trample that horse in front Merryweather," called Joiner. That explained Garth's desire to distance himself from the following horse. "It's no good just legging that horse Merryweather; you have to steer him around."

We rode on, but there was still no sign of the rear file appearing on my right.

"Don't trample that horse Merryweather! Steer around! Are you listening to me Merryweather?"

There was no verbal response from behind, but I could tell that all was not well.

"Merryweather will you bloody well listen to me? Sit still; stop flailing your arms around! Steer that horse! Apply a little left leg and feel the right rein!"

I could hear the commotion from behind but could still see nothing.

"Merryweather listen to me! Merryweather; oh shit! What the hell! Jeezuz! Merryweather what the hell are you doing man?"

---

[10] *The area between the top line of a horse's hindquarters and the dock of the tail.*

The flurry from behind continued and finally, out of the corner of my eye, I began to see the shape of a horse come into view on my right. I kept looking dead ahead, kept the pace, and kept my dressing.

"Merryweather hold tight! Do not fall... What the bloody hell? For God's sake what the...? Hold tight Merryweather!"

The rear horse was now right alongside me. I could resist no longer and looked to my right. At first I thought my eyes were deceiving me, but no - I was in fact witnessing a feat of riding that rivalled any daredevil display I had ever seen on TV in the annual Christmas Circus.

"Merryweather! You raving maniac! Stop that horse before you kill yourself!"

The horse continued to trot past at a rapid pace, wild eyed, spurred on ever faster by the flapping reins and stirrups that were banging against its sides. The saddle was vacant, and Merryweather was still on board - but only just.

PC Merryweather and his steed were definitely now seeing eye-to-eye. Literally. He was looking directly into his horse's face, his arms wrapped around the horse's neck and his legs similarly wrapped around further down. How he'd got into such a precarious position I will never know, but he hung grimly upside down, beneath the frightened horse's neck. His eyes were firmly closed as he overtook me.

"Woah! You can stop now! Merryweather! Listen to me, Merryweather. WOAH!" cried the sergeant in vain.

The confused horse carried on hurtling around and around, faster and faster until he finally broke into the canter. This only increased Merryweather's problems as his skinny rear end was severely pounded by every step of the horse's front legs. Eventually the leading file took the initiative and brought the ride to a halt, watching stricken as the wall of death display team continued thundering crazily around the perimeter of the school.

"Merryweather will you stop that bloody horse!"

"M-E-R-R-Y-W-E-A-T-H-E-R!"

It was the horse, however, that finally came to its senses, listened to the furious sergeant's orders and bought the situation under control; it just ran out of steam, turned into the centre of the school and screeched to a shuddering halt. As the horse stood breathing heavily, Merryweather just hung there, eyes firmly closed and looking uncannily like a waking sloth desperately clinging to the branch of a shaking tropical tree. There was a pause before the sergeant broke the silence:

"Merryweather you have now safely landed at Tally Ho. You can come down now; please have your passport ready and return to terra firma."

There was a round of roaring laughter, followed by a further pregnant pause while we watched with bated breath, waiting for him to release his grip with his legs, stand on the ground and finally put an end to his hell ride. Merryweather, however, never one to follow the crowd, had other ideas and inexplicably chose to let go with his arms while maintaining a firm grip with his legs. With a shocking lack of dignity, his head and shoulders unceremoniously crashed to the ground with a worrying thud, before being followed by the lower half of his body. There was an audible gasp around the school, as he lay flat on his back, motionless. The silence was only broken when the confused and flustered horse lowered its head and snorted into Merryweather's face. The sudden blast of spray shocked him back to consciousness, and to add insult to injury also blew the cap, that had so far been so firmly attached, from his head.

Everyone burst into uncontrollable laughter. I had only recently completed my own riding course, and during that nine weeks had witnessed some real drama, but nothing had been as funny as the exhibition of sheer slapstick we had all just witnessed. Where had this bloke been when Billy Smart[11] was recruiting clowns?

Right on cue, and to the relief of everyone, the doors opened and Steve Durran came in with a tray of mugs; we all dismounted and stood holding our horses, chatting and drinking tea. No comment was made about the drama of the previous half hour and Jack Merryweather quietly joined in with the conversation. He seemed unperturbed, as if nothing at all had happened, and if he didn't look as if he had just climbed out of the shit pit, no one would have been any the wiser.

Jack Merryweather, without doubt, had an appalling seat[12], which is why he constantly fell off of his horse. In addition, his lack of balance, bizarre ever-changing position in the saddle and spasmodic hands sent a stream of conflicting signals to the horse, which resulted in confusion, panic and erratic behaviour. Consequently, it was often impossible to predict what calamity would happen next.

After the break Steve Durran carried poles into the school and, under the sergeant's direction, arranged them on the ground along the centre of the school. Ground poles are often used in the training of both horses and riders.

---

[11] *Billy Smart's Circus was reputed to be the world's biggest circus for a large part of the 20th century.*

[12] *A rider with a good seat has the ability to be able to sit on a horse in a relaxed, well balanced and secure manner. It allows the rider to move in harmony with the horse at all paces, and to control and influence the horse with leg, reins, and flexion of core muscles.*

They can be laid in succession to be used at the walk, trot and canter; the set distance between the poles varied depending on the gait and size of the horse. On this occasion the poles were laid out evenly spaced for a trotting exercise.

We resumed with familiar exercises but with the addition of the trotting poles. Every time the ride turned down the centre of the school in single file the horses trotted over the poles. At first the exercise was carried out normally, with reins and stirrups, then without stirrups, and later with hands on heads. Often the horses negotiated the poles more fluently without reins or any other interference from the rider.

Towards the end of the session, a small jump of about two feet high was made using the last two trotting poles, so the run down the centre of the school became three trotting poles and a tiny jump, with a sharp turn left or right at the end of the school. The dressing between each of the horses was increased to a horse's length and we continued to follow each other around the school and over the poles.

"Last five minutes gentlemen," called the sergeant. "On my command leading file to trot ahead, turn down the centre with hands on head and no stirrups, negotiate the poles and jump, and re-join the back of the ride. All at the trot please. Off you go leading file."

The leading file trotted away from the others and around the school, before eventually turning down the centre, where he took his feet out of the stirrups, put his hands on his head and allowed the horse to carry him over the small obstacle course. After re-joining the ride at the rear, two of the trainees repeated the exercise in turn without incident. Then it was Merryweather.

"Okay Merryweather. In your own time, off you go; no acrobatics please!"

Merryweather increased his pace and promptly trotted away, leaving the remainder of the ride behind. As he continued his lap of the school I watched as he 'boinged' to the left and to the right, fascinated with his inability to sit upright as he rode around the track. His hands were held almost at shoulder height, his reins were far too long and the animation in his arms and hands was mesmerising. The horse must have misinterpreted the flurry of conflicting signals and broke into the canter just at the moment that they turned down the centre. The sensible course of action would have been to feel the reins and slow the horse back to the trot, but the old soldier obeyed the last order and removed his feet from the stirrups at the same time as putting his hands on his head as he approached the poles.

The poles were set far too close together for a cantering horse, and consequently the horse clumsily clattered into the second and third one. Wrong footed and now thoroughly confused, the poor horse braked hard and stopped dead at the small jump. The sudden loss of impulsion immediately launched the unsuspecting Merryweather out of the saddle, into the air, and over the horse's head. The moment seemed to span out in slow motion; I remember watching him fly gracefully through the air before contorting into some sort of gymnastic like somersault. I was astonished to see that even when he hit the wall boards upside down and face first, he still had his hands firmly placed on the top of his head. This was taking the 'obey the last order' policy to a new and ridiculous level.

There was a sickening crunch before he slowly slid down the wooden boards; at first standing momentarily on his head before finally crumpling to the floor. He lay, quietly curled up, with his hands still determinedly clutching his cap to his head.

"Bloody hell Merryweather! What are you doing down there?" groaned the sergeant. "If you damaged those boards you'll bloody well pay for them!"

"I'll bear that in mind sarge," mumbled the casualty without opening his eyes.

"Have you any idea of the amount of paperwork involved if you kill yourself? Get up man, for God's sake!"

"I'll bear that in mind too, sarge."

In time honoured mounted department fashion, we expressed our sincere concern and sympathy by indulging in hearty group laughter.

"I don't know how he does it without killing himself?" I said to the trainee next to me.

"He's very good at it, isn't he?" he laughed in reply, "and in fairness he does have lots of practice!"

"I reckon he'd make really good money as a Hollywood stunt double."

"Really!" he laughed. "Who have you ever seen in Hollywood that looks like Jack Merryweather?"

It was a fair point which reduced us to fits of laughter again.

Jack Merryweather was an enigma. He had served with the army, seen the world, achieved the rank of sergeant, and was consequently a very mature recruit when he initially trained to be a police officer. Later, and well into middle age he had applied to join the mounted branch and was dangerously hopeless from the start. He never improved and no one really knew why he wanted to be a mounted officer, or why he continued without complaint while constantly enduring innumerable dramatic falls and crashes. It could have been sheer grit and determination, or perhaps one of the earlier falls onto his head may have clouded his judgement. Whatever the reason, his falls, flights, and considerable crashes are legendary and still provide plenty of material for hilarious reminisces at reunions forty years later.

A few days later I was working from Tally Ho. Steve Durran had taken a couple of days leave, and I was standing in for him as stableman and helping out with the riding course. I had started at 7am, so had already completed the mucking out and groomed the sergeant's horse, and was now bedding down the loose boxes while the horses were working in the riding school.

With the bulk of the morning chores completed, I was about to go upstairs to prepare tea for the mid-morning break when two horses rode into the yard. They rode past me and up to the large entrance doorway of the riding school; one of them was Len Hunter and his remount Jackson. I heard Joiner's voice from inside:

"Good morning gentlemen, what can I do for you?"

"Morning sarge," replied Len. "Any chance of us joining in for a while? He needs a bit of work around other horses."

"Come in, come in; the more the merrier."

They pushed the heavy doors open and rode through into the school.

I allowed myself a few minutes to watch from the viewing gallery. It ran across the entire width of the riding school and was elevated, so gave a bird's eye view of the whole scene. I watched with interest to see how the young trainee horse would integrate with the others in the close confines of the indoor school. The session continued more or less as normal, but with the inclusion of some extra exercises for the benefit of the remount. Len wanted to concentrate on exercises that involved Jackson riding away and leaving the other horses, and also where other horses rode away from Jackson.

A police horse needs to be able to work calmly alongside other horses without squabbling, and the close confine of the indoor riding school is a perfect place to learn this. Additionally, a horse needs to stay calm when horses ride away and leave him alone, and also to be happy to ride away independently and leave other horses behind. Both manoeuvres go against the horse's natural herding instinct and are an essential part of remount training.

During the early part of their training remounts are generally less fit than the experienced horses; consequently, their work load has to be gradually increased to fall in line with their increasing stamina levels. Their training needs to be interesting and challenging but not exhausting. Tired horses become bitter, so it was something that needed to be considered when working remounts in the school with fitter, more mature horses. On this occasion fatigue wasn't an issue however, because Jackson was allowed several short rests during the session. They weren't planned, but regular interruptions were a way of life with this group because Jack Merryweather was still dramatically hitting the dirt with alarming regularity.

Jackson was an impressive looking young horse; he was tall at almost seventeen hands high, not too heavy, and moved well around the school. He worked well with horses riding alongside him and seemed to be unperturbed when they rode past him. Each time he rode away independently Len would lean forward, pat his neck and praise him with a "Good Laaaad" or a "Well done". I was intrigued by the close bond developing between horse and rider. Len Hunter was obviously a naturally talented and vastly experienced horseman, with a wealth of knowledge and years of acquired wisdom. Unfortunately, his undeniable communication skills were not so well tuned towards his fellow man, so a great deal of that experience and wisdom remained locked away and sadly unshared.

"Mr Wild!" called the sergeant. "Wakey wakey; don't sleep on the balcony, get the kettle on man."

Disturbed from my day dreams, I went into the bunk and switched the kettle on.

Five minutes later I walked into the riding school with tea for the morning break. Everyone dismounted and crossed their stirrups over their saddles, before gathering together for a chat and a recap of the morning's lesson. Having no horse for the day I joined in, waiting with my tray, so I could collect the mugs when everyone had finished.

Len Hunter didn't take part in any conversation and purposely stood alone with Jackson away from the group. I watched as he talked to the horse whilst feeding him morsels from his pocket. He walked a couple of paces away from the horse, called him, and praised him with pats and verbal encouragement when the horse walked towards him. Every time he walked a little further back until there was about three metres between horse and rider. Each time Jackson quietly walked towards Len and nuzzled his pocket for a treat, which he was given along with more hearty pats and praise. There was an obvious strong bond developing between Len and his horse. It was beginning to feel cold standing around though, and the horses were becoming fidgety, so I began to gather the mugs ready for washing up.

I suddenly jumped and almost dropped the tray at the sound of a very loud fart; I spun around just in time to see Jackson buck for the second time and canter away from the group to the other end of the school. He stopped and stood, head held high, snorting, looking at the remaining group of horses standing in the middle of the school.

"Loose horse!" called the sergeant. "You blokes hold on to those other horses; Wildy stand by the door please."

I walked over to the exit to prevent anyone entering the school, and watched as Len walked calmly and slowly towards Jackson.

"Jacko, you silly bugger," he said softly. "Come on now, come on."

He approached steadily before standing quietly about three metres away with his hand extended; the horse slowly walked towards him just like he had done several times before only a few minutes earlier.

"Good laaad, good laaad," he almost whispered. "Come on now, come on."

Jackson slowly crept towards Len with his neck outstretched, and appeared to be about to surrender his soul for a snack when he suddenly turned away and bucked and farted again, before cantering around the track of the school. He began heading towards the exit where he suddenly noticed me and turned away, cantering back in the opposite direction. He stopped again. Len approached, speaking to him softly, but again he bucked, farted, and hurtled away. He was just a young adolescent horse, acting daft; embarrassing, but it happens.

He began to increase his speed, and following another explosive buck, the stirrups that had been crossed over the saddle came free and began to bounce against his sides. He went faster and faster, galloping along the straight sides of the school and banking around the bends at either end. Len, having given up any hope of catching him, stood in the centre of the school waiting for him to tire and return to the fold. I watched in awe as he rampaged around the school and marvelled at the power, speed and freedom of movement that is so much more evident in horses without a rider.

"Everyone keep hold of their horses," ordered the sergeant. "The last thing we need is a stampede. He'll calm down in a minute; just hold tight."

Jackson seemed to have other ideas. He continued to hurtle around the school at ever increasing speed, occasionally stopping, leaping in the air, and immediately charging off again in a different direction. I wasn't sure about his motive, but he was clearly enjoying himself.

Jackson's performance, sadly, ended as quickly and as dramatically as it had begun: with the eyes of everyone in the school watching intently, he accelerated along the straight side of the school and tripped over the reins that were now dangling close to his fore legs. The forward speed, power and impulsion ensured that the resulting summersault was to be a good one; the big grey horse turned completely over in mid-air and travelled for several more metres before hitting the ground head first to the sound of a ghastly 'crack'.

The whole building seemed to tremor as he hit the ground. There was quiet, then more quiet. Jackson lay motionless as Len Hunter and the sergeant carefully walked towards him. I didn't have a clear view, but the signs were clearly ominous - a tangible sense of doom spread around the now silent group.

Len and the sergeant dropped to their knees and examined the now prostrate and motionless animal.

"Someone go to the office and call the vet. Make sure he understands that this is a real emergency," ordered the sergeant authoritatively but calmly. "The rest of you leave the school quietly. Put your horses away and keep yourselves busy for a while."

The school was cleared and the vet was called. Fortunately, McDougal the vet was at his surgery at the time of the call, so was informed immediately; his practice, however, was eight miles away in West Bromwich. Eight miles along the busy congested roads of the industrial conurbation; it was going to be a long and tense wait. I went back down to the riding school to update the sergeant. He was standing looking over Len Hunter who was kneeling beside his horse and stroking its neck. Jackson's eyes were wide open; he seemed to be listening while his rider reassured him, but was still laid flat out where he had fallen.

"The vet is en route and he's coming by police car; the control room have fixed it up."

"Good that'll speed things up a little," replied the worried looking sergeant. "Go and get a couple of day rugs, he'll be feeling the cold in a minute."

I returned a few minutes later with two rugs and stood by while the two men covered the horse except for his neck and head.

"It doesn't look good does it?" I asked Joiner.

"No it doesn't. I was hoping he was just concussed but that's looking more unlikely every minute."

I went back outside and joined the others in the yard. After a surprisingly short time, I heard the distinctive two-tone notes of a police car in the distance. Just a few minutes later the familiar sight of a 'jam sandwich[13]' approached along the drive at great speed. It screeched to a halt in the yard and the front passenger jumped out, opening the back door to reveal McDougal the vet.

He struggled out of the back of the car clutching a leather Gladstone bag, and made his way straight into the riding school without acknowledging anyone. Mr 'Mac' was generally a serious man of few words, but today he looked ashen faced, wobbly, and definitely a little bit under the weather.

---

[13] *Traffic patrol cars of the time were white with a thick red line painted along each side. They were commonly known as 'jam sandwiches'.*

We waited quietly for a few more minutes until the sergeant and Len joined us in the yard. Joiner closed the large school doors firmly behind him and told us to close the top doors to the horses' loose boxes. Before we were able to indulge in any further conversation, the ominous sound of a loud single shot reverberated around the complex. The school door opened and the shaken looking vet walked out. "It's done. I need a cup of tea if there's one available," he said, packing a revolver back into the Gladstone bag.

Upstairs in the bunk the atmosphere was gloomy. Joiner and the vet were smoking while they talked; the rest of us quietly listened while drinking tea. Len Hunter sat, head in hands, in complete silence at the end of the table.

"His neck was broken. I was surprised he was still alive," explained Mr Mac. "Would you like me to arrange the knacker[14] or will you do it?"

"No, we'll fix it up thank you," answered the sergeant. "You did a good job; I appreciate it."

"It's not the nicest part of my job, but someone has to do it," he explained while shakily lighting up his second cigarette in as many minutes.

"You seem shaken Mr Mac?"

"You're right, I am shaken. But it was the ride here that shook me," he took a long drag on his cigarette. "Eighty miles an hour down the busy Soho Road, and a hundred miles an hour along Pershore Road! I'm not a great lover of speed and may need to change my trousers when I get back to the surgery."

---

[14] *A person employed in the disposal of animal carcasses.*

The image of the vet sitting in the back of the traffic patrol car, gripping the seats and cringing in terror, brought a smile to several faces. It lightened the mood a little, but there was still a quiet sombre atmosphere around the building for the rest of the afternoon.

A short while after the vet had left, for hopefully a more sedate journey home, Big Ben walked into the bunk. We all stood up, only to be waved back into our seats while he sat down and listened to the sorry story of Jackson's demise.

He nodded in silence while the sergeant summarised the incident, and then walked down to the school with Len Hunter where they both looked at the lifeless Jackson. I watched from the gallery as they talked for a few moments, and saw them turn away and walk out of the school. Len was obviously crestfallen. He looked the most miserable man in the world; they both got into Ben's car, and without coming back upstairs, left Tally Ho to return to Duke Street.

I drove home that afternoon deep in thought. I had spent nine weeks on my riding course at Tally Ho, and had visited on many more occasions since the end of my course. I had fallen off numerous times, and I had lost count of how often I had seen Jack Merryweather hit the dirt. I had seen horses rampaging out of control with screaming trainees clinging to their backs, and the same lads flying through the air with the greatest of ease when their horses stopped suddenly at jumps. But it wasn't until that morning's shocking incident that it suddenly occurred to me the riding school was a dangerous place.

I had looked into the school from the gallery before I left for home; it was empty apart from the lifeless corpse of poor Jackson, still awaiting collection by the knacker. Earlier he had done so well in the school; I had quietly looked on while he was following

Len Hunter for morsels of food, and smiled with everyone else as he cavorted with defiant youthful exuberance around the riding school. Now, in the blink of an eye, he was dead. One moment an eye catching, beautiful young grey horse, the subject of much hope for the future; the next a routine collection for the knacker man. It wasn't the first time I had seen a loose horse charge around the riding school and it certainly wouldn't be the last. The general attitude was that if the door was closed it would be fine and nothing to worry about. After that day, however, it always made me cringe, and while others laughed at the antics I would close my eyes, think of Jackson, and hope that history wasn't about to repeat itself.

It had been a sad day indeed. It had also been thought-provoking; despite all the laughs we had, the riding school was a dangerous place, and the lesson of the day was that none of us are immortal.

CHAPTER 18

NAME THAT TUNE

Chief Inspector Stuart Hancock and Inspector Benjamin Scott were men of another time, but even in the days of 1970s policing their attitudes and methods were simply twenty years out of date. Both had seen National Service in the 1950s, in cavalry regiments that were steeped in tradition. Ben Scott had served with the Household Cavalry, whilst Hancock had been a gunner with the Royal Horse Artillery, so both men were weaned into adulthood amid spit, polish, shouted orders, and bugles.

On completion of their National Service they both joined their local police force; Hancock the Metropolitan Police, and Scott Birmingham City Police, but served only short terms on the beat before transferring to their respective mounted sections. Police mounted sections of the time were exclusively male, and almost entirely made up of former army horse soldiers. Military traditions were maintained and strictly followed; detached from mainline police duties it is easy to see how they clung to their 1950s attitudes, oblivious to the fact the wider world around them had changed into a more liberal and less regimented place.

One of their more noticeable traits was that they addressed everyone by just their surname, so to both of them I was quite simply 'Wild'. Civilian members of the department - such as the grooms and the store man - had their names prefixed with Mr, but the police officers were always abruptly addressed by surname only. Elsewhere, this really was a relic of the past; back on division even the most senior officer would formally address me as 'PC Wild'. Informally, they would routinely address me as 'Stefan' or even 'Stef'. Big Ben Scott would - in rare moments of joviality- smilingly greet me with 'Wildy', but Christian names were never used.

Many, many years later, long after they had both retired, I bumped into a much aged and mellowed Stuart Hancock at a reunion event.

"Hello Mr Hancock, good to see you. I'm not sure if you remember me?" I asked, whilst introducing him to Becks.

"Hello Wild, and Mrs Wild; it's a pleasure. Of course I remember you." He shook my hand with unexpected warmth.

"You're looking very well. You haven't aged a bit," I lied politely.

"You always were a charmer, Wild," he laughed. "I'm sorry, I can't call you by your first name."

"Don't worry Sir; my memory isn't what it was either."

"Oh I haven't forgotten it Wild, I just never knew it!"

And that was the simple truth of it. Even after years as my boss, he had never seen the need to know my - or anyone else's - first name. To Stuart Hancock, Duke Street stables in the 1970s, was no different to Woolwich Barracks in the 1950s.

Paradoxically, and with the benefit of hindsight, the ways of the two old soldiers were good for morale and had a strange unifying effect on the men. Everyone was treated the same, albeit dismissively; there were no favourites, no internal politics, and everyone was united in their collective underling status. Stuart Hancock treated everyone with disdain, and in all of my thirty years of police service, he was probably the only boss I ever worked for who genuinely didn't give two pence for what anyone thought of him. Behind his fiery outbursts, Ben Scott was actually far more amenable - but he loyally toed the line, firing the metaphorical bullets loaded in the chief's office. Neither were properly appreciated until after they were gone, but that's a story for the future.

A complete antithesis of the 1970s mounted department was the West Midlands Police Male Voice Choir. The choir was a popular attraction at many concerts, an enjoyable pastime with membership open to any singing male employee of the West Midlands Police, civilians and officers alike. The membership covered all ranks and positions from Assistant Chief Constable to the mounted branch store man and everyone in between. All members were strictly known to each other by their first names. Membership wasn't an option open for me because I sing like a hippo, but several of the other mounted officers were enthusiastic members, including our civilian store man Maurice Lawrence.

Maurice, affectionately known as Loz, was a quiet-natured mature gentleman who had started work with West Midlands Police later in life, after being made redundant from a long career in engineering. His initial job description was purely to run the department's stores, order stock, and make sure that the stables were regularly replenished with the required equipment. Inevitably, however, his natural skills soon led to him being regarded as the departmental 'Mr Fix-it'. He saw to all minor repairs of saddles, bridles, and other miscellaneous equipment in a pleasant and efficient manner in his recently opened, well-equipped workshop. Loz was a very useful man to keep on the right side of.

At the time of my arrival, the mounted department was going through a slow, inevitable, but irreversible change. The old National Service men from the 1950s had largely disappeared into retirement, and been gradually replaced by younger men whose only military experience was gained from listening to the tales of their fathers and grandfathers. Nowhere was more typical of this change than the bunk and tack room at Duke Street.

Tack cleaning after riding was a social occasion, where current affairs were debated, football discussed, and opinions on a whole range of topics freely expressed. Towards the end of the working day, it was 'bloke time', and it was also amongst the saddle racks and bridle hooks that the generation gap was most apparent. For every middle-aged man in an apron, quietly stripping and diligently polishing his brow band and buckles, there were two or three youngsters in jeans, trainers, and baggy t-shirts doing the same.

Looking back now, through much older and hopefully wiser eyes, I can feel the pain of the older officers of that time. After so many years of order and quiet routine, they were rapidly being swept aside by an invasion of cheeky kids who spurned their comfortable traditions, laughed at their rebukes, and generally made too much bloody noise! The tack room, with its painted brick walls, and timeless smell of leather, saddle soap, and carbolic, was once such a haven of calm and decorum. It was, however, slowly transforming into a much livelier place of shouts, laughter and laddish behaviour, with the smell of Brut and Hai Karate[15] overpowering everything else.

One of the more memorable characters to noisily burst onto the new mounted scene, at about the same time as myself, was PC Martin Morris.

[15] Both very popular men's after shaves in the 1970s and 80s, regularly featuring in humorous TV advertising.

Martin was widely known as 'Johnny' Morris, after the comical TV presenter of Animal Magic[16], and was a six foot two pressure cooker of bubbling, ready to burst, nervous energy.

He was a wiry, athletic lad with an almost permanent grin, and spent his working hours enthusiastically and energetically trying to impress and please everyone.

He was friendly, noisy, animated and tactile, dominating any room with his genuine warmth and gesticulating, arm-waving laughter. One to one conversation with Johnny was both captivating and exhausting, because in addition to being locked into his inescapable eye contact, you were also subjected to well-intentioned but constant, painful back slapping and hugging. Forty years on, and having not seen him for many years, I still find it difficult to supress a smile whenever I think of 'Johnny' Morris.

It was during one of these riotous tack cleaning sessions that Derek Joiner walked into the room carrying his usual large mug of tea. His entrance was perfectly timed to catch Johnny Morris standing bolt upright on the tack room table.

He had leapt up a few moments earlier, in an attempt to escape a whipping from someone who objected to being drenched by a wet cleaning swab, which had just mysteriously propelled itself from Johnny's bucket of mucky lukewarm water.

"What are you doing up there Morris?" enquired the sergeant.

"Up here sarge? Up here, I'm just checking the ceiling of course," he replied, tapping the ceiling and listening to the noise.

The whole room erupted into laughter.

"I think your head needs checking before the ceiling Morris.

[16] *A hugely popular BBC children's television series which ran from 1962 until 1983. Johnny Morris provided jovial voiceovers for the animals in his character of a zoo keeper.*

You're never right (Harrumph). You are never right. Now come down from your podium because the boss wants to see you." He punctuated his statement with a slurp of tea.

"What does the inspector want me for?" he asked, looking worried as he jumped to the floor.

"The inspector doesn't want to see you, Morris, it's far worse than that. Mr Hancock wants to see you immediately. Don't keep him waiting because he's not in the best of moods."

"What have I done?"

"I have absolutely no idea; he chose not to share the details with me. Just hurry up, don't keep him waiting, and tidy yourself up first," he said, shaking his head in exasperation as he left the room.

There was an immediate increase in chitter chatter. Not all of it was reassuring, and the general consensus was that 'Johnny Morris was in the shit'. However, he wasn't allowed to leave before everyone joined in to prepare him for his certain impending doom, so by the time we pushed him out of the door he looked suitably industrious - wearing a uniform shirt and tie, and with his clean apron comically overloaded with brushes and dusters of every description.

He looked really comical as he marched out of the door, straight as a die, swinging his arms in a demented fashion, and we all watched nosily through the window as he straightened his tie, smoothed his hair, and buffed his shoes on the back of his trouser legs, before knocking the door and disappearing into Hancock's office.

It was about five minutes later when Johnny returned to the tack room with a puzzled look on his normally laughing face. Everyone was desperate to know what had happened, so immediately bombarded him with questions.

"I've got to go to Steelhouse Lane right away," he said.

"Steelhouse Lane? Why? What for?"

"I've got to tune the piano in the band room."

The tack room erupted into laughter. Eventually everyone paused for breath, and as order was momentarily restored, I took the chance to speak.

"What the hell do you know about pianos?"

"Sod all to be honest," he replied, shrugging his arms in an 'I don't know' manner.

"Can you play the piano?"

"Come on! What do you think? Of course I can't play the bloody piano."

"Well what did he say to you about the piano?" I probed.

"He said the Assistant Chief Constable had called, and instructed that I was to go to the band room at Steelhouse Lane Police Station, this afternoon, and tune the piano. That's all I know."

"But you don't know anything about pianos?"

"Mate I know that, and you know that. I don't even know where the bloody band room *is* at Steelhouse Lane!" He shrugged again.

"This is crazy. What did you say to him?"

"I asked why he wanted me to tune a piano and he just shouted at me. He said '*Who are you, Morris, to question the orders of the Assistant Chief Constable?*' Then he told me to bugger off, do as I'm told, and hurry up about it."

"That's it then," advised one of the aproned old - school quietly, from the back of the room. "Obey the last order. No questions asked." This pearl of wisdom precipitated mutual mutterings of agreement around the room; encouragement which I sadly suspected was more inclined towards mischief than genuine support.

So, it was decided by a majority vote. Johnny Morris was off on a mission to Steelhouse Lane Police Station to tune the piano in the band room. There were to be no further questions, no dissent - he just needed to obey the last order, and get on with it. Worryingly, it didn't take very long for Johnny to be swept along with the growing ebullience in the room.

"What tools have you got?" someone asked.

"I've got my socket set in the car," replied Johnny enthusiastically.

"Take some out of the forge as well, just in case," another officer suggested.

"He's got to tune it, not bloody shoe it!" The room erupted in a roar of laughter.

"I thought he was a German composer?"

"Who?"

"Shoe it."

"That's bloody Schubert. You ignoramus."

The jocular mood continued as we all marched him noisily through the stables and into the forge in search of a suitable tool kit. Johnny, being as daft as a brush, was now completely absorbed into the mood of the crowd, and was revelling in all of the attention. I couldn't help thinking it was ironic to see such a happy victim swept along so joyfully by his own lynch mob.

We watched through the window as he marched purposefully out of the yard with his great long stride. He merrily carried an old hessian sack loaded with a selection of dirty tools borrowed from the forge, although what operation he was hoping to perform with a large striking hammer, several long chisels, and a huge pair of tongs, I had no idea. Either way, I strongly suspected that no good was going to come of it.

Half an hour later, with the tack cleaned, polished and hanging neatly, and the horses groomed, rugged and put to bed, we sat at the bunk table, drinking tea and waiting for home time. Derek Joiner had sat down with us, and we were filling him in on the latest details of Johnny Morris and the mysterious mission to tune the band room piano. He looked concerned.

"Well that can't be right. I've never heard of anything so daft! Why did he just bugger off without coming to my office first?"

"He was obeying the last order sarge," someone answered.

"Well it's a bloody good job no one ordered him to go and drown himself in the trough, that's what I say," replied Joiner, just as Big Ben walked into the bunk. Everyone jumped to their feet.

"Sit down. Sit down everybody. Pour us a cup of tea Wild." The inspector waved me off towards the teapot.

"We're just discussing this bloody piano and Morris fiasco, Sir. What's it all about?" asked the increasingly concerned sergeant.

"Buggered if I know anything about it; it came straight from the ACC direct to Hancock. Very insistent that he drop everything and get the job done this afternoon."

"But Morris knows sod all about pianos Sir!"

"Obey the last order Derek. You know the drill, just obey the last order," Big Ben explained, nodding sombrely around the table.

We were all listening so intently that hardly anyone noticed the door edge open and Loz the store man sidle sheepishly into the room. He stood next to Derek Joiner, before quietly speaking.

"Sorry to interrupt sarge, but do you know if Mr Hancock has had a call from the ACC today?"

"He most certainly has Mr Lawrence. What do you know about it?"

"Well… we were at choir practice last night and were struggling because the piano was so terribly out of tune. I said I could probably tune it, so Ken said that he would call Mr Hancock and arrange for me to do it today. I've been waiting to hear all afternoon," Loz meekly explained, ever polite.

"Ken? Ken, who the bloody hell is Ken? And if Ken wanted you, why the hell did the ACC ask for Morris?" demanded Ben, who by now was probably the only man in the room who hadn't worked out the riddle of the tuneless piano.

"I'm afraid it's all first names in the choir sir," Loz whispered, looking increasingly uncomfortable, "Ken is the ACC, and my name is Maurice sir, Maurice Lawrence."

"Maurice Lawrence. Really? Maurice and Morris? Really? Ken is the ACC? Really? What a lot of first name nonsense. What a load of bollocks. This is not good, Derek. In fact this is a right bag of shit." He looked worried and thought for another moment or two. "Sadly I have to go and visit West Bromwich. You'd better sort this out Derek, and quickly, or I foresee a 'finale tragico' for that damn piano. Sort it out Derek. Just sort it out." He shook his head in disbelief, and retreated from the room.

Unusually the mystery had been solved before the plot had run its final course. It was difficult to imagine what havoc was, at that very moment, unfurling in the band room at Steelhouse Lane, where an innocent piano was at the mercy of an eager to please Johnny Morris and his bag of medieval torture tools.

Everyone was on a high as we walked out of the yard together to find our cars, which we always parked in the crowded side streets around Duke Street. There was much laughter and speculation, when hearing the sound of screeching tyres, we all leapt back on to the pavement and watched as Derek Joiner sped past us in the departmental Morris Marina Estate. Sitting next to him, looking terrified in the passenger seat, was Mr Lawrence the store man and talented handyman - better known to his friends, of course, as Maurice.

One of the major benefits of life on the mounted branch was that most days I was home nice and early. Even when I dropped Jim Hardwick off first, I was usually back at home before 4pm. Although still far from sure that I wanted it to be a permanent posting, I was fully aware of how much Becks was enjoying it. The three of us now always sat together for our evening meal, so I became more involved in little Mel's latest efforts to feed herself, and never ceased to be amazed at all the places a toddler could find to spoon food into. It was, without doubt, a major change in our lifestyle - and I couldn't deny that I had never been fitter. The constant tiredness that dogged me whilst working shifts had all but disappeared.

My future career had become a regular topic of discussion during our evening quality time, and though it was far from certain that I would actually be offered a permanent post, we both agreed that it would be nice to have an answer should the offer be made.

It was me that was undecided. There were so many things I enjoyed about the branch, but there were many things that annoyed me too. I missed the atmosphere, camaraderie, and variety of work on the shift, and the foot stamping, saluting, and routine of the mounted branch irritated me - but I was really beginning to enjoy working with and riding the horses. I needed to make up my mind, and soon, but not tonight. Tonight, I had a gem of a funny story to tell.

"You'll never guess what happened today," I began.

"You fell off your horse again?" she answered with a twinkle in her eye. There was never a chance of becoming too cocky in our household.

"No, it was much funnier than that. Johnny Morris had to tune the choir's piano," I said, laughing already.

"Wasn't he an electrician? I never knew he was a musician as well. He doesn't seem the type."

"He isn't, that's the point, and I've no idea if they've even got a piano anymore." I continued to tell her the whole story: the Maurice and Morris fiasco, how everyone had egged him on, and him borrowing the farrier's tools to do the job. She sat listening with tears in her eyes, shaking her head in disbelief.

"Poor old Martin, he's such a fool, he truly needs help. So what happened?"

"I won't know until tomorrow when I go back to work."

"I want to know now!" she insisted. "Why don't you call him?"

"He'll tell us all tomorrow. Be patient."

"Come on," she wheedled. "Call him - you know you want to."

She was right of course, I did want to, and I didn't need too much convincing, so I called Johnny at home, not really knowing what to expect when he answered the phone.

"Hello is that the Maestro Morris, piano tuner to the Queen?" I began.

"Who are you calling a Morris Maestro, you cheeky git?" he laughed. "Mate, it was terrible. Why did you let me do it? You should have stopped me. Where were you when I needed you?"

"Nothing to do with me mate, you just got swept away with the atmosphere and followed the crowd. You daft tit! Anyway, did you tune it?" I asked.

"No, but I took the bloody legs off it. Mate, you should have been there, it was quality!" He roared between fits of hysterical Johnny Morris laughter.

"You're joking. Why did you take the legs off?"

"Because I didn't have a clue how to tune it," he reasoned, "and it was actually only one leg, because Joiner and Loz arrived and stopped me."

282

He told me he had arrived at Steelhouse Lane and been shown up to the band room, where a battered old baby grand piano stood in the corner. After putting his tools down he had a little tinkle on the ivories, but realised that to his tone deaf ears none of the notes sounded any better or worse than the others. It finally dawned on him he had no idea what to do. The only tools he had that were of any possible use were his sockets, kept in the boot of his car, which fitted the leg bolts. With nothing else constructive to do, he decided to remove the legs from the now very vulnerable piano.

"So tell me again, why did you take the legs off?" I had to ask.

"I suppose I thought that if it was on the floor I'd be able to reach inside more easily," he reasoned.

"I thought pianos are really heavy?"

"You're not wrong there, mate. It hit the ground like a ton of bricks; no joke. I could have been killed. At my age! Can you imagine?" Clearly the scare had done him little lasting harm, as he roared with laughter again.

"What did you do then?"

"Joiner and Loz appeared. He started to give me a right bollocking but couldn't carry on because he was pissing himself laughing. I told him I was only obeying orders, and then he said *'Well obey this order Morris. Bugger off out of here before you do any more damage. Go home, and I'll see you tomorrow.'* I offered to stay and help but he started to swear a lot. So I went home."

I put the phone down with my sides aching from laughter. I don't think I had ever worked with anyone quite as barmy as Johnny Morris. His whole life tumbled along like a perpetual pantomime. I related his story back to Becks and we both sat on the sofa in fits of laughter, but it wasn't too long before she grabbed the opportunity to swing the conversation by making a crafty observation.

"You know Stef, you keep going on about missing the lads on the shift, but you've got some right old characters where you are now. It sounds like an asylum and you're daft enough to fit in perfectly, so I can't see the problem."

She made a valid point, and the truth was that I was slowly beginning to feel at home on the branch. I still wasn't convinced, but I knew I needed to make a decision soon.

Characters don't come much bigger or more memorable than Martin 'Johnny' Morris and he is still a mounted branch legend who we can't help but discuss over beers at reunions. I haven't seen him for many years, but we keep in contact via social media. We now operate in different hemispheres because he moved to New Zealand, many years ago, after retirement from the police, and now lives with his wife, dogs, and a small menagerie of animals on their small holding where he cultivates special grass that is used for high quality horse feed. Like me, he's got older, and like me he's no longer a lanky wiry youth, but has piled on a few extra pounds. We often exchange photographs, and his usually show himself dressed in shorts and bush hat, often sitting on a tractor, and always closely followed by his two dogs. His face is more wrinkled but still wears the same ear to ear crazy grin, and you can almost hear the laughter in the messages we exchange.

I don't know what the Kiwis make of Johnny Morris, but I'll bet the neighbours can't ignore him; especially if they're piano owners.

CHAPTER 19

UP THE ALBION

By 1979 police officers mounted on horses had been a familiar part of British Policing for many years. There had also been a longstanding debate regarding their usefulness, financial viability and operational value in the modern mechanised world. Mounted officers, in the main, were detached from most of the stresses of daily frontline policing, and so mainstream officers generally believed the Donkey Wallopers had a really cushy number. To a certain extent it was true, because the hours were good, the paperwork was minimal, and the very physical nature of the job ensured a good level of personal fitness.

What was never disputed, however, was the value of police horses for policing large crowds, and many police officers have tales to tell about how they were 'saved by the donkeys' at a football match or some other violent demonstration. Sitting on a horse, high above the heads of a crowd, gave a wider view and a much greater appreciation of a crowd's behaviour than was possible from ground level. Likewise, an officer on horseback was far more visible, so could communicate more widely; crowds push from the back not from the front, and mounted officers could see the problem areas. The half passes and full passes learned in the riding school were effective measures for gently holding or pushing passive crowds needing guidance, whereas more vigorous action could be used to break up more violent gatherings.

The West Midlands area, at the time, was home to six professional football league clubs, five of which were in the old First Division[17]; so at times, and especially during the winter months, the horses and men of the mounted branch were spread thinly and kept busy. My first posting to a football match was a big one. The players of West Bromwich Albion were enjoying an exceptionally good season under new manager Ron Atkinson. They were riding high at third place in the first division, winning most of their games and consequently drawing larger crowds than they had done for many years. On Saturday 5th May they were playing Manchester United at home at The Hawthorns, and a capacity crowd was anticipated.

I arrived at West Bromwich stables at about 9.45am and drove the Mini into the yard to unload my kit. I had been looking forward to working my first football match and counted myself lucky that I'd had the opportunity before the end of my attachment to the branch. I went into Dai Owens' office, checked the posting book, and saw that Cuthbert was to be my ride for the day. This was good news because though he was cranky and challenging in the stable, and I still had the scars to prove it, Cuthbert had a reputation for being bombproof and solidly dependable when working with crowds. I was keen to make a good first impression and it was going to be easier if I didn't have to worry about the behaviour of the horse that I was riding.

Grooming was completed without incident or further violence, mainly because I had sneaked into the loft and dropped down a section of hay for Cuthbert to munch on whilst I got on with the brush work.

[17] *The top flight of the football league in the days before The Premiership.*

I then prepared my saddlery for crowd control and attached the sword stick, chain rein and a Perspex eye shield to Cuthbert's bridle. The equine eye shields were a recent addition to the equipment, and reflected the steady escalation in the violent behaviour of football crowds that sadly was to peak at even higher levels during the next few years.

Four of us rode out of the yard at 12.50pm; we were to meet a match day special train carrying approximately six hundred Manchester United supporters at Rolf Street Station at 1.30pm. It was the first time that I had ridden with more than one other alongside of me. Dai Owen rode at the front on the offside, and I was positioned at the back on the nearside.

Rolf Street Station is in Smethwick, a heavily populated borough located close to The Hawthorns between West Bromwich and the outskirts of Birmingham. We took a back route, through an industrial estate and eventually beneath the M5 motorway by way of a pedestrian underpass. I was third in line as we descended in single file down a steep concrete ramp to the underpass; the noise from the four horses' hooves on the concrete slabs was considerable inside the narrow enclosed tunnel, and I had to bend low and right forward with my head lower than Cuthbert's to avoid scraping my helmet on the roof. It occurred to me that I had little or no control over my horse whilst in this awkward position and I was at the mercy of his mood, but it was obviously a regular route for them because they all walked briskly, unconcerned by the racket from their hooves and close confinement. Leaning forward with my head low, I watched my horse's ears gently rub against the tunnel roof until we finally emerged into natural light at the other side to find ourselves in Smethwick.

It was just a short walk to the station and we arrived with five minutes to spare before the arrival of the first train. Rolf Street was just on the edge of the centre of Smethwick town centre, and the railway station, like the rest of the surrounding area, was old, decrepit and a ghostly reminder of the town's former industrial prosperity. Next door was Rolf Street Baths, another dour Victorian civic building which was easily identifiable by the words 'ROLF STREET BATHS' painted in large blue and white letters on the expansive red brick exterior wall. These letters, and indeed the entire baths building, now stand proudly six miles away at the entrance of the Black Country Museum[18] in neighbouring Dudley, and induce feelings of nostalgia every time I visit the museum.

Our object was to greet the United supporters as they emerged from the station, keep them together as a group and escort them along the streets to the football ground. The purpose of the escort was to prevent any disorder or property damage on the way to the ground. Potential disorder could be caused either by the visiting supporters, or by home supporters attacking the group as they made their way along the one mile route.

The chants from the visiting crowd could be heard before they appeared at the exit gate and continued loudly as they suddenly spilled out onto the pavement. There were a lot of red and white hats, scarves and other clothing, and several large flags and banners, as we moved into a line with officers on foot to contain them on the pavement.

"UNITED! UNITED! THERE'S ONLY ONE MAN UTD!"

---

[18] *The Black Country Living Museum is a popular open air working museum located in Dudley. It takes the form of a working Victorian Black Country town, and has been built from demolished and reconstructed significant buildings from around the industrial Midlands.*

The sudden appearance of so many noisy people caused the horse in front of me to shy into the road before its rider brought it under control, but Cuthbert stood firm and unruffled, his ears pinned back as if he was going to bite one of the noisy red and white heads that were bobbing around perilously close to his mouth. We spread ourselves evenly along the length of the crowd and eventually moved them away towards The Hawthorns.

"IF YOU ARE A CITY FAN… SURRENDER OR YOU'LL DIE… WE ALL FOLLOW UNITED!"

Escorting these noisy convoys was a skill in itself; whilst any obvious misbehaviour needed to be nipped in the bud swiftly and firmly, it was important to keep everyone grouped together and moving at a reasonable pace. Order was usually maintained by the use of conversation and friendly banter - it was a definite advantage to have some knowledge of football, and especially of the visiting team.

"HI HO! HI HO! WE ARE THE BUSBY BOYS!"

Cuthbert, who had seen it all before, was obviously underwhelmed but compliant. He stopped and waited whilst I encouraged stragglers to catch up and then trotted forward to slow down the front runners to keep everyone in a group. It occurred to me that it was a little like herding cattle; I smiled as I recalled some of the TV westerns I had enjoyed as a child, and thought how nice it would be if the noisy shouting and swearing that was disturbing the peace of local residents could be replaced with a steady restful mooing.

"ONE MAN UNITED! THERE'S ONLY ONE MAN UNITED! ONE MAN U-N-I-T-E-D!"

After a busy but uneventful twenty minute roundup, we eventually reached the ground in Halfords Lane and guided our convoy noisily along the long rising ramp at the back of the Smethwick End before handing them over to the crew of three men and horses that had earlier ridden from Ladywood. The four of us formed back into our section of four and trotted steadily back to Rolf Street Station to collect a further five hundred fans due to arrive on the second train.

Both of the train escorts were noisy but trouble free, and at 3pm as the game kicked off we met up with the rest of the mounted contingent in Halfords Lane. Three horses and men from Ladywood, three from Thornhill Road, plus ourselves made a total of ten; after a few minutes a large roller shutter door opened and we rode into the ground. Inside we all lined up and, when settled, most of the men dismounted and covered their horse's back and saddlery with their long riding mac. It was rest time for horses' backs and men's bums alike. We were under cover beneath a seated area located in a corner of the ground between the Smethwick End and the Halfords Lane stand. The game was now in progress, the crowd was noisy, but where we were was free from supporters, and I could see that there were toilets and a burger bar trailer sharing the space with us.

Much to my surprise, someone arrived from the police office with a cardboard box and handed around packed lunches. I hadn't been expecting it, but like everyone else I tucked in and began to make short work of it, but not without a little harassment from Cuthbert, who seemed convinced that the unexpected snack was for him and not for me.

"Cyril never eats his lunch so Cuthbert usually gets it all," laughed one of the guys.

"Well he can't eat all of this because there's a ham sandwich and a sausage roll in it," I replied.

"And?"

"Well horses aren't carnivores so they don't eat meat," I replied with the confidence of a man whose depth of knowledge stemmed from his riding course and was only learned a few weeks previously.

"Cuthbert was poorly educated and no one ever told him about the meat thing. He'll eat anything," he replied. "And if you don't give him something there'll be big trouble. You'll regret it."

It was sound advice. It soon became obvious I wasn't going to have a moment's peace from Cuthbert unless I shared my packed lunch with him. He wouldn't stop butting me with his head, so I succumbed to pressure and fed him my apple and half of my Kit Kat; I stuck to my guns on the meat issue, however, and ate the sandwich and sausage roll myself. Happily the compromise worked, and he contentedly crunched his Granny Smith whilst I took care of the meat.

The match was obviously a cracker because the crowd was animated and constantly noisy; there was continuous loud chanting from both sets of supporters which created a palpable feeling of atmosphere and excitement around the ground. After our snack I remounted and joined two of the others who were watching the match from the edge of the stand. We were right by the corner flag, so it was a grandstand view of the pitch and an excellent training exercise for the horses, surrounded by thousands of noisy fans to their left, right and behind them above their heads in the seated area. The other two horses were younger, and though they stood their ground and behaved, it was noticeable that they were very aware of the crowd and the level of noise around them. Cuthbert just stood, and the two younger horses seemed reassured by his quiet acceptance of his surroundings. He was completely underwhelmed by the occasion, but after a while began to scrape his feet on the ground to signal that he would rather be back under cover with the rest of the horses. He was without doubt a curmudgeonly old bugger, and obviously not a keen football fan.

Shortly before half time we returned to the others under the stand, remounted, and sat in line waiting for the sound of the referee's whistle and the following sudden rush as hundreds of fans surged into the area to use the toilets or to buy food from the trailer. Instead of the anticipated whistle, however, there was a sudden almighty roar from the crowd and the ground began to shake from the stamping of feet in the stand above our heads. Someone had obviously scored.

A couple of the horses jumped at the sudden eruption, one of them raising its head in surprise, but then settled immediately. Cuthbert just grumped, while the rest of us waited to hear who had taken the lead.

"ALBION...! ALBION...! ALBION...! WE'RE GONNA WIN THE LEAGUE... WE GONNA WIN THE LEAGUE... NOW YA GORRA BELIEVE US... WE GONNA WIN THE LEAGUE!"

The Albion had taken the lead just moments before half time; psychologically this was a great time to take the lead and the crowd knew it. They kept up a terrific barrage of noise which almost drowned out the halftime whistle when it was eventually blown. There was a sudden urgent rush from the terraces towards us, and in no time at all we were surrounded by a swell of noisy home fans. There was a tremendous level of excitement as a horde of noisy men queued for the toilets and for burgers from the trailer. Everyone seemed to be shouting loudly, describing the goal even though they had all been there and witnessed it for themselves. It was a tradition; it had to be done, and the more beer that had been consumed, the louder it needed to be done.

Football grounds in the 1970s[19] were primitive by today's standards. Beer was on open sale, and it wasn't long before a noticeable smell of burgers, sweat, and urine from the overflowing toilets began to permeate the area. It was the stench of the match-day cocktail; unnoticed if you were excited, intoxicated by the atmosphere and a belly full of beer, but all too obvious to the line of mounted policemen sitting quietly and talking amongst themselves whilst watching over the melee of the half time rush.

"ONE CYRILLE REGIS… THERE'S ONLY ONE CYRILLE REGIS… ONE CYRILLE R-E-G-I-S… THERE'S ONLY ONE CYRILLE REGIS!" was now being loudly 'belted out' by the ecstatic Albion supporters. Cyrille Regis was their hero; he had put them into the lead moments before half time, and so now had to be loudly saluted whilst they queued for their burgers. It was a true party atmosphere - noisy, unruly, high spirited, but mainly good natured.

A few moments later, however, there was a sudden and noticeable change of tone and an increase in the noise from the crowd; as I looked across I could see evidence of a fight taking place at the burger trailer. Had I been on foot I would have been unable to see past the man standing next to me, but my elevated position from the back of Cuthbert enabled me to clearly see and assess the situation. It was just the sort of incident that could escalate and spark a major disturbance in such a tightly packed emotive environment.

[19] *Later in the 1970s the standing terraced areas would be segregated and separated from the pitch by tall metal mesh fencing. This was to prevent crowds from invading the pitch, as violent pitch invasions were sadly to become an unfortunate feature of many matches. The fences came down again after the tragic incident at Hillsborough in 1989 where 96 Liverpool supporters died when they were crushed against the perimeter fence. Standing terraces disappeared from grounds at the same time.*

I instinctively legged my horse forward and was joined by my colleague on the horse to my right. Two horses were enough; any more could have provoked panic in such tight conditions. We reached the edge of the crowd around the trailer and I could see that the actual fight was between two men close to the serving window.

One had thick black curly hair and the other was a closely shaved skinhead; they were furiously exchanging blows whilst being cheered along and encouraged by the tightly packed crowd around them. It was my first football match on horseback so I looked across to my colleague for guidance.

"You go first. I'll follow you in," he said and nodded towards the fight.

"Me first? Really?"

"Yes, Cuthbert will lead. My horse won't."

Needing little further encouragement I applied firm leg to Cuthbert's sides and he immediately walked into the crowd. He didn't rush and he didn't hold back, but just pushed his way through with no fuss while I addressed the crowd.

"Mind your backs… coming through… mind your backs… let us through…"

When you push into a tight crowd on a horse it generally generates a fair amount of verbal abuse, and occasionally a disgusting flurry of spittle. This occasion was no exception, but the crowd complied and parted, albeit noisily, and we soon reached the cause of the problem. The two men, completely oblivious to our presence, continued unabated to knock lumps out of each other.

Cuthbert stopped, and I paused for a moment to assess the situation before deciding what to do next. My next course of action was decided for me, however, when Cuthbert, without warning or instruction from me, lunged forward and fiercely bit the skinhead on the very top of his bald head.

"AAAAAAAAAAAAGGGHHHHH!" The scream could be heard clearly above the rest of the crowd noise.

Not content with a quick nip and a crafty retreat, Cuthbert held on and managed a vigorous shake of the shaven man before finally dropping him to the ground. The surrounding crowd was hushed with shock as the unfortunate victim staggered back to his feet.

"AAAAAAAAAAAGGGGHHHHH! Me bleedin' head! AAAAAAAAGGGGHHHH!"

It was a pretty good early diagnosis, because from where I was sitting I could clearly see blood beginning to ooze from the huge set of teeth marks on the top of the victim's shiny dome. The closer members of the crowd, clearly horrified by the savagery of my trusty partner, began to back away from the situation as the skinhead clutched his head with visibly blood stained fingers. He howled hysterically as I leaned forward and took hold of the other fighter's thick curly hair with my right hand.

"You are under arrest for threatening behaviour in a public place. Contrary to Section Five of the Public Order Act 1936. You don't have to say anything, but anything you do say will be taken down and may be used in evidence against you!"

"Whatever mate! Whatever! I ain't arguing. I'll come quietly. Do what you like, but don't let that big bastard bite me!"

I'd never reined back in anger before, or while using only one hand, but still holding onto my prisoner with my right hand I applied leg, resisted a little with the reins in my left hand, and Cuthbert walked steadily backwards like a dream through the parting crowd. I dragged the now submissive thug with us until we reached the line of horses.

Before I had time to think about what was to be done with the man in my clutches, two foot officers approached, took hold of him, and marched him through a door into the police office.

"Section 5?" one of them called over his shoulder.

"Yes!" I replied.

They were closely followed by two other officers, who were half carrying the semi limp skinhead with the bloodied head. He was still groaning incoherently as he followed close behind his adversary before disappearing through the door to the police office. As I still had the scars from a Cuthbert kiss visible on my rib cage, I quietly empathised and felt his pain.

"Well done; I'm impressed," said the guy who had followed me into the disturbance.

"Cheers. That's my first prisoner while sitting on a horse."

"Remarkable; there are some here who've never had a prisoner while sitting on a horse," he laughed and nodded towards the rest of the crew.

"What happens now? Do I need to go in and deal with him?"

"No, stay with your horse. They'll sort it out in there; someone will probably ask you for a statement later."

This was both a revelation and, in my mind, a very fine arrangement. Paperwork had long been the bane of my life, so the thought of someone else completing the formalities for my prisoner was very acceptable.

"I guess I'm going to get a complaint about the skinhead's head wound?"

"I doubt it. He's well pissed and probably won't remember a thing. He'll think he's been bottled when he sobers up."

I laughed and leaned forward to pat Cuthbert's neck. "Good lad. Perhaps you'll have to stand on an ID parade," I joked. He promptly replied by kicking out and shaking the brick wall behind us.

"You're a cranky old sod. What's the matter with you?" I asked.

"I did warn you that there'd be trouble," laughed my colleague. "He's meat deprived and no one's safe when he's craving blood; he's not too keen on Kit Kats either."

The game was obviously good old fashioned 'end to end stuff' during the second half; the regular gasps of loud "OOOOHHHHs" and "AAAAAHHHHHs" from both ends of the ground confirmed several near misses for both sides, and the corresponding mounting tension as Albion clung to their precious but slender one goal lead. The final score was of obvious importance to passionate supporters of both sides, but was also of great interest to officers policing the match, because the result of the game often determined the behaviour of fans when they left the ground at full time.

About ten minutes before the sound of the final whistle, the roller shutter opened and we all rode out into Halfords Lane, which was now closed to traffic. The three from Thornhill Road stables made their way to Birmingham Road, where they were to mingle with the fans that headed towards Birmingham at the end of the game. Despite all of the efforts to segregate the opposing supporters, Halfords Lane was a potential flash point where fights often broke out. We were left with seven mounted officers and about thirty officers on foot to escort the hundreds of travelling fans from the two trains back to Rolf Street.

The end of a game is always more chaotic than beforehand, because supporters tend to arrive anytime during the ninety minutes before kick-off, whereas at the end everyone swarms out into the street at the same time.

The final result was Albion 1 Manchester United 0, which meant that the disappointed visiting supporters had begun to drift out of the ground shortly before the final whistle, giving us a little time to begin gathering the train convoy together before the final rush at the end of the game. There were still isolated scuffles amongst the mingling crowd, but we were able to concentrate our efforts on gathering our flock together. The route back to Rolf Street was busier and more confused because of the sheer volume of people, but also quieter due to the subdued atmosphere amongst the United supporters.

The route between the ground and the station was a mixture of industrial premises and terraced houses. A typical feature of many Black Country streets, at the time, was waste land. These were areas where old decaying properties had long been demolished in slum clearance schemes, but the land had been left, undeveloped and littered with the debris of demolition. There was one such large plot on the right hand side of the road about halfway along the route to the station; as we approached I could see a gang of about fifty youths gathering. They were vocal and abusive, but were on the opposite side of the road to the convoy, so we kept them in view and carried on.

Their chants of "ONE – NIL! ONE – NIL! ONE – NIL!" drew little response, apart from the occasional expletive, from our convoy - most of whom now just wanted to get back to the station to catch the train.

"SHITE ON UNITED! WIM GONNA SHITE ON UNITED! SHITE ON UNITED!"

The level of verbal abuse rose, and the severity of the situation escalated further when the idiots on the waste land began to throw handy old half bricks at the passing column. A car window smashed noisily just in front of me, so three of us broke away, crossed the road onto the waste ground, and broke into a canter towards the offending large group. They immediately turned and fled.

Cuthbert was an old timer who, despite plenty of bluster and snorting, was soon left trailing behind the two younger horses. I could see them ahead and watched as they drove the gang from the waste land into the next street, and with the scene now clear I decided to break down to the walk. Cuthbert, however, had other ideas, and contrary to my instructions, continued to charge on, head down, at a lumbering canter. I hadn't noticed the limping yob who was straggling behind the fleeing main herd, but Cuthbert had. At the very last moment I attempted to steer to the left as we thundered towards him, but Cuthbert resisted all of my efforts, carried straight ahead, and bowled his target over leaving him flattened face down on the ground. I paused for a few moments to see him struggle to his knees; a tirade of foul language punctuated with a splutter of turf and soil poured in my direction. It confirmed that he was still very much alive, so I looked away, feigning innocence, before carrying on to join the others.

"You got one then?" laughed one of the other riders who had obviously witnessed our solo stampede.

"Well he did; it didn't have much to do with me, I'm afraid."

"Good answer; dumb animals are immune from prosecution."

"I don't think there is much dumb about this animal. He may be bloody horrible, but I don't think he's dumb for moment!"

We all had a good laugh before joining the others to continue with the escort. A large group of violent and unruly youths running away from just three police officers was a new phenomenon to me, and another perfect example of the value of police horses when working with crowds. I was enjoying myself. It was fun, and Cuthbert, bless him, was 'the man'!

Without further incident, we delivered the convoy safely to Rolf Street, where we formed them into a long line along the pavement. After a wait of about twenty minutes, amidst a flurry of cheeky banter, the first of two trains pulled into the station, and we were eventually able to hand the remaining supporters over to British Transport Police. As the last red and white scarf disappeared through the station gate we parted company with the three Ladywood guys, and headed back to West Bromwich stables.

Back at West Bromwich we watered and fed the horses before putting them to bed. I'd just made a final check on Cuthbert's rug and was watching him devour his last meal of the day. He was a miserable grumpy old sod, but it couldn't be denied – he was an excellent and unflappable police horse.

"Why are you such a miserable git?" I asked, without really expecting an answer.

He never lifted his head from the trough, but replied by kicking out with his off hind leg, adding another notch to the brick work of the back wall. I was just contemplating the paradox that was Cuthbert when I noticed Dai Owen standing at the door.

"Is that horse okay?"

"Yes sarge."

"Did you dry him off properly?"

"Yes sarge."

"Have you checked his feet?"

"Yes sarge."

"Right, shut the door then and leave him alone," he mumbled, walking away, before stopping and turning with an afterthought. "You did well today."

Before I could reply he'd turned again and disappeared back into the saddle room. Dai Owen was a man of few words and little praise, so his few mumbled words were treasure indeed.

Back in the saddle room we cleaned our kits, hung them up and tidied up, before adjourning to the bar to finish the day with a final match debrief. 'Debrief' at West Bromwich was a euphemism for a couple of pints in the police club after work. Police social clubs are now a thing of the past and have largely disappeared, but back in the day they were an important part of police culture, and the club at West Bromwich Police Station took up the whole fourth floor of the building. It was a friendly warm environment in which to wind down with colleagues, discuss the working day and swap heavily embellished funny stories. The beer was very cheap too; what was there not to like about police clubs?

There was a further debrief when I got back home after work. Mel was already in bed and Becks was watching Larry Grayson and The Generation Game, but ready and eagerly waiting for a full report about my first football match on horseback. I told her how good the horse had been, and she laughed uncontrollably when I described how he had ravaged the skinhead's bald head and railroaded the other yob into the ground.

"So Cuthbert is your buddy now?" she asked.

"Sort of, until the next time he bites me."

I unfastened my shirt and we both inspected the faint remaining traces of Cuthbert's teeth marks that were still visible on the side of my rib cage. We laughed at the thought of having a similar pattern permanently visible for all to see on the top of a bald head, and concluded that the yob would have to grow his hair again to hide his war wound.

I described how we had rounded up hundreds of noisy fans as they left the station, and walked them in fairly orderly fashion for almost a mile before delivering them safely to the football ground. I went on to tell her how, with just three horses, we put to flight a large gang of stone throwing idiots who had attacked the Rolf Street convoy.

"You can see so much more from the back of a horse," I enthused, "people listen to you, and do as they're told because they're afraid of the horses."

"With good cause too; that Cuthbert sounds positively dangerous to me. Are they all trained to eat people?"

"No they're not. He can't help it though; apparently his grannie was a T-Rex."

We continued to laugh at the poor skinhead's misfortune and debated whether his injury really was the result of me denying my horse a ham sandwich; the thought of him sitting in the queue at Sandwell General waiting for a painful tetanus jab in his bottom made us laugh even more.

"It sounds to me like you really enjoyed yourself Stef?"

"I did. All that pain and training... it all came together today and suddenly made sense and seemed worth it. I knew we were doing something really useful."

"What about a transfer? Have you made your mind up yet?" she asked, looking straight into my eyes.

"I think I need to go for it. I've sort of made my mind up. I think I have anyway."

"I wouldn't put it like that if you get an interview."

"No, you're right. I am enjoying it. I didn't want to admit it though. I'll type my application tomorrow morning; it's quiet on a Sunday."

"Are you sure?" she asked. "You mustn't do this just because I want you to. It has to be because you want to do it."

"I do want to do it. I've made up my mind; I've got nearly four weeks left to bust a gut and make a good impression."

I could tell by the change in her facial expression and tone of voice that she was delighted with my change of mind. She would never have tried to push me into it against my wishes, but now that I had made my decision she enthused about how the more sociable working hours would affect our daily lives. I knew then that it was the right thing to do, but I had only a short time left to prove my worth back at work; I hoped that my late application didn't suggest a lack of commitment.

"Come on. Let's have an early night and celebrate," she said as she encouraged me to my feet.

"Celebrate? What are we celebrating?"

"One – nil to the Albion of course," replied the girl who I knew had absolutely no interest in football.

We switched off, locked up, and began to make our way up the now warm and silent stairs. Halfway to the top I stopped and prevented her from going any further. She looked at me in surprise.

"You're not going to do a Cuthbert and bite me are you?" I asked.

There was a short pause. "No I'm not. Well not on the top of your head anyway."

"Well; trot on Wildy!" I laughed as we ran up the few remaining stairs.

CHAPTER 20

THE LONE RANGER

There were around forty men of varying levels of competence and experience serving on the mounted department, and as a novice, the level of your ability and rate of personal development could be measured by the calibre of horse you were allowed to ride. Remounts and novice horses were allocated to, and trained by, the more experienced and able officers, while the steady old schoolmasters[20] were generally ridden by the least experienced. In between these two extremes was a variety of animals of different character, temperament, physical ability, appearance, and desirability, and whilst there was generally very little interest for promotion through the ranks amongst the men, the desire to be allocated a good horse was high, and often the root cause of any internal politics within the department.

Only full time officers who had been permanently transferred to the department were allocated their own horse, and those horses were generally ridden on the officers' rest days by a 'spare' man who was often, like me at the time, an inexperienced attached officer.

---

[20] *A schoolmaster used to be a horse that was so dull and insensitive anyone could safely ride him.*

Initially, irrespective of the horse's ability or experience, attached officers always went out on patrol as a pair whilst being escorted by a more experienced colleague.

A significant milestone and rite of passage for an attached man was being allowed out on independent patrol without an escorting officer. It could, however, sometimes be nerve wracking and eventful.

It was 1979, so the days of shiny police whistles and Dr Who type police call boxes located on street corners had long gone, and patrolling police officers had routinely been using personal radios for over fifteen years. Mounted officers still, however, routinely patrolled without radios. It had nothing to do with operational policy, but was simply down to the limited technology of the time. Local police officers were controlled locally, so used short range UHF personal radios which were tuned into the frequency of their local police station. A mounted officer, however, could sometimes travel between fifteen and twenty miles whilst on patrol, so could transgress several radio zones in a single tour of duty. A VHF force wide radio, like those fitted to traffic patrol vehicles, required a large heavy battery pack which needed to be carried in a harness; they had been previously tried and rejected as impractical for mounted use. The two main issues with not carrying a radio were that you could be in the vicinity of an on-going incident and would know nothing about it, or you could happen upon a serious incident and have no means of relaying information or seeking further assistance. It was not an unknown sight, in those days, to see a police horse standing patiently outside of a public telephone box whilst the officer was inside - telephone handset in one hand and reins in the other, dialling 999.

After my eventful introduction to football match duties I had started to take the job more seriously, and my desire to complete my attachment and return to divisional duties as soon as possible had waned. I had discussed it at length with Becks, and although she hadn't openly cheered out loud at my decision to try for a permanent transfer, I knew she was quietly delighted at the prospect of more social working hours and the effect that would have on our family life. Decision made, I had formally applied for a permanent transfer to the department and had set out to impress; I was always punctual, kept my kit in tip top order, went out of my way to get along with everyone, and tried to display a willingness to learn and improve. I rode whatever horse I was allocated and never complained at the nomadic nature of my job when I was given my postings for the week.

During my first few weeks I had been posted to all of the stables except for Bordesley Green. I had absolutely no idea where Bordesley Green was, so was interested when I was finally instructed to work a 10am until 6pm shift there for just a single day. Birmingham as a whole, in those days, was a bit of a mystery to me, so I plotted my journey the night before with the help of my much thumbed A to Z map of the city. It was a couple of miles to the east of the city centre, and given that I would be travelling during a very busy rush hour I knew that I was going to have set out nice and early.

The journey went well and I arrived at the stables at about 9.30am. Bordesley Green Police Station was a large three storey, double-fronted Victorian building; it fronted directly onto the pavement of a road of the same name, and sat next door to a fire station of similar age and proportions. Like most of the surrounding area it looked drab, run-down and daunting.

I turned into a gate to the left of the building and spotted the stables at the end of a long driveway to the rear of the main building. It was a very old stable, and had obviously been built at the same time as the main police station. The stable door opened directly into stalls where there were three horses standing, one of them saddled for riding, and a door to the side that opened into the bunk; I knocked, walked in and found a trouser-less man changing into uniform. He momentarily abandoned his routine, and shaking my hand, greeted me like a long lost friend.

"Hello young Stef, my name's Laurie Lord. Welcome to Bordesley Green. It's lovely to meet you; we've heard all about you," he enthused whilst continuing to shake my hand furiously with both of his firmly clasped.

"Crikey! What have you heard?" I asked with interest, not realising that I already had a reputation.

"Well hopefully you won't need to punch me, and you don't have to sing to our horses because none of them bite; so you're quite safe here for the day," he laughed, and playfully punched my shoulder.

I put my kit down on the floor and made myself at home whilst Laurie made me a cup of tea. Laurie Lord was a slightly built man sporting a sizeable moustache; he was probably twenty years older than me, but very fit and, even standing in his boxer shorts, looked polished from head to toe. He had spent most of his service as a mounted officer, and was, with few exceptions, one of the nicest people that I have ever had the privilege to work with. Laurie Lord was a true gentleman.

"I've got two to ride this morning Stef, so I'll be in to change at half time. You'll be taking Daemon out this afternoon," he said to my surprise.

"What, without an escort? I haven't been out alone yet. Will it be okay?"

"Well that's what the posting says, so someone must think that you're up to it. There's a first time for everything Stef, so you may as well break yourself in with old Daemon; he'll look after you."

So that was that. He rode out of the yard leaving me alone in a strange stable, where I quietly groomed my strange horse before finding my way to the forage store, bedding down, and finally swilling down. I made Laurie a cup of tea when he came in to swap horses, and then tidied up before getting myself ready to go out on patrol alone.

Daemon was a quiet and gentle horse and had behaved impeccably whilst being groomed and saddled; he was cobby[21], but his attractive, dark dappled grey wouldn't have looked out of place on rockers in the corner of well to do nursery, or in a picture book harnessed to Cinderella's magic coach.

Laurie had returned from his second patrol and was cleaning his saddlery when I mounted up in the yard. He came out, dressed in his apron, to see me off.

"Off you go then," he said whilst patting Daemon's neck. "Good luck on your maiden solo; keep out of trouble."

"I may never be seen again," I sighed.

"You won't get into trouble on him; he's as good as gold."

"I don't doubt you, but I haven't got a clue where I'm going. Who knows where I'll end up?"

"Just give him his head if you're lost. He knows where he lives and where his bed and supper are," was a reassuring reply, but I was beginning to regret leaving my A to Z in the Mini. I rode out of the yard and turned left into the unknown, trying to create the impression I had some idea of what I was doing and where I was going.

[21] *A short coupled thick set horse.*

I'm not sure where I went, or how far away I was from the police station at any given time, but Daemon was a treasure. I couldn't have chosen a better ride for my first solo patrol. He needed a little leg to keep him going forward, but didn't pull and wasn't fazed by any situation that we encountered on the streets of Bordesley Green.

I, however, was less impressed by Bordesley Green, which seemed to mainly consist of run-down Victorian terraced houses in a never ending maze of dour, neglected Victorian streets. Once proud, smart, tree-lined avenues were now dirty, littered, and lined with endless rows of tatty parked cars; there was little doubt I was in the heart of inner city Birmingham.

Having no means of communication between myself and the rest of the West Midlands Police, I was relieved that the patrol had been without incident and the horse hadn't put a foot wrong, but becoming increasingly concerned that I had no idea how to get back to the police station. It was decades before the arrival of mobile phones and the magic of Google Maps. I reached a set of traffic lights at a busy crossroad and couldn't decide if I should turn left, right, or carry on straight ahead. As the lights changed to green I decided to follow Laurie's advice and ask Daemon, so I lengthened the reins and surrendered the feel on his mouth.

"Go on son; walk on."

He turned left without hesitation and walked purposefully on, so I collected up the reins again but didn't offer any feel to the left or right and just let the horse go exactly where he wanted to go. Horses are a little like homing pigeons in that they can almost always find their way home. They are creatures of habit and soon learned the routes and streets of the areas that they patrolled daily. A lot could be learned about where an officer frequented on his daily patrols by riding his horse on his rest day. Horses show no loyalty, have no secrets, and would unknowingly betray you for a slice of carrot or a lump of sugar.

Half an hour later, Daemon turned through the gate and back into the yard at Bordesley Green Police Station. He had, just as Laurie said, kept me safe and brought me home without me having a clue of where I was. I put him to bed and cleaned my saddlery, before watering and feeding the three horses at about 5.30pm. At 5.45pm I finished the final de-litter of the stalls and picked up the telephone before dialling Big Ben's extension number at Duke Street.

"Inspector Scott," answered the familiar voice.

"PC Wild at Bordseley Green Sir; all the horses are fed and feeding."

"Good man Wild. First time independent today, I believe?"

"Yes Sir," I replied with some surprise.

"Nothing to report?"

"Nothing at all Sir, it was all plain sailing really."

"Good man. Don't get cocky though Wild, shit will happen you know. Shit will definitely happen. Now get yourself home, and good night," he said as he put the phone down. It just left me to lock the door behind me, before retracing my steps across a very busy Birmingham during my second rush hour of the day.

I arrived home later than normal that day, and ate my meal from a tray because the girls had already eaten. I moaned to Becks about the length of the journey, the terrible traffic, and the dreariness of Bordesley Green and its depressing samey streets.

"You wouldn't want to work there full time then?" she asked.

"No not at all. It's too far, would cost us a fortune in petrol. And it's a shithole."

"Really, it's as good as that?" she laughed.

"It's as good as that yes, but I did go out all alone without anyone with me and without a parachute."

I went on to tell her about my first independent patrol; that I had no idea where I was or where I was going, and that the horse had had to take me back to the stables because I was lost.

"Yes, but think about it Stef; they must think something of you or they wouldn't let you go out alone, would they?"

"Good point; I must be good. So in future you can call me the Lone Ranger[22]; if you don't mind of course?" I joked.

"I see… and I suppose you'd like me to be your Tonto?"

"Now you're talking babe; so in future you must obey all of my commands and show me blind loyalty, without question as we ride the range together. Is that understood?"

"Listen matey, just because you've been out alone on a big grey horse doesn't mean that it was Silver, you're not in charge here, I'm not Tonto, and you aren't The Lone Ranger. This is my prairie too you know," she replied, fiercely attacking my ribs with a poking finger and forcing me to retreat backwards whilst squealing like a giggly girl. My latest attempt to install male supremacy into the homestead had, sadly, failed again.

My second independent adventure happened the following week whilst I was posted to West Bromwich. West Bromwich is the principal town in the Metropolitan Borough of Sandwell, and though I wasn't completely familiar with the local streets, I knew all of the main roads and would certainly be able to find my way back to the police station without any need of assistance.

---

[22] *The Lone Ranger was a popular TV masked cowboy hero of the 1960s. He rode a white horse named Silver, and had a loyal Native American companion named Tonto.*

West Bromwich was, at the time, a typical Black Country town. It was densely populated with an ethnically diverse, largely working class community; the sky line was a gloomy mixture of grimy heavy industrial factories and poor housing. Its outer boundaries were blurred, because like elsewhere in the Black Country conurbation, one borough just seamlessly merged into the next without any open space between two towns to define their individual identity. However, in complete contrast to the rest of the neighbourhood, and only a few minutes from the police station, was Sandwell Valley Country Park.

Sandwell Valley Country Park is a large open park, of almost two thousand acres, that creates a dividing oasis of green between West Bromwich and the city of Birmingham. Historically it was once the estate of the medieval Sandwell Priory, but is now a popular public space, and includes park facilities, nature reserves, a bird sanctuary, several lakes, and large expanses of open parkland. It was an excellent place to exercise and school horses, so was a regular feature of the mounted patrols from West Bromwich Police Stables, and was simply referred to by the men as 'Over the Valley'.

My ride for the day was to be Big Seth, whose name had been well chosen, because Seth was the biggest horse of the whole department. He was heavy, ugly brute, stood at about 17.3 hands, and if he hadn't been so naturally chicken hearted, could have been a truly formidable beast. Like some of the other horses, he would flatten his ears in an attempt to intimidate when you entered his stable, however unlike Cuthbert, a raised voice "Boo" would leave him cringing remorsefully whilst you got on with your job.

I mounted up with the others at 10am, and was pleased that after a double hop I managed to get into the saddle without having to stand on the shit pit wall, like I had seen others do. I collected my reins, and Dai Owen came out to speak to me before we rode out of the gate.

"Take care out there and look after this horse," he said whilst patting Seth's massive neck.

"I'll do my best sarge."

"You'd better, and have a look over the valley while you're out. A couple of dog walkers have been flashed at over the last week or two. Pob lwc.[23]"

I hadn't the slightest idea what he was talking about, but nodded knowingly as I rode out of the gate - feeling very tall, conspicuous, and more than a little self-conscious.

I spent an hour or so patrolling around the streets close to the town centre before heading towards Sandwell Valley. My route took me through Dartmouth Park, which was a traditional urban park laid out mainly to formal gardens, before passing the visitor centre at the old Sandwell Valley Farm, and then over a footbridge crossing the M5 motorway. The bridge spanned high above the busy, fast moving traffic and the handrail was very much lower than my eye line, so 'eyes front and don't look down' was very much the order of the day.

Once over the motorway the landscape immediately changed to a mixture of rough parkland, woodland, and water, which included a boating lake and a wetland bird sanctuary. The whole area was served by a network of hard-core footpaths which were well used by the public on the weekends, but relatively quiet during the week.

[23] *Good luck in Welsh.*

There wasn't a soul to be seen, so I congratulated myself on managing to keep out of trouble during the morning's patrol, and, now we were off the road and out of the traffic, felt I would be able to relax and enjoy a gentle hack in the countryside. Seth, however, had other ideas.

We began to walk steadily along a wide track with open ground to our left and a tall, thick, hedgerow to our right, and I lengthened his reins a little so he could stretch his neck. The eagle-eyed Seth, however, succumbed to a bout of paranoia and responded by spotting a horse-eating monster hiding in a hawthorn bush. Without warning, he leapt to his left onto the grass, and stood staring into the bush with his head raised, snorting, nostrils flared and in obvious terror. I recovered my composure, applied a little leg pressure, and looked to see what had terrified the not-so-bold Seth.

There was absolutely nothing to be seen, but the horse was still frozen with fear and refused to take even a single step forward. I would, in time, learn that a horse's ability to spot invisible gremlins at the most awkward of times was unfortunately not rare. They are, after all, animals whose natural instinct is to flee from danger; Seth, despite his size, was exceptionally chicken hearted with a finely tuned instinct for flight, but he was also coarse and insensitive to the leg, which I was now applying more firmly. It was an unfortunate combination, and no amount of leg and spur had any effect.

"Come on you bloody great cowardly lump; there's nothing there!" I growled in vain as I frantically kicked his sides with my heels.

The situation deteriorated further when he began to respond to my leg pressure by rapidly retreating backwards. This wasn't in the book; there was no logic in the situation because there was absolutely nothing in the bush, but his snorting through flared nostrils suggested that he was genuinely afraid. I was alone with no one to ask or assist, and I could have walked off to the left, in our original direction and pretended nothing had happened, but felt that would have created a poor precedent for the future. So, I turned him right and walked back in the direction from which we had come, before turning to approach the lurking bush monster for a second time.

Nothing; he walked on past the bush without missing a step, or any hint of a sideways glance. It was as if the previous fractious minutes of our lives had never happened. I leaned forward and patted his neck. "Good lad, well done, walk on, well done," I praised, quietly wondering what on earth was going on in his huge, stupid head.

There was, inexplicably, a complete change in Seth's mood, and for whatever reason he decided that he no longer had a care in the world. He walked on with a new spring in his step without any encouragement from me, so I began to relax and enjoy the ride; could there be a more pleasant way of earning a living?

My enjoyment, however, was short lived; just a little further down the track, and again without warning, Seth raised his head and ripped a branch from another large bush with his teeth. By the time I realised what had happened, he had continued to walk boldly forward, now with a sizeable shrub, of about four feet long, hanging out of his mouth.

"You bloody daft donkey. Give it here!" I snapped, reaching forward in an attempt to grab and remove the offending foliage.

Seth continued to walk on defiantly, raising his head high out of my reach and refusing to surrender his newly won trophy. I leaned as far forward as I possibly could without actually sitting on his neck, but each time I reached out he just stretched further forward until his mouth was tantalizingly just out of my grasp. I didn't feel secure leaning so far out of the saddle, so I pulled him

315

up whilst I considered the situation - which, in fairness, wasn't really impeding our progress. He continued to happily chomp on the branch while I mentally debated my next course of action. I soon concluded that though we were making progress along my chosen route, I wasn't prepared to be seen in uniform riding a horse with a small tree hanging out of his mouth. It didn't seem professional, so I decided I would have to dismount and remove it.

I dismounted, crossed my stirrups over the saddle, and hung on to the end of the reins while I reached out and took hold of Seth's oversized morning snack. I pulled and so did Seth, who showed no signs of surrender. The harder I pulled, the higher he raised his head, until at one point both of my feet were lifted off the ground.

"Loose the bloody thing you long nosed fool," I growled, wrestling in vain. "Put the damn thing down… put it down… DROP IT!"

The battle moved into another phase when he began to rein back and pull me along the path; I dug my metal tipped heels into the gravel but was no match for the dinosaur sized horse, and was dragged along, ploughing two shallow furrows in the pathway. We both stopped pulling and paused to glare at each other. I looked around to make sure there was no one nearby to witness my humiliation.

"Have you any idea how stupid you look with that tree in your mouth?" I asked in desperation. "You're supposed to be a police horse. Where is your pride? Where is your dignity?" It occurred to me however, as I was looking into his big goofy face with a tree growing from his green foaming mouth, that pride wasn't really his thing. I would need another plan, other than verbal negotiation, if I was to win this battle.

After a little thought, I looped my arm through the reins, held onto his bit with one hand and prised his mouth open with my thumb whilst twisting the branch with my other hand; after a final moment or two of defiance he finally dropped the hotly disputed foliage onto the ground. He stood with his head held high, lips wide apart, and the whites of his eyes showing; he was not happy as I uncrossed my stirrups and thankfully managed to re-mount.

As we walked on along the track in the original direction, I gathered the reins, re-established my seat and re-gained my composure. I was beginning to reconsider my views regarding the joys of a carefree ride in the countryside as opposed to the usual street patrol, when Seth suddenly and without warning burst into song.

I had no idea why he was doing it, or if I should try to stop him, but he began to grunt loudly in time with the beat of his footfall. This alarming vocal performance was accompanied at regular intervals by a long, loud neigh. I had not heard a horse neigh at all during my riding course or attachment, and had no idea if it was in any way normal, or if he was in pain. Whatever the reason, this was a performance to behold.

Ugh... ah... ugh... ah... ugh... ah ugh... WHINNIEEEEEEEEE!
"Shut up you bloody fool. Someone will hear you."
Ugh... ah... ugh... ah... ugh. Ah ugh... WHINNIEEEEEEEEE!
"Shush! You muppet! Shush!"
He threw his head high into the air and raised his lip to expose his teeth every time he let out the neigh, and I was completely puzzled as to why he was doing it.

Ugh... ah... ugh... ah... ugh. Ah ugh... WHINNIEEEEEEEEE!
Just ahead the track disappeared around a bend, and as we approached I saw a line of horses and riders walking towards us. The reason for Seth's serenade was now apparent.

Ugh... ah... ugh... ah... ugh. Ah ugh... WHINNIEEEEEEEEE!

"Will you belt up?" I snarled. "They're going to think we're a right pair of clowns." I gave him a sharp dig with my heels to no avail.

Ugh... ah... ugh... ah... ugh. Ah ugh... WHINNIEEEEEEEEE!

As we drew closer I could see that there were six riders in line. At the head of the column was a middle aged woman, followed by a teenage girl on a slightly smaller horse, with the line behind gradually reducing in both size and age, until finally a little girl of about six, riding a typically Thelwellian Pony[24], brought up the rear.

Ugh... ah... ugh... ah... ugh. Ah ugh... WHINNIEEEEEEEEE!

"My word, he's a great big noisy boy," greeted the smiling leading lady, whilst raising her crop, as we came into earshot.

"Yes. Hello. He's just very pleased to see you," I replied with a smile through gritted teeth. I dug my heels into Seth, who had slowed obviously intending to stop for a chat. Somehow, I managed to keep him moving forward, but couldn't straighten his head from the acute bend to the right as he looked longingly at every one of the passing ponies.

"Hello... hello... hello... hello... hello...." I continued with my false smile, nodding as I greeted every one of the passing young riders whilst still frantically legging the reluctant Seth along the line of little girls. I consoled myself with the small bonus that he had, at last, stopped his ridiculous singing.

Finally, as I drew level with the tiny girl on the Thelwell at the back of the line, I stopped kicking my horse forward as the girl's head was roughly level with my leg, and prepared to continue en route along the path.

---

[24] *Norman Thelwell was an English artist well known for his humorous illustrations of small fat, unruly ponies, ridden by adventurous tiny girls.*

Seth, however had other ideas. With a speed and agility that belied his bulk, he suddenly spun around to his right, before falling neatly in at the back of the line behind the tiny Thelwell.

I was completely stunned. I had worked so hard to overcome his highly tuned herd instinct and had kept him going forward against his wishes, but now in the blink of an eye he had wrong footed me, and I was tail end Charlie at the back of a pony club hack. I increased pressure on the reins, but to no effect - eventually I was sitting back in the saddle hauling with all of my strength to try and stop the infatuated but wilful Seth.

"Whoa! Whoa! Come here! Will you whoa, you big daft bugger. Whoa!" I desperately struggled with the reins, but he was smitten and not listening.

In front, somewhere down below Seth's nose, the little girl was nervously looking over her shoulder at the huge animal following her, and breathing down her neck.

"Whoa Seth! Whoa! WHOA!" I cried with ever increasing desperation.

"Mrs Wimbury! Mrs Wimbury! The police horse is chasing me!" I heard the girl cry.

"Shush! You'll be okay. We're going in a minute," I reassured, but not very reassuringly.

"Mrs Wimbury! Mrs Wimbury! I'm frightened Mrs Wimbury!" she continued to blub with a now quivering lower lip.

"Shush! Don't shout," I pleaded desperately. "It'll be fine. Shush!"

Inevitably, however, Mrs Wimbury finally heard the child's cry and was somewhat surprised when she looked around and saw a policeman riding a rhino sized horse at the back of her hack. She raised her arm, halted her ride, and trotted to the back of the line to investigate. She nervously looked me up and down with growing suspicion.

"Can I help you officer?" she asked in a rather matronly fashion.

"We've had reports of a man exposing himself in this area, so I thought I'd join you for a few minutes; if that's okay of course?" I lied unconvincingly.

Mrs Wimbury was a far more experienced horsewoman than I was horseman and she saw through me immediately.

"You can't control that horse, can you officer?"

"It's not a matter of control; it's just a momentary lapse;" I heard myself spluttering, "nothing to worry about, no harm done. It will be fine!"

"I don't think that Charlotte's silk would agree with you officer."

I looked to my front, where to my horror I saw Seth was now nodding his head at full height, like a dog shaking a rat, but with little Charlotte's silky hat cover dangling from between his clenched teeth.

"My new silk; that's my new silk! My Nana bought it me for my birthday!" the child cried with tears rolling down her cheek.

Seth continued to triumphantly wave his trophy aloft for all to see, like a cheerleader at a basketball game. I angrily dismounted, and by taking hold of the bit managed to lower his head so that I could reach the brightly coloured silk. Predictably, he had no intention of giving up his prize without a fight, so it was only after another determined tug of war and a very loud talking to that Seth finally relented and allowed me to wrench the silk from his clutches. I apologised and handed the now mangled, soggy hat to the heartbroken Charlotte.

"There you are luvvie, stop crying; it's all fine now."

"It's all wet and gooey," she sobbed.

"It will wash lovely; don't worry Charlotte," I assured.

"It's all horrible and green, and foamy… Mrs Wimbury, it's all foamy."

"Ah. That'll be the leaves from the tree," I cringed.

"He's pulled my pompom off," she continued to bawl.

It was difficult to imagine how the situation could possibly develop to any higher level of embarrassment, but it did, because when I looked up at Seth he defiantly eyeballed me and returned my glare, this time with a large, pink, woolly pompom firmly clenched between his front teeth. He looked ridiculous with the colourful pompom held high between his sludgy green and brown teeth, and I had a disturbing vision of dancing a violent and sweaty battle to retrieve it. The very thought of it terrified me, so after some not so careful consideration of the situation, I took the only sensible course of action appropriate; I got back on my horse, trotted on, and left town in a hurry.

Back at the stables, I confessed my sins and painfully relived my tale of woe by confiding in Cyril Riley. He sat with an expressionless look on his face, listening intently to the whole sorry story before erupting into a fit of laughter.

"Old Seth; what a star," he chuckled. "What would we do without him?"

"I couldn't do a thing with him. Is he always like that? He made me look a complete tool in front of all those kids."

"He always takes the piss, but you'll get better and you won't fall for his tricks when you know what you're doing."

"I thought that I did know what I was doing," I moaned.

"And that was your first mistake son. Babes and sucklings, babes and sucklings; lambs to the slaughter. You'll learn by your mistakes son, you'll learn."

"Big Ben warned me that shit would happen."

"Well there you go, Ben's not stupid."

"Well you say that, but everyone at Duke Street says he's mad."

"He's as mad as a bloody hatter, but that don't mean that he's stupid," he tried to explain. "When you understand the difference you'll be cleverer than Seth. Now let's crack on; I'm going to see to Cuthbert." He got up and walked out of the room singing, whilst I contemplated his words of wisdom. I listened as his voice faded away into the yard; I didn't, however, notice the song returning to the room, and so was jolted back to my senses when he looked around the door and spoke to me.

"I forgot. I was supposed to pass you a message."

"A message? Who from?" I asked.

"Seth wants his pompom back. What have you done with it?"

I couldn't help but laugh at myself, and now more fully appreciated the limitations of my little practical experience; Big Ben was right. *"Shit will happen. It will happen."*

A few weeks later, towards the end of my three month attachment, I was posted to 3pm until 11pm shift at Kings Heath to work my first night football match at Villa Park. I hadn't previously ridden in the dark and it was almost seven miles from Kings Heath to Villa Park, so it was definitely going to be a new experience.

I arrived at Kings Heath a few minutes before three, just as the early shift guy was putting on his coat to go home. I had never met him before and he was keen to get out of the door and go home, but he did take sufficient time to tell me that my partner for the night had phoned in sick. I was to be working alone - a strange stable, a strange horse, darkness, and worst of all, having to find my way to Villa Park when I wasn't even entirely sure which way to turn out of the gate.

There were two unridden horses in the stable, with no indication in the duty book as to which one I was to ride and which one was going to stay in bed. I looked at them both and chose a large grey with the name 'Jemadar' displayed over his stable door. Parade time at Villa Park was 6pm for a 7.30pm kick off; it was a lengthy ride and I didn't want to be late, so I planned to leave at 4.30pm.

I groomed my chosen horse, who was thankfully friendly and compliant, prepared my kit and uniform, attached my red light to my right stirrup, and made time for a last minute cup of tea before saddling up. After feeding hay to the remaining horses, I mounted as planned, and rode out of the yard at exactly 4.30pm. It was still light, and having looked at my A to Z for the shortest route I was worried I might get lost, so decided I would follow the main roads through the city centre; a longer but vaguely familiar journey.

Jemadar was a delight to ride. He didn't require any leg to keep him moving, he stopped when I asked, and seemed happily unfazed by the busy traffic that we encountered. The route took us along Bristol Street and through the city centre via the Bull Ring, which in those days was still fully open to through-city traffic. It was the peak of the rush hour as we steadily trotted around the fast moving, multi-laned, Bull Ring roundabout. I couldn't help but reflect that just a few weeks earlier I couldn't even ride a horse, and was now trotting all alone around one of the busiest road junctions in the Midlands during evening rush hour, on a horse I had never previously ridden and with no radio. The roundabout was a sea of beeping, braking and lane changing traffic, and at the time it may have been exhilarating; now, in hindsight and from the comfort of my reclining armchair, it was sheer craziness that would have sent modern day health and safety professionals into apoplexy.

Emerging from the city centre, I rode below the high flyover, turning right around Lancaster Circus and then onto the busiest roundabout of the journey at Dartmouth Circus, which seemed even crazier as dusk drew in and headlights were switched on. We trotted briskly around the roundabout because it seemed safer to keep up with the traffic, before eventually breaking away into the relatively quiet streets of Aston.

For the final mile we slowed and walked through the dark streets of endless aging terraced houses, arriving at Villa Park just before six - safe, sound, and with me feeling a little pleased with myself. My new best mate, Jemadar, had been faultless; I liked him a lot.

I met up with the some of the others who were sitting waiting at the main entrance in Trinity Road, and joined the end of the line just as Derek Joiner arrived with the Duke Street contingent. The Duke Street officers lined up, whilst Joiner stood in front to brief us on our duties. He took a sheet of paper out of his pocket and looked up and down the parade of officers.

"Good evening gentlemen. Let me see who we have got and who we haven't got." He studied his paper further before looking again. "Wild, who are you with?"

"I'm on my own sarge, my other half called in sick."

"Don't tell me that you've ridden from Kings Heath alone tonight."

"I'm afraid so," I answered, wondering if I perhaps shouldn't have.

"What horse is that Wild?"

"It's Jemadar, sarge," I replied, with a slowly increasing realisation that I'd done something wrong.

"Ye Gods Wild, who told you to ride that horse tonight?"

"No one told me which horse to ride so I just chose one. He's been very good though. I like him a lot."

"I'll bet you bloody do. You may not like him so much on the way home tonight. I can't believe this! Talk about an accident waiting to happen. Wait here until I've posted everyone else."

Everyone, when posted, moved out to their pre match positions to man the entrances located around the perimeter of the huge football ground. I had never been to Villa Park before and was keen have a look around, but before I had a chance to see anything I was further cross-examined by the sergeant. It seemed that Jemadar was a relatively young, not yet fully trained horse, and was definitely not in the available pool of horses that I was allowed to ride. Additionally, it seemed that he was regarded as a difficult horse to ride, and had earned himself a reputation for taking hold of the bit and galloping home at great speed, often with better, more experienced riders than me. It seemed that Jemadar had not only an unusually finely tuned compass and homing instinct, but also an insatiable longing for his bed and dinner.

No one knew at the time, but just two years later in 1981, Jemadar would be one of two grey horses proudly loaned to the City of London Police to lead the parade at Prince Charles' marriage to Lady Diana Spencer. The horses were duly delivered to London but were ridden by City of London officers for the parade. There was a full rehearsal along the entire route on the day before the wedding, and apparently both of our horses behaved perfectly. On the big day the streets were packed with throngs of cheering and waving people; the noise, excitement and atmosphere was incredible, and obviously a huge challenge for any horse in the circumstances. Jemadar, it seems, was completely unfazed by the occasion and never flinched at the flags, banners and electric atmosphere. However, such was the accuracy of his compass, that after only being in London for twenty four hours, Jemadar knew that when the parade moved away from St. Paul's Cathedral he was heading back towards the comforts of his new stable. His rider reported back after the horses returned to Birmingham, and he had nothing but praise for the bombproof bravery of our Jemadar. Unfortunately, he also said that on a few occasions after St. Paul's, he thought his arm muscles were about to explode as he fought to prevent the horse from taking off and leading the parade at thirty miles an hour through a cheering London to terminate at the police stables. Now that would have been good television!

Even without the ability to see into the future, Sergeant Joiner was deeply troubled about the prospects of my return to Kings Heath aboard my new friend Jemadar. He was angry with me for not calling him, but even angrier with whoever had posted me to my first night match from a distant stable without stipulating which horse I was to ride.

"Right Wildy, pin your ears back. As soon as they kick off at 7.30pm do not come 'round for a cuppa; just head off back to Kings Heath. Take it easy and take your time. Do not trot that horse, and don't let him piss off with you. Do you understand?"

"That means that I'll miss them coming out of the match at the end," I complained.

"I don't give a shit about the end of the match. Just do as you are told. Are you listening to me?"

"Yes sarge."

"I repeat - do not trot, take your time, and don't let him piss off with you. With a bit of luck you'll get back alive, and I'll call you after the match, the moment that I get back to Duke Street. Have you got that?"

"I've got it, but if I don't answer; you could try The Accy," I laughed.

"Don't! Just bloody don't!" He rubbed his forehead before turning his horse around and riding away.

So, at exactly 7.30pm as the whistle blew to signal the start of the match, I began the long lonesome trail back to Kings Heath. The streets around the football ground were strangely deserted, but packed with parked cars and eerily illuminated by the bright floodlights of Villa Park. I tried not to let the sergeant's obvious concern worry me unduly, but even with my limited experience, there was a noticeable extra spring in my horse's step from the moment we began to head home. He wasn't pulling, but I hadn't had to ask him to slow down yet, and we had a long way to go for him to build up to an uncomfortable speed.

"You just take it easy. It isn't a race. Be a good lad. Are you listening to me?"

He was listening to me, and I knew that he was because every time that I spoke to him his ears pricked up and showed that he was paying attention. I tried a little experiment by remaining quiet whilst feeling the reins, and was met with resistance. The more I talked, the more animated his ears became and the more he responded to my feel on the reins without pulling. After just a few minutes the one way conversation was in full flow; his ears were vigorously responding and he was comfortably mouthing the bit as we approached Dartmouth Circus at a nice brisk walk.

The roundabout was much quieter than it had been two hours earlier, so we walked steadily around without being hassled by rush hour traffic; my conversation, however, was struggling as it was completely one sided and I was rapidly running out of topics that we had in common. There was no one around to eavesdrop, so I moved on to fairy stories in funny voices, which he seemed to enjoy very much.

"Once upon a time there were three bears…"

He seemed to approve.

"Daddy bear," I said in my gruffest voice, "mommy bear and little baby bear…" I continued in my squeakiest tone.

I seemed to have struck gold. Jemadar was now so engrossed with his story that he had forgotten all about his warm bed and feed bucket. He plodded on steadily oblivious to his surroundings, and by the time I had reached the scary part with "Who's been eating my porridge?", we had completed Lancaster Circus and were well on our way towards The Bull Ring.

The city was now alight, and as we walked beneath the giant bull on the side of the overpass, there was already evidence of early revellers beginning to appear on the streets. A little further on along Smallbrook Queensway, which is located on the edge of Birmingham's Chinese quarter, I was accosted by a group of drunken young women. I had no option other than to stop and talk to them, because a big heavy girl wearing leopard print hot pants that were a size or two too small, stood in front of me in the roadway. One of her friends produced a small instamatic camera from her handbag and Jemadar and I were suddenly surrounded by giggling women taking turns to pose next to us. The girl bulging out of the hot pants suddenly grabbed hold of my leg with both hands.

"Oooh Darlin' are you gonna give us a kiss for me birthday?"

"Goodness that's tempting," I lied, "but sorry it's not allowed; not while I'm in uniform anyway," I joked.

"Well we can soon get you out of your uniform, can't we girls?" shrieked one of her friends as they all began to cackle with laughter.

Not wanting to be de-bagged in the city centre, I decided that it really was time to make my exit. In order to prevent any danger of a chase, I disobeyed my orders from the sergeant and put my legs to the horse to trot away. He went away briskly scattering beauties left and right, but still under control, so I decided to continue trotting as we turned into Bristol Street. It's not easy telling a story at the tempo of a rising trot, so after making sure that there no one in earshot, I tried him with a song.

"Horsey, horsey don't you stop… just make your feet go clippity-clop…"seemed to go down very well as we made rapid progress along Bristol Street. "Your tail goes swish and the wheels go round…" saw us into Belgrave Middleway, and "…giddy up we're homeward bound," kept him happily trotting nicely in hand along Pershore Road. After another song or two, and with no further incidents, we eventually walked cool, calm and collected into the yard at Kings Heath at about 9.45pm. Despite all the warnings it had been a perfect journey, because the much maligned Jemadar had behaved like a gentleman. After feeding the horses, putting them to bed, and cleaning the saddlery, I answered the telephone in the bunk at about 10pm.

"Is that you Wildy?" asked an obviously concerned sergeant Joiner.

"Yes, it is."

"You've got back safely then?"

"Safe and sound; no problems at all, he's been brilliant."

"You managed alright then?" he asked with obvious surprise. "Didn't he pull your arms out?"

"No, not at all; I think he's a great horse. He's got a good ear too," I replied with tongue in cheek.

"Well, thank the lord for that. Well done young man. I have to say I'm mightily impressed. Right; we're all going over the Sack for a couple of pints when we've tidied up. Why don't you pop in on the way home?"

It was good to be invited to join the crew for a post-match drink and I did seriously consider the offer, but I also had a long drive home. If I left immediately I would probably get home whilst Becks was still awake. She always enjoyed listening to my funny stories about the horses, and I had a good one to tell her tonight.

The call of the pub was strong, and it did occur to me that some social bonding with the sergeant and the lads may be beneficial given my recent application to transfer, but the thought of some cosy horizontal story telling back home was even more appealing. So I turned left out of the gate and, bursting into song, began to find my way towards the M6 North.

CHAPTER 21

THEY THINK IT'S ALL OVER

It was almost the end of May, the week before the scheduled end of my attachment, and I had been summoned to Duke Street to see the Chief Inspector. Just a week earlier I had submitted an application for a full time transfer to the department, and I suspected that this meeting was to confirm whether my application had been successful or not. I knew that I was one of four applicants and that there were only two vacancies. I had discussed the situation with Becks only the night before, and told her that realistically there were only three serious candidates because the fourth was Jack Merryweather - a nice bloke, but who was still falling off his horse at least six times a day. I, on the other hand, was fairly confident; I had worked hard during the final weeks of my attachment and had had some very positive comments from a couple of the sergeants regarding improvements in my riding and my contribution at the few football matches I had worked.

The other two applicants were Paul Garrett and Jim Hardwick, both of whom I regarded as good friends, since the three of us had gelled as a team whilst completing our riding course together at Tally Ho. On my arrival at Duke Street, I was surprised to find that all three of my adversaries were there too. It was, it seemed, decision day for all of us. We all stood together chatting in the bunk, and were all in agreement that while we all wanted to stay, none of us felt very comfortable about any of the others being rejected at our expense.

Paul Garrett was the first to be called into the office, leaving three of us waiting expectantly in the bunk for his return. Hardly two minutes had passed before he walked back through the door, initially with a noncommittal look on his face, before finally busting into laughter and punching the air in jubilation. We all congratulated him, but before we could interrogate him too closely, Big Jim was called in. I felt terrible. Jim was a mate - we had shared lifts - and realistically I knew that it was now between him and me. Therefore I also knew that if he came back in with a smile on his face, it meant I had been unsuccessful and would have to return to division. I needed Jim to fail, and that didn't feel right.

It was a full ten minutes before he returned to the bunk with a grim look on his face.

"That's it then. I'm off next week. It's been good fun. I'll miss it," he said in a very matter of fact manner.

"What did he say Jim?" I carefully asked.

"He said I could have a job, but he was concerned about my weight. The old bastard had bathroom scales ready and waiting! I couldn't believe it. He told me if I was below fourteen stone the job was mine. I knew it was a waste of time so I declined his offer to be weighed."

"Are you over fourteen stone Jim?"

"I'm over seventeen stone, but don't tell him," he laughed.

"What, even after all the exercise on the riding course? Are you sure?"

"Oh I'm sure alright. All that exercise just made me hungry, so I ate more pies!" We all erupted into laughter just as I was called into the office. I walked in and saluted with the bittersweet confidence of a man who had just seen his friend and rival fall at the last fence.

This time Hancock was alone behind his desk, holding papers in his hands. Predictably, just as before, he didn't ask me to sit down before he spoke.

"I've just read your report from your riding course and sergeant's comments from your attachment, Wild. You've tried hard and done well. Thank you for your effort, and I'll be sorry to see you go, but I'm afraid that there isn't a permanent place in this department for you, so please make arrangements with PC Parfitt to return your kit. Thank you again Wild; that's all. Goodbye."

I was speechless, and had almost opened the door to leave before I actually heard any words splutter out of my mouth.

"I understood that there were two vacancies, Sir?"

"Yes that's right, and they will be filled by Garrett and Merryweather. Is there a problem Wild?"

"Yes! Jack Merryweather is bloody hopeless!" I heard myself say.

"So now, after only a few weeks, you are already an expert, are you Wild?"

"No I'm not. But you don't have to be an expert to notice a bloke fall off his horse at least every half hour. He's hopeless."

"Merryweather has maturity which you have not, and he has an excellent military background. We need more men of his calibre on this department. Now you may go," he said sharply.

"You need more men of his calibre to fall off at football matches?" I snapped defiantly.

"How dare you Wild?! You thick Black Country oike; how dare you come into my office and question my decisions. Get out of here, now! Go and get your bloody beat helmet back on your head and get back to where you belong. GET OUT!"

So I got out. I didn't go back into the bunk, didn't look back, and didn't speak to anyone on the way out, but just got into the Mini and drove home. I was incredulous, and bloody angry. All of the ridiculous bullshit, orders, saluting, and fixation with surnames that I had only recently began to accept as normal, had unexpectedly kicked me in the teeth. Jack Merryweather was a nice enough bloke - he had certainly been around a bit, and I enjoyed listening to his stories about the troubles in Belfast and of serving in Berlin during the height of the Cold War - but what use was a wealth of life experience to a mounted policeman who couldn't ride a horse? It was ridiculous and I told myself I was probably better off out of it. Now I just had to tell Becks.

She was disappointed of course, but was as usual accepting and supportive.

"Never mind Stef. You had great fun while it lasted, and we'll be fine. At least I can tell everyone at the nursery that my hubby can ride a horse."

"Which is more than can be said for the bloke they chose instead of me."

"I know, so you keep saying! But honestly Stef, I don't think that you were really sure you wanted it full time anyway. It's just a pity we can't keep those breeches, boots and spurs," she laughed, trying to lighten my mood.

"I wasn't sure until he told me that I hadn't got it. Now I'm really sure, but it's too bloody late! It's back to shifts, and Mel won't see me for half of her life, and she'll miss her Sunday water and feeds. I feel like I've let you both down," I groaned.

"Whatever you end up doing is fine by me," she said, trying hard to smooth the waves. "You haven't let anyone down and I'm sure you'll be fine when you start back and have a laugh with the crazy gang. Now if you're looking for more sympathy Stef, you've almost emptied the tank - so come on and cheer up."

She was right of course; rejection is a hard pill to swallow and my ego was bruised and dented, but it was only recently that I'd had any intentions of applying for a full time position. I would just have to return to division, slide back into the routine and carry on with life as it had been before my riding course.

"Two control calling one two. Over."

"Go ahead. Over."

"Stef; what was the result of the sudden death at Wood Lane? Is it a coroner's report by you? Over."

"Negative sarge. The GP issued a certificate for pneumoconiosis, so it'll be an OB[25] entry by me. Over."

"Smashing, thanks Stef; now if you've got your pen ready I've got a couple more jobs for you. Over."

It was a bright, warm summer's evening, was my second week back in the old routine of driving Panda 1-2, and I was working a late shift until 10pm. It had been a busy afternoon and I had only just noticed that it was already 6pm - it would be teatime at home. Becks and Mel would be sitting down at the kitchen table to eat their evening meal, and I was here, alone with my uneaten sandwiches on the back seat. I wouldn't be home for Jackanory[26]. It would be at least 10.30pm before I got home at the end of the shift, and I was due back on duty again at 5.45am the following morning.

[25] The occurrence book was kept in the front office. All occurrences that required no further action were entered into this book. Deaths were always entered in red.

[26] Jackanory was a 1970s-80s fifteen minute children's story programme that was shown daily by the BBC before the evening news.

Tomorrow was a designated 'Zombie Day'. It was the name given to the twice monthly quick changeover days that all the men found so exhausting and all of their wives found so demanding. It was the day when you were home bright and early in the afternoon, with a window of opportunity to do happy family things, but just crashed out with exhaustion and snored on the sofa instead.

I was really fed up; things didn't seem like they were before. In fact, things weren't at all like they were before; I had only been away for a little over five months, but in the meantime there had been a couple of significant personnel changes to our previously happy crew. My former opposite number, who had driven Panda 1-3, had moved on to greener pastures and been replaced. We had always worked well together, shared the load, and backed each other without needing to be directed at some of the trickier jobs, but his replacement was a shirker.

He could always find a reason not to be available for a job, and couldn't always be relied upon to answer his radio when needed. He was an 'old sweat' with about twenty years' service who really didn't want to be working shifts.

His attitude to me was that I was a young sprog who should be happy to do all of the work, and that he was there in an advisory capacity only. He was simply bone idle. We had already squared up over breakfast a few days before, but nothing had become of it and I was just contemplating how this unsatisfactory issue with my new partner could be resolved when the radio burst into life again.

"TWO CONTROL CALLING PANDA ONE-TWO. OVER!" came a booming voice over the radio. It was Shout. I groaned. Perhaps things could get worse after all.

"Go ahead. Over."

"Are you committed Ostler? Over."

"Negative Sir. Nothing desperate at the moment. Over."

"Well get yer skinny arse over here; I want to see you. Over."

"En route Sir, about ten minutes. Over."

It was always a worry to be personally summoned by Shout. Even though I had no real reason to be concerned, he was just that sort of bloke - scary. I turned around and began to head in the direction of the sub-divisional headquarters to see why my presence was so urgently required, and was approaching the humpback bridge over the canal that we used as the boundary between our two police stations when I experienced a little moment of déjà vu. Fortunately I had slowed, engaged second gear, and was about to cross the brow of the bridge when I was confronted by a familiar sight. Trotting over the bridge towards me, in the centre of the road, was a large, shaggy, black and white horse.

Fortunately there were no following vehicles, so I stopped and engaged my handbrake as I watched him trot by, dragging a long rusty chain behind him.

I sat for a while and watched through my rear view mirror as he disappeared out of view further down the road. I had absolutely no desire to turn around and chase him; I'd been there before and was always quick to learn from my mistakes, so I said nothing, moved away and continued with my journey to see Shout.

I did wonder if it was actually the same horse that I'd done battle with the year before - and whether the damn thing had a name. I decided that he was called Horace; he just looked like a Horace. As I drove, I reflected on the way that my career had taken a complete loop since that infamous Horace incident. It certainly looked like the same horse and if it hadn't been for obstinate Horace I would never have had the opportunity to spend that short time with the Mounted Department, and I would never have learned to ride.

I felt a cold shiver go down my back when I thought of our potentially fatal tug of war on the railway crossing, and of how slimy Ted had dropped me in it with Shout. Just the memory of the resulting bollocking sent me wobbly at the knees. What still made me laugh, however, was that one of the lads - whose identity was still a mystery - had forged an application for me to attend my riding course. He'd unwittingly opened a window for me into a bizarre, out-dated, equine environment, that against all the odds I had enjoyed immensely, and was now surprisingly missing so much.

I was still really sore at, what I perceived to be the injustice of, my rejection in favour of a man who, at the end of his riding course, still couldn't ride a horse without falling off. I had spoken to and commiserated with Big Jim, who was more philosophical than I about his rejection; he knew that he was too heavy, and also knew he wouldn't be able to lose sufficient weight and maintain it indefinitely; he was just a big bloke. He was, however, completely sympathetic with my situation and agreed that the final choice was senseless.

But, what was done was done. I'd had my fun and it was over; I was now back in the real world and had to get over it, and quickly, because I had just pulled up outside of the police station and had the more pressing worry of Shout to deal with. I walked through the double front doors, turned right, straightened my cap and knocked on the first door on the right.

"SOD OFF! …UNLESS YOU HAVE TEA!" boomed the familiar voice from the other side of the closed door, so I quietly turned around and walked back along the corridor to put the kettle on the stove. Five minutes later, with a mug of tea in my hand, I knocked for the second time.

"COME IN ONLY IF YOU HAVE TEA!" I walked in and closed the door behind me.

"Ostler; good to see you lad. Didn't you make yourself one? How's the lovely Becks and the bab?" Thankfully he seemed in a very good mood.

"We're all fine thanks Sir. You wanted to see me?"

"I did, I did," he replied whilst gesturing for me to sit down. "We need to have a chat and I haven't seen much of you since you came back to us."

He had a piece of paper in his hand that I could clearly see to be a telephone message form.

"Ostler; how's it been since you came back?" he asked whilst eyeballing me with a raised eyebrow. "Because a little birdie tells me that you are well and truly pissed off."

"I'm fine Sir; just settling back in."

"Settling back in, are you? Well I've already batted off two complaints since you came back. One from when you gave that mouthy kid a short caution[27] in front of his gobby mother, and the other after you ripped into that drunken teacher and his slag of a missus at that domestic."

"The kid was obnoxious…"

"I know, but she saw you slap him! Don't get sloppy, and don't get caught!"

"…and I just told the teacher and his missus that they lacked dignity, were a disgrace to his profession, and that I was half their age and wasn't paid to referee their ridiculous, petty squabbles."

"True, true, but you also told them that if they really wanted to kill each other they should take pills, and not call the police.

---

[27] *Black Country police euphemism for a swift punch.*

I can't fault your sentiment lad, but you need to be more careful. I think you're more pissed off than you realise."

I opened up more than I would have thought possible, and told him about how I thought I'd made good progress on my mounted attachment, and genuinely believed that I'd earned a transfer, but finally been rejected in favour of an old bloke that kept falling off his horse.

"I hear that you gobbed off at the chief inspector when he told you?" he interrupted. "That wasn't too clever."

"No, in hindsight it was stupid and pointless," I conceded, wondering where he had got his information from.

"Now what's the problem back on the patch?" he asked, probing a little deeper.

I told him that, under the circumstances, I was disappointed at returning - but also that things were quite different following the changes in personnel since I'd been away. I also told him I'd sort it out myself, and that I would have to snap out of it and get on with the job.

"That's the nature of working on a shift, lad. Most people eventually want out, so they jump ship when the first opportunity comes along. I told you all this before you went, when you wanted to withdraw your application. Never turn down what you want to do just because you like your mates, because they'll be gone in the blink of an eye and you'll suddenly find yourself working with a load of wankers."

I nodded in agreement, and whilst I didn't entirely agree with his load of wankers analogy, I was impressed with his insight into my mood and situation. He had hit the nail right on the head; whilst I was away with the mounted department I'd missed the camaraderie of the shift, but when I came back it had gone. What I had been missing so much was no longer here.

"Would you go back if they asked you and if we could spare you?"

"Yes I would, but it's not going to happen is it? They've got no vacancies and I think I've shot myself in the foot with the Chief Inspector," I replied.

"How do you get on with Inspector Scott?"

"He shouts a lot," I laughed. "They call him Big Ben because he goes off every hour."

"Well I've had a good chat with him this afternoon and he seems to rate you." I was intrigued and my attention was now completely focussed on the piece of paper that he held in his hand. "He called earlier and asked if we were prepared to release you at short notice. It would appear they've had an officer long term sick with a back injury, and he's just confirmed that he isn't going back. The problem is that they want a replacement to start this Monday."

"I guess that isn't possible?"

"Well everything's possible, but there's no time to mess about; I've already been in and discussed it with the superintendent this afternoon and he's prepared to let you go. I think you're lucky because we're still well under strength, but he's a fair bloke if you talk to him properly. So - what do you want to do?"

I couldn't believe my ears, and at first struggled to get my head around how my immediate future had potentially changed so dramatically in the passing of the previous few minutes. Of course, I immediately confirmed that I would accept the completely unexpected opportunity I had been so suddenly offered.

"Good! Let's get the ball rolling then. It's quick change tonight so I'll call your Inspector Big Ben in the morning. Get yourself back to the nick and sort out all your paperwork, your locker and kit; I don't want any sign of you left here after you've gone on

Monday. Don't leave the nick until you've cleared your work and don't get involved in anything that you can't get rid of. Understood?"

"Yes sir."

"Good. Bugger off then; you've got a lot to do."

I could feel myself grinning. I tried to suppress my excitement, but my facial muscles seemed to act independently of my brain. Overwhelmed by my involuntary exuberance I leapt from my chair, stamped my right foot hard on to the parquet floor, vigorously flung my right arm wide out to the right, up into the air, and then snapped it down short and smart back to my side.

"Bloody hell Ostler; what are you doing?" gasped Shout while frantically wheeling his chair backwards to distance himself from me.

"Saluting you."

"Is that what it was?" he said, looking relieved as he slowly scooted himself back into striking distance. "Don't do it again; it scares me."

"Sorry; we have to do it every time we go into the office at Duke Street. I forgot where I was for a moment," I tried to explain. "It's all about the longest way up and the shortest way down."

"I bet it is," he replied while shaking his head in disbelief. "You've only been there a few months and you're already as daft as they are. Now bugger off - you're making my head ache."

I was still in a daze as I walked out of his office and back to the panda car. It seemed ironic that the two inspectors that had always struck the most fear into my heart had, between them, put themselves out and looked after me. They were old school blokey blokes who shouted a lot and shook their fists, but their hearts were genuine and their barks worse than their bites.

The last part of the journey back to the nick took me along the same route that I had taken with the cursed Horace almost exactly a year before. I looked across at Ecka Rushton's yard and saw that the same fearsome Alsatian dog was still slathering and chained to the gate post. Further on as I drove across the railway level crossing, the lights were on green, ensuring that this journey was in complete contrast to the hard fought, almost deadly tug of war of the previous year.

I strode through the front door of the police station, bouncing on an adrenaline high. Without a care in the world I went straight to the report writing room so that I could call Becks.

"Hello?" she answered.

"Is that the undeniably irresistible Mrs Wild speaking?"

"Yes, it is - and is that the undeniably annoying Mr Wild interrupting the undeniably irresistible Mrs Wild halfway through Coronation Street?"

"Never mind Corrie! Sit down; I have an important announcement to make."

"Should I be worried?" she asked suspiciously.

"Well I'm not on nights next week, so you'll have to stay on your own side of the bed."

"Stef... you haven't been fired, have you?"

"No, but if you look under the sink I think there is some of that surgical spirit left in the bottle."

"Meaning?"

"Meaning that I start at Duke Street at 7am next Monday morning."

"Wooooooo-Hooooooo!!"

I told her about the unexpected conversation between Big Ben and Shout, explaining the sudden change in our circumstances, and the reaction from the other end of the telephone confirmed my suspicions that she had, in fact, been as disappointed as I had at my initial rejection.

"I'll have to go now because I've got a fair bit of paper to clear and my locker to clean out and only a couple of days left to do it. I'll see you at about ten thirty."

"Don't be late because I'll have the surgical spirit and the towel ready," she laughed. "The night is young and we've got some prep work to do."

"Calm down tiger; it's quick change tonight and I've got to get up early in the morning."

"Lightweight!" she laughed as she put the phone down.

It was 9.15pm and the light was just falling to dusk. I had finished one or two reports, cleared the desk into my basket, and was about to put the kettle on when my lazy partner strolled into the kitchen.

"Don't you ever go out of the nick?" he sneered.

"I've got a lot of paper to clear."

"You've always got something to write about; all bullshit, I suppose."

"It's what happens when you do some work; you have to write about it. You should try it occasionally; it makes the time go faster."

"You really think you're good, don't you? You think you know the lot, but let me tell you, when I was-" He was interrupted as the radio burst into life.

"Two control calling Panda one-two. Over."

"Go ahead. Over," I answered.

"Stef; I know it's late but we've got reports of a big black and white Oss rampaging around gardens in Canal Street. Can you make it please? Over."

I paused for a moment or two, thought of Horace and wobbled a little at the knees, before gathering my thoughts and replying:

"Negative sarge. I'm confined to the office for reports on the inspector's orders," I could feel a sly smile beginning to corrupt my features as I contemplated the second battle of Horace v Police. "One-three is uncommitted; you'll have to send him. Over."

EPILOGUE

Stef Wild's anticipated short spell on the Mounted Branch unexpectedly extended to almost thirteen years, after which, coincidentally, he returned to the same little Victorian police station that he had left in such a hurry in 1979. Many things had changed during his absence; the Police and Criminal Evidence Act had changed the face of policing, the panda cars were more modern and the faces at the nick were new, but the area and public had not. Feral horses still roamed the streets.

During his thirteen years with the branch he became a proper mounted man, and eventually regularly represented the force in many competitions, sporting events, and displays around the country; he also followed the traditional practice of the branch and trained young remounts along the way. He never did feel completely at home in Birmingham, and though he became familiar enough with the streets to ensure that he didn't get lost, many of the surrounding districts remained a mystery, ensuring the pages of his trusty A to Z were always well thumbed.

The 1980s, sadly, became synonymous with the shame of mindless, escalating violence at football matches, and was also a time of regular civil unrest; the miners' strike and many other violent demonstrations against the thrice-elected Thatcher government's reforms kept the branch busy and relevant throughout the decade.

Sadly, however, following an impressive decade of rapid growth, modernisation, and expansion, the branch was suddenly disbanded in 1999 on the grounds of cost and manpower shortages. With ruthless speed and efficiency the older horses were retired, the younger ones and the masses of equipment were sold at auction to the highest bidder, and the personnel thinly re-distributed to other duties around the force. The long awaited 'showcase' modern central stables, which were eventually opened at Aston Cross, were demolished without trace when barely ten years old, and the wonderful indoor riding school at Tally Ho is now a garage for the parking of driving school cars. Spookily, the A.K.E.H.C.M.B.F[28] signs and marker boards still gather cobwebs on the internal walls.

Inevitably, most of the older characters in this book are sadly no longer with us, and even the rowdy youngsters who joined the branch around the same time as the author are now drawing their old age pensions. Paul Garrett remained on the branch, rising to the rank of sergeant before its final demise, and now lives in Spain very close to a golf course.

[28] *ALL-KING-EDWARDS-HORSES-CAN-MAKE-BIG-FENCES*

Big Jim Hardwick escaped from further whippings and found a ride more suited to his stature in a Range Rover, working as a specialist motorway patrol officer until his retirement from the force.

Stef Wild, after a short spell in uniform back on division, unintentionally (a familiar story) fell into the CID where he remained a plain clothes detective for the remainder of his service. He finally retired from West Midlands Police in 2005, after serving with the Murder Investigation Unit, where he was known as the only 'Donkey Walloping Homicide Detective' in the force.

When questioned after retirement about the diversity of his two main roles, he states that early in his career he used his brawn because he was brainless, whereas later in service he reverted to using his brain because he was brawn-less.

He and the long suffering Becks are still happily together, having been married for over forty five years, and spend their time touring in their motorhome, walking, gardening, enjoying their kids and spoiling their grandkids. Sadly they've thrown out the leg warmers and no longer keep surgical spirit beneath the kitchen sink, but do now have good carpet on their stairs, and, happily, no longer need to hide from the milkman.

A WORD FROM THE AUTHOR

Thank you very much for reading 'Longest Way Up Shortest Way Down'. This my first book, has been a long time coming, and I hope that you've enjoyed reading it as much as I enjoyed writing it. If you could spare just a few more moments, an honest review on Amazon would be greatly appreciated.

FOLLOW THE AUTHOR

You can follow me on Twitter (@TalesofStefWild), or Facebook (Stefan Wild). To read reviews, to view images, or to learn more about me and the characters in this book, please check out my website: www.tales-of-stefanwild.uk

A FREE CHAPTER

The sequel to 'Longest Way Up Shortest Way Down', is already work in progress. If you would like to preview the first chapter, completely free of charge, please visit: www.tales-of-stefanwild.uk and check in with your email address.

Again, many thanks

Stef
October 2021

Printed in Great Britain
by Amazon

79268834R00200